I0747600

Woodpusher

Azaes Realm, #2.0

S. Morgan Burbank

Woodpusher, Book 2.0 of the *Azaes Realm* series

Published by Iocusia Press, a division of Job at Place LLC, PO Box 256, North Olmsted, OH, 44070

©2024

Paperback ISBN: 978-1-7353190-5-6
Digital ISBN: 978-1-7353190-6-3

Cover art by Lauren Restivo
Edited by Charlotte Laidig

Second Edition: JuneF 2024

This book is a work of fiction. Names, characters, places, and incidents are fictional. Except for the cats. All cats can be willed into existence if you believe in yourself and you're willing to knock things off of counters. Any resemblance to actual persons, living or dead, companies, events, locations, or politicians is purely coincidental. Any resemblance to actual cats is, however, intentional.

For Morgan. Thank you for your patience.

1
Pioneer to the Falls

December 27, 2034/5:17, Day 93, Year 10311

Erika woke up with a pounding headache unlike anything she'd ever experienced. She didn't remember drinking the night before. That in and of itself wasn't an odd occurrence. The last thing she remembered was going on a walk to the beach with Abby. There was a bright light and then...nothing. Just a pulse in her skull that screamed for her to keep her eyes shut.

She felt around, expecting to find her phone or tablet somewhere nearby. Not only did her search turn up empty, her nightstand wasn't there.

"Abby?" Erika called out. She flinched from the sound of her own voice.

"Yeah?" replied Abby.

Erika felt Abby roll toward her. At least she was nearby and, presumably, in the same bed.

"Are we upside down?"

"That's an odd question."

"My nightstand is gone," Erika stated.

"I'm sure it's still there," replied Abby.

Erika felt around again, her arms swaying haphazardly in an attempt to find the table.

"No," she said after repeated failed attempts. "It's gone."

"That's not what I mean. I'm sure it's still there. We're just not home."

"How drunk did I get? Also, when did I drink?"

"You didn't," replied Abby.

"Well then where are we?" asked Erika.

"That's not a simple answer."

Erika opened her eyes. She looked around at the dimly lit room they were in, happy that the only light on came from a lone lamp in the far corner. It looked like a large hotel suite, complete with a small kitchen, a living area, and the bedroom they were currently in. Presumably, there was a bathroom somewhere. But this didn't look like any hotel Erika had seen before. Something was off.

Erika turned toward her android girlfriend. Abby put down the book she was reading and met Erika's gaze.

"What is this place?" asked Erika.

"This is our room," replied Abby. "At least for while we're here."

"Where is here?"

"It's apparently called the Azaes Realm. This book was on one of the tables in the other room."

She handed the thin paperback to Erika. *"The Azaes Realm and You: A Guide to Navigating Your Time In-Between"* its cover read.

"Is this a joke?" asked Erika.

"Pretty sure you're dead. This is purgatory. You managed to be just good enough not to go to Hell immediately, but not good enough you'll avoid it forever."

Great, Erika thought. An unfamiliar room with post-death literature, and Grace. The voice that drove all her worst mental moments didn't even go away after she stopped living.

"We're dead?" Erika half asked, half said.

"I don't think so," Abby replied. "I can't imagine an afterlife that conscientia and humans would share. Or really any robotic beings and humans."

"Then what the fuck is this place?"

"I'm not sure. I did find this envelope on the table."

Abby handed a cream-colored envelope to Erika. Their names were written in delicate handwriting across the front, the ink used giving off a slight shimmer as light hit it.

"What's in it?" Erika asked.

"I haven't opened it," said Abby.

"Why not?"

"It's addressed to both of us."

"I think it's okay to open shared mail when we might be in Hell."

"Would Hell have shared mail?" asked Abby. "From what I understand about the concept, I'd just assumed that all you'd ever get would be ads with coupons for things you'll never buy. And bills."

"You've thought about this way more than me," said Erika.

Erika opened the envelope, pulling out a neatly written letter. The same shimmering ink caught Erika's eye as she read it.

Hello Abby and Erika! Welcome to the Azaes Realm!

I want to begin by apologizing for your abrupt and

unannounced arrival here. While this is not standard practice, I assure you that we have a good reason for needing both of you here ahead of when you'd otherwise be scheduled. Rest assured that your affairs will be taken care of while you're here.

"Is this another one of Amy's projects?" asked Erika.

"Not that I know of," said Abby. "I know she hasn't told me everything she's ever done, but I'd like to think she'd at least tell us before she relocated us. Again."

Erika nodded and continued reading.

I know it can be an adjustment for those coming to the Azaes Realm. I would encourage you to take the time you need to rest and recalibrate. Your work and training will start in earnest at 16:00. My personal envoy, Quaid, will be by to take you to the main facility at that time. There you will meet the rest of your team and learn about why you're here.

Erika looked around the room for a clock, but her still sleepy eyes couldn't focus well enough to find one.

"What time is it?" she asked.

"I'm not sure," replied Abby.

"How do you not know?"

"I mean, I know it's 5:17 right now. But something's not quite right with the time."

"Like you can't get the time to sync with a server?"

"Like time is literally different."

Erika set the letter down and stared at Abby.

"How can time be different?"

"Time seems to move slower here," replied Abby. "And here is apparently the Azaes Realm."

"How much slower are we talking?" asked Erika.

"I haven't worked that out yet. That's why I was reading. Maybe it's in the letter."

You'll find food in the storage area of the kitchen in your room. If there's anything specific you'd like to eat, we'll do our best to accommodate it. Due to the nature of our location, although we will do our best to fulfill any and all dietary requests, please note that the following items are unavailable within the Azaes Realm.

- *Alcohol*

- *Certain meats (Note: plant or lab-grown substitutes of similar or better quality, taste, and nutritional value are available)*

- *Certain synthetic sugars*

"Hahahaha. Oh my god. You are so fucked."

There are a few differences between how things operate within the Azaes Realm versus what you're used to on Earth. While most of these items are covered in the book, "The Azaes Realm and You: A Guide to Navigating Your Time In-Between", that you'll find in your living area, if you're reading this letter, there are an additional set of discrepancies that apply to you.

Although you are in the Azaes Realm right now, you will have the ability to return to Earth under certain circumstances. While the primary criteria for this is the completion of your mission with your team, it is possible that you'll return to Earth to complete

"That would explain my time confusion," Abby said.

"I'll finish this later. I need something to eat," Erika said. "And apparently we're being fed. Want anything?"

"I should eat," replied Abby. "I haven't found an outlet in here yet, so I haven't been able to charge."

Erika climbed out of bed, noticing her clothing for the first time. She was wearing silky-soft pajamas, far nicer than anything she owned. They were her favorite color, orange, and were surprisingly warm despite the cool temperature of the room. Abby wore a pair of her own, albeit red instead of orange, and with buttons down the front of the shirt rather than a pullover top.

"Distracted?" Abby asked.

"What?"

"You're staring intently at the unbuttoned part of my shirt."

"I like how you look."

"Go get breakfast," replied Abby. "We can examine the buttons together later."

"I can't tell if you mean that literally or not."

Abby shot Erika a smile, then pointed toward the door with the book.

"Go," she said.

Erika entered the kitchen area of the suite. It looked like kitchens she'd seen on Earth, though there was an overwhelmingly sterile feel to the room that she couldn't shake. She opened the refrigerator, expecting to see some amount of food and drink inside. Instead, Erika was greeted by a flat screen with a large, touchscreen picture menu on it.

Erika began tapping through the various choices, overwhelmed at the number of choices at her fingertips. There wasn't just a lot of food to choose from – it felt like virtually every food Erika had ever heard of was available for selection, not to mention countless other foods that Erika hadn't heard of.

"Abby," Erika said. "Is there something specific you want?"

"Just surprise me," Abby shouted from the other room."

"I don't think you understand how many options there are."

Abby joined Erika in the kitchen and began filtering her way through the choices in the fridge's menu. Outside of the first few days after Abby was implanted in an android, Erika didn't see Abby get overwhelmed easily. But even she seemed awestruck by the number of options she was being given.

"I want to try so many things," said Abby. "I don't know where to begin."

"Me either," replied Erika. "We could always get something we know we like then figure this out later."

Abby nodded, choosing a bowl of oatmeal topped with bananas and blueberries, a mug of black coffee with honey, and a single scrambled egg. The fridge made a series of noises, followed by the screen splitting apart and a gray tray protruding from the newly opened space, Abby's meal atop it.

"Why is the hot food coming out of a fridge?" asked Erika.

"It might be best not to think of it as a fridge," replied Abby. "Though I'll be damned if I could tell you what it's called."

Erika acquired her own food – a diner-style omelet with green peppers, tomatoes, spinach, and mozzarella cheese, straight black coffee, and hash browns – and walked to the table to join Abby.

"Hadn't you just started that book when I woke up?" asked Erika.

"It's short," replied Abby. "I'm almost done."

"What have you learned?"

"It seems that the Azaes Realm is a mix between a parallel universe and the concept of purgatory. But I feel like the book isn't telling me everything I need to know to fully understand what's going on."

A knock at the door interrupted Abby's explanation. Erika walked over to the door, where she was greeted by a tall, slender, dark-skinned person. They were dressed in black denim pants and a yellow halter top, wearing a shimmering pearl necklace.

"I've been informed the two of you are awake," they said, voice calm and soft. "Is there anything either of you need?"

"Hey!" Abby shouted from the table. "You're who we saw right after the flash of light!"

"Who are you?" asked Erika. "And um...how did you know we were awake?

"My name is Svieva, guardian to the goddess Adelina," they said, extending their hand toward Erika's. "And I knew you were awake because I received a notification that your pantry had been used for the first time."

Erika stared at Svieva's hand before cautiously shaking it. The handshake had fallen out of favor on Earth across the early 2020s, though there was a devoted -- typically older or male -- contingent of those who used it. Svieva didn't strike Erika as the type who viewed anything other than a handshake as disrespectful. Nevertheless, she cautiously grasped Svieva's hand, then immediately moved to wash her hands at the sink.

"Ah, yes," Svieva said. "You come from one of the post-pandemic times. Sorry about that. The sink has a sanitization setting. Just tap the faucet twice."

As Erika began to wash her hands with the bubbly liquid that poured out of the faucet, Svieva turned her attention to Abby.

"I thought one of the envoys was coming to get us, not an actual guardian," Abby said.

"Is this not better?" asked Svieva.

"It is. I just would have assumed you had plenty else you have to do."

"Have you begun reviewing the literature Revaus instructed our couriers to leave you?" she asked.

"I'm working on it now," replied Abby. "When does it need to be read by? I can stop eating if it's urgent."

"You have plenty of time," said Svieva. "Please, eat. You'll need the energy for your training."

"What do you mean, training?" asked Erika as she dried her hands.

"I see you haven't finished the introductory letter," replied Svieva.

Erika squirmed a bit, remembering she'd left it in the bedroom.

"We wanted to eat first," she said. "I promise it's on my to-do list though."

"Well, no matter," answered Svieva. "The two of you are here to help prevent the end of the world on Earth."

"*Fuck.*"

2
Where is Now?

"What do you mean we're here to stop the end of the world?" asked Erika.

"I mean exactly what I said," replied Svieva. "You've been brought here by our gods under the understanding that you have an integral part to play in stopping a catastrophic downfall of humanity on Earth."

"Just the two of us?" asked Abby.

"There's a team you'll meet later," replied Svieva. "I've met the rest of them already and—"

"So, we're the last ones here?" interrupted Erika.

"You are," said Svieva. "I feel this would likely be quicker if you both just read the literature that's been provided to you --"

"A letter isn't going to tell us why we're here – "

"I frankly don't know the entire story about why you're here. Or why you were chosen. Or the plan. I just know that it's my job – on top of my actual job – to make sure the six of you are comfortable transitioning here until you begin your training."

Erika stared at Svieva, who was still standing outside the doorway. They seemed frazzled.

"Would you like something to eat?" asked Erika.

"When did you become a gracious host?"

Shut up, Grace, Erika thought.

Svieva sighed, then entered the room. They walked over to the refrigerator – apparently referred to as a pantry – and began selecting.

"It's rare that I'm invited in by the newly arrived," Svieva said as the machine produced a mug of cocoa. "Thank you for your hospitality, though I will need to keep my time here brief."

"Brief by time on Earth or by Azaes Realm's standards?" asked Abby.

"The latter."

Svieva took a seat in the living area, sipping at their cocoa as Abby went back to eating.

"Would it be better if I changed?" asked Erika. "I'm sorry we're both in pajamas."

"I am interrupting your morning, not the other way around," replied Svieva. "Only change if you feel uncomfortable around me. Otherwise, please, sit. Ask away. I'll answer what I can. If I cannot answer, I'm sure I can find you someone who can."

Erika paused, waiting to see if Abby would start off with any questions. Whatever Abby had to ask would sound much less stupid than whatever came out of her own mouth, she reasoned. But surprisingly, Abby stayed silent.

"Forgive me, but I'm terrible with names. You said your name was Stevia?"

"It's Svieva," they replied, chuckling. "Though that is one of the sillier mispronunciations I've ever gotten."

"That's a sugar," Abby added.

Erika sighed. "Sorry. Svieva. I'll work on that. You said there's more of us?"

"Indeed," replied Svieva. "There are four others – Lorena, Shaw, Lace, and K'Andre. You'll meet them all later today. They're much closer being your contemporaries than I am."

"What do you mean?" Erika countered.

"You're from the 2030s, are you not?"

"We are. Aren't you?"

Svieva let out a hearty laugh that seemed to fill the entire room. The laugh itself lasted for several seconds, though Erika swore the echo of it lingered on for a full minute.

"You really should finish the literature," Svieva replied. "But no. I am from a time much before yours."

"How far before?" Abby interjected.

"I came to the Azaes Realm in 1872."

"So you're like 175 years old?" asked Erika.

"That depends on how you calculate it," replied Svieva. "I was born in 1852. As you'd calculate it on Earth, I'm 182 years old. But I came here just before my twentieth birthday. When considering the rate at which the Azaes Realm ages humans, I'm roughly the equivalent of 34 years old."

"What the Kentucky fried fuck?" Erika mumbled. Though she thought she'd said it quietly, it was loud enough for Svieva to pick up on.

"You're the second person to react to my age that way," Svieva said. "Is that a common expression of surprise in your time?"

"It's really not," replied Erika. "Who else used that?"

"Shaw. He's an odd character."

Abby, having finished her meal, left the table and took a seat on the couch to Svieva's right. She picked up another book off the table and began to read through it. As Erika worked through what she wanted to ask next, she watched as Svieva took interest in Abby.

"You're the special one Gersemi spoke of," Svieva stated. They continued to examine Abby, meticulously looking her over as if she weren't real. "I didn't believe it, but my eyes tell me it's true."

"Special?" asked Abby, looking up from her book.

"You're a machine," replied Svieva, "but you look human. With all the amazing technology that I've seen in the Azaes Realm, you'd think I would have caught it sooner. But the work is astounding."

"We're called conscientia," said Abby. "Or androids. Or a litany of derogatory terms. It depends on who you ask."

Svieva nodded, their face growing sad.

"It's a shame to hear humanity's hatred of those who are not like them continues," they said. "Not that I expected it to stop. But I had hope that things would be different from when I was there."

"Where exactly were you?" asked Abby.

"I was born in the town of Cape Coast in the Gold Coast," Svieva said. "I lived there until I was 12, at which point I was relocated with my father to Moncton in British Canada."

"Relocated?" asked Erika hesitantly. "Like...slavery?"

"No," replied Svieva. "Slavery was outlawed in the Crown Colonies and the British Empire as a whole before I was born. My father worked for the government. I suppose I should say my adoptive father, but I think the point still largely stands. Even so, I had trouble fitting in both places."

"Why's that?"

"Mid-century colonials had no time for what they considered to be a woman dressing like a man. It's much easier to be non-binary in this universe than yours."

"So call you they?" asked Erika.

"I prefer my name," replied Svieva, "though they is my preference otherwise."

Svieva shifted their focus back to Abby.

"How long will it take you to finish that book?" they asked.

"If I'm actually trying?" Abby replied. "Or if I'm killing time while waiting on Erika to do something."

"If you actually try."

Abby began to flip through the pages with startling speed. In the span of ten seconds, Abby went from near the front cover of the book to closing it shut with a thunk.

"Done," she said.

"That book is nearly 600 pages!" Svieva gasped.

"583 if you don't include the table of contents, appendix, and title page," said Abby. "591 if you do."

"Does she do this to you too?" asked Svieva.

"Not frequently, but yeah," replied Erika. "It's useful. My memory is shit."

"Simply astounding," Svieva said, marveling at Abby. "May I?"

Abby nodded, letting Svieva touch her hair and the skin on her face.

"The world does not cease to amaze," continued Svieva.

"I can do other cool things too," said Abby. "But I'm sure you have plenty to do."

"I do," stated Svieva. "I really must be going now. But I'd love to learn more about you when we have some time."

"That's code for they want to fuck your girlfriend."

Stop.

"F U C K."

Wouldn't you be fascinated by technology 200 years more advanced than you grew up with?

"Your fridge is a store, restaurant, and computer. The sink washed your

hands with foam and light. But an android is special. Bullshit. Sounds to me like they want that robot booty."

Shut up.

"Good luck with that. Booze is banned."

...fuck.

Alcohol is 'unavailable'. She'd read it before, but the words hadn't sunk in. Granted, since they'd moved to Canada, Abby had kept a close eye on how much Erika drank. But it had always seemed to be enough to avoid any sort of withdrawal. Not now though. Now there was no alcohol to be found. Period.

"I've missed you. We'll have plenty of time to get reacquainted in here."

"Erika?"

Erika snapped out of her mental trance. Both Svieva and Abby were staring at her.

"Are you alright?" Svieva asked.

"Yeah," Erika said softly. "Just spaced out there for a minute. Can we go back to the whole needing to save the world thing? What are we saving it from?"

"It's not a what so much as a who," Svieva replied. "Janus is the guardian of time here. Or at least that was the case until recently."

"What happened? Did they die?"

"Though guardians can travel to and from Earth, we generally try to avoid doing it regularly as our abilities are much stronger in the Azaes Realm. One of our other guardians, Gersemi, has taken quite a liking to the people of Earth."

"That makes sense for the guardian of love," Abby said.

Erika stared at Abby; confusion riddled on her face.

"What?" Abby asked. "It was in the book."

"Gersemi and Janus hold fundamentally different views toward humans," Svieva continued. "While Gersemi sees the inherent beauty of humanity, Janus is much more pragmatic. Being the guardian of time, she sees the flaws that have plagued humanity over time. War, pestilence, slavery, bigotry, genocide, misinformation, they're all cyclical. The methods change, but the actions don't. Janus made the decision help humanity break that cycle."

"That doesn't sound like a bad thing," Erika said.

"Janus intends to do it by helping to hasten the downfall of humanity. If there are no humans, humanity cannot do bad things."

Erika leaned back in her chair, staring off into space. She heard Abby and Svieva begin talking again, but she couldn't focus her mind long enough to make out what they were saying. She'd just been on the beach in Nova Scotia. Now she was in another world being told about how some all-powerful being was plotting to accelerate the demise of humanity. Not only that, but it was partly her job to stop it.

"Run. Get out. They're trying to put responsibility on you that you can't handle. You know you can't. Take Abby with you and go."

"You there?" Abby said.

"Yeah," Erika said, shaking her head in an effort to refocus. "Just tired."

"If you need some more rest," Svieva replied, "I'd encourage you to nap. There's a lot of training ahead. You'll need your strength."

Svieva left the room, the door latching with a near-imperceptible click behind them. Abby walked behind Erika, draping her arms around Erika's shoulders, leaning in close to her.

"She's loud today isn't she?" said Abby.

Erika nodded. She leaned back into Abby's embrace, though the back of the chair prevented her from getting too close. She could feel Abby's warm breath against the back of her neck.

Of all the human behaviors that conscientia had, realistic breathing was the one that always caught Erika off guard. There was no need for Abby to breathe. She didn't have lungs. She didn't need to cry. Or develop bad habits like biting her nails. Abby did all those things to make Erika feel more comfortable around her. But breathing – one of the most basic automatic systems of human anatomy – seemed foreign whenever it came from Abby.

She kissed Erika on the cheek, then walked back over to the couch and continued to read. Erika stared at her food for a few moments, her appetite gone. She took a step toward the fridge, briefly considering getting a different meal in hopes she'd be hungry again, but ultimately decided against it.

"I think she's right," Erika said. "I should go back to bed."

"It's a lot to take in," replied Abby. "You rest. I'll catch you up with anything important."

Erika curled back up in bed, pulling the pillowy comforter up to her chin. As she tried to drift off to sleep, she noticed the light from the living area peeking under the bedroom door. Then she noticed the time on the clock. And then –

"Tick tock. Time's a wastin'"

*****

Loud pounding on his front door woke Youles from his slumber. He rolled over, his still cloudy eyes wincing at a clock that read just after one in the morning. The pounding continued, constant and panicked. Cops didn't knock like this. He'd had enough of them show up in the past. While there was always the chance it was someone with an actual emergency, Youles grabbed his bedside pistol as he made his way to the door. Good news never arrives at this time of night.

It was nights like this that Youles wished he'd invested in video equipment for outside his home. None of those video doorbells that connected to some far-off database. Too much potential evidence could be turned over to the police that way. A closed-circuit video system was more his speed, but Youles lacked the technical knowhow – and if he was honest with himself, the funds – to get it set up. Unexpected visitors in the middle of the night made for a lot of regrets.

Youles peeked through the peephole of the front door, hopeful that whoever was outside hadn't covered it up. Though it was dark outside, he could make out the shivering form of an old man holding himself up with a cane. Youles holstered the gun in his waistband behind his back and opened the door.

"Greg, it's the middle of the night," Youles said.

"Janus knows we fucked up," said Greg, his voice shaky both from the chilly wind and fear.

"Of course she does. She's known for a while. I just got back from Ohio staking out the real target's parents in case she came home for Christmas."

"She knows it's my fault. She knows you killed the wrong person. We're loose ends, Youles."

"Shit like this happens all the time, Greg. You make a mistake. You do some cleanup. You move on and go after the right target again. Occupational hazard"

"I don't think you understand!" Greg shouted. "This isn't a normal job. Janus has goals, big ones. And if you're not directly helping Janus achieve them, you're expendable."

Youles reached in the door, grabbing a cigarette and lighter off the table. He motioned to Greg, offering him one, then lit his own after Greg turned him down.

"Everyone has plans, Greg," Youles said. "When those plans are big, the person with the balls to pull the trigger isn't the one who takes the fall first. It's some unimportant underling who fucked up the assignment in the first place."

"I'm telling you!" Greg said, his reply panicked. "She's coming after everyone who messed up. This is bigger than you or me."

"So's the fucking sun but you don't see me hiding from it. Now get off my porch and let me go back to bed."

3
Gorilla

December 30, 2034/11:39, Day 93, Year 10311

"I think we should venture out," said Abby. "Even if our training session isn't until this afternoon. Let's walk around and see what it's like here."

"How do you know we can do that?" asked Erika. She was lying on the couch, her eyes covered by the sleeve of a hooded sweatshirt she was using as a pillow.

"Because there's a door. And it can be opened. And we can exit the room."

"Okay, smartass. I mean how do you know we can go exploring? What's to say there's not security at the end of our hallway that'll tell us to turn right back around and get in our room until we're told to come out?"

"Svieva was in here earlier," replied Abby. "They're a guardian. And that seems like a really important thing. I don't think they'd just send someone important if we're prisoners."

"Abby. Guardian has the word guard in it. It's not a ridiculous leap to assume we can't leave."

"Well then I'm going to go, you can stay."

"No, don't do that," replied Erika.

"Why not?"

"Because we need to stick together until we know it's safe."

Erika waited for a reply, but one never came. She groaned and lifted the sleeve from her eyes, expecting Abby to be staring at her, pleading for her to come with. Instead, Abby was nowhere to be found, the door softly latching behind her as she left the room.

"Goddammit," Erika mumbled.

Erika hopped off the couch, pulling the hoodie over her head as she headed toward the exit. As she opened the door, the only thing Erika saw was Abby jumping at her.

"Boo!" Abby shouted.

Erika tumbled to the ground, an ear-piercing screech emanating from her throat. She took a sharp breath in, then let out a second, slightly quieter scream.

"Jesus H. Tapdancing Christ, Abby," Erika said, her voice frantic as she worked to catch her breath.

"It was fun!"

"What part of making your girlfriend nearly piss herself is fun? About had a fucking heart attack."

"I'll have you know that in the event you have a heart attack, I am fully capable of providing you the necessary medical attention until we can find you a doctor."

Abby offered her hand to Erika, lifting her from the ground.

"How do we get back in the room?" Erika asked. "I didn't see any keys or anything."

"Come out of the room and I'll show you."

Erika exited the room, letting the door shut behind her. Abby gently pulled her away from the door, waiting until a soft click sounded. She held up a finger to Erika, then walked in front of the door. The face of the door changed from its woodgrain appearance to a blank, gray screen. Within a few seconds, Abby's picture appeared on the screen, along with a name and confirmation that she could enter. The door shifted back to its wooden appearance, followed by another soft click. Abby opened the door and walked into the room.

"Try it if you want," Abby replied.

Erika waited for the door to shut and lock behind Abby, then repeated the process. Her name and picture appeared on the screen, the sight of her own face causing Erika to cringe.

"They really couldn't find a better picture?" she said as she opened the door, letting Abby back out into the hallway.

"You look great," replied Abby. "Now let's go."

Erika followed Abby down the hallway toward what appeared to be a pair of elevators. Before they got too far, Erika stopped in the middle of the hall, surveying the scene around her.

"What?" asked Abby.

"There aren't rooms," said Erika. "It's just a pair of long walls."

"So?"

"So we're in a long hallway that should be filled with lots of doors on both sides. Our room is basically a hotel room. You've seen how hotels work, right?"

"Yes, but –"

"But there should be doors for oth—"

Erika stopped speaking, staring back down the hallway from the direction they'd came.

"Where did our door go?" she asked.

Erika ran to where the room's exit had been, her heart pounding in her chest. The problem with the door not being there, however, was that Erika had no idea when to stop to look for the door. By the time she noticed that the door had manifested itself back into existence, Erika had nearly run by it.

She came to a stop, backpedaling to the door. As was the case before, Erika's name and picture appeared on the screen, followed by a small click.

"They just disappear?" Erika said, bewildered. "What in the magical fuck is this?"

"Yeah, the doors are trippy. You'll get used to them though."

Erika looked up to see a tall, athletic white man coming down the hall, his own doorway disappearing behind him. His messy, ash brown hair came down just above his eyes, never quite getting in his line of sight. He was cleaning off his glasses when he came to a stop near Erika and Abby.

"I don't get why they do it either," he said. "But it's easy enough to find your room so long as you know what floor you're on."

"And you are?" asked Erika.

"Oh, right, sorry," he replied. "Shaw Felix. You must be the new recruits."

"We're still not sure what that's all about, but that's us," said Abby. "I'm Abby Lin. And this is Erika Edens."

"Nice to meet you both. Are you both doing anything before our group meetup?"

"I don't think so," replied Abby.

"You could come watch my training?" said Shaw. "It sounds like none of us know exactly what you'll be doing, but it might be useful for you to know what I do. Since this is a mission and all."

Abby looked at Erika, hoping she'd give some sort of answer. With a shrug from Erika, they followed Shaw down the hallway toward the elevators.

"We've got an interesting crew here," Shaw stated.

"Have you ever done something like this before?" asked Abby.

"Save the world?" asked Shaw. "Not even close. But it sounds like our goal is limited. I think we can do that. Plus, we've got a diverse skill set, so we should be able to handle for most contingencies."

The elevator doors opened to reveal a sparkling obsidian car. The three of them piled in, doors shutting behind them.

"Where to?" a fluttering female voice asked.

"The practice arena, please, Sadie," Shaw said.

"Yes, Mr. Felix."

The elevator lurched upward, moving much quicker than Erika had expected. She stumbled, her body colliding with Abby's.

"Falling for me again?" Abby said, chuckling.

"Very funny," Erika mocked.

The elevator came to a stop, opening its doors to a massive room with high, vaulted ceilings. It reminded Erika of a gymnasium, only without the bleachers, basketball hoops, and volleyball nets teenage Erika would have associated with such a room. There was a row of chairs lined up along the far wall, along with another set on portions of each of the perpendicular walls. A series of balconies – not unlike press boxes or suites in sports arenas, Erika noticed – lined the long sides of the room, though they were a story above the ground floor of the room.

The near wall of the room housed a series of cabinets, some tall, some short, along with a small seating area. Both side walls of the room were nearly empty aside from their chairs, though both walls themselves featured a series of speakers – seven a side in total – that ran the length of the room at set intervals.

For a space this large, Erika expected there to be some sort of staffing around. It seemed to be just the three of them, and only Shaw with any idea what this room was used for.

Shaw walked over to a tall cabinet along the near wall, retrieving a pair of wood-like sleeves with leather gloves on the end.

"What are those?" asked Abby.

"They're training gauntlets," said Shaw. "They let me learn the weapon and the elemental magic of the real weapon I'll be using without risking injuring myself until I understand how it works."

"Elemental magic?" Erika interjected; her face glazed over with confusion.

"Have a seat," replied Shaw. "I'll give you a demonstration."

Erika and Abby took a seat along one of the side walls. Shaw strapped the training gauntlets onto his arms, taking care to double check each of the connections he'd made as he did so.

"Sadie?" Shaw yelled into the arena.

"Yes, Mr. Felix?" came a response that filled the room. It was the same voice from the elevator.

"Set up a basic training scenario for Apidae Gauntlet training. Low level and small size, ideally. I'm just trying to demonstrate training weapon usage and safety."

"Understood. Generating demonstration scenario, version 9.0.1.136b, Apidae Gauntlet combat training."

A large black wall began to materialize, cutting the room down to about one-fifth of its initial size. A clear screen also appeared in front of the chairs. Erika reached out and touched it. It felt like plexiglass, though Erika had no idea how such a substance could materialize out of thin air, never mind the fact that nothing appeared to be holding it up.

A series of mannequins appeared around Shaw, the closest just outside of his arm's reach. By quick count, Erika estimated there were a couple of dozen of them around though she couldn't say for certain.

"Are you ready to begin, Mr. Felix?" Sadie asked.

"I am."

The lights lowered slightly and a chime echoed through the room. Shaw immediately charged at the mannequin closest to him, delivering a swift flurry of punches that knocked it to the ground. With a nimble stride, he made his way to a second target, dispatching it as quickly as the first.

"Is he serious?" Erika whispered to Abby. "This looks like a bad action movie."

After taking down a third target, Shaw waited as a line of mannequins began to form in front of him. He chuckled to himself, fiddling with dials on the gauntlet on his left arm.

"Sapphire Haze!" he shouted, pointing his left arm forward at the targets.

Within moments, a glimmering mist formed in front of Shaw. He raised his arm high in the air, the sparkling cloud rising in concert with his motions. After a few seconds – and what Erika was convinced was a wink in their direction – Shaw threw his hand down. The misty cloud turned into a volley of blue dagger projectiles, crashing down on the dummies, and obliterating them.

Erika stared at the scene as the daggers began to disappear. She couldn't believe what she was seeing. There had to be some sort of scientific explanation to all of this, though the simpler answer was that this was all a dream. Or that she'd walked into the plot of an anime.

"How the fuck is he doing that?" Erika wondered.

"I think the special effects budget is starting to kick in," Abby whispered.

Shaw was readying for another attack, a scattered formation of enemies already beginning to appear in front of him. This time he used his right arm as a base, steading the gauntlet on his left hand as he lined up a shot.

"Terra Pulse!" he yelled.

A halo of rock and earth shot out of the gauntlet, expanding from a small ring to a massive circle as it arrived at its targets. Unlike the first maneuver, this attack didn't seem to damage the mannequins so much as it did slow their movements. Shaw was quick to capitalize on this change, darting in and delivering a series of punches and kicks to some of the closer enemies.

"Final wave incoming," Sadie's voice said.

"Have it move with some purpose," Shaw replied.

"Yes, Mr. Felix."

The largest set of dummies yet appeared on the arena floor, practically surrounding Shaw. Instead of attacking – or even appearing to line one up – Shaw knelt on the ground. He used the left-hand gauntlet to create a barrier around himself, holding his right arm high in the air. As the barrier was closing, Shaw began to shout his command.

"Chrysidoidea Cyclone!"

A low buzzing sound filled the room, overpowering everything else around it. Erika could feel the sound coursing through her entire body, suddenly thankful for the barrier between her and the training area. A swarm of jewel wasps began to fill the arena, attacking the mannequins. In a matter of moments, the targets were on the ground, shredded and tattered from the attack. The few lingering dirt-covered mannequins didn't fare much better, though the damage was harder to see. Sadie's voice was faint, barely audible over the cacophony of the insects.

"Scenario complete. Retracting all battle elements."

As quickly as the buzzing had begun, it stopped. The mannequins vanished off the ground, leaving Shaw alone on the arena floor, still kneeling. His barrier had vanished, though he seemed to be waiting for the simulation to completely end before moving.

"Removing barriers and safety protocols," said Sadie. "You may exit the training floor at this time."

Shaw stood up and walked over to Erika and Abby, unbuckling the gauntlets from his arms as he moved.

"That was so cool!" Abby said gleefully.

"It's so fucking cool!" Shaw replied. "And these are just the training versions. Can you imagine what the real ones are like? I'm curious to see what they give the two of you to use."

"Why do we need something like that?" Erika asked. "That could kill so many people."

"These are training weapons," Shaw stated. "Everything I'm doing there is based on simulations Sadie is creating and how they're interacting with the actions I'm taking. But for the real weapons, the magic only works inside the Azaes Realm. If I were to take these – or the real Apidae Gauntlet – to Earth, they'd basically be useless to me. I mean, getting a forearm to the face with one of these things would hurt like hell. But the mineral shards and the wasps stay here."

As Abby quizzed Shaw on the mechanics of how the gauntlets worked, Erika sat back in her chair and began to think. She really needed to get back to the room and finish reading about the realm. Or at the very least, she needed to know what Abby had learned. Something wasn't adding up.

If the goal of their mission was, as Svieva had said, to stop the end of the world, why train them on weapons that would have limited use on Earth? And while Shaw seemed competent enough at fighting (at least the best that Erika could tell), she certainly had no hand-to-hand combat or weaponry skills to speak of. While Abby had taken a few self-defense courses, they certainly weren't enough to bring her to Shaw's level of skill, never mind considering her a trained fighter.

"Have you considered the possibility you're a human sacrifice? You like getting kicked when you're down."

There were still more people to meet, but Erika couldn't tie it all together. Maybe Abby could be the tactician for whatever this master plan was. But if she couldn't connect to the internet or the various databases she learned with, there'd be limitations on what she could do. Not that Abby wouldn't figure things out. She'd learned to love despite being born a computer program.

"In spite of you."

But why bring her here?

And where exactly was here? The explanation seemed simple enough to Abby, even if Erika didn't understand it herself. She got the concept of an intersecting universe, even if she couldn't fathom how they existed or why she'd never heard of one before coming here. What she couldn't get was why everyone here was from Earth. Why would they care more about a place they weren't in than where they were? And why didn't any room in this building seem to have windows?

No, Erika thought, something wasn't right about the Azaes Realm. She just didn't know what yet.

4
Commedia di Guerra

January 1, 2035/16:02, Day 93, Year 10311

Erika and Abby sat quietly in a small room with a round table, as they waited for whoever would be running the meeting to show up. Though they had met Shaw earlier in the day, everyone else in the room was new to them. And though everyone had been polite and introduced themselves, Erika was certain she'd forget their names by the time the meeting was over.

To Erika's left sat a slender, short Black man named K'Andre Jones. He was, aside from Abby and Erika, the quietest person in the room. Beyond his name, he hadn't said a word since Erika and Abby got there. He looked calm and collected – or desperately tired. Erika couldn't tell which one. Considering how he was sipping on coffee in the afternoon, Erika assumed the latter.

According to Shaw, he and K'Andre were childhood best friends. They seemed like polar opposites at first glance, though Erika knew well that those kinds of friendships can work out for other reasons. If nothing else, it seemed likely that K'Andre had his work cut out for him trying to keep Shaw in line.

Shaw sat to K'Andre's left, then to his left came a muscular, middle-aged woman with slicked back hair. She'd introduced herself as Lace, though Shaw was quick to mention that her actual name was Sara. Her impeccable posture and constant scanning of the room initially gave Erika cause for concern, though she quickly reasoned that Lace would be shutting everyone up if they were in real danger.

Lace spoke with a thick Scottish accent, words spilling out of her mouth quickly. Erika found her accent difficult to understand, though it seemed she was the only one not following along. Maybe she was more tired than she realized.

Seated between Lace and Abby was Lorena de León. Lorena looked to be the youngest of the group by far – Erika estimated her to be in her early 20s, while everyone else was at least in their early 30s, if not older – but certainly didn't act her age. She was reserved in speaking, but when she did, she commanded the attention of everyone in the room.

Shaw seemed to be particularly enamored with Lorena, finding a way to work in subtle flirts whenever the opportunity presented itself, as well as occasionally when it didn't. Lorena, for her part, either ignored Shaw's flirtatious comments entirely or snapped back at him with an insult. A quick jab to the ribs from K'Andre's elbow stopped him, but not for long before Shaw was right back at it.

Poor girl, Erika thought. At least he's not hitting on me.

In the back of the room, a group of individuals that Abby identified as envoys of the various gods sat, talking amongst themselves. First was a balding, middle aged man with olive skin and tufts of wavy black hair combed from front to back. His name was Tevarius, Tev for short, envoy to Brigid. He spoke with a nasal, fluttering voice, driving Erika to cringe if he got going on a long tangent.

To Tev's left was Revaus' envoy, Quaid. His high-and-tight haircut looked freshly barbered, clean lines all around the edges. His brown eyes sagged as those around him talked, betraying the fatigue he was so desperately trying to hide. Erika assumed he was older than Tev, though she couldn't tell if that was because Quaid was actually Tev's senior or because he looked like he'd just pulled back-to-back all-nighters.

Next was Adelina's envoy, a young woman named Kuhla. She wore her baby blue hair in a braid that went halfway down her back, accented by bright silver accessories throughout its length. Kuhla occasionally peeked up from the book that she was reading to input her thoughts into the conversation going on around her, but largely couldn't be bothered to focus on what the other envoys were talking about.

Much of the conversation between the envoys was focused between Tev and the final envoy, Vermilion. Dau's personal envoy was by far the most vocal of the group, as loud and brash as she was alluring. Strange that Shaw would choose Lorena over Vermilion, Erika thought. Then again, hitting on the envoy to the god of chaos likely wasn't the most sensible plan. Nevertheless, Erika's gaze lingered on Vermilion's piercing mahogany eyes.

"I don't know who she is, but she's really pretty," Abby whispered.

Erika nodded slightly, relieved to hear Abby agree. Even with their history, things still felt too new to say Abby wasn't the only attractive woman Erika noticed. Finally ending up here had taken too long for to risk fucking it up for a pretty face.

The door to the room opened, a lanky, athletic woman with long, braided carmine hair entering the room. She was dressed in a red and black argyle sweater with black dress slacks, making her the only person in the room not in casual clothing of some sort. She passed out a stack of folders to each person in the room, then walked to the head of the room and began to speak.

"Good afternoon," she said. "My name is Nell. I am the lead elemental weapons researcher and armory chief here in the Azaes Realm. I haven't had the pleasure of meeting any of you yet, but I assure you that we'll have time for pleasantries after we cover the purpose of our meeting today."

"Oh good. She's one of those people."

"For now," Nell continued, "I'd like to give a bit of an introduction to the rest of the team for our final recruits. I'd like everyone to meet Abby Lin and Erika Edens."

"I thought you said there was only going to be one more member of our squad," Lace said.

"Plans change, Lace," Nell stated. "You of all people should know that. Now, who wants to go first?"

Shaw eagerly bounded up from his chair.

"We've already met," he said, "but I'm Shaw Felix. Back on Earth, I was from Davenport, Iowa. I'm a high school history teacher and an independent pro wrestler. And I've been best friends with K'Andre here since we were in the first grade."

"Shaw will be part of our Alpha team," Nell added, "which will act in more of a supportive role to the Omega team."

Shaw sat back down, slapping K'Andre on the back. K'Andre stood up and, with a voice much more confident and louder than he'd initially told everyone his name in, spoke.

"Yeah, so, I'm K'Andre Jones," he said. "I'm a doctoral student in chemistry at Case Western Reserve University."

"Like the one in Ohio?" Erika interjected.

"One and the same," he said.

Why was it that everywhere Erika went she managed to find someone who was either from Ohio, had family in Ohio, or lived there? Her dad had always joked that Ohio was like the crazy uncle of America – always around when you least expect him to be, whether you want him to be or not – but Erika hadn't expected to run into this problem in whatever the Azaes Realm was.

K'Andre started to sit back down, seemingly thankful for Erika's interruption. Before his butt could hit the chair, Shaw piped up, encouraging him to stay standing.

"You didn't tell them the most exciting part about you, man," he said.

"That I like sitting down and letting other people take their turn?" K'Andre retorted.

"K'Andre here is a standup comedian," Shaw said. "And a pretty good one too. I'm not just saying that because he's my friend either."

"That's pretty cool," Abby replied. "How did you get into that?"

"Emotional abuse and racism, mostly," K'Andre said.

The room fell silent for a lengthy, awkward pause. The stillness hung in the air for what felt like an eternity to Erika...only for K'Andre to fall apart laughing.

"I'm kidding," he said between wails of laughter. "I had a friend convince me to go do an open mic night in high school and I was hooked."

A beat passed.

"But also, the emotional abuse. And the racism," he finished, his voice back to being deadpan serious.

"Always have to end with a downer," said Shaw.

"You know it."

"K'Andre will also be on the Alpha team, along with Shaw," said Nell.

Lace stood up next.

"I'm Sara Ross, though everyone calls me Lace," she said. "I'm from Ayr, Scotland, and spent part of my adult life in Afghanistan and the US. I'm an ex-RAF pilot and a hand-to-hand combat specialist. I'll be responsible for most of the combat training you all will receive."

"Lace will be heading up the Omega team," added Nell, "though, as she said, you'll all be working with her in some fashion to improve upon your pre-existing skills, in addition to the work most of you will do with the guardians to hone your elemental weapon training."

Pre-existing skills?

"Unless it's downing scotch, I don't know what the two of you have in common."

Just because she's Scottish doesn't mean she drinks scotch. Or drinks.

"The only thing you've fought is a cold. It tends to kick your ass."

Lorena rose from her chair next.

"My name is Lorena de León," she said. "I'm from Palma on Mallorca. Prior to coming here, I was a personal assistant for the CEO of a major Spanish bank. I have a background in organizational management and electrical engineering."

"That's an interesting combination," Abby said.

"I couldn't make up my mind what I wanted to do in university," Lorena continued. "So I did both. I was awarded a Rhodes Scholarship, but I turned it down so that I could take the job I had before being in the Azaes Realm."

"Wait," said Erika. "You've finished school, turned down a Rhodes Scholarship, and are an assistant to a C-level executive and you're how old?"

"Twenty-two," said Lorena. "Well, no. It might be twenty-three at this point. The maths of aging in the Azaes Realm are not my thing. Let's just call it twenty-three."

Fuck. How has she done so much?

"How have you done so little."

"Lorena will be leading the Alpha team," said Nell. "I believe you're up, Abby."

Abby smiled and bounded out of her chair, her energy nearly

matching that of Shaw.

"I'm Abby Lin!" she said excitedly. "I'm a conscientia and a receptionist from Indianapolis."

"A what?" asked Lace.

"A conscientia. It's pretty much a self-learning computer program in a robot body."

"So a robot?" Lace said.

"Kind of," interrupted Lorena. "It's too simple to call what Abby is 'just a robot'. Think of it like an android if that's where you need to start. But a conscientia has the brain of a supercomputer and it has the emotional learning capacity of a human."

"That's...a better explanation than I've ever given," said Abby. "And I am a conscientia."

Lorena shrugged.

"I explain smart things to stupid people all day," Lorena stated. "The fact that I don't have to completely dumb things down in this room is a welcome change."

"Not completely? Only a little bit then?" asked Lace, her eyebrow raised.

"No that's not what—"

"Abby will be part of the Omega team," Nell interjected, "though you'll be training a little bit differently than the rest of the group since you aren't human. You'll still meet with Lace to cover some basics, but most of your training will be conducted either by Svieva, Brigid, or me."

"Neat!" Abby exclaimed. "Wait. Am I the only one getting trained by a god?"

"How does she know Brigid's a god?" asked Shaw.

"Unlike you, she can read," Lorena retorted.

"It's true," K'Andre added. "So illiterate you can't read body language."

"Hey!" yelled Shaw.

The corners of Nell's mouth perked up at the argument. When she noticed herself on the verge of smiling, she took a small breath, composed herself, and carried on.

"And finally, Erika."

"Do it."

No.

"Come on. It'll be funny."

Remember what happened last time.

"Yes, but that was with Minerva. And she was a little too –"

High-strung?

"--Bitchy for her own good."

"Hi. I'm Erika Edens and I'm –"

Erika paused. She thought about making the same joke she had the first day at the Friends of AI meeting – the same one that had set Minerva off at her. Erika shot a quick glance at Abby. Her face held an encouraging smile, her eyes soft and kind. Erika couldn't repeat her mistakes from before, even if she was sure the joke might go over better with this crowd.

"I'm a data analyst at a call center," she said. "And Abby's my girlfriend, though we've known each other much longer than we've been together."

"Erika will also be part of the Omega team," said Nell.

As Nell went on talking about it was the envoys turn to introduce themselves, Erika felt Abby's hand brush up against hers. Erika clasped her fingers around Abby's, shooting her a slight smile. Abby mouthed a silent thank you in Erika's direction, then squeezed her hand before letting go and focusing on the folder that Nell was directing everyone's attention towards.

*****

The meeting ended nearly two hours after it started. Erika hated marathon meetings on Earth, but when she took the time to consider the time conversion within the Azaes Realm, realizing that she'd just sat in a room for nearly 22 Earth hours, her brain was ready to melt.

Everyone had filed out of the room save for Erika, Nell, and Abby. While Abby was busy packing up the various papers and materials from the meeting – items that she had taken copious notes on despite not needing the notes herself – Nell came over to them, taking a seat beside Erika.

"How are the two of you adjusting to life in the Azaes Realm?" she asked. "I know it's only been a day and might be too early to tell, but I'm curious."

"It's different," Erika said. "I don't know what I'm supposed to think about it. Truth be told, I don't fully understand what it is."

"The reading's kind of heavy, isn't it?" Nell questioned.

"I'm just not much of a reader."

"I get it. I'll try to help you out where I can."

"How long have you been here?" asked Erika.

"I'm assuming you want Earth years," Nell replied.

"It's really the only way I have context right now."

"Let's see. It's 2035 on Earth now."

"Wait," Erika interrupted. "The year changed?"

"Yeah, while we were in the meeting," Nell responded.

"Happy new year!" Abby added, feigning a small celebration.

"I don't have access to champagne, but I bet there's black eyed peas in the pantries. Or ham. Or whatever you're supposed to eat for good luck when a new year starts. I could never keep track."

"That's a thing?" asked Abby. "We never did that celebrating a new year."

"That's because every year was exactly the same," replied Erika.

"That's not true at all! You had me there last year."

"I also had no money."

"Well had I known there was new year luck foods, I could have bought some," said Abby. "Can you make your own new year luck foods? I'd pick Chinese food. Or donuts."

"Or bacon," Nell stated.

"Oooo! Bacon!"

"Abby," Erika interjected.

"I was 29 when I came here," Nell continued. "That was 1999, so 36 years. There are others who have been here five or six hundred years."

"That's insane," Erika replied.

Nell shrugged.

"You get used to it," she said. "Besides. I've always found it easier to live in the Azaes Realm, regardless of when it is, than to be on Earth, whenever it is."

As Abby finished packing her materials, Nell stood from her chair.

"We'll have dinner as a team in about 90 minutes," Nell said. "Though I'd like to get the two of you outfitted with some training weapons in the interim. Care to join me on a trip to the armory?"

"I mean, sure," said Erika. "But why?"

"We have to get the two of you outfitted with weapons so you can begin your training. Hard to do that in a meeting room."

"It's just that –"

Erika's voice trailed off. She wasn't sure what she was getting herself into here, but wielding any sort of weapon wasn't part of what she had in mind.

"It's just that she's more of a lover than a fighter," Abby said, trying to finish Erika's thought. "Frankly, I think we both are."

"So was I when I came here," Nell replied. "I certainly wasn't a fighter. And while I hope teaching you how to use weapons is unnecessary, I'd rather you know how and never need it than to need to know how and have no clue."

"That seems reasonable," Abby said.

"Yeah. Reasonable," Erika replied.

5
Quartermaster

January 2, 2035/18:15, Day 93, Year 10311

"We need to swing by my room first," stated Nell. "While the vast majority of the weapons we house are stored in the armory, there are a small handful of special weapons that we keep under tighter security."

"So they're stored in your room?" Abby asked.

"Not at all," replied Nell. "That wouldn't be safe. I need a key to get them."

"That makes much more sense."

A short elevator ride took them to the top floor of the building. Unlike the long hallway that was found on the floor Erika and Abby's room, this corridor was quite short, tight enough that the three of them fit in it comfortably, but a larger group would have felt clustered. As they arrived at the end of the hall, three doors appeared out of the walls, one on each side of them and one straight ahead. Nell paused while the door on the left scanned her, then entered the room.

"What are the other doors?" asked Abby.

"It's not important right now," answered Nell. "We have a schedule to keep."

"So she's hiding something."

"Feel free to come in," Nell continued, "I won't be long."

Nell exited via a door in the back of the room, presumably to her bedroom, leaving Erika and Abby alone. Nell's room was quite tiny in comparison to the suite Abby and Erika shared. The living area and kitchen were condensed into an area small enough that Erika could nearly stretch her arms out and touch both walls. At five-foot, one inch tall, this wasn't a feeling Erika was accustomed to. It made her chuckle a bit.

"What?" asked Abby.

"It's just so tiny," Erika said. "I love it. It's like the room was built for me rather than you giants."

"Nell's not *that* tall," Abby replied.

"You're five foot eight and she's got at least four inches on you. I don't know how she lives in here."

"Comfortably," Nell said, laughing as she came back into the room. "And it's closer to six inches. Last I checked, I'm six foot one. But I used to have to share a one room home with my entire family. This is luxury."

They exited the room and made their way to one of the lower levels of the building. Nearly immediately after exiting the elevator, Nell stopped at a narrow wooden door. She pulled a bronze key out of her pocket and carefully unlocked it.

"All of the fancy technology in this place and this room opens with a key?" inquired Erika.

"Literally? Yes," replied Nell. "Though you wouldn't be able to use the key. It only works when it senses the fingerprints of those who can use it. If you're not one of the people authorized to use the key, it won't work for you."

She opened the door, leading Abby and Erika into a room no bigger than a broom closet. There were five safes in the room, two on each of the side walls and one on the back wall. Nell turned to the second safe on the right wall, carefully taking her time to unlock it. From inside, she produced a small hatchet and a thin black book.

"These are for you, Abby," Nell said. "This hand axe is named

Longhouse. It's a weapon capable of stunning opponents in melee combat or knocking them unconscious with pulses of energy."

"That seems dangerous," Abby said.

"It certainly could be," replied Nell, "though I will point out that Longhouse is one of the few elemental weapons in our possession that's completely non-lethal. While you could certainly incapacitate someone with it, you needn't worry about ending their life. As for the tome, that's the Book of Eterna. I will be giving you training on how to use that tome personally, as it is incredibly dangerous if misused."

"So why give us the incredibly deadly weapons now?" Erika asked. "We're not properly trained. And you don't just want any idiot running around with something that can kill someone. That's how mass shootings happen."

"There's no practical way to avoid it," Nell countered. "For those who need to learn to use tomes, the spells themselves take practice, study, and memorization. You'll be getting training versions of the elemental weapons to practice with. But there is an importance to having an understanding of – and a respect for – the weapons you're learning to use."

"Can I leave it here until I've had time to study and learn the weapon? Abby asked. "That just seems safer."

"As you wish."

Nell took the Book of Eterna back, placing it back under lock and key in the safe.

"You're free to head back up to the training area," said Nell. "Floor seventeen. Lace will be there to set you up with a training version of Longhouse and to show you how to use the room. She'll bring you down to dinner when you're done."

Abby left the room, heading up the elevator to her next

assigned task. For the first time since arriving in the Azaes Realm, Erika was without Abby.

"Welp. This is how you die."

She's just going off to train.

"I'm sure Abby's fine. You on the other hand."

Not worried about me either.

"You're stuck here with a stranger, in a place you neither understand nor trust, heading to get weapons you certainly don't know how to use."

"Are you ready to go in?" Nell asked.

Erika had been following Nell during her brief interlude with Grace, not noticing that they'd made their way to the opposite end of the hallway.

"I think so," Erika said.

"Anything I can do for you?" Nell asked. "I know these transitions can be difficult."

"Open bar? Hell, I'd settle for malt liquor right now."

"It's nothing you can help with."

"Alright. If something changes, let me know."

Nell placed her hand on a screen by a set of double steel doors, waiting a moment while the sensor read her palm. A light above the doors flashed blue, followed by the doors retracting into the walls beside them.

The room beyond the doors was unlike anything Erika had ever seen. On each side of her, the walls were lined with weaponry of all shapes and sizes. From swords and spears to knives and guns to weapons Erika didn't recognize, it was clear the room was an armory of some sort. But unlike rooms like this that she had seen in movies, the weapons were not lined up near one another. Each weapon was given a bit of space surrounding it, complete with a small wooden placard beneath it with a description of the weapon. The display was more reminiscent of a museum than anything Erika would have expected.

On the far wall of the room, a series of books were mounted in a similar manner to the weaponry on the side walls. Each of the books had its own placard as well, though the books were mounted open, obscuring their covers from sight. While Erika could quickly identify what each of the weapons on the walls appeared to be – presuming she knew what the weapon even was to begin with – the books looked like gibberish from a distance. Some featured beautiful artwork, while others were hand-written scrawls filled with messy penmanship. Still others held intricate diagrams that Erika assumed were alchemic in nature, though that guess was based on watching anime as a child and nothing more.

Down the middle of the room was a row of four tables, each about ten feet long, with a series of smaller weapons under glass cases on each. Like the weapons and books on the walls, each item was labeled with some sort of notation as to what it was, though the opulent placards had been replaced by simple cards. The colors, both under the glass cases and along the walls, were vibrant and beautiful, the striking purples, greens, reds, and blues, complimenting the sparkling golds, silvers, and bronzes adorning several of the items.

"See anything that interests you?" Nell asked, gesturing at the walls around them. "Or, better yet, anything you have a passing knowledge of how to use?"

"I've never used a weapon," replied Erika. "At least not seriously. I stole my cousin's nunchucks once and played with them."

"We have few sets of nunchaku around, though most of the ones in this room are for more advanced users. I wouldn't recommend using any elemental weapons until you have some training though, which limits what you can use right away."

"People keep saying elemental weapons. What exactly does that mean?"

"We'll be training your group how to use both elemental and non-elemental weapons," said Nell. "There's a tradeoff that goes with them, but if you're in a serious fight, it's worth it."

"How so?" Erika inquired.

"For most wielders of elemental weapons," Nell said, "the weapon uses up part of you as it does what it does. Water weapons damage your skeletal structure, fire weapons impact your blood and vocal cords, earth weapons damage your musculature, metal weapons impact the respiratory system, while wind weapons take a toll on the brain."

"Shit," said Erika.

"The tradeoff is that, depending on the weapon, you can generate immense power in whatever element you're using. We have healers – users of either light or dark aligned magic – that can help remedy this. You'll even build up some level of tolerance to the damage over time, meaning that you can use stronger and stronger weapons with enough practice. But even with consistent healing, humans will eventually feel the effects of their weapons."

"What about Abby?"

"That's the beauty of Abby," said Nell. "As a non-human entity, she doesn't experience the same effects that you will. She will lose power much quicker than normal, but I'm seeing what we can do to work on that."

"That still seems like a bad thing for humans to use," Erika continued. "I don't want something fucking up my lungs."

"We have healing staves to help with that, provided someone doesn't overuse their elemental weapon."

"What happens if you overuse it?"

"The damage has the potential of becoming permanent," Nell replied. "Or, assuming you can't get healed in a timely manner, you could die."

"That seems drastic," Erika said.

Nell shrugged.

"Learn your limits and heal frequently. That's what I always tell people."

Erika wandered along the tables in the room, examining the weapons under the cases in front of her. She paused at the second table, pointing at a silver and red chakram near the front edge of the case.

"What about this one?" Erika asked.

"That is a fire elemental weapon," said Nell. "It's known as the Lotus Quoit. If we can get you adept at using a training chakram, it's not a particularly difficult weapon to use."

"How does it work? Do I have to call out my attacks?"

"No," Nell replied laughing.

"Then why did Shaw do it when we saw him training?" Erika asked.

"Because Shaw thinks it looks cool."

Erika kept walking through the room, a bit overwhelmed by the number of choices she had available to her. A black boomerang eventually caught her eye, leading her to call Nell over.

"What about this one?" she asked.

"That's an earth element boomerang known simply as Wyrie," Nell replied. "It's a bit of an odd weapon — one more advanced than I'd recommend for you – as it's a non-returning boomerang."

"I thought boomerangs came back?"

"Not always. You have to be fairly adept at hand-to-hand combat to use this one. Have you had martial arts training?"

"I have not."

"Any sort of hand-to-hand combat at all?"

"Nope."

"Have you been in any fight in your life?" Nell asked, growing impatient.

"Not since I was in kindergarten," replied Erika. "I got in a shoving match on the playground with this one girl because she kept stepping on the back of my shoes."

Nell walked over to the farthest table, opening the case and raising up one of the trays of weapons underneath.

"Why can't I use a healing stave?" asked Erika. "I'm not exactly a physical specimen here."

"You could," replied Nell. "I'd still give you a weapon to defend yourself with if you need it."

"Awesome. Where do I get my healing stick?"

"That said," Nell continued, "being a healer is quite the responsibility. If everything goes perfectly, you might not even be needed. But when things don't go as planned – as is often the case when a real fight breaks out – you're the person who's responsible for making sure your friend doesn't lose a leg or die. And while others may not blame you for someone dying, you're going to blame yourself if you can't heal them. It's a role with minimal praise and significant potential for criticism."

Erika cringed at Nell's explanation of the realities of being a healer.

"Can't I just heal people once they come back from...wherever they're going?" Erika asked.

"We do have a staff of healers that work here. I'd be happy to introduce you at some point. But I do need to train you for combat situations, be that as a healer or not."

"On second thought, I'll stick with just a weapon."

Nell produced a pair of small wooden boxes, taking them over to Erika.

"I'd like to recommend these as your weapons," said Nell. "Granted, these are both training weapons, but there are elemental versions I can introduce you to when you're ready."

Nell opened the first box, revealing a set of brass knuckles.

"Lefty or righty?" Nell asked.

"Righty."

"Put these on your right hand then."

Erika did as Nell instructed. Nell then opened the second box, producing a shimmering butterfly knife.

"Oh my god," said Erika excitedly. "I used to do tricks with these."

"That's...that's not the point to this weapon," Nell replied, her voice lacking any semblance of amusement or joy that Erika held.

"But I *could* use it for that, right?"

"I mean, yes, but..."

"Sold."

Nell sighed and handed Erika the knife.

"Your training will start this evening," she said. "Since you lack any combat experience whatsoever, I'm going to have Lace train you in that first before we even consider any sort of elemental training."

"Didn't she say she was ex-military?" asked Erika.

"Yep. Good luck."

6
Fifteen Seconds to Midnight

January 6, 2035

"What do you mean, you can't locate them?"

"Exactly what I said. I can't locate them."

Youles Kift sat alone on a chair in the middle of a warehouse. He'd been to this location several times. It was one of the more secluded places he knew of in the Midwest – somewhere he could reliably lay low without suspicion in the event he was being tailed. An unguarded warehouse without cameras or closed-circuit television was nearly unheard of anymore. Quick access to I-65 let him get to Chicago and the Upper Midwest or Indianapolis and the Lower Midwest. No one knew him in the area. He'd never even bought gas at the same station within a two-county radius more than once. To have had this place as a reliable overnight safehouse for the past ten years was a godsend.

To be interrogated by a client was one thing. Things happened in his line of work. People are creatures of habit. Some are better about being unpredictable than others, but everyone has a price, and everyone has a weakness. That wasn't the concern.

He had worked with unstable, irrational, and even unpredictable clients before. There was a housewife in Tupelo who wanted her ex-husband to pay up on his child support. Give him a scare, but don't hurt him. People wanted that much more often than an actual hit. Youles did the job, pocketed the money, and went on his way. But then this woman started stalking him. She drove from Mississippi to Virginia following him, all to try to get her money back because she didn't think Youles had scared the poor bastard enough. Youles knew how to deal with that kind of crazy. Eleven years later, the housewife from Tupelo still hadn't been found. Even better, the ex-husband took the fall, then offed himself in prison.

Then there was the cabbie from Grosse Pointe, Michigan who wanted to fake his death to get away from a loan shark. Making someone disappear was hard enough. When the person wanting to disappear has people with a vested interest in their continued existence, it adds a layer of complexity to the matter. A small explosion in the cabbie's garage, a package with a rib and three fingers showing up on the shark's door, and a one-way ticket to Tampa set the cabbie free. All Youles had to do was to pay a mortician a few hundred bucks for some spare parts.

Youles loved when there were no loose ends.

But this client – or more accurately, these clients – were different.

"I've been looking for them since October," Youles said. "There's no record of them anywhere. Credit cards stopped getting used. Cell records stop the same day. I spent time staking out the one woman's parents at Christmas. I showed up pretending to be a cop looking for her for a made-up crime. They never even heard from her. It's like they vanished into thin air."

"If you'd done as I asked, they never would have had the chance to vanish."

These two clients were peculiar. Normally, they worked through intermediaries they insisted on referring to as envoys. They were good at covering their own trail. Youles hadn't been contacted by the same person more than once. It was always a new face bringing information from the same duo. They referred to themselves as Janus. No last name. No organizational affiliation. Just Janus.

Youles has tried to find them online, but when your client

happens to share part of their name with both a very large, very famous investment firm and a Roman god, results for individuals get buried – never mind two people co-using a single name.

He'd met with one of them a handful of times before, if you could call it a meeting. A courier – or envoy as Janus was particularly insistent upon calling them, even though no one had used that term in decades – would contact him, inform him of a meeting place and time, and then he'd be expected to show up. Youles would be alone in a room, much in the same way he was tonight. They'd be obscured from view, by darkness or some sort of sight line obstruction. In the event money needed to change hands, an intermediary would do the deed.

The first 'Janus' was a wealthy, middle-aged woman. Probably in her fifties at most, Youles figured. Polite and business-savvy, all the negotiation was done through her. Youles preferred her, if only because she wasn't the other 'Janus'.

Youles couldn't quite put his finger on anything about them. Sex, gender, age, economic status, education – he couldn't pin down any of it. They were the sterner, less personable of the two and tended not to come to the meetings. But if something went wrong, they were always the one that came calling. That's who'd come tonight.

The most frustrating thing, at least in Youles's eyes, was that Janus – whoever they were – had managed to find *his* hideout and use it for meetings with him. This warehouse had been his domain for years. He'd paid good money to the previous owner to ensure the building would be his without being traceable to him. There'd been shell corporations setup in the Bahamas, Dominica, and Nauru that deeds and finances had been filtered through. It cost a pretty penny, but the anonymity and stability of having a dedicated base of operations that no one knew about – and that next to no one realized wasn't part of the larger complex the building sat in – was an invaluable asset.

None of that seemed to matter with Janus. Even before their first meeting, it was clear to Youles that someone had managed to get access to the building without him knowing. They'd make him leave first, only for them to leave well after he was gone. There'd be no trace of them or their associates. And that pissed him off.

"It wasn't a mistake," Youles said. "I was given the wrong target. I ended up in some gentrified neighborhood in Carmel whacking some naked fat bitch. I didn't know until after the fact that you were looking for a firecracker and her robot friend."

"The envoy who brought you the initial assignment has been dealt with," the voice said.

"You mean Greg?"

"The source of your misinformation has been addressed."

"The fuck's the problem then?"

"You're an expert in your field, are you not? Part of what makes someone an expert is the foresight to know when to ask questions if something doesn't add up. Your inability – or unwillingness, whichever it may be – to do so turned a moderate error into a catastrophe."

"I can go get the mom or the dad," Youles replied. "Missing parents are usually enough to draw someone out of hiding."

"It won't matter."

Youles was getting frustrated.

"Did you hear me? The parents go missing, the children turn up."

"Neither you nor I are in a position to retrieve them now," the voice replied again.

"If they're abroad, I can get there," Youles insisted. "I've got contacts enough places that I can work something out. Where are they? France? Mexico? China?"

"It is not a matter of logistics. It is now a matter of patience."

Youles was at a loss. He wasn't one to mind waiting, but Janus was shooting down every plan. He could be taking other jobs once this was completed, if only they'd let him. Money wasn't an issue under Janus's employ – this was the first time he'd ever been paid a consistent salary in his life – but the money wasn't the point. It was the lack of control that he suddenly had over a business and reputation he'd built over the past 20 years.

"There will be a time when I need your services again in the future," Janus continued. "I encourage you to work on improving your craft in the interim. That is all."

"What do you mean im—"

"An envoy will be in contact with you soon. I assure you this one will not make the same mistakes."

"But wh—"

"Now leave before you find that your involvement in my plans is no longer required."

7

Dismantle & Repair

January 7, 2035/5:29, Day 94, Year 10311

"Why are we awake?" asked Erika, pulling a blanket back over her head.

"Because we have training at six," said Abby. "And while it's my second day, it'll be your first. And I don't want you to be late on your first day."

"This isn't school, Abby. It's okay if you're a couple of minutes late."

"I'd still rather not test that theory."

Erika felt the blanket lift off her face. Abby was standing over her, already dressed for the day, holding the blanket aloft. Erika stretched her arms out in a futile effort to pull the blanket back toward her body.

"But it's so warm!" Erika whined.

Abby leaned down, kissing Erika softly on the lips.

"Please get up," she said, smiling.

"I'm cold!"

"If you get out of bed, I'll make you breakfast."

"Just five more minutes?" Erika begged. "Please?"

Abby sighed and threw the blanket on the floor and headed toward the kitchen. Erika stared down at the blanket, feebly trying to grab it. Her arms were well short of the task, not even making it halfway to the foot of the bed. Her feet were able to reach the blanket, though its weight stopped her from being able to pull the comforter from the floor and onto the mattress. Faced with the dilemma of feeling slightly chilly or having to get up, Erika grabbed Abby's pillow from behind her and held it close, trying to squeeze any residual warmth out of it.

"What should I get you from the pantry while you get dressed?" Abby shouted from the kitchen.

"Right," Erika grumbled. "Magic fridge. Insane science-y crazy world place."

"If it helps you choose, I already made you coffee. Or at least the magic fridge did."

"Oh, praise be to the magic fridge," Erika stated. "For I have seen its light and basked in its glory. And it has rewarded me with a bounty from the heavens. We shall sing about its beauty forever and ever. Amen."

Abby peeked her head in the doorway, shooting a glare in Erika's direction.

"That's a little dramatic, don't you think?" said Abby.

"Abby. Darling. When you choose breakfast for me, please bring me a second cup o--"

The speed at which Erika was pulled off the bed and dragged on the floor caused her words to catch in her throat, leaving her short of breath and thought. She tried to catch the casing of the bedroom doorway as Abby dragged her to the kitchen, only to flail helplessly as she missed. Abby came to a stop by the table, dropping Erika's legs, then bringing food to the table.

"Alright," Erika said. "You've made your point."

"Point?" countered Abby. "That was for snarking me and acting like you were getting breakfast in bed. I'm going to make my point by drinking your coffee right in front of you."

"You wouldn't dare."

Abby raised the mug to her lips, shooting a coy smile just before she began to drink. Erika stumbled to her feet, nearly taking the dining table to the floor in the process.

"You win," said Erika. "I'm up. I'll have breakfast. I'll get dressed. I'll be a good student for the teacher on my first day."

Abby handed Erika the mug of coffee before leaning forward and planting a kiss on Erika's forehead.

"Good."

*****

Lace was imposing. Erika couldn't recall seeing anyone with as much muscle tone as Lace had in person. Outside of professional athletes, she didn't think it was possible. And yet, Erika had to train with her. One wrong move and Lace could snap Erika in half.

"Somebody's gonna get their ass kicked."

"What's your background?" asked Lace.

"Like where I'm from?" Erika replied.

"Fighting background. Muay thai? Boxing? Bar brawls?"

"I've never been in a real fight."

"Ah. I see. Keepin' it close to your chest so you can learn from me on the fly. Smart woman."

Lace tossed the towel she was holding off to the side, nearly hitting Lorena, who was standing off to the side, chatting with Abby and Quaid.

"Well, c'mon then," she stated. "Square up."

"No," Erika said. "I really mean I've never been in a real fight."

"First time you said it was funnier. Let's go."

"I'm not kidding, Lace."

"Really?" Lace asked, dropping her guard. "Not even like self-defense classes?"

"Nope."

"No brothers or sisters beating you up as a kid?"

"I'm an only child," Erika stated.

Lace took a deep breath and walked to the far side of the room. She was pacing and talking to herself, and though Erika couldn't hear what she was saying, it was clear Lace wasn't happy. While Quaid and Abby continued their conversation, Lorena had made her way to the training floor, watching Lace and Erika's interactions.

"Alright," Lace stated as she walked over to Erika. "This is both good and bad. It's bad because I thought everyone here knew something."

"Oh good. You're making new friends already. I'm so proud of you."

"But good in that you're a blank slate," Lace said. "Let's start as basic as we can. Let me move you around."

Erika let her body go limp. She waited awkwardly as Lace picked her legs up and moved them around the floor, carefully adjusting them repeatedly.

"That's your base," Lace said. She stood in front of Erika, mirroring Erika's stance. "Rock back and forth for a bit. Sway your hips. Move every part of your body except your feet but come back to right where you are. Remember how it feels. Whatever we do, you're going to bring yourself back to it after. Got it?"

"I think so."

"Good. Wait. You're not a southpaw, are you?"

"No," replied Erika. "Why does everyone keep asking me that?"

"Dominance," said Lace. "Most people have a dominant hand when they're doing anything, even fighting. I set you up in an orthodox or right-handed stance. You'll guard with your weak – left – side, allowing you to protect your strong side for when you need to attack."

"And I'm assuming you're left-handed because your right foot is forward?" asked Erika.

"Good eye, but no. I'm right-handed but made my stance southpaw because it confuses people when I fight. But I learned orthodox, so I can teach it to you."

"Were you a boxer?"

"I was a kickboxer before I joined the RAF and a personal trainer after I left," Lace stated. "And I'm cross-dominant. While I do most things right-handed, my dominant leg is my left one. My stance protects my strong leg, not to mention deliver more powerful kicks with it."

"You've put a ton of thought into this," Erika replied.

"And that's why I'm teaching you and not Shaw."

Erika heard Lorena let out a sigh.

"He's a wrestler though. That's not real fighting," said Erika.

"A common misconception that'd immediately put you at a disadvantage if you tried to fight him," Lace said. "Pro wrestling is a staged fight, but that doesn't make the combat any less real. He's got an amateur wrestling background and some judo experience, not to mention the Kalari training he's received from Dau. He'd fuck most people up."

Lace steadied herself in her stance.

"Now," she continued. "Attack me the best you think you can."

"You'll kick my ass," Erika said.

"If I were trying, yes. But I'm not. I want to gauge what your instincts are. Your coordination too."

Erika took a deep breath, doing her best to calm herself. She felt pretty good that Lace wasn't going to try to hurt her. But that doesn't mean she wanted to fight her. She paused, readied herself, then swung as hard as she could with her right hand.

Please don't hit her. Please don't hit her.

"Coward."

Erika watched as her fist made its way toward Lace. Time moved in slow motion as Lace stared down her oncoming punch, then deftly took a step back to get out of the reach of the strike.

Oh thank god.

Erika attempted to follow up the first punch with a second, quicker jab with her left hand. As she started to throw the punch, her hair flew in front of her eyes, blocking her vision. The strike missed. By the time Erika brushed her hair out of her face and was ready to deliver a third shot, she felt her feet leave the floor. Her eyes turned skyward, staring at the piercingly bright lights on the ceiling. Though they were practicing on a padded floor, the shock of hitting the ground stung Erika's head and shoulders.

"Fucking fuck," Erika grumbled, her muscles tensing up.

"Rule number one of a fight," Lace said. "Tie up your fucking hair."

Lace extended her hand and helped Erika off the floor. Erika dusted herself off – though with how pristinely clean the room was, she felt silly doing so – then walked to her bag. She grabbed a hair tie out of the pocket, restraining her hair in a tight, high ponytail.

"Not like that," said Lace.

"It's a ponytail," Erika retorted. "It's how I've always tied my hair up."

"Let me show you why that won't work."

"This sounds like I'm going to get my legs swept out from under me again."

"I promise I won't sweep your legs out from under you again."

Erika walked back over, taking the time to set herself up on her base as Lace had shown her.

"You're learning," stated Lace. "That's good. Now try that combo punch you tried before. I'll dodge, but I want you to keep coming at me."

Erika took a deep breath, then took a hard swing with her right hand, followed by a quick jab with her left. As was the case before, Lace easily dodged both shots.

"Keep comin'," Lace said. "You can do better than that."

Erika took a few quick steps forward, now delivering quick, alternating punches with her left and right hand. On the third punch, she felt her ponytail whip her in the left cheek. It smacked her in the right side of the face with punch number four. By the fifth punch, her long ponytail had smacked her in the face – and then she was flying. Erika felt Lace's grip release from her wrist just after she slammed on the ground.

"Told you I wouldn't sweep your legs," Lace said between laughs.

"This is going to be a running theme, isn't it?" Erika asked.

Erika made her way back to her feet. She winced as she stood, her back in much more pain now than she had been a few moments prior.

"A bun is your best friend," Lace said. "Unless you want to cut your hair like mine. But somethin' tells me you're not going for the Tilda Swinton look."

Erika carefully tied her hair up into a bun. She hated having her hair up at all, but especially in a bun. She always managed to tie it up too tight and hurting her head in the process. But if it kept her from unexpectedly ending up on the ground, it was worth it.

"Can we please go back to you teaching me things without giving me a concussion?" Erika asked.

"If I wanted to give you a concussion, you'd have one," Lace replied. "But sure. Let's get back to some basics. You've got a lot to learn and your body will need a break at this rate."

Great.

"I told you."

After an hour of training and sparring, Abby and Erika left the arena and headed back to their room. Quaid waited behind for Lace, who was stopped by Lorena as she cleaned up her stuff.

"That was tough to watch," Lorena said.

"She's never fought before," Lace replied.

"Maybe her time would be better used somewhere else."

"She's got to learn sooner or later. Best to get it out of the way now."

"Maybe your time is better used somewhere else."

Lace stopped packing her gym bag and looked up at Lorena.

"What are you saying?" asked Lace.

"You're being asked to train someone with zero fighting experience," Lorena replied. "You should be focusing on making people who already know how to fight better. Give her to Shaw."

"She won't take Shaw seriously. You heard her today."

"And she listened to you once you corrected her. She's open to learning. Let her learn, just let it happen with someone whose time isn't as important as yours."

"I appreciate what you're trying to do, but it's not your call. She's not part of your team."

"She should have been," Lorena insisted.

"And I should have Shaw," Lace snapped back. "It is what it is."

"Then let me have her."

"Not my choice."

"No one has to know."

"Lorena," Lace said, frustration seeping into her voice, "the chain of command exists for a reason. Plans aren't made arbitrarily. Even if I don't agree with it, I follow it. It's my duty."

"Isn't part of your duty speaking up when you know a plan is flawed?" Lorena countered.

"You saying I don't?"

"It's not just that she needs work—"

"I'm well aware—"

"She literally knows nothing about fighting—"

"If I may," Quaid interjected as he joined Lace and Lorena on the arena floor. "I think there's a better way to handle this."

"What do you suggest?" asked Lace.

"Bring your concerns to the guardians and the envoys. All of them. Making your case to one person can be effective, but only if they're on your side. If you really feel that Erika is better off being trained by someone else, say it."

"She shouldn't even be here!" Lace shouted.

"No, she shouldn't," Lorena concurred. "Give her to me and you take Shaw. I can help her learn everything she needs without the worries of teaching her to fight. You get an experienced fighter who doesn't flirt with you half the time."

"Oh. That's what it is?"

"No! Not like th—"

"I get it. You want peace. Put him in my way."

"I'm trying to make things easier for everyone."

"Bring it to the guardians and envoys," Quaid said. "Since Gersemi isn't here to provide direct input herself, it's the best you can do. And if you can convince them to the point of consensus, the next time someone sees Gersemi, it will be easier to change her mind."

8
In a Safe Place

"Holy fuck." Erika shouted over the sound of running water. "I have never been so excited to see a bathtub in my entire life."

"Why?" Abby yelled back from the living area.

"I feel like I got hit by a truck. Lace kicked my ass this morning and that's before we had to run this evening. I hurt in places I didn't know I had. How is that even possible?"

"I don't feel pain quite in the same way you do. But I can tell she's a very adept fighter. You're very lucky to have someone of her caliber to set the foundation for your combat training."

"Tell that to my spleen," Erika groaned.

Erika slowly lowered herself into the bathtub, the hot water and steam providing an amount of relaxation she hadn't anticipated. For as long as she could remember, Erika hated baths. The entire premise of sitting in the liquid you were using to clean yourself while the dirt was still in it freaked Erika out. The only reason she'd even considered the idea was because she'd showered first. But, as much as she hated to say it, this was nice.

With her eyes closed and the steam rising around her, Erika tried her best to forget about the entirety of the day. The training schedule for the team was structured – one day physical training, two days strategic planning. Repeat three times, then one day off. Erika and Abby had arrived mid-cycle, so she wouldn't have as many training days before a rest. That didn't make Erika hurt any less now though.

And then there was the lingering feeling that something

about the Azaes Realm wasn't right. Svieva and Nell seemed nice, as did everyone in their training group. But there was talk of gods and guardians. Aside from Svieva, Erika hasn't seen nor heard of any of them. Maybe that was coming with the strategic planning sessions, but it felt to Erika like something was being hidden.

"Are you going to bed soon?" asked Erika.

"I'd planned to be up until you went to bed," replied Abby.

"Can you come give me a summary of everything you've read about this place?"

"Literally everything?"

"As much as you can until I get bored or freak out. Don't worry about having to talk all night. I'm sure it'll be quick."

Erika waited for Abby to join her in the bathroom, expecting to hear her sit down on the toilet, the edge of the tub, or the counter by the sink – or knowing Abby, possibly the floor. After a long pause, Erika opened her eyes and looked around, finding herself still alone in the bathroom.

"Are you coming?" Erika asked.

"It's your time," said Abby. "And you're in the tub."

"How long have we been together now?"

"If you mean 'how long have we been dating' and if you're going by Earth time, a little under two months."

"First off," Erika said, "the whole Earth time versus here time thing is going to take me a while to get adjusted to. So sorry if I ask you stuff like that a lot."

"It's fine."

"Second, you've seen me naked. Much closer than this, I might add."

"I'm trying to respect your boundaries," Abby insisted.

"Abby. Please come here."

Abby walked into the bathroom and stood by the side of the tub. Erika pulled her down toward the tub, kissing her while also being careful not to pull Abby in the tub with her.

"Stay," said Erika. "Please. I need to figure out more about this place. And I like you around. So, I'd like you here."

Abby smiled and took a seat on the floor a few inches away from the edge of the tub.

"What do you want to know?" asked Abby.

"How are you okay with all of this?" Erika countered. "It doesn't make sense to me. I thought you were made to love wholly and unconditionally. Being able to fight seems to directly contradict that."

"Not necessarily. I could be play fighting you as a form of affection. Or I could be taking a taekwondo class for fitness and for fun."

"But that's not what this is. You're learning to use actual weapons. No. Scratch that. Hyperpowered weapons with the ability to do fuck knows what. That's not even remotely the same."

Abby leaned her head back against the edge of the tub, taking a moment of silent contemplation. Erika leaned over and kissed her on the side of the neck, sending a shiver up Abby's spine. Abby leaned her head against Erika's, quietly considering her response.

"I don't really know," Abby said. "I feel conflicted about it, don't get me wrong. I can learn the technique and the theory just fine. I'd like to think that it's because I was built to learn to love and protecting you means protecting the thing I love. But that seems a bit counterintuitive. What if my actions accidentally hurt you? What if my being good at fighting with these weapons makes you a bigger target? I'm just trying to figure it out as I go."

"But what reason is there for you to protect me?" asked Erika.

"I feel like saving the world implies some level of protection to those you care about."

"So you can just go from lover to fighter like that?"

"I wouldn't be able to if you weren't involved," Abby countered. "I'm certain of that. I don't get how that makes it okay to learn the skill to harm others. That doesn't seem particularly fair. And I still don't know if I'll be able to fight when it really comes down to it. But I'm of the mindset that if I'm going to need to protect you – even though it might be incredibly unlikely to happen – I might as well learn to do it the best I can."

Erika leaned back in the tub, letting the warm water envelope her as she relaxed. There was something oddly charming about Abby's willingness to fight for her. Though she didn't feel like she was in any sort of imminent danger, Abby's logic was sound enough.

"Shame you're useless protecting her."

Erika felt Abby begin to run her fingers across her cheek. Even though they'd been together for a little time now, it still warmed Erika's heart to have someone care for her the way Abby did. Erika smiled and closed her eyes, her skin tingling from Abby's touch.

"Anything else?" asked Abby.

"Go on to the whole gods, guardians, and envoys thing," said Erika. "That seems pretty important, even if I don't get it."

"There are five gods and five guardians within the Azaes Realm. Each of the gods and the guardians has a concept that they're the keeper of, though their powers vary in strength based on whether they're a god or a guardian."

"Svieva's a guardian, right?" asked Erika.

"Right," Abby replied. "Svieva is the guardian of memory.

There's also Janus, the guardian of time, Kedi, the guardian of justice, Tane, the guardian of peace, and Gersemi, the guardian of love."

"And is it something like where they need to be alive for their virtue to exist?"

"What? No," Abby said incredulously. "That'd be insane."

"How am I supposed to know!" Erika mocked. "The only God I learned about as a kid likes to have His name capitalized. Now I'm somewhere with enough gods to make a polytheist blush."

"The Romans alone have Azaes beat. They had 12 gods. The Greeks had the 12 Olympic gods, the Egyptians are believed to have had over 2,000 separate gods. That's not even getting into modern religions like Hinduism where there's believed to be about 33 million gods and demigods. If anything, five gods and five guardians seems like a very reasonable number of all-powerful beings to keep track of."

"Well when you put it *that* way."

"I can see how it'd be hard to follow," said Abby. "Aside from what the guardians protect and the fact that they can fight with elemental weapons and open portals to Earth, I really haven't found a ton of information about them yet."

"Do the envoys have powers?" Erika asked.

"Not in a magical or fantastical sense like the gods and guardians do, though they do wield power in their own right."

"As in they get to boss us around because they're designated to do so by the gods?"

"They do have power vested by the gods themselves," continued Abby, "though there's more to it than that. They're trusted with elemental weapons, much like the gods and those who work in the armory. But yeah, a lot of it is symbolic power that you get when the person you work for is all-powerful."

"This explanation is..." Erika trailed off.

"Boring?"

"Like reading a high school biology book."

"I can make some finger puppets if you'd prefer," Abby snarked, an obnoxiously large smile plastered across her face.

"I feel like I should be terrified you're that eager," Erika replied.

"We could be done?"

"No. I'll be a big girl and tough it out. What about the gods?"

"The info on them is even more vague. There are names given for three of them: Dau is the god of chaos, Brigid is the goddess of life, and Revaus is the goddess of order. All the literature in the room was written by Revaus, or at least on her behalf."

"It makes sense that the goddess of order would want everything documented."

"Agreed," said Abby. "But that doesn't explain why any of them aren't described well – nor why two of the gods aren't nearly non-existent."

"What do you mean?" asked Erika.

"There is a direct reference to a god of knowledge named Adelina. That said, what I've read states that she's reclusive and must be sought out."

"That seems like a very standard god of knowledge thing to do."

"I wouldn't know," replied Abby. "Are there a lot of mythological gods of knowledge on Earth I don't know about?"

"I mean it's like a movie thing," said Erika. "Wise old man or woman, hiding up in the mountains of Tibet or an African jungle or a slum in Bangkok or something. And that's not even counting space sages like Yoda. It's a whole thing."

"Maybe this god is who all of those things are based off of?"

"Seems unlikely. How many times have you heard of the Azaes Realm before coming here?"

"Fair point."

"You'd think her envoy would have an in with her," Erika suggested. "Or at the very least know where she is."

"We could try to find her envoy. If nothing else, it might point us in the right direction. Especially because it sounds like the recluse thing is a recent development – even though everything I've read presents it as fact."

"Who was her envoy again?" Erika asked.

"Kuhla," replied Abby. "Young girl with the long blue braid."

Erika stared at the wall of the bathroom, digging through the whirlwind of time since they'd arrived trying to remember Kuhla. She had to have been in the meeting where Nell introduced everyone, but nothing was coming to mind.

"Not the hot one," Abby sighed.

"I've got that much," Erika replied. "Did she even talk?"

"I don't think so. She seems pretty quiet. Maybe she's just introverted and will talk more if we spend some time with her."

"I don't get how I could completely forget someone with blue hair. It's not like that's a normal color."

"I'm sure once you see her, you'll remember her. Or fake it well enough that she thinks you do."

"What about the last god?" asked Erika.

"There's a god of death referenced in the literature as well," said Abby.

"That makes some sense," Erika interrupted. "If you have a goddess of life, you need some kind of counteracting death force."

"Agreed. But there's no name given to them. No description, no date of arrival to the Azaes Realm. Nothing of any real substance. I was able to find out that the god of death exists, even the other gods fear them, and that they make themselves known when it is most needed."

"Well, that's not ominous at all."

"And what's interesting," Abby said, "is that the god of death is new here, so to speak. There's a previous god of death, but they ceased to exist at an unrecorded date in the recent past."

"That feels like a weirdly important thing to leave out of records," Erika said.

"It's not like the Azaes Realm is an easy place to get in and out of. Either someone new would have arrived – and I'd think that'd be an obvious tell as to who's the new death god – or their powers transferred to someone who was already here. In theory. It's always possible they were on Earth and got brought here after the fact."

"Oh good. Glad to know the grim reaper is sulking around here somewhere with a scythe and a creepy ghost dog waiting to kill again."

"I don't think it's that ominous," Abby said.

"What if you're the god of death?" asked Erika.

"I'm pretty sure the power must transfer to a living being. Considering there are no animals around here, if we assume the god of death is already here, they'd have to be human."

Erika sat up and raised her hand out of the tub, motioning with her finger for Abby to come closer.

"Am I death?" Erika whispered.

"I don't know," Abby said. "Do you feel extra grim today?"

"I feel like I'm about to die."

"Then I think you're fine."

Erika rested her head back against the wall of the tub, allowing her body to sink back into the water.

"Okay good," she said. "I don't need that kind of responsibility. Did you ever tell me how the gods and guardians are different?"

"From what I could tell, "Abby said, "there really aren't many noticeable differences between the gods and the guardians in terms of powers aside from the fact that guardians can go to Earth. Gods cannot, aside from the goddess of life. And then there's the god of death, who seems to be more powerful than all of them, even though they each have their own unique powers related to the thing they're responsible for."

"How does that work?" asked Erika.

"From what I read, the goddess of life, Brigid, can shapeshift into many different forms. The guardian of time, Janus, has a limited capacity to see into the future. Revaus, goddess of order, can manipulate probability. And so on with each of the others."

"What makes the god of death unique?"

"Two things," Abby said. "First, they can be summoned by someone with access to a special spell. This allows to that person to kill a single target, but at the cost of their own life as well."

"That sounds like a horrifying proposition in the wrong hands," stated Erika.

"The other unique thing is that the god of death is the only entity in the entire Azaes Realm capable of summoning magic without the use of elemental weapons or staves. Of course, there's also the fact that Death doesn't have an envoy until they make themselves known. So even if we wanted to find them, it's not like we'd have any leads."

Erika shifted her weight, causing the bath water to ripple and wave. She slid down further into the tub, trying her best to avoid the air she could feel chilling as the room cooled. Even if everything else about the Azaes Realm was weird, the fact that the tub was long enough for someone much taller than her to stretch out in without having to bend their knees was a fantastic surprise.

"This thing is huge," she said, splashing water around with her legs.

"Bored again?" asked Abby.

"Not bored so much as I am trying to keep track of everything."

"I can come up with a mnemonic device or something to help you remember everything. The offer of a puppet show is still on the table too."

Erika shrugged.

"It's not even that," she stated. "It's just a lot."

"When you're done with your bath, I'll give you a massage," Abby replied.

"I can guarantee you I will fall asleep if you do that."

"I can give you a massage that helps you stay awake?"

"Abby Lin!" Erika said, her voice filled with faux surprise. "Are you propositioning me?"

"How can it be propositioning if we're dating?"

"I don't make the rules."

"No but...how?" asked Abby.

Erika pulled the plug from the drain, then slowly stood up from the tub, careful not to lose her balance.

"Hand me that, please," she said, pointing to a towel on the counter by the sink.

Abby obliged, giving Erika the towel, which she then used to dry off her hair before putting it up in the towel. A second towel soon followed.

"You know what I never got in high school or college?" said Erika.

"Laid."

"Bad grades?" asked Abby.

"I never got an attractive study buddy to study with."

"Flattery will get you everywhere, Miss Edens."

9
Council

"We're running a serious risk to the plan if we let Erika be part of the forward team," Lace said.

Lace, Lorena, Shaw, and K'Andre were seated along one side of a table in a meeting room. Across the table from them sat, the four envoys to the gods, Vermilion, Kuhla, Quaid, and Tevarius, along with Svieva and Nell. The room was tense, nearly everyone with a look of frustration on their face, save for Kuhla, who very clearly wanted to go to bed.

"This isn't anything against Erika," Lorena stated. "Lace and Shaw have said she's willing to learn. But she's going to get in the way."

The panel in front of them was largely quiet, save for the occasional sipping sound Kuhla made as she drank her tea. Vermilion, envoy to the god of chaos, was the first to respond.

"What makes you all think that her inexperience is not offset by other skills she might have?" asked Vermilion.

"She can't fight," Lace stated.

"Neither could Lorena when she arrived," Vermilion replied.

"But I'm not part of the team that has to fight," Lorena insisted. "She is."

"It's too late in the process to get her up to speed," Shaw added. "Lorena has been here nearly an Earth year and she's just now comfortable. We've barely got that long until the mission is scheduled to begin."

"Presuming everything goes to plan," Quaid said.

"It *will* go to plan," Vermilion retorted.

Svieva stood up and began to pace around the room. They held a certain sway whenever they entered the room, especially when the envoys were involved. Svieva had originally entered the Azaes Realm as the envoy to the previous god of death, Pollux. After he died, Svieva began to develop magical abilities of her own, leading the other gods to wonder whether they were the next god of death. Though it quickly became clear that Svieva had merely gained the powers of the guardian of memory, it was still the first time in thousands of years that an existing inhabitant of the Azaes Realm had developed the powers of a god or guardian after they were already in the realm.

The envoys showed a sort of reverence toward Svieva normally reserved for the gods they individually served. Even the outspoken Vermilion would defer to Svieva whenever they were in the room. Though most figured it was, rightfully, due to Svieva's natural kindness, there were some who wondered if the respect shown to Svieva was only because the envoys themselves wished to have a similar transformation of their own in the future.

"The concern here," Svieva began, "is less so with the viability of Gersemi's plan and more with the personnel needed for it to succeed within the timeline that's been set forth. Am I understanding this correctly?"

"You are," confirmed Lorena.

"You've been leading her training thus far, Lace. Do you think she'd ever be able to learn what you're teaching her?"

"With enough time, yes," Lace replied. "Nowhere near the time we have."

"Can you get her combat abilities to the point where they're passible?" Svieva continued.

"Define passible."

"Good enough that she won't actively harm herself or others by trying to help."

The room went quiet as Lace contemplated her answer. The silence was broken by Kuhla turning a page in her book, the movement of paper rippling through the room like the waves from an acorn dropped by a squirrel from a branch high above a serene lake.

"I don't think she's going to be competent enough to not be a danger to others," Lace said.

"Let me train her then!" Shaw interjected. "Please?"

"Shaw, shut the fuck up," Lorena said, rolling her eyes.

"I'm not saying I have to do it by myself. What if Lace and I both train her? In theory she should pick up enough from the two of us that she should be able to fight alright."

"Or she becomes an incoherent mess confused by two teachers with differing styles," Tevarius interjected.

"Thank you!" Lorena shouted. "She needs a consistent teacher. And she shouldn't be fighting at all."

"Oh no, I don't agree. I'm merely playing devil's advocate."

"Tev's got a point though," Vermilion said. "If one person can't fix her, adding a second voice would only give added information for her to forget."

Kuhla looked up from her book, seeming to notice the escalating debate around her for the first time.

"It's diminishing returns for sure," Kuhla said, "but I don't see the harm in trying. Maybe it's an issue of compatibility in learning and teaching styles."

"I don't get why we even need her as a combatant!" Lorena said. "Please. She really should be back with me and K'Andre. Shaw fighting shouldn't be a backup plan."

"Dude knows how to fight," K'Andre added. "And Erika knows...something?"

"Barely," Lace mumbled.

"There's a plan," Svieva said, cutting off any of the envoys before they had a chance to speak. "Gersemi has never led me astray before. I have no reason to believe she's doing so now."

"But what is the plan?" K'Andre asked.

"She's only revealed information on an as needed basis," Tevarius interjected. "She's Brigid's guardian and I'm her envoy. If anyone would be in the loop here, it'd be me."

"What *do* you know?" asked Lorena.

"I know as much as anyone in this room—"

"Then tell us what you do!"

"Oi! Lorena!" Lace snapped back. "Enough. He said he doesn't know. Shouting doesn't change that."

"Yes ma'am," Lorena replied sheepishly.

The room went quiet again. The envoys looked at each other, each waiting for the other to speak, save for Kuhla who had gone back to her book. Lorena and Lace both stared off into space, taking care not to look at one another after their brief spat. K'Andre, convinced Shaw would do something stupid to break the silence in an otherwise serious meeting, gave Shaw a swift kick to the shins under the table.

For the first time since the meeting began, Nell cleared her throat and began to speak.

"It's clear there are a lot of concerns floating around right now," she said, "both in this room and in this complex. Gersemi's desire to venture outside of the Azaes Realm for extended periods of time is, indeed, a point of contention. The four of you are worried about the addition of Erika to the team, not to mention the already short timeline that everyone has been provided to execute Gersemi's plan. Then, of course, there's the fact that Gersemi has only provided us information as needed for that plan."

Nell turned to Svieva, who was still pacing around the back of the room.

"Svieva," Nell continued. "When you saw Gersemi on Earth, did she say why the plan changed?"

"Only that she'd been in touch with Death and that this was the new plan," Svieva answered.

Vermilion sighed.

"Of course," Vermilion said. "Do you really wish to go against Death? Literally the one entity that could end us all is the one helping Gersemi plan this."

"You're just jealous you didn't get promoted to death god when the old one died," Quaid snarked.

Vermilion grabbed Kuhla's book out of her hands, careful to stick her finger in between the pages where she was reading. With a swift motion, Vermilion delivered a powerful slap with the book across Quaid's face, placing the book back in Kuhla's lap before Quaid had time to react.

"I wish they'd be more forthcoming with their decisions," Nell said. "That said, I understand the need for secrecy, particularly if Janus is not working alone. If this is what Death has planned, then there must be a good reason for it."

"Do you think Janus isn't working alone?" asked Lorena.

"It's not my place to speculate on that."

"It'd be foolish of Janus to work alone," said Kuhla, not bothering to look up from her book. "While it's certainly easier to keep a secret that way, plotting the downfall of an entire civilization – especially one that you were once a part of but have long since separated from – is not a one person job."

"Then Janus is working with someone on Earth, clearly," Quaid said. "It's not like any of us can go back, save for Svieva, Brigid, and these four."

"K'Andre," Nell said. "You haven't said a word. Do you agree with the rest of the team on this matter?"

"It's not my place to judge this plan," said K'Andre. "I'm here to do a job. Nothing more."

"A man after my own heart," Tevarius said, smiling.

"I would encourage you all to remember that those who do not fit neatly often show themselves as being useful in other ways," Svieva stated. "It's probable that Erika may not look to be of use to you now, but that doesn't mean she won't in the future."

"Then why not put Shaw with me and Abby?" asked Lace. "Give me the best fighter we have to go along with our new superweapon, not some desk worker with no coordination."

"If I may," said Nell.

"Of course," Svieva replied.

"I will be meeting with Erika and Abby tomorrow to help them to better understand the history and purpose of the Azaes Realm. Brigid will also be joining us for part of the session. I think that between the two of us, we should have a pretty good gauge of how accurate the team's concerns are after our lesson."

"And you are certain of this how?" Vermilion asked.

Nell gestured to the team of four across the table from her.

"Part of why they're as unified as they are is because of the work we – and they – have put in so far," Nell said. "Let me do what I do best."

*****

"Lydia, are you a hunter?"

"Never got into it. Why?"

"Step closer. I have something for you."

Lydia rose from her seat, walking further into the spotlight shining down from the rafters. An old theater was a strange meeting place, but she'd encountered weirder people in more bizarre places. And no job was paying close to what this one was promising.

She opened the mahogany box on the floor of the stage, revealing a shimmering steel cutlass with a silver-toned hilt. Beside the sword lay a long-barreled pistol, along with a box filled with several large caliber bullets.

"Is this a choice or do I get both?" Lydia asked.

"They're both yours, along with whatever other weapons you need. I make sure that those who protect me are well outfitted and similarly compensated."

"These are a great start. When do I get to test them out?"

"All in due time, my dear. Now. Take your gifts and rest up. I'll need you to be my eyes, my ears, and my face soon. I'll make sure you have all you need to handle that too."

"You're very generous, Janus."

"And you are very wise to believe in my vision."

10

Runner's High

January 13, 2035/7:17, Day 95, Year 10311

"Good morning!" Nell said excitedly as Erika and Abby walked into the armory. "Ready for the day?"

Erika groaned, sipping at her coffee.

"You brought this on yourself."

"Late night?" asked Nell.

"She's still sore from training with Lace yesterday," Abby said.

"I can help you with that."

Nell walked to the back of the armory, grabbing one of the staves off the back wall. She walked back over, holding a short maple staff in her left hand.

"Give me your coffee," Nell said.

"Fuck off," Erika grumbled. "It's the only thing keeping me upright."

"I'm not drinking it. Hand it over."

Erika gave Nell a puzzled look, slowly handing her the coffee cup. Nell smiled, taking the cup and setting it on the floor in front of her. She pointed the stave at the drink, a soft, white light pouring out of the end and absorbing into the liquid inside. After a few seconds, Nell handed Erika back her coffee.

"Don't worry, the flavor hasn't changed. I'm picky about my coffee. I wouldn't lie."

Erika took a sip. The flavor hadn't changed, though she was convinced the coffee was slightly warmer. Within a few seconds of drinking it, the stiffness and pain in her lower back and shoulders began to dissipate. The headache that had begun the first time Lace knocked her to the floor faded away shortly after.

"How did you do that?"

"It's a healing stave," replied Nell. "Before I was in charge of the armory here, I was a healer."

"I thought only the gods and guardians could use magic," Erika said.

"It's a bit more complicated than that," said Nell. "While they are the primary wielders of magic within the Azaes Realm, there are others capable of using very narrow subsets of magic. This is usually with elemental weapons, but some people can use healing staves. My specialty is light and healing magic. While I can't use every healing staff or tome we have, I'm adept with most of them.

"Anyone can walk in here, grab an elemental weapon and start using it. Some take more skill to use well or to use at all though, so you do have to know a bit about what you're doing. Of course, there's also using them safely, which is particularly problematic for anything other than healing staves."

Nell took a quick look around the room, then reached into her pocket and produced a small book. Its cover was green and black, the color changing depending on how the light hit it.

"This is my personal tome, so to speak," she said pointing at the book. "It's one of the few healing tomes capable of using elemental magic – albeit to heal. Well, not magic, per se. But I've found that in trying to explain it to the rest of your group that it's just easier to say magic and leave it at that."

Erika examined the book, noting the fading gold letters on the spine of the book. She could make out the letters 'IEM', though the rest of the word was obscured by Nell's hand. The rest of the title – whatever it was – had rubbed off.

"Any healer can do what you just did?" asked Abby.

"Presuming they've got enough experience, that is."

"Literally that? Probably," replied Nell. "That was a basic healing spell. It's not something we teach the first day, but anyone with a decent grasp on light or order energy properties could do it."

"I thought order was one of the things the gods ruled over?" Erika interjected.

"It's also a kind of energy in the Azaes Realm. There are four types of energy present here – light and dark, order and chaos. Even the elemental weapons are bound to these four energies."

"Is that why Shaw's gauntlets are so unpredictable?" asked Abby.

"Partly. The Apidae Gauntlet does have a chaos-aligned energy in it. But there are several factors that impact how a weapon behaves, including its element, its energy, the skill level of the wielder, the type of attack being used –"

Erika interrupted, listing off her own factors. "The alignment of Mercury versus Jupiter, the percent of alcohol by volume used in their construction, the airspeed velocity of an unladen swallow."

"Two of those three aren't as far-fetched as you'd think," Nell replied, chuckling to herself.

"Wait. What?" asked Erika. "Which two?"

"That's not important," Nell said. "It's time for the two of you to learn more about why you're here. Brigid asked that she be part of this session too, so frankly I'm stalling while we wait for her to get here."

"Brigid is..." mumbled Erika under her breath.

"Goddess of life," replied Abby. "Is she typically late?"

"I run on my own schedule," said Brigid from the doorway, overhearing Abby's question. "Some people view that as being late, but I prefer to think of it as having my own plan."

Brigid walked over to everyone else, giving a subtle bow as she arrived.

"I presume you're our two new recruits," said Brigid. "I trust Nell has taken good care of you."

"She has. I'm Abby!" said Abby cheerfully.

"Wonderful to have you aboard."

"And I'm Erika." Erika's voice was peppier than when she'd initially arrived in the room. Though even the sudden relief of back pain didn't change the fact that it was morning.

"And it is a pleasure to meet you," Brigid said, flashing Erika a quick smile. "Now that that's out of the way, what are we covering today, Nell?"

"We're getting into more of the specifics of exactly how the Azaes Realm works," said Nell. "And, of course, why that's relevant for the need to save the Earth from itself."

Nell led everyone over to a small table in the back corner of the room. She seated herself with her back to the corner, allowing everyone else to have the less tightly cramped chairs. As everyone was getting settled, Nell pushed a wooden button on the wall. The armory wall filled with weapons shifted backward slightly, a large screen materializing and taking its place in front.

"Is everything here cool sciencey shit?" asked Erika.

"You could say that," replied Brigid.

"It understates the work that those before us have done," added Nell. "But it is, at its core, accurate."

The screen lit up, a giant white question mark on a black field appearing on it.

"Oh good. A fucking slide deck."

"I'm going to begin by asking you what I've gathered to be a particularly contentious question on Earth," Nell said. "What happens to a human after they die?"

"Are you asking what I was taught, what science says, or what I believe?" asked Erika.

"The fact that there are potentially three different answers there concerns me a little bit," Nell replied.

"It's my understanding that when you die, your body decomposes. And that's it for you. Your memory lives on with the people whose lives you've touched. But for you, that's all she wrote."

"Quite an eloquent way to put it. Is that what you were taught?"

"Not totally," Erika admitted. "There's only so long you can live in a white, middle-class neighborhood without hearing about Jesus. I think I made it to preschool."

"Fair enough," Nell replied. "And the third thing you mentioned: what do you believe?"

"I'd love to believe that reincarnation is real," Erika admitted. "The entire idea that you can live a life, learn from it, and then live your next life in a better or worse place because of your actions in the current one is calming. I'd like to believe you get to learn from the mistakes and successes you've had in the current life when you move onto the next one. Either that or everyone gets to go to the Heaven they believe in – whatever it is they might call it. I know this isn't how it works. But I wish it were."

Abby glanced at Erika, a look of amusement on her face.

"What?" Erika said.

"I never knew that about you," Abby said. "It's charming."

Erika stuck her tongue out at Abby, eliciting laughter from

Abby. Brigid chuckled to herself as well, though Nell insisted on carrying on with her lecture.

"From a purely literal standpoint, your scientific assessment is accurate," Nell said. "Following death, the body does decompose, eventually becoming part of the Earth again. Yadda yadda, circle of life."

"Spoken like someone who's going to live significantly longer than you."

"Did you just yadda yadda the entire life cycle?" Erika asked.

"I did," Nell replied. "That said, there is some truth to the spiritual component that many religions believe as well. Granted, each religion seems to take it a little differently, putting their own spin on it to make it fit more accurately with their specific narrative. But the idea that there is an afterlife spiritually is real.

"Though to simplify the Azaes Realm in such a way would be an underselling of the history of this place. To this point, who all have you met here? Not names specifically. Just generalize for me."

"Gods, guardians, envoys, other random folks floating around here and there," Erika said.

"But what do they all have in common?" asked Nell.

"They're all human," Abby replied.

"Exactly. Or at a bare minimum, they all once were. It depends on if you want to classify gods and guardians as still human considering their amplified powers and responsibilities. I personally do, but I know some don't."

"Wait, back up," Erika interjected. "Why is everyone here human? Is this some sort of secret government facility where people are turned into superheroes, only they have to be called gods and guardians for copyright infringement reasons?"

"Define here," Brigid said.

"Are you really playing the 'oh we're all not human in this room' card knowing full well Abby's a conscientia?" asked Erika.

"That's not what she means," Nell replied.

"I mean, a little bit," Brigid mumbled.

Nell continued, ignoring Brigid. "Putting aside Abby's status, she's right to say that those you've met – and that you'll continue to meet – in the Azaes Realm are human. Even if they've spent far longer in the Azaes Realm than they ever did on Earth, they're still humans. Though it's been that way for quite some time, this universe wasn't originally inhabited by humans."

"Like at all?" asked Erika. "What was here first? Aliens?"

"Oooo. Offensive Erika is coming out. Spicy."

"Alien wouldn't be the term I'd use," Brigid interjected. "If anything, we're the aliens here."

"Offended. Nailed it."

"Long ago, there was a race of beings in the Azaes Realm known as Azaeans," Nell said. "Hence the name. They were the original inhabitants of this place. They lived through wars and turmoil, through visits from beings in several different universes. This place was bountiful in the creatures that lived here. Not just the Azaeans, but all kinds of flora and fauna thrived as well."

"There used to be this creature called a ragauormelet," Brigid added. "Think of them as tiny tree frogs, but they had soft little kitten ears, wooly fur, and walked around on three legs. They were extinct long before we got here, but I'm fascinated by them."

"Aww," Abby said. "Like the little tripod doggies? Those poor things."

"Kind of. They had two legs in the back, but the front one was centered. Apparently, they walked by doing this weird gyrating maneuver that kind of looked like if you put a wool hat on a terribly slow frisbee."

"What did the Azaeans look like?" asked Erika.

"From what I've read, they weren't all that different from humans in a basic sense," replied Brigid. "They're featherless bipeds. They stand on two legs. They love corn."

"...a plucked chicken?"

"Then there's the eyes on the sides of their heads."

"Wait what," said Erika.

"The Azaeans are definitely not ambush predators," Brigid continued. "Don't get me wrong, they've gotten into quite a few battles and held their own surprisingly well. But there's a reason they were able to build all of this. Evolutionarily, those of their species who survived did so by adapting through planning, hyperintelligence, community building, and compassion."

"They seem to have a leg up on humans in that regard," Abby said.

"They do. Which is weird, because you'd think with a species with a three-sided head that comes to a point would be much more adept at fighting via headbutt."

"Is no one going to address how crazy this sounds?" Erika asked.

"Why aren't the Azaeans here anymore?" Abby asked, trying to move things along before Erika had a mental break.

"Around 8,000 years ago, the great Anphanalia outbreak began," Nell said. "It started slowly, depleting a lot of native plants and microorganisms, but nothing the Realm couldn't overcome. When it made the jump to larger fauna, and eventually to the Azaeans, things got more dire. For a while, it was believed that humans were immune to Anphanalia, though the disease eventually mutated and began to infect them too."

"Did we bring it here?" Abby asked.

"No. It originally came from the Halycon Realm, which was another universe that the Azaes Realm briefly intersected with. Though considering how utterly terrible we've been at controlling diseases and human behavior around them throughout history, I could understand assuming that."

"What happened then?"

"When an Azaean got infected with Anphanalia, there was a chance that they'd die, though that was fairly uncommon," Nell continued. "The bigger problem for them was that the disease made them sterile. Though Azaeans remain fertile for a much larger portion of their lifespans than humans, this still slowly killed off the population."

"So, they all died off and we took over?" Erika asked.

"Humans do control the Azaes Realm now, yes, but to say the Azaeans are dead is inaccurate. But that's more Brigid's area of expertise than my own."

Brigid leaned back in her chair and took a deep breath in. She let it out with a long, pensive sigh, taking a moment to collect her thoughts before speaking.

"The truth about life is that it's inherently a complex thing," Brigid began. "Think for a moment about the variety of life on Earth. From single-celled organisms to the tallest redwood trees and everything in between, the variety of life on Earth is quite literally awe-inspiring. But there are things that can happen in other universes that the physics of our reality just wouldn't support."

"Like what?" asked Erika.

"Like a self-dividing universe."

Erika stared at Brigid for a long time, a series of blinks the only sign she hadn't short-circuited. Erika barely paid attention well enough in school to understand the concept of cell mitosis.

To imply that a universe could do the same thing – and the one that she was now in at that – was beyond the bounds of her understanding.

"Don't worry," Brigid said. "It's not going to divide again with you sitting here. There's been enough research conducted to determine that it won't happen again for another 20,000 or so years, if it does at all. It's more likely for the other universe to split off of this one and become completely separated than for the Azaes Realm to divide again."

"The other universe Brigid keeps referring to is known as the Diaprepes Realm," Nell interjected. "The native Azaeans were able to go there after the split. For most of them, it's cured and often reversed the effects of their Anphanalia infection. That, combined with the fact that time moves even slower in the Diaprepes Realm means that their population is slowly on the rebound. From data Sadie has gathered, it's looking like they're up to around 500 or so. Even if things were to divide again, you'd stay here...or at the very least you'd want to. The one time we tried to send a human through, they died. It was a guardian even, so I can't imagine a mortal would fare any better."

Erika remained silent. Not only was she away from her world. Not only was she having to learn how to fight, but now it comes to light that this whole intersecting universe was really two universes that split apart.

"We still get a lot of information and technological advancement from the work being done by those in the Diaprepes Realm," Nell continued. "Their continued involvement in the well-being of our intertwined universes allow us to operate the Azaes Realm on what would otherwise be a skeleton crew, especially with Sadie's existence."

"So many ways to die and you don't even have to leave. Magic weapons and a killer twin universe? What luck!"

"Did you know about this?" Erika asked as she turned to Abby.

"Yes?" Abby said cautiously.

"Why didn't you *lead* with that? That seems like a big detail."

"A 'world filled with gods and guardians separate from Earth' implied there's a lot going on here. You seemed overwhelmed enough that I figured a second universe would likely just make you mad."

"She's right. Dumbass."

"Is that all?" Erika asked. "Is there any more crazy science you're going to hurt my brain with?"

"There's no more crazy science," Brigid assured her.

"Define crazy science," Nell said.

Brigid shot Nell a glare that could freeze water, only for Nell to mouth a quick 'what' at her in return.

"What's the rest of it?" Erika asked.

"It's not important," Brigid said.

"Tell me."

"Let's take a break. We can come back to—"

"For fuck's sake, tell me," Erika insisted.

"There is – and I don't have a more delicate way to put this – a bit of an afterlife component to the Azaes Realm and Diaprepes Realm," Nell said.

"Which is?"

"Because of the fact that the Azaes Realm is an intersecting universe with your own, there's a bit of inter-universe crossover that happens from time to time. Most of that just so happens to occur with souls en route to the next step toward their afterlife."

Erika stared at Nell.

"Are you telling me we're dead?" Erika asked.

"I'm—"

"Because I don't feel dead. But there's a refrigerator that makes you literally anything you could dream of, so maybe I am."

"You're not dead," Brigid reassured her.

"Well, I mean..." Nell stammered. "That's mostly true."

"What is?" Erika replied. "Am I in a coma? How are you here if this is a coma?"

"No, nothing like that," said Nell. "As Brigid said, you're not dead. You are very much alive. If you were to go back to Earth, you'd be just as alive as you were the day Svieva brought you here. However, the perception on Earth is that you've gone missing."

"Like kidnapped?" Erika asked.

"Just missing," Nell answered. "It's rare that a live human is brought to the Azaes Realm, though it certainly does happen. Everyone in this room in this room is evidence of that – not trying to exclude you Abby, but I think you get the larger point I'm trying to make."

"I do," Abby said.

"In most circumstances, such as the one that Brigid and I had," Nell continued, "the belief on Earth is that we died. This is because there's no intent for us to come back as the people we once were on Earth. In rare cases, such as yours, we give the message that you're missing, as we do hope to have you return to Earth once your mission is done."

"So my family thinks I'm just...gone?" asked Erika.

Nell was quick to reply. "Well yes, but –"

"There's no but to that!" Erika shouted. "What about my dad?"

"It's always a challenge for those back on Earth when a

member of their family comes to the Azaes Realm –"

"He should know I'm alright. He doesn't deserve this."

"The fact that you're missing rather than dead is more comforting to them."

"How the fuck is that comforting? I can't imagine what I'd do if Abby went missing. At least if she were dead, I'd know it's final!"

"Erika," Abby pleaded.

"They can't do this to people! Most of my family might not like me but they deserve the truth."

"This bigger than us."

"I don't want to be here. I want to be home!" replied Erika. "I want to be home. With you. Like we finally got to have after so fucking long. Nothing is bigger than that. Now that's gone, my family thinks I'm missing—"

"There's more to it than that," Nell insisted.

"More than 'your planet's boned unless you can save it' or 'oh yeah, everyone thinks you're dead'?"

"They don't think you're dead," Abby stated. "Nell just said that."

"Gone is as good as dead," replied Erika. "Can't have them having closure. That would be too kind. Mom won't care, I've been dead to her for years. But Dad..."

Erika went quiet, taking a moment to wipe a tear away from her cheek.

"They're not getting younger, Abby," she continued. "People die from less."

"If you're that concerned about your family, I'm sure there's something we could do," said Nell.

"Do I need to be here or not? Which is it? Is the world

imminently about to be destroyed? And from what? Aliens? Nuclear war? Racism? Is the moon haunted?"

"Now you're just being absurd."

"Am I though?" Erika asked. "If the world needs saving, why not pick the best and brightest minds from Earth. Instead, you chose me."

Erika stood up from her chair and walked toward the door, only for Abby to stop her.

"What are you doing?" asked Abby.

"Leaving," said Erika.

"Don't run out just because you hear something you don't want to hear. You're not a child."

"This is purgatory. We've been kidnapped, we're as good as dead, yet everyone is acting like this is totally normal."

"Of course it's not normal," Abby stated. "You're still trying to wrap your head around changes to cornerstone knowledge you've known all your life. We're in a universe no one on Earth knows exists. There are others that cross paths with both this one and our own. And a second universe was born from this one yet is somehow still connected to it."

"And?"

"We're here to make sure that something catastrophic doesn't happen to everyone left on Earth. Why wouldn't we? We know we're not alone now. There's always been speculation, but you're standing in the proof."

"I didn't want proof!" Erika said. "I didn't want to leave!"

"We can!" Abby interjected. "Eventually. This is just an interruption. Hopefully a short one."

"How can you be so calm about this? Were we not enough?"

"You're still with me. We can be part of something that's beyond our understanding."

"They kidnapped us."

"Would you stop?" asked Abby. "I know you're worried. It's not like this the first time your parents haven't heard from you for a long time. Your mom won't even notice. I'm sure your dad will be fine."

Erika let out a frustrated groan, then turned and walked out of the armory.

"Bye!" Abby shouted after her.

"Will she come back? asked Nell.

"You did just tell her that her family thinks she's missing," Abby said. "She loves her dad – hates her mom – but it's still a lot. Knowing her, that's going to take more than a minute or two to work through."

"Would you mind if I try to talk to her?" Brigid said.

"You can try," replied Abby. "She's stubborn."

Brigid left the room, heading off to try to track down Erika. Nell sat back down in her chair, sighed, and closed her eyes.

"I hate this part of my job," Nell said. "I always hurt someone. And it's never anyone who deserves it."

"I'm sorry," Abby replied.

"Don't be. If everything works out with Gersemi's plan, it'll all be worthwhile."

"Gersemi seems wise from what I've read about her," replied Abby.

"She is," said Nell. "I see a lot of her in you."

"Does Erika really need to be here? I'm glad she is, don't get me wrong. But she's going through a lot – has gone through a lot for that matter. There's no way to avoid this?"

"I'm afraid not. You might be the lynchpin to Gersemi's plan, but without Erika, it can't succeed."

Abby stared blankly at Nell, perplexed at her previous statement. She tried to run every plausible scenario through her head as to why a plan to save the world not only needed Erika to succeed, but apparently required her involvement. Even with the advanced calculation and assessment her body provided her, Abby was at a loss.

"You're going to have to help me understand that one," Abby said. "She is trying her best, but she's not exactly a trained soldier."

"If and when I'm allowed to do so, I will," Nell replied. "Until then, just do what you can to help her. Oh. And maybe don't mention her importance to the plan to anyone. Even to Erika."

"Why not?"

"Like you, a lot of the others realize she's fighting an uphill battle. I don't think Erika needs the added pressure. Do you?"

"Not when you put it that way," Abby said.

Nell stood from chair and stretched her body, contorting and twisting as her back popped loudly. Abby cringed at the sound. It was bad enough when Erika absentmindedly popped her knuckles. But hearing a person crack their entire back multiple times in the span of a few seconds made Abby happy she didn't have bones.

"I need a quick break," Nell said. "Want me to bring you back a snack? Coffee?"

"I think I'm good," Abby replied.

Nell left the room, leaving Abby alone in the armory. She rose from her seat and walked around the room, perusing the various tomes and staves on the wall closest to her. The covers were weathered and dusty from age, though most appeared to be lightly used. Several of them even featured brilliant, though faded, art on the edges of the pages, creating beautiful images with the tomes closed and on display.

Plaques beside the tomes gave basic information about the weapons, their magical type and alignment, and history. One book in particular caught Abby's eye. The tome had a brilliant white cover, clearly much newer than the others around it. The crimson lettering on the cover looked freshly printed, though it seemed nonsensical to Abby. Even with her ability to master languages quickly, as well as technologies within the Azaes Realm that made it easier to verbally communicate with others, this script was still unintelligible. This frustrated Abby, a feeling which only compounded when finding the tome's plaque contained merely a single word: Olimaw.

"It's a gorgeous book, isn't it?" came a voice from behind Abby.

She turned around to find Adelina's envoy, Kuhla, standing a few feet away, sipping a mug of coffee. She had a bookbag draped over her shoulder, giving off a look that she was much younger than her actual age. In a few books, Abby had encountered characters who were full-fledged adults, but were mistaken for children due to their size and looks. Abby figured it was nothing more than a literary trope. Now, staring at a 27-year-old woman who barely looked 16, she understood where the concept came from.

"It's very elegant," Abby replied. "Are you looking for Nell? She just stepped out."

"Not really," Kuhla replied. "I wouldn't mind finding her. I just like looking at the tomes. Even though I'm not supposed to read them."

"Why not?"

"Envoys shouldn't play with magical weapons. That's what Revaus says. And since she's the god of order, that logically means she's the best at making rules. And because she's the best at making rules, I don't touch the tomes. Even if I want to."

A look of child-like wonder washed over Kuhla's face as she looked at the tomes. Even if Revaus encouraged the envoys to use magical weapons, Abby was convinced that Kuhla would be too awestruck and careful to touch the tomes, lest she accidentally rip the corner of a page.

"What do you know about this one?" Abby asked.

"I wish I knew much of anything about it," Kuhla said. "That tome is Olimaw. It's a wind magic tome, we think."

"You're not sure?"

"It's not just me – no one is. It hasn't been used in thousands of years."

"How can it be thousands of years old?" Abby questioned. "It looks brand new."

"The only other thing any records about it indicate are that it's meant to be used in conjunction with healing staves," replied Kuhla. "There aren't many tomes with that kind of power, but the ones that do use magic in such a way deteriorate significantly slower than others."

"Hey, you're Adelina's envoy, right?" Abby said, recognizing she finally had an opportunity to act on Erika's idea.

"I am. Though it's not like I have much to do right now."

"Do you know where she's hiding?"

"What do you mean hiding?" asked Kuhla.

"Huh? Every text I've read says the god of knowledge likes to hide until they're sought out."

"Oh, that. No, that's a common misconception. A lot of the early humans who filled the role of god of knowledge leaned into the whole wise, reclusive monk lifestyle. Adelina is super outgoing."

"If she's not hiding, where is she?" Abby asked.

"I wish I knew," said Kuhla. "She's been missing for weeks now. I think that...I've got to go."

Kuhla quickly left the room, flashing a smile to Nell as she reentered.

"Kuhla came by to look at the tomes again, I see," Nell said.

"Yeah, she really loves them," Abby replied. "It's a shame the envoys aren't allowed to touch them."

Nell stared at Abby; her brow furrowed.

"There's no such rule. Where'd you hear that nonsense?"

11

Cain & Abel

January 13, 2035/8:08, Day 95, Year 10311

Dau and Revaus sat across a long table from one another in a dimly lit room. As Revaus carefully reviewed her notes and plans, Dau stared a hole through her, his eyes unyielding in their persistence.

Revaus adjusted her bifocals, ignoring Dau's gaze. At 78 years old – 66 of them spent within the Azaes Realm – she was the elder statesman, both human residents of the realm, as well as of the gods in terms of tenure. She'd grown up in the town of Lienz in the County of Gorizia, itself part of the Holy Roman Empire at the time. Not only was the country of her birth long gone, so was the Earth that Revaus knew, having survived calamities from the Black Death and COVID-19, along with several atrocities of all shapes and sizes in between.

"Say whatever is on your mind," Revaus stated without looking up from her work. "You haven't been this focused on something since you came up with the idea for lotteries funding education."

"I know you're behind this," Dau said. "Janus wouldn't act alone. They're a seer, not a terrorist."

Dau was an older man, having aged to the Azaes Realm-adjusted equivalent of 63 years. His gray hair still showed some specs of black here and there, though the color of his youth had largely disappeared from his head. Like Revaus, he too came from a nation that no longer existed on Earth, having been born in the Mataram Sultanate in 1628. Though he'd been fortunate enough to move to the Azaes Realm before the arrival of Dutch colonizers, Dau held a soft spot for the chaos that changing nationhood brought, despite his personal distaste for the overwhelmingly negative consequences that colonization itself brought both to his former people and to the world as a whole.

"Janus isn't even my guardian," Revaus said. "If anything, you should blame Death – who I might add we haven't seen in person since the last one met his end."

"You know as well as I do Death only makes themselves known when it's time for a guardian or god to die. Or whenever they feel like. It's part of why Death amuses me so in this realm."

"How do you know they're even in Azaes right now? Janus is on Earth. Gersemi's there regularly. Brigid practically lived there for the better part of the past two years. A foolish thing to do as the goddess of life, but what do I know."

"Have you forgotten how things work?" replied Dau. "The only god that can travel between our realm and theirs is the god of life."

"We don't know that for certain," Revaus interrupted. "We make that assumption because no previous gods of Death left the Azaes Realm following their identity becoming public knowledge. We don't know what they're capable of until they're known. A being that powerful outside of the control of our world is terrifying."

"That's because you lack the appreciation for the spontaneity of Earth life," Dau said. "It's got a little bit of something for everyone. Brigid loves cats. Gersemi has her thing with clocks. Tane has opened my eyes to the world of theater and television in her travels. You'd fit right in as a bureaucrat."

"And you'd make for a hell of a painter if you had any talent," Revaus retorted.

Dau stood from the table, stretching his limbs as he slowly moved around the room. He knocked on the door to the room, which cracked open slightly.

"Bring us some water, if you would, please," he said to someone standing outside.

The door closed again behind him, Dau continuing his stretching to go along with some slow pacing.

"If I were to believe you," Dau said, "and let's say that I do for sake of this discussion, what do you think Janus's plan is?"

"What do I think it is?" asked Revaus. "Or what do I think you've done? Because this reeks of your hand."

"You've always been quick to blame me."

"And you do the same."

"I do. But since you asked, I'd like to know both."

Revaus finally looked up from her papers, her face stoic and harsh.

"I think Janus is attempting to sow discord and hate on Earth. Humans are many things, but they're easily trained to fear above all else. If their survival instincts are running hot – and it doesn't take much to get them there – they'll turn on whoever they fear quickly. They become isolated and self-insulate with those like them. It makes them feel safe."

"And in turning inward, they shift toward those who think and look like them," Dau replied.

"Thereby burdening humanity with the pack mentality that has plagued them for millennia," Revaus continued.

"That same mentality allowed for the building of community. It created shared heritage among small towns, countries, religions, people. You and I both experienced that in our time there."

"I'm not trying to argue that human traits are solely positive or negative. I'm merely saying that the same habits that create beauty and order in one circumstance can create hatred, discord, and chaos in others."

"Pity you find what I'm tasked to protect so detestable."

"It might not have been your choice to be called to be the god of chaos," Revaus replied, "but you did have the chance to decline the title. Just as every god and guardian in the Azaes Realm is given."

"Someone would have taken my place," Dau countered. "And they may have let you get out of control long before now."

"I don't see why you're accusing me of being the source of all Janus has done. This, again, is your ideas incarnate."

"As if those who seek control don't gain power by whatever means they deem necessary."

"You're doing nothing to deny your involvement," Revaus said.

"I don't see why I need to prove a negative," Dau replied. "What I have done is to support Gersemi's plans in bringing people here for Earth, then training them to go back and stop Janus."

"I've done that too. I fail to see how that matters."

"Because the argument you're making is predicated on my own action or inaction – when in fact you're handling things in the exact same way that I am. It is neither chaotic nor orderly. It is merely acting in the best interest of protecting this realm and one we have a connection to."

"Like you care about people," Revaus replied. "Weren't you the one born during a siege of the city you lived in?"

"Order cannot exist without chaos," Dau said. "It's only natural. My mere existence is practically required by the idea you swear by."

"Perhaps. But –"

"There's no but to it."

"But just because I believe in that balance," Revaus continued, ignoring Dau's interruption, "doesn't mean that everyone does. There is much to be gained by disrupting the balance of things in a place that none of the gods can directly influence."

"And that's why you think Janus did this?" Dau asked.

"You answered that question yourself," Revaus replied. "Janus is a seer. The future is unwritten to all except for Janus."

"The future may be unwritten, but anyone with a modicum of critical thinking skill can work out the long-term implications of Janus's actions. Especially if there is nothing but inaction from anyone else."

"And if there is a way to save humanity, or to save it from itself, it's Janus's duty to do so."

"I genuinely can't tell if you think Janus is in the right in their actions or not."

"That's not my place to say."

"Then why are we going along with Gersemi's plans? She certainly doesn't think Janus is in the right. We wouldn't have these humans here if she did."

"It's best to have a contingency plan," said Revaus. "And besides, if this ends the way I think it will, we'll either need a new guardian of time or a new guardian of love. It's in our best interest to begin the vetting process now."

*****

"How does she fucking find everything?" Youles muttered to himself.

In the five months since Janus had originally contacted him, Janus – or more typically one of her associates – had shown up at his home in Illinois, both the safe house apartments he rented in New Jersey and Tennessee, respectively, and his vacation home in Florida. He'd even gotten a call from his mom saying a suspicious man had been staking out his childhood home in North Dakota.

As annoying as all those things were, it's not like finding them took a ton of effort. The home purchases were public record. The safe houses were owned by a company he owned. And though the house was in his mom's name, looking up a maiden name was a trivial task for someone who really wanted to learn information about Youles. He'd looked up more information for less promising dates.

The warehouse was the first thing to truly annoy him. Had that been the only place Janus found, he could have chalked it up to oversight. The place was too abandoned, so any change at all could cause someone to start asking around if they'd been monitoring his movements. From there, it was only a matter of time before they found out who owned the place and, ultimately, found him.

Today, Youles found himself tearing apart a hotel room in Tuscaloosa, Alabama looking for something, anything, that let him know how Janus knew he was here. He'd paid for everything he could in cash. The card he'd left at the hotel front desk was a pre-paid credit card from a gas station. The license plates were picked up from a forgery artist in Colorado, mailed to a shipping supply store in suburban Chicago seven months ago, only for him to pick them up two weeks ago. The car was registered under the name Drop Table, which would cause most outdated police record systems to crash if he was stopped along the way.

And yet, despite going on a job that he'd mentioned to no

one else, there was a gift basket waiting on his hotel room bed. Not just one of those subversive gift baskets that nice hotels put on the bed that you think is free, but everything except the coffee pods bills a charge to the room either. It was a basket filled with high end whiskeys, chocolates, and cigars, carefully selected to match his tastes and preferences. The note on the card featured no words, only the word "Janus" typed into the card by what looked to be the markings of a vintage typewriter.

Youles had searched every piece of furniture in the room. He'd taken apart the bed layer by layer, unscrewed every outlet, lamp, and light switch in the room. He'd even blacked out all the curtains and shined a laser around the room, hoping to reflect off a camera hiding somewhere in the nooks and crannies. But nothing. The room was totally clean.

After taking time to put the room back together, lest someone else under Janus's employ come by and become aware he was onto them, Youles went down to the front desk. An elderly man was seated behind the counter, reading through an adult magazine.

"Hi, I'm up in room 217," said Youles.

"Ya locked out?" asked the old man.

"No. I was hoping to find out what to do if I found some stuff that the last person who stayed in my room left behind."

"Lost and found's over there. Just drop it in. Someone wants it bad enough, they'll come back."

"Look, is that girl who checked me in still here?" asked Youles. "Maybe she can help me."

"Who?" the man asked, finally looking up from his porno.

"There was a younger girl. Black hair, heavy eyeliner. I think her name was Linda."

"There ain't no Linda that works here. But if you see her, send her my way. This is my fourth time through this today. I need something real."

Youles left the clerk alone and wandered back to his room. He knew how the basket likely got into his room now. But he still had no idea how Janus always knew where he was – or even why killing one specific android was so critical to her plan.

12
Don't Dead Open Inside

January 13, 2035/8:22, Day 95, Year 10311

"So...you're dead now."

I'm not dead.

"No one knows you're still alive. No one can prove it. And if no one can prove you're alive, you must be dead."

But no one can prove I'm dead either.

"So you're Schrödinger's lesbian. If you get the cat, you can fulfill two tropes at once."

Erika leaned back against the headboard of the bed. Though Grace had been around since coming to the Azaes Realm, she'd faded to the background as Erika worked to get adjusted. But ever since learning that her parents thought she was missing, Erika couldn't get Grace to shut up.

"Step one: read the pamphlets. Couldn't even do that. Now we're days behind."

Stop. I need to figure this out.

"You barely passed science class in high school, but you can work out the details of interdimensional space travel?"

Erika got up from the bed, slowly making her way to the bathroom. She stood in front of the sink, trying to turn the tap on with cold water. Instead, a disinfectant light poured out of the spigot.

Right. Future shit.

The bath faucet worked out much better, producing a steady stream of water. Erika knelt on the floor, splashing the freezing cold water against her face. It had been a reliable tactic for quieting Grace in the past, even if only briefly. But she just needed

111

a minute to think – to figure out what in the hell was going on.

After hitting herself with six or seven bursts of water, Erika turned off the faucet, toweling off her face the best she could. She turned and faced the mirror over the bathroom sink. The shoulders and neck of her shirt caught more water than she'd hoped. Her hair was even worse off.

"Fucked up washing your face? Impressive."

Goddammit.

"You look like your collarbone got caught in a downpour."

Of course it doesn't work today.

"For someone who can't swim, I always wondered why you never considered drowning yourself. You've thought of every other way to go. Now I know why. You'd miss the fucking lake."

Erika retired to the bedroom, swapping out her wet shirt for a new one. She dried her hair off the best she could – most of the water had missed her hair in favor of landing on her face and her top. For the first time since arriving in the Azaes Realm, Erika put her hair in a bandana. It was something she did nearly every day back on Earth, thinking nothing of it when she did. But here, it felt like a big step. It was something to link her back to the Erika she knew on Earth. Something to show that the Earth version of her wasn't gone.

Out of instinct, Erika pulled open the drawer of her nightstand, expecting to find the flask she'd kept there at her old apartment or even the carefully measured bottle Abby allotted her at their home in Nova Scotia. But there was nothing in the drawer. No booze. No bottles. No Gideon's Bible mocking her failures to keep her addiction in check. Just a white drawer bottom so clean Erika could nearly see her face in it.

Erika picked up the book from the table in the living room. She flipped to a random page in the middle of the book, thinking she could get some instantaneous answers to her questions rather than having to read the book from cover to cover. She read a few words, hopeful that the information would be what she needed, only to realize she had turned to the middle of a section explaining the rules and regulations of usage of the Azaes Realm armory.

"Fuck," Erika muttered.

A knock at the door startled Erika's concentration. Didn't the door automatically unlock for Abby? Erika sighed and answered the door.

"Would it be alright if we talked?" Brigid asked, a peppy smile plastered across her face.

"Do I get a choice?" Erika replied.

"You get a choice as to the location of our talk. And the when."

"Why?"

"Coming here is quite the adjustment," Brigid said. "I speak from experience there. So, let's talk on your terms. It's the least I can do."

Erika looked back into the room, thinking through her options. Brigid was giving her an out now – but that only delayed the conversation. Choosing the where wasn't ideal, though at least it gave her the power to pick somewhere that Abby wouldn't walk into mid-conversation. In Erika's experience, it was better to have awkward conversations one at a time.

"Somewhere else," Erika said. "Ideally with comfortable chairs."

"Easy enough," replied Brigid.

Erika followed Brigid to the elevator, always staying a few steps behind her. There was always a chance to turn back. Not that there was necessarily a need to do so, nor did Erika have anywhere to go other than her room if she did leave. Having the option in the back of her head was nice, even if it was merely a placebo.

"Where do you want to sit?" Brigid asked.

"Like outside or inside?" replied Erika.

"Not q—"

"In," Erika said, cutting Brigid off. "There's too much nature outside."

Brigid laughed, her bubbly voice filling up the elevator car.

"I personally don't mind it," she said. "I quite like most plants and animals. But I get how it's not everyone's thing."

After a quick ride, they exited the elevator to a familiar hallway. This was the short, cramped corridor that Erika had been in the day prior.

"Isn't this where Nell's room is?" asked Erika.

"Her room is across from mine," said Brigid. "For now, that is."

"Why is that a temporary statement?"

"My personal guardian, Gersemi, has been on Earth for quite some time. And being a goddess, it's frowned upon if I don't always have some sort of protection near my room. So when a guardian isn't an option, the head of the armory and a stellar healer all in one is the next best option."

"Is her room not normally here?" Erika asked. "Wouldn't that be difficult to move stuff room to room whenever Gersemi comes back?"

"It's super easy," replied Brigid. "Barely an inconvenience."

"Oh really?"

"The rooms can be moved. When Gersemi's away, Nell's room moves up here. And when Gersemi's back, her room takes this place, while Nell's moves down by the armory."

"Wouldn't that be weird?" asked Erika. "Like you go to bed one night in one hallway and wake up the next morning, walk out, and you're somewhere else."

"Nell doesn't seem to mind," replied Brigid. "At least if she does, she's never mentioned it.

Brigid opened the door between Nell's and the one she'd called out as her own room. Inside was a cozy lounge space, complete with a pantry, several plush chairs, and a screen against the far wall.

"I can promise you that you will not find a more comfortable, softer chair in existence, be it on Earth or in the Azaes Realm," Brigid said.

Erika sat in one of the chairs, its plush, charcoal-colored fabric squishing as she sat in it. As she moved around the chair seemed to move with her, as if she were floating on air.

"Brigid," Erika said. "I have fucked up."

"I mean, I wouldn't say leaving the meeting this morning was that bad —"

"No. I mean I sat in this chair without getting a muffin and now I don't want to leave it."

Brigid laughed again, going over to the pantry and retrieving a pair of warmed orange cranberry muffins. She handed them to Erika, along with a steaming mug of black coffee.

"You're very kind," Erika said.

"You've been through a lot today," Brigid said.

"I mean, not really. I learned one thing, flipped the fuck out, and left."

"Be kind to yourself, Erika. If you're not, who will be?"

"I hear that a lot," Erika stated.

"From Abby?" asked Brigid.

Erika nodded. She looked over at Brigid, who was busy peeling the skin away from an orange. Brigid didn't look that much older than her – maybe in her mid-30s, Erika guessed, though figuring out anyone's actual age in the Azaes Realm was a crapshoot. Her fair skin and flaxen hair stood in sharp contrast to her chocolate-brown eyes and her midnight blue top. Erika had always imagined God – or gods or goddesses or whatever – would be cloaked in light and togas. Instead, this one looked like she should be on the cover of Vanity Fair rather than doing...whatever it was goddesses did.

"She's the one you all actually wanted, isn't she?" Erika asked. "I got drug along for the ride because I happened to be there when Svieva showed up."

"Abby is a critical component to the success for this mission," Brigid said. "Gersemi is an excellent strategist and I trust her with my life. She was insistent that Abby be part of this, even after we'd compiled the rest of the group. And I've never seen her so adamant about the inclusion of anyone in anything before."

Brigid paused, peeling away one of the segments of her orange and taking a bite from it. She chewed slowly, contemplating her next sentence.

"That said," she continued, "if you were not needed and you were not important to this mission, you would not be here. You would be back in the tiny hamlet just outside Halifax, alone, in a house by yourself. We would have told you that Abby had gone missing, much in the same way that those who are privy to your existence were notified of your disappearance. You are here because you matter to our success."

"But how?" Erika asked. "I can't fight like Lace. I'm not a leader like Lorena. I'm not a brilliant mind like K'Andre, a supercomputer like Abby, or a...Shaw."

"Shaw is a capable fighter and exceedingly good at reading people," Brigid said. "Unless he's interested in them, that is, but I'm pretty sure every human suffers from that."

"You say that like you're not human."

"I've met more than my fair share of people that caused me a lustful blind spot. You just kind of lose association with it once you've been here long enough. You start to learn the tendencies of the gods and the guardians, as well as the actions of repentant individuals. But the average human is, admittedly, foreign to me at this point."

"Then why are we so important to you?"

"To me literally?" asked Brigid. "Or to the Azaes Realm as a whole?"

"Both, I guess," Erika said.

"I don't know if I'll explain this as well as Nell does, but I'll certainly give it my best go. The Azaes Realm is an intersecting universe with your own."

"Don't you mean a parallel universe?"

"I don't," Brigid replied. "Our universes briefly overlapped in the past. That's how so many humans ended up here, along with the resources to allow us to be able to create the technology we have in Azaes."

"But they don't overlap now?" asked Erika.

"No. They're still very close, but they are drifting apart. Right now, the guardians and I can come and go as we please to and from Earth, even without portals. To take a human across, we have to use them due to the fact that our universes are already separating a bit. There was a point where as long a guardian was with a human, we could just jump between realms. In time, it'll be much more difficult for us to do so, even with portals."

"How long is 'in time'?"

"Unless you suddenly decide to permanently live in the Azaes Realm, and you were to live an exceedingly long time for a human while you're here, it won't be within your lifetime," Brigid said.

Erika let out a deep breath. She hadn't realized she'd been holding it in since she'd asked her question, leading her to chuckle.

"Oh, thank god," Erika said. She quickly began to backtrack. "I mean, I'm sure this place is fine for you. Oh god, did I insult you by saying god? Shit. I did it again. Fuck."

Brigid smiled, leaning forward in the chair. Though she'd only sat up a few inches, Erika felt like Brigid had moved significantly closer to her somehow.

"You didn't insult me," Brigid said. "Despite the fact that I'm a goddess, I'd much rather be a human. It's much more fun. I try to visit whenever I can."

"Isn't it obvious when you come though?"

Erika thought back to when Svieva had come to get her and Abby on Earth. There was a massive set of circular doors surrounded by a glowing blue ring of glyphs. That's certainly not a subtle way to arrive to a new planet, particularly in an age of cameras being everywhere.

"Not really," said Brigid. "I just kind of s—OH! You mean the glowy gate things! Those are just for show or for when we're officially going to get a human to bring them back like we did with you and Abby. Once Azaes gets far enough away from your universe, that'll be the only way we can travel, though."

"How do you get onto Earth now?" Erika asked.

"We all have different ways. All of them are portal based, but some are more visible than others. My personal favorite is manifesting out of a tombstone or some other graveyard monument. It really freaks out middle of the night stoners."

"I'll have to see that sometime."

Brigid took the last few bites of her orange, waiting for the next question from Erika. When none came, she took the opportunity to speak.

"Why not just ask to leave?" Brigid said. "It's not like you have to go along with this."

"Where would I go?" Erika asked.

"Home. Nova Scotia. Indianapolis. Somewhere other than here."

"It's not like I can cast a magical portal and get myself back to Earth."

"If you're really set on going, I can take you myself," Brigid said.

"You're a god," Erika countered. "Don't you have responsibilities here?"

"Being a god also means I have some level of autonomy to do what I want. Since I can go to Earth freely, I do. And you're dodging the question."

"I can't leave Abby behind."

"So then your commitment is to her, not to the mission?"

"I mean," Erika replied. "It'd be kind of nice to still have an Earth around to go back to."

"You're free to go back now," said Brigid. "You know it's there now. While I'd assume it'll be there in the future, there's no guarantee of it. Go while you have the chance."

"It's not that."

"Then what?"

"Nothing," Erika mumbled. "I'm fine."

"Whatever it takes to get you to buy in," replied Brigid. "If you have to be all-in for Abby to give a damn about what we're doing, that's what I want you to do."

Erika nodded. For all of Brigid's talk about not feeling human, she seemed to get what Erika was feeling more than any of the actual humans here. Not that she'd gotten to spend much non-combat time with any of them yet.

"How long have you two been together?" Brigid continued.

"A couple months," Erika said. "But there's years of history."

"Good. Hang onto that. It's more fleeting than you realize."

"How so?"

"I have my own history of finding love and losing it," replied Brigid. "Usually painfully."

"I'm sorry to hear that," said Erika.

Brigid shrugged. "It's the cost of being who I am. At least since I came here. One of the things that epic poems and romance novels do a poor job preparing you for is that loving someone forever has a very different meaning when you both have roughly the same lifespan. Things really can be forever then. When you're functionally immortal, you can be a lot of people's forever without ever feeling it yourself."

"Did you ever have someone on Earth? Before you ended up here, that is."

"I used to," replied Brigid, "though saying someone implies one. Being in the Azaes Realm has let me age slower than normal and my shapeshifting abilities, and you've got a recipe for having multiple relationships over time."

"Oh," Erika said. "I guess I hadn't thought of it that way."

"I really hadn't until I came here. My shapeshifting abilities were something I was just starting to learn. I got told a lot as a kid that I could be anyone I wanted to be when I grew up. I ended up being able to take that literally. But..."

Brigid trailed off, her eyes glazing over as she stared out into space. Erika diverted her own eyes from the god of life, choosing instead to gaze at her own shoes.

"Even all-powerful beings aren't immune from your bullshit."

"One of the drawbacks to being able to be anyone at any time is that you never really get truly close to anyone. Combine that with immortality and the nagging knowledge that you'll outlive any partner you have ten-fold and..."

Erika looked up at Brigid, tears welling up in her eyes. She took a deep breath in, sighed, then re-composed herself.

"Let's head back down and join Nell and Abby," Brigid said. "I'm sure there's still plenty for you to learn with them."

13

Fourteen Seconds to Midnight

March 9, 2035

Turnpike food never failed to turn Youles's stomach. It didn't matter that most of the restaurants were the same ones he could find in any decent-sized town in the country. There was just something about stopping and eating somewhere that was part of a controlled-access highway that gave him indigestion, no matter what he did to prevent it.

Youles picked at a soft pretzel, dipping small pieces into a container of caramel sauce. This was his second pretzel of the day. That was part of the disadvantage to this plan. 'I'm the man wearing a University of Kansas hat eating a soft pretzel in the South Somerset travel plaza' seemed like an apt enough description for someone to find him. But you never know with some people.

After their meeting in the warehouse, Janus had sent an envoy to Youles with his next set of instructions. As a hitman for hire, he played more than his fair share of false identities. Some of them greatly amused him. He particularly liked any situation that allowed him to have a Brooklyn accent or to talk about pizza. The former led to enough stereotypical descriptions that it made it hard for him to be tracked down. The latter was generic enough that it gave nothing to go off. Who doesn't love pizza?

The fact that the meeting had to take place outside of Indianapolis wouldn't have been weird under most circumstances. Several of Youles's previous clients had made efforts to separate the location of their discussions from the area where their requested act would be committed. It gave both the client and him some level of plausible deniability, particularly if he worked under a pseudonym.

For this meeting to be in Pennsylvania specifically was strange, as both he and his new contact would have to drive from central Indiana to have this meeting. Take it out of the metro area? Sure. Cross multiple state lines for what would likely be a fifteen-minute conversation in a public place? That felt like overkill, even if the state they were travelling through was Ohio. No one willingly went to Ohio unless they had to.

His cover today, at least per the envoy who had called him, was that of a food critic. Marty Gunnselman, roadside restaurant connoisseur and magazine contributor. The envoy was insistent that he should frost the tips of his hair to better fit undercover, but Youles could have sworn he heard her giggling at the mere suggestion of the idea. No matter how many times he read over it, the job always managed to sound dumber each time. Who on Earth would actually fall for that?

"Marty Gunnselman?" Youles heard a voice behind him ask.

"Who wants to know?" Youles asked.

A salt-and-pepper haired man in a navy blue cable knit sweater walked around the table, sitting in the chair across from Youles.

"Sam Sawchuk," he said, "and it's a pleasure to meet you."

His face plastered with a smile only a used car salesman could love. Youles could tell there wasn't an honest bone in this man's body. At least he knew what he was getting himself into. Honest men and liars were easy to predict. It was the ones who lived in the gray area in the middle he had to worry about.

"The pleasure's mine, Mr. Sawchuk," Youles said. "I'm told you're familiar with my work."

"I am," Sam replied. "You're one of the most respected food critics in the Midwest. Your pieces on the cuisine of the triple I states is a must-read for anyone looking to open a restaurant in that area of the country."

Janus had clearly put a ton of work into this persona. If Marty Gunnselman was half as respected as this guy was letting on, he was going to believe literally anything Youles had to say. Or his plan would blow up in twenty seconds. There wouldn't be any in between.

"Then why ask to meet me in a truck stop in Western Pennsylvania?" Youles asked. "I can get one of these pretzels at the mall down the road for a lot less gas money."

"I'm opening a restaurant in Indianapolis," Sam replied. "A good friend of mine that you did a review for several years back suggested I talk with you."

"And who's your friend?"

"Lino Cano. He owes a little Italian place called Boerio's Eatery."

Though Youles had no idea who this Lino person was, he was familiar with Boerio's. Calm atmosphere, charming decorations, and most importantly for this discussion, great food.

"I know their linguini with clams well," Youles admitted.

"I'm more of a manicotti guy myself," Sam said, "but you've got good taste. Look. I'm opening my place in about six months. There'll be a pre-opening dinner there about a week before it opens. We'll invite family of the crew, special guests, and, of course, critics like yourself."

"That's all well and good. But why did you want to drive all the way to Pennsylvania to tell me this? You could have called my office. We could have met at a coffee shop that didn't make me get up at 4am just to get to it."

Sam looked around for a few moments. Once he was satisfied with the lack of whatever he was looking for, he leaned in close, his voice barely above a whisper.

"My accountant is one of those...you know."

"A Jew?"

"What? No!" Sam said, his voice growing loud. "I can say that out loud. Don't be a dick."

Sam went back to speaking in hushed tones.

"She's one of those robot people."

"Oh," Youles said, drawing out his response. Janus hadn't told him this would be a meeting to find his next target.

"She's very good with money," Sam continued. "She's even helped some friends of mine better manage their assets for greater profits than they otherwise would have had."

"There's a but coming."

"But she doesn't like the fact that I'm doing my best to ensure I get great reviews. Not just good reviews, Marty. Great ones. What kind of food do you like?"

"In general?" Youles asked.

"That I might be able to serve you at the dinner," Sam said. "Look, I'll make you something off menu if that's what it takes to make sure the review is good. But I'd much rather you try something we'll be preparing normally. It adds some credence to the review. Gives people something to sink their teeth into, both literally and metaphorically."

"What kind of shellfish will you have on the menu?"

"Ever had clams casino?"

"No. Heard the name, but never tried it."

"It's basically a clam with smoked bacon and breadcrumbs, then broiled," Sam said. "One of my chefs was insistent that we put it on the menu. I was skeptical, but the hints of garlic,

Worcestershire sauce, and lemon in it make the dish an experience. I'm not just saying that to sell it to you either. It's phenomenal if you're a shellfish person."

"I'll have to try it then," Youles said.

Sam grabbed his wallet out of his pocket. He counted out twenty $100 bills and slid them across the table. He was about to put his wallet away, only to open it back up and add two more to the stack.

"Ten thousand for a stellar review," Sam said. "Two thousand now, then another eight once it's published. Feel free to put a couple of minor nitpicks in here. Something to make it believable that we're still the new kids on the block, but nothing that'd sink us. The rest is to cover your travel today."

For the first time the entire meeting, Youles was convinced Sam was serious. He didn't know that Youles was a hitman at all. He truly believed he was a food critic. What had Janus gotten him tangled up in?

"Um..." Youles stated, trailing off.

"You don't have to decide here," Sam said. "I get it. Your job is important. But think it over. If you're interested, come by. August 5th. 6pm. L'ostrica Reale is the name. It's in Meridian Hills. That should be enough for you to find it when it comes time. If the review is good enough, I'll make sure you get something a little extra after your meal."

Sam stood up from the table, leaving through doors on the far side of the lobby. Youles took a moment to count the money Sam had given him. Once. Twice. Three times. He pulled out his phone and sent a text to a number that had been given to him several months ago – a number that never responded, but that always got him a phone call or a visit from an envoy.

"Information received. We need to meet about next steps."

14

Amplification

March 18, 2035/6:06, Day 101, Year 10311

"Why did we agree to this again?" Erika asked as she shuffled her feet down the hallway.

"Because Lorena asked nicely," Abby said. "And if we're going to be here, we might as well make friends with people kind enough to invite us over."

"And her idea of a good way to make friends is to make me wake up to have breakfast at six in the morning on our day off?"

"Just give it a chance. Please? At the very least just be polite to her."

"I'm going back to bed after we eat," Erika replied. "I might even sleep for the rest of the day."

"If you're good, I'll join you," Abby said.

They stopped at Lorena's door, Abby knocking on the door loudly. Despite the early hour, there were abundant sounds of life coming from inside: music, clanging metal, and singing.

"Ah fuck," Erika groaned. "She's a morning person."

The door flew open, Lorena's beaming smile greeting them. She wore a red apron covered in white polkasquares over a pink and yellow sundress.

"Good morning!" Lorena said cheerfully. "You two look lovely this morning!"

"You do too!" said Abby. "I love your dress!"

"I'm in jeans and a tank top," Erika grumbled. "This took less than thirty seconds to put on."

"Being lovely is not about how you look, Erika," Lorena said. "It's about your spirit. Your aura. Your entire mood!"

"This bitch is crazier than you."

A timer on the counter went off.

"Oh shit!" Lorena exclaimed. "I have to start making my omelets now. Breakfast isn't quite ready yet. The ensaïmadas just went into the oven."

"The what?" asked Abby.

"Ensaïmadas. They're sugary bread covered in even more powdered sugar. The omelets are for if you want something savory."

"Can't the pantry just make these things for you?"

"It can," Lorena said. "And they're really good. But there's just something different about making food with your own hands. You enjoy it more, even if it doesn't taste as good. It makes it more rewarding."

Erika sat at the kitchen table, watching as Lorena bounded around the kitchen, gathering ingredients she'd previously retrieved from the pantry as she cooked. How someone could have this much energy at any time of day was baffling, never mind before the sun rose...

...had the sun risen here? Erika was certain she hadn't been outside since she arrived in the Azaes Realm. Nor had she seen a window. Looking around Lorena's room – which was laid out nearly identically to her room – only went further in confirming this. There had to be sunrise and sunset. That's how things worked on Earth.

But this place wasn't Earth. It was, as Brigid had called it, an intersecting universe. And while many of the basic rules she'd been used to on Earth still applied, that didn't mean there was a sun. Maybe there were no windows because the air outside wasn't safe for humans to breathe. Maybe they had to stay inside because solar radiation would melt their skin if they didn't.

"Maybe that's how they get rid of shitty recruits. You go outside. Breathe in the fire and brimstone – really let the sulfur into your lungs – and then poof!"

This isn't Hell, Erika thought. I'm safe. Safe enough.

"I wonder if that's where they keep the demons?"

This isn't Hell. This isn't Hell.

"Nell said all the religions are a little bit right about the afterlife. I bet if we make a break for it, we can find a door out of here and see what's really going on."

I'm having breakfast. There are people I know here. I'm not in Satan's butthole.

"Sunday School really did a number on you."

"I'll be right back," Erika heard Abby say, snapping back to reality as she felt Abby's arms wrap around her shoulders.

"Where are you going?" Erika asked.

"I have a scarf I wanted to show Lorena, but I forgot it. I'll be back in a minute."

Abby kissed Erika on the cheek, then left the room. While Erika was confident Abby wouldn't be gone long, there was still something unsettling about being in the room alone with Lorena. It was awkward enough watching someone cook without helping – not that Erika had been shamed for that multiple times in childhood or anything. But the general lack of closeness Erika felt with anyone else in the mission team didn't help matters.

"You two make such a cute couple," Lorena said as she chopped green onions.

"Thank you," Erika replied.

"I've never understood how people can dislike a conscientia. They're always so kind and thoughtful."

"You've been around others?"

"Oh yeah," Lorena replied. "My neighbor was one."

"Was?" Erika asked. "As in they're dead?"

"I hope not. I mean was as in I'm not his neighbor anymore. With being here."

"Oh good. You had me worried there for a minute."

"His name was Carlos Velazquez," Lorena said. "Super kind. Really into coffee. I can't tell you how many kinds of espresso I tried because of him. He taught me how to help my flowers grow a little better too."

"That's nice of him. I kill every flower I touch."

"Do you know any conscientia other than Abby?"

"A couple," Erika said. "There's a lady named Tara. She's an accountant. Insanely smart. She's one of those people who plays chess for fun."

"She'd get along with Gersemi from what I've heard," replied Lorena. "I don't know much about her, but I do know that she's obsessed with chess."

Abby came back into the room, a white scarf with thin black pinstripes on it wrapped around her neck. Lorena gasped with delight.

"May I try something?" Lorena asked.

"Go for it."

Lorena pulled the omelet she was making off the stove, plating it, and turning the burner off. She bounded over, removing the scarf from Abby's neck and wrapping it around her face in a gaiter mask-like style. Lorena stepped back, taking a moment to admire her handiwork.

"You can do the thing where you can change your hair

whenever you want, right?" asked Lorena.

"Yeah," said Abby.

"Give yourself razor-cut layers and some bangs that swoop down in front of one of your eyes."

Abby followed Lorena's instruction, much to Lorena's delight.

"You look like you walked out of a fucking action movie," Lorena said. "All you'd have to do is dress in all black and carry around a tonfa or some shit. You're a morally gray enforcer sex symbol that would make millions at the box office."

"That's an oddly specific description," Erika said.

"But am I wrong?"

Erika looked Abby's outfit up and down.

"You are not," Erika replied. "It's a real good look."

Abby smiled, her excitement visible even behind the scarf.

"Very classy!" Lorena replied. "I'd wear it."

"You can borrow it or even have it if you really want it."

She makes friends so effortlessly.

"Because you're fucking awkward."

"Oh my god!" Lorena exclaimed. "I can finish the look!"

Lorena ran to the pantry, quickly tapping a series of menu options. Within a few seconds, a bright green apple came out.

"You've been practicing your knife skills, right?" she said.

"Yeah?" Abby replied.

Lorena grabbed a butterknife out of the drawer and handed it to Abby, along with the apple.

"Throw the apple in the air and stab it with the knife," Lorena said.

Abby tossed the apple a few inches above her head, then carefully stabbed upward, impaling it on the end of the knife.

"That's not fair," said Erika. "You've got advanced tracking or an aimbot or something in your mind."

Abby pulled the knife out of the apple, handing the fruit to Lorena.

"Lorena, you throw it," Abby said.

"Where? How far?"

"Just somewhere to my left. Doesn't matter beyond that. I'll count you down."

Abby fixed her gaze on Erika, her unblinking eyes flashing a hint of arrogance.

"Aimbot!" Erika insisted.

"I can't track it with my eyes if I'm not looking at it."

"Fine."

"Three," said Abby. "Two. One."

From behind Abby, Lorena tossed the apple across the kitchen and living room, its trajectory making a beeline for the couch. Just as the apple crossed the divider between the two rooms, Abby flung the knife with a flick of her wrist. The knife came to rest in the living room wall, the apple impaled along its blade. A seed slid down the wall, leaving a thin trail of apple juice behind it.

Abby pulled the scarf down from over her mouth, revealing a coy smirk.

"I'm getting there," she said.

"Incredible," Lorena muttered.

"I am scaroused," Erika said breathlessly.

The timer on the oven rang out.

"Breakfast time!" Lorena shouted, running over to remove the ensaïmadas from the oven.

*****

Despite Erika's insistence on going back to bed as soon as breakfast was over, as the clock turned to the 9 o'clock hour, she found herself still in Lorena's room, sipping strong coffee and snacking on sugar-drenched pastries.

The fact that Lorena was a gracious host was not particularly surprising to Erika. She was bright and kind, an endearing combination. It wasn't even Lorena's desire to make them breakfast from scratch that was the most surprising thing about her. Instead, it was her openness to talking about nearly any subject with deep fascination. In Erika's experience most people were either reserved, but thoughtful in their communication or they were open, but direct and crude in the way they felt toward other people's feelings. For Lorena to have struck that balance, particularly at such a young age, was unexpected.

"I think the thing I miss the most about being on Earth is getting to see my therapist," Lorena said. "I love talking to her. Mai helps me walk through things I can't figure out for myself."

"It's always nice to have someone to be able to talk to like that," Abby said. "Having a non-judgmental influence in your life is great."

"Those people can fuck off. Life's significantly easier if you just assume that everyone is judging you. Constantly. Then you can be at peace with the fact that they all expect you to fail. Exceeding expectations makes everyone happy, but when do you ever do that?"

"I'm sure she has judged me," replied Lorena. "I certainly would have had I known me from the outside when Mai met me."

"What were you like? If that's not too personal."

"Mierda. Well, that's not fair. Circumstances made life difficult for me, but I didn't help myself along the way."

"She certainly sounds like a therapist."

"How so?" asked Abby.

"Are you okay with me bringing the mood down?" Lorena replied.

"Yeah."

"Erika?"

"You'll be fine. If you can't have mimosas with brunch, being crazy is the next best thing."

"Sure," she replied.

"I'm pretty open about things," Lorena said. "But it can be hard for others to listen to."

"We're fine," said Abby. "If we're not, we'll let you know."

"Alright," Lorena said. "I was thrown out of my house at fifteen. Apparently telling your drug addict parents to get a job when they ask you for money isn't the right answer.

"One of my teachers took me in. The stability allowed me to succeed. I ended up graduating at the top of my class and finished secondary school early. Then I went to university, finished that ahead of schedule too, all while doing a program that typically takes five years.

"Life was great. I'm in my early twenties. I'm done with school. I've got a good job and a fun roommate. But then, both of my parents overdosed and died on the same night."

"Fuck," Erika mumbled.

"I was crushed," Lorena continued. "You'd think if someone treated you like shit for most of your life, you wouldn't feel bad that they're gone. It's a confusing feeling. I started drinking. I thought it was helping, but before I knew it, I couldn't stop. Then I started having these thoughts. You know...how to end it.

"I was lucky to have the support system I did," Lorena continued. "My roommate, Rose, was an ex-pat from Australia that was only there for half of the year. Had this happened any earlier in the year, she wouldn't have been back in Mallorca. And I'd been seeing Mai for about a year when my parents died. Between the two of them, they got me through a lot of dark times."

The room went silent. Abby walked over and embraced Lorena, who had started to tear up as she'd told her story. Erika watched them, trying her hardest to think of something to say. She couldn't begin to imagine losing her own parents...or how her parents must feel not knowing what happened to her.

"You're here against your will. No reason is good enough."

This isn't about me. It isn't about you.

"You're captive. Your parents don't even know you're alive. And it's killing them."

God. Stop.

"You thirsty? I'd kill for a vodka right now."

Erika took a long, deep breath in, then began to count in her head as she held it.

One. Two. Three.

"There's always alcohol to be found. Even when it's prohibited."

Four. Five.

"You just have to know who to ask."

Six. Seven.

"And I think you already know who that is."

"Stop!" Erika groaned as she exhaled.

"It's just...a hug," Lorena said, her voice filled with confusion.

"Who's the crazy girlfriend who won't let her woman hug people?"

"She's not yelling at you," Abby said.

"Is she okay?" asked Lorena.

"Oh my god, no," Erika said, "Sorry. I was talking to myself and –"

"And what?"

"I—I—"

"It must be so embarrassing not to be able to form a basic sentence like a functional adult."

"I'm sorry, I—"

"Failure."

"I need to go."

Erika bolted up from her chair, flinging the coffee mug that had been sitting on her lap into the air. It landed on the floor in a loud crash, shards of porcelain scattering everywhere. Erika felt one jam into the sole of her left foot, letting out a small whine of pain as she headed toward the door.

"Is she alright?"

"I'll help you clean up later."

15
Black and White Flags

March 21, 2035/12:33, Day 101, Year 10311

Tara snuck around her dark house, gathering what needed to for work. Despite the arrival of a heavier than expected snowstorm, the idea of working from home never crossed her mind. It's hard enough to take care of a small child. She wasn't about to make the Foggs feel guilty for a baby crying while she tried to work.

Having the ability to move in with Jericho and Caroline always seemed like an unnecessary luxury to Tara. But after seeing a fellow conscientia, Cecil Hughes, die at his own wedding to a mob of angry zealots, moving in with friendly humans seemed like the safest choice.

It was a mutually beneficial relationship. Tara was already Caroline's accountant for her small business and had known Jericho for several years. She gave the beleaguered parents a much needed in-house babysitter, and in return, she got a basement to herself. With the Foggs, she was safe.

As she gathered her bags in the kitchen, Tara listened for any sounds of movement upstairs. It had been a rough night, with both Jericho and Caroline up multiple times with baby Steffi. Tara felt guilty that she wasn't taking turns with them, but they argued strongly against it. They weren't about to ask a tenant to wake up at two in the morning to feed their baby, even if Tara was willing to do so.

Tara closed the back door as softly as she could, making her way to her car in the garage. She had spent weeks trying to convince Jericho to let her pay for a plow service for the driveway and had never felt more vindicated than she did this morning.

Flakes of snow pounded Tara's car as she backed out of the driveway, heading down the side street she lived on and toward the accounting firm's offices. As she pulled away, a gray sedan idling in a driveway four houses down turned its lights on and backed onto the residential street. It slowed as it passed the Fogg's home, a light turning on in the nursery thanks to an angry baby with a poopy diaper.

*****

"Thank god for healers," Abby said as she held the door open for Erika.

Erika entered her room, expecting to have to adjust the stance of her crutches as she did so. The doorway, much to her surprise, expanded to meet the increased clearance that a human on crutches would need to come into the room.

"Okay, that's cool as shit," Erika said.

"No kidding," Abby agreed.

Erika hobbled her way to the couch, collapsing down on it as soon as she got close. Her crutches clattered to the floor, landing in the space between the couch and the coffee table.

"There's one positive to being a colossal embarrassment," Erika said. "I get out of training tomorrow."

"It was a recommendation more than a requirement," Abby replied. "They said you'd likely be fine tomorrow, but you did have an inch-long piece of coffee mug in the arch of your foot."

"So much blood. So, so much blood. Do you think they'll charge me for it?"

"Like an American insurance bill? No, they seem to have compassion here."

Erika moved herself to a laying position, repeatedly making minor adjustments to get comfortable.

"You'd think if the door can expand for crutches that this couch could do the same for my hips," Erika said.

"It's called a bed," Abby replied.

"That's so far away."

"It's literally in the next room."

"Abby," Erika whined. "I'm injured."

Abby walked over to the pantry, pressing a series of commands on the screen. After a few moments, a tray came out. Abby brought the tray – complete with two mugs of hot cocoa – over to the coffee table. She handed the first mug to Erika, before taking the second one for herself and having a seat on the floor next to the crutches.

"Bold of you to trust me with one of these after the morning I had," Erika said.

"What can I do to help you?" asked Abby.

"Plastic cups would be a good place to start. Maybe a fall risk bracelet. Bubble wrap?"

"With Grace."

Erika went quiet. She leaned over and sat her cocoa on the table, laying back on the couch and thinking.

"I mean, I assume it's Grace," said Abby.

"Oh no, I've been caught! Wonder what she'll do. Hit you? I might like that. I already know you do."

"Are you with me?"

"Are you? Were you ever?"

After a few moments, Erika felt Abby reach her hand over and feel for hers. She grasped Abby's hand tightly, her fingers stinging from the tight grip.

"It can wait. I don't mind."

Abby pulled Erika's hand to her lips, then stood and walked away.

"I need a drink, Abby," Erika mumbled as Abby neared the doorway. "She won't stop."

"Is she there constantly?" asked Abby.

"Not every second. There's stuff that triggers it."

"Lorena?"

A long pause filled the room.

"No," Erika said quietly.

"I'm sorry," Abby replied after an extended pause of her own.

"There's got to be some way to get booze here."

"Wouldn't medication be better? I'm sure there's something that Nell or one of the healers has that could help you."

Erika quickly pushed herself up, nearly falling off the couch in an attempt to get standing. She grabbed her crutches off the floor, swiftly hobbling to the door.

"Where are you going?" asked Abby.

"To find Nell," Erika answered. "I can't believe I didn't think of this before."

"I never said she could get rid of Grace."

"She can try!"

Abby rose to her feet, jogging to get in front of Erika and open the door. She'd hardly shut the door behind her when she noticed Erika halfway to the elevator, practically jogging on her crutches.

"You're going to find a new way to hurt yourself if you keep that up," Abby shouted after Erika.

"Doesn't matter!" yelled Erika. "The magic healing light is going to fix my brain!"

"You don't know that!"

"Magic. Healing. Light."

As Erika and Abby rode the elevator down to the armory, the car came to a stop. Brigid joined them, holding a glimmering gold and silver sword.

"Are the two of you heading to see Nell too?" Brigid asked. "I assume so if you're on crutches."

"Yeah, but not about my leg," Erika said.

"Well, depending on what's wrong, Nell might have something. I'm off to the armory to sharpen Caér here."

"Is that your sword?" Abby asked.

"It is," Brigid replied. "It's the personal weapon that all the gods of life within the Azaes Realm's history have used. It's one of the few elemental weapons capable of using true electrical waves. I believe you have the other one."

"Me?" Abby said, a hint of surprise in her voice.

"The Book of Eterna is capable of summoning lightning and electrical energy spells," Brigid said. "It's the way you'll want to use it in nearly every situation."

"I'd been focusing on learning my axe, so I hadn't really even thought about it."

"Probably for the best that you learn one weapon at a time. You'll get to tome training soon enough."

The elevator came to a stop, Abby exiting the car first. Brigid held the door open for Erika, who moved swiftly on her crutches.

"You know the way to medical, right?" Brigid asked.

"End of the hall, take a left," Erika said, already making her way in the direction she stated.

Even with her partner on crutches, Abby had to jog to catch up with Erika, the two of them leaving Brigid well behind as she went off to her own devices.

"I don't think I've seen you move this fast ever," she said. "Crutches generally slow people down."

They reached the lobby of the medical bay – a small, brightly lit room with comfortable chairs and the faint scent of lavender wafting through the air. The receptionist was nowhere to be found, a piping hot mug of coffee sitting on the desk a sign of their recent departure.

"Is there a ring bell for service option?" Erika asked as she surveyed the room.

"Be patient," Abby insisted.

"You're telling me to be patient now? How?"

"I'm telling you that you need to wait for someone who knows what can be done."

Erika tossed her crutches to the ground, standing on her own feet. A dull pain shot across the arch of her injured foot. It was enough to make Erika wince, but nothing more.

"Look at this!" Erika said. "We're in a world where I can jam a knife through my foot, stand on it and have it barely hurt a few hours later. They can fix me. I know it."

"Fix what?" a voice rang out from the room behind the reception desk. "What's wrong?"

Erika looked around, unable to locate the source of the voice. Even after leaning over the desk – the ends of her hair dangling precariously close to the receptionist's open coffee mug – she couldn't spot anyone.

"Yes! It's me! I'm broken!" Erika shouted. "Wherever you are, that is."

The door on the side of the room opened, making Erika quickly stumble her way off the top of the desk. She crumbled in a heap on the floor, the bulk of her body weight landing on her injured foot. To her surprise, the pain was manageable, though she did let out a small groan.

She stared up at the short woman with sandy blonde hair in front of her. Her red scrubs indicated she was one of the healers like Erika had seen earlier, though Erika's attention was drawn to the woman's face. A black eye-covering with shimmering silver and navy accents covered her right eye, along with a significant portion of her forehead and cheek. The covering was shaped like a kite shield, its wider, rounded part extending nearly up to the woman's hairline, teardropping down to a point just below the woman's nose. The patch paired in stark contrast to the brilliant blue-green shimmer of her left iris, which seemed to twinkle and sparkle with every wink and blink.

"You're the coffee mug in the foot from earlier," she said.

"Did I meet you?" Erika asked.

"No, though I did hear about what happened."

"Even the doctor's office is laughing at you. You're a medical marvel."

"I'm sorry," the healer continued, "it's terribly impolite of me to start talking about your medical history without introducing myself. I'm Iris. I'm the newest healer here."

"Hi Iris," Erika said frantically, "my brain is broken. Can you please fix it?"

"Broken how?"

"Name it. You're probably right."

"She has a persistent – and loud – inner critic who amplifies her severe anxiety and its corresponding spirals," Abby interjected. "She also exhibits signs of alcoholism and complex post-traumatic stress disorder. While neither of those are formally diagnosed by any medical professional from when she was on Earth, symptoms are present and persistent in the case of both conditions."

"That was exceptionally thorough," Erika said.

"Is the lack of diagnosis because of no attempt to diagnose either condition or because of failures to achieve a diagnosis?" Iris asked.

"I –"

Erika stared at Iris in a stunned silence for a few moments before attempting to respond.

"I just want it to stop."

"We can't do anything for that."

"We as in you the newbie healer or the royal we?"

"I know I certainly can't," Iris replied. "And though I don't think there's anyone of royal descent here, I can't rule it out. Either way, it's not within the scope of what healers can do here, regardless of any possible noble lineage."

Erika bounded off the floor, grimacing as pain began to build in her foot again. She grasped at her crutches, nearly falling over in the process. Abby was barely able to hand them back to her before Erika spun on her injured heel, screaming in pain as she exited the room.

"Where are you going now?" Abby shouted after her.

"To find Nell," Erika yelled back. "If they can fix my foot, they can fix my head. It's about finding the right person."

"Based on that scream, I don't think her foot's fully fixed yet either," Iris said.

As Iris talked to herself, debating exactly how long it'd take Erika's foot to heal, Abby left the room and chased after her girlfriend. Abby quickened her pace to a jog and caught up with Erika. With a quick sidestep, Erika tried to dodge, only to lose her balance. She crumbled down into Abby's arms, crutches landing on the ground at her sides.

"Why are you stopping me?" Erika asked.

"I'm not," Abby insisted. "I don't want you to hurt yourself on the way there."

"Is that really it?"

"Why are you being such a jerk to me today?"

"How am I being a jerk?"

"Have you been listening to yourself?" asked Abby. "You spent the entire time before we got to breakfast whining about how you didn't want to be awake. I basically carried you to medical after you cut your foot, not even a thank you before you ran out the door again. Look at you."

Erika relaxed her body, resting on the floor and allowing her weight to lean against Abby rather than trying to flee.

"You don't need to try to fight me when I'm helping you. I'm on your side."

"Did I really not say thank you?" Erika asked.

"Not once."

Erika looked around, finding that no one had followed them down the hall out of the medical area. She'd expected Iris to follow, if nothing else to see what the crazy lady was doing.

"Can I – can we – please go find the lady who will tell me the newbie is wrong?" Erika asked.

Abby tightened her grasp on Erika, wrapping her arms around her shoulders and pulling her in close.

"What?" asked Erika.

"I hope you're right," Abby said.

Erika kissed Abby on the cheek, then attempted to pull herself up. She stepped on one of the crutches, slipping, and falling back to the ground.

She held her arm out and helped Erika to her feet.

"Do you need me to carry you again?" Abby asked.

"No, I can do this," Erika replied.

"Because I will. Big spoon carrying her little spoon."

"Now you're just patronizing me."

"That's not true," Abby replied. "I'm mocking you."

Erika gave a small chuckle, then started hobbling down the hall on her crutches, Abby in tow close behind. They arrived at the armory shortly after and nearly bowled over Nell, who was exiting the armory while reading a book.

"I see you've been to the med bay," Nell said.

"Yeah, I hurt my foot, whatever," Erika said. "I need you to fix my brain."

"Can you be a little more specific?"

"The newbie with the eyepatch said it couldn't be done. But my foot's healing. I can almost walk. And you had that magic that made my back stop being sore after training. I'm sure you or someone else can do the same to my brain."

"Still needing some specifics," Nell said. "What happened to your head?"

"I have a voice. A critic," Erika began, "And she gets in the

way. It takes me to really dark places. I break down, I drink –
please. You fixed my back. The healers fixed my foot. Where do
we need to go to fix my brain?"

Nell's brow furrowed. She looked Erika over, her eyes
occasionally darting to Abby as she did so.

"I'm not joking," Erika insisted.

"I don't doubt that at all," Nell said. "I'm just worried you have
a fundamental misunderstanding of what can and can't be done
with the healing tools we have."

"So you can't fix me?"

"What did your back pain and your injured foot have in
common?"

"They both hurt like fuck," said Erika.

"Yes, but that wasn't what I was going for," said Nell. "They
were both acute injuries. Your back was inflamed. Your foot
was...what exactly was wrong with your foot?"

"She cut it open by stepping on shards from a shattered
coffee cup," Abby interjected.

Nell shuddered.

"Glad you took that one to med bay and not to me," she said.
"But what it sounds like you're dealing with is one or more chronic
mental illnesses."

"Right," Erika interrupted, "Exactly, you got it."

"And unfortunately," continued Nell, "that isn't just
something that you can poof away. It takes time to build new
neural pathways in the brain. I can't just go into your brain and
replace your critic with something else. That's not how the human
brain's infrastructure works."

"Can't you try?"

"To literally replace your brain's infrastructure? It's called a lobotomy and it's a barbaric procedure that never should have been practiced. You wouldn't be you. It would fundamentally change who you are, who you remember yourself to be, and everything about you."

"Oh," Erika said meekly.

"Now, if you're asking me if I can help you with symptoms while you work on building those pathways, that I can do," Nell said. "Were you on any sort of medication for this on Earth?"

"Does Grey Goose count?"

"Does it come in prescription strength?"

"She is not on any medication," Abby interjected. "I don't know that she's ready for it."

"Well while that could be a possibility down the line, I think what Erika is looking for is two things. First, she needs something to help her when her spirals overwhelm her. Is there anything you can do specifically to address this symptom?" Nell asked.

"Possibly, I haven't thought about it, What's the second thing?" Erika replied.

"Honestly, I think you need to work through things with a non-judgmental third party," said Nell.

"Therapists haven't worked," Abby sighed. "I've tried but living together, being together, it always ends in an argument."

"We can find you that person for sure," Nell said. "The medical team has several folks I think could do a good job. I'd even be willing to be that person if you felt most comfortable with me. At its worst, its darkest, what worked for you best on Earth?"

"If I was drunk enough, the voice stopped," replied Erika. "Or too out of it to notice."

"I see," Nell said. "I could give you something, Erika. Though

I really do think we should find you a way to help work through this. You've already met Iris. She's fantastic at what she does. If you sat down with her and talked through some of what yo—"

"Thanks anyway," Erika said. "I appreciate your help."

Erika began to hobble away on her crutches, her movement slower and less steady than it had been on the way down.

"Coward. Always running from your problems."

Abby quickly caught up to her, stopping a few steps in front of her.

"I need to be alone," said Erika.

"She's giving you hope!" Abby exclaimed.

"There's no hope, just therapy. And that's not fixing me."

"You don't know t—"

"I said I need to be alone!" Erika growled, her voice breaking. "Please?"

Abby started to say something, but changed her mind, taking a few steps out of the way. Erika passed her by, making her way back to the elevator. As the door started to close, Abby darted into the car to join her.

"You don't have to talk to me," Abby said. "But I'm talking to you. Even if you don't listen."

As the door clicked behind them, Erika slowly made her way to the bedroom. She threw herself on the bed, letting the crutches clatter to the floor in the process.

"There's no such thing as a free lunch. Therapy and meds may be free, but you'll pay for it somehow."

Erika closed her eyes tightly, hoping to block out any light from the other rooms coming through the open door. She felt the mattress shift as Abby crawled into bed beside her, intertwining their fingers together as they curled up under the blankets.

Erika sighed. She opened her eyes to find that Abby had shut all the lights off save for one of the lamps, leaving the room dim and calm. She felt Abby's hands warming as they held her own. The change was subtle, calming in its own way. It gave her a sense of belonging. She was meant to be in this moment, in this place, with Abby. Sometimes that thought alone would stop a spiral in its tracks.

Today she had no such luck.

"They're trying to help because they care," said Abby. "Even if it's not the way you want. We'll get you through this. But you can't do it alone. You can't keep doing the same things you've done in the past and expect things to get better."

Abby moved closer to Erika, wrapping her arms tightly around her shoulders. Erika rested her head on Abby's chest, closing her eyes as she allowed herself to listen to the soft sound of Abby's synthetic heartbeat. Tears trickled down her face as she felt Abby softly kiss her forehead.

"You won't get through this."

16
Gemini

Erika watched as Shaw and K'Andre prepared for a practice battle with their respective elemental weapons. Though she expected that two people with such contrasting personalities would go about their training in different manners, she didn't expect it to be so stark.

It was surprising that Shaw's high-energy warmup didn't wear him out. He was bounding back and forth between two points in the room, alternating between sprinting and leaping. After a few moments, he'd come to a stop, aggressively bending and twisting to stretch out his upper body. In the moments he wasn't running, Shaw was singing something loudly, though Erika didn't recognize the song.

By contrast, K'Andre barely moved. He sat on the floor, using an exercise band to stretch his legs and his arms. Though Erika was pretty sure she'd seen K'Andre doing a light jog when she entered the arena, his measured, slow manner of getting ready still surprised Erika. After all, Shaw was the athlete of the two. He had to know something about getting ready for combat, right?

"One minute until combat begins," Sadie said over the room's sound system. "Please put on your protective wear at this time."

The term, protective wear, was a bit of a misnomer according to K'Andre. The weapons used in this battle would be a middle ground between the training weapons Erika had seen Shaw use and the actual elemental weapons they'd use in a battle. Though the suits did provide protection against the low levels of elemental magic, the primary purpose of the gear was to monitor damage dealt by the weapons and to provide feedback to the wearer accordingly.

K'Andre used a scaled back version of an elemental weapon called the Aquarius Sledge. A sledgehammer in design, its element water, it moved around in K'Andre's grip as if it was liquid.

As for Shaw, he had a toned-down version of the Apidae Gauntlet again, albeit stronger than the one Erika had previously seen. He checked the arm straps multiple times on each arm, before finally deciding they were to his liking.

"They should really give us entrance music for this," Shaw said. "It'd make the battle feel a lot more epic."

"You do realize this is practice for actual combat?" K'Andre replied.

"I stand by my statement. I'm getting tired of having to sing it myself."

"That was your entire gimmick! You sang your own entrance music and made fun of your opponent with parody songs."

"Was my entire gimmick. You're two tweaks behind. And besides, that's just a character," Shaw countered. "If I'm going to save the world as Shaw Felix, I want proper entrance music."

"Return to your starting points at this time," Sadie said. "Combat will begin in fifteen seconds."

Shaw and K'Andre made their way back to their designated locations.

"Are you actually going to give me a challenge this time?" Shaw shouted.

"You should be beating my ass," K'Andre replied. "The fact that I even keep things close with you says you're not trying hard enough."

"Oh yeah? Well, you wouldn't want to see me at full power!"

"What, is it over 9000 or something?"

"Very funny."

"I thought so."

"You can suck my kamehamecock."

Plexiglass-like screens dropped down in front of Erika and the other spectator chairs. A buzzer sounded, initiating the battle. Shaw began running toward K'Andre, cutting the distance between the two of them in half in a matter of seconds. K'Andre held his ground, his sledgehammer at his side.

"Try some of this!" Shaw shouted. "Opal wave, lance form!"

A brilliant white shield formed in front of Shaw before morphing into a slender javelin. Shaw chucked the spear at K'Andre who was still in his starting position, watching Shaw's moves. Once the javelin left Shaw's hand, K'Andre lifted the sledgehammer off the ground, transforming it into a large, rectangular shield. The projectile clattered off and landed on the ground at K'Andre's feet.

"Really?" K'Andre said.

"I've been practicing that for a week and you just block it?" Shaw replied, disgusted.

"Get good, scrub."

Shaw let out a whining growl, then began to charge at K'Andre.

"Hornet's blades!" Shaw yelled.

The gauntlets on each of his hands morphed into small daggers, a violet light reflecting off them as he ran. K'Andre quickly made his shield smaller, changing it to be a circular shape that he held on his left forearm. Part of the sledgehammer shifted to his right hand, forming into a double-headed mallet.

"His weapon can split?" Erika mumbled to herself. "Can they all do that?"

K'Andre blocked with his shield as Shaw took his first strike with his right hand, deflecting the punch to the side. Anticipating this, Shaw quickly countered with a pair of quick jabs from his left hand, the first missing, but the second glancing off K'Andre's armor. By the time K'Andre counterattacked with his mallet, Shaw was out of reach. He waited for the swing to finish then came at K'Andre again, this time leading with a left hook.

With a nimble motion, K'Andre was able to dodge the left hook, but not the follow up jab. Shaw was able to get a couple of more shots in, staggering K'Andre. He retracted the daggers into the gauntlet and began to circle.

"Emerald flowsion!" he shouted.

"Wait, what?" K'Andre replied.

Shaw picked K'Andre up into a powerslam position, causing K'Andre to drop his weapon in the process. As K'Andre punched at Shaw's armor with his bare hands, Shaw dropped K'Andre onto the right side of his torso. Shaw leapt to his feet, taunting K'Andre with an invisible championship belt around his waist.

"Woo!" Shaw shouted. "You come at the champ; you best not miss! I can do this all day! Woooo! All d—"

Shaw was cutoff mid-sentence as his legs were swept out from under him. K'Andre had regained control of his weapon, turning it into a long staff and tripping Shaw. Outside of the battlefield, Erika chuckled to herself as Shaw tumbled to the ground.

"Man, shut up," K'Andre said.

Shaw laughed to himself, rolling away and making his way back to his feet.

This time it was K'Andre on the offensive, his weapon back in sledgehammer form. The hammer moved slowly, giving Shaw time to dodge out of the way of the path.

"Spider's silk!" Shaw yelled.

A delicate white thread began to form around K'Andre's feet. He tried to run away, but his legs churned slowly and deliberately, as if he were trying to sprint through a pool of molasses.

"That hardly seems fair," Erika said to herself.

"Do you give?" Shaw shouted. "I have you trapped and can finish this however I want."

K'Andre took a moment to assess his position before shifting the sledgehammer to its smaller mallet form, then chucking it at Shaw. He ducked out of the way easily.

"Oh, we're do—"

Before Shaw could finish his sentence, the second half of the weapon – also in the form of a mallet – hit Shaw in the chest, knocking him to the ground.

"Now I do!" yelled K'Andre. "You get your win, but I got you to shut the hell up for a second."

Shaw climbed off the ground, laughing as he rubbed his neck.

"Sadie, end the battle, please," he said.

"Yes, Mr. Felix," said Sadie.

The projected plexiglass wall disappeared from in front of Erika, as did the remnants of the magic spider web holding K'Andre in place.

"I can't believe you insist on having Sadie call you that," K'Andre said as he worked to remove his armor. "What's wrong with her calling you Shaw?"

"Where's the fun in that?" Shaw replied. "Makes me sound like I'm a secret agent."

"Sounds like you can't get yourself out of a classroom, even in a whole other world."

"At least I don't have parents yelling at me here."

Erika hobbled her way over to Shaw and K'Andre, her crutches scuffing the floor with each step.

"How are you two still standing?" Erika asked. "Doesn't that hurt?"

"K'Andre's tougher than he looks," Shaw said. "When we were in high school, I powerbombed him onto my kitchen table. It wasn't a gimmicked table, so he didn't go through. But he popped right back up like nothing happened."

"She means the training weapons," K'Andre replied. "And that fucked my back for a week."

"Oh, yeah, these don't hurt at all so long as you're wearing the armor. No more than getting hit by a regular punch or hammer, that is."

"Getting hit by a punch isn't pleasant," Erika said. "Lace has hit me enough to teach me that for a lifetime."

"What he means is that you don't run the risk of the same harm with the practice weapons and armor as if you used the real ones," K'Andre said. "There's no harm to any of your bodily systems for using them. The contact stings, but it's not going to set you on fire or freeze you. Think of them more like laser tag guns on steroids."

Erika stood quietly pondering this information. Every time she felt like she had a handle on how the Azaes Realm worked, there was a new piece of information that caught her off guard.

"Anything else you saw you have questions about?" asked Shaw.

"I'm surprised how much of the weapon training involved

traditional fighting," Erika said. "Is it always like that?"

"Shaw likes to show off, but you're right," K'Andre replied. "There's more to using these things well than letting them do all the work."

"I tie my wrestling and judo background in because it's what comes natural," added Shaw. "But if you watch Lace, you can see her boxing and martial arts experience in how she moves. K'Andre's cunning and looks for openings to counterattack. It's about knowing what you're good at and using that along with your weapons."

"I'm still on the training wheels program," said Erika.

"You'll get there," K'Andre said. "It's not like you have to be the badass fighter on your team. You've got Lace for that. And Abby seems to be picking up on things pretty well."

"Yeah..." Erika trailed off. She'd seen Abby training a bit with Lace. To say it was coming naturally to her was an understatement.

"So just try your best," K'Andre said. "We'll work with you where we can."

"I can teach you hand-to-hand combat if you want someone who isn't Lace doing it," Shaw added. "She can be a bit tough to work with."

"Thanks," said Erika. "For someone whose job is to constantly kick me to the floor, she's surprisingly nice about it."

Shaw and K'Andre finished putting their armor away and packing up their training weapons. As they left to get cleaned up, Erika slowly made her way to the elevator to head back to her room. As she was waiting for the car to arrive, a voice called after her from further down the hallway.

"Wait for me, please!" Svieva shouted, sprinting toward the elevator.

Erika held the door, allowing Svieva to slow to a light jog.

"Thank you so much," Svieva replied as the doors shut behind them and Erika. "It's been a crazy morning."

"Don't mention it."

"Say, I'm heading to Earth a bit later this week to do some intel gathering from Gersemi. Would you like me to check on anything for you while I'm there?"

Erika thought for a moment. She'd heard Brigid mention that Gersemi was on Earth but didn't think about the fact that others might go to her from time to time.

"Are you sure I can't go with you?" asked Erika.

"I'm afraid not," Svieva said. "You'll only be allowed to go with your team as a whole."

"Well, then can you just check and see if my parents are alright? My dad more than anything."

"Of course. I'll do my best for you."

Svieva exited the elevator, running down the hall to wherever they were in a hurry to get to. The door closed behind them, leaving Erika to continue her trip to her room.

As the elevator arrived on the floor with Erika's room, she noticed Brigid standing in the hallway in front of where the door to her and Abby's room would be. Erika made her way out of the elevator, doing her best to flag Brigid down as she moved.

"Are you looking for Abby?" Erika asked. "I think she's in one of the arenas training with Nell and Lace."

"I'm actually looking for you," Brigid replied. "How are you feeling?"

"I could probably get off these things now. I'm just being cautious like I was told."

"And mentally?"

"Finding out your magic can't fix my broken brain was kind of a killjoy, if I'm honest," Erika stated.

"I'm sorry about that," Brigid said. "If I would have known it was something you'd get your hopes up about, I would have had Nell warn you earlier."

"It's fine. Well, it's not. There's no magic cure for it. The only reliable thing to shut it up is alcohol, which is banned from this god-forsaken place. Instead, it's meds and therapy, which everyone seems intent on using to fix me."

"Smooth."

"Fuck," Erika spit out. "I didn't mean to insult you."

"How?" Brigid asked.

"I called it a god-forsaken place in front of a god. Who lives here."

Brigid shrugged.

"We all get stressed. I've said worse."

"They're no help anyway. Probably rather sedate you. Make you something other than you."

"I was under the impression that therapy was a bit more normalized in America than it used to be," said Brigid. "Is that not the case?"

"It is," Erika replied.

"Were you ever discouraged from going to therapy? Maybe as a kid?"

"I mean, my mom wasn't a fan of the idea when I first mentioned it. But it was more of an eyeroll moment than anything else. Dad's always been non-committal, but supportive."

"Did you have a bad experience with a therapist? Finding

someone you can talk to openly and honestly while feeling comfortable is arguably just as important as any help they might give you."

"I tried a few," replied Erika. "They were nice enough."

"Did you not feel comfortable talking to them?" Brigid inquired.

"I just said they were nice."

"That's not the same thing as being comfortable with them. Think of it this way. You're walking down the street. You drop your water bottle. A stranger picks it up and hands it to you. Do you still drink out of it?"

"Yeah, of course."

"Okay, let's take that same stranger and he walks up to you on the street," Brigid continued. "He hands you a water bottle. It's not yours. He offers you a drink. Do you drink out of it?"

"No. I don't know what's in it," replied Erika.

"Right. Now say Abby walks up to you with a water bottle, unprompted, and offers you a drink."

"I drink it."

"It's because you're comfortable with her," said Brigid. "You trust her. Those are critical emotions to feel. If you don't trust someone enough to open up to them, you can't really make progress. It's not an instantaneous process. But it does work if you put the time in with someone you trust."

"I couldn't afford to keep going to any of them," Erika replied. "Even with insurance—"

"You do realize we're not going to charge you to get help, right?"

"Why do that when I could have something I know works?"

Erika said. "I don't know whoever it is you're going to find. And maybe they're great at what they do, maybe I'll like them, maybe I won't. But I do know that if you give me a fifth of vodka, not only do I stop feeling like this for one night, but it also stops until I run out."

"I want to help you," said Brigid. "There are ways we can make things better. There's probably not a silver bullet to this, but a mixture. I have some ideas, but I need some time to get everything together."

"Like what?" Erika blurted out. "Tell Nell to suggest meds to me in a slightly different way? It's not like other people haven't tried that before."

"Erika," Brigid said, "let me see what I can do for you. Please?"

Erika stared at Brigid. Something seemed different about Brigid's pleas to let her help. Erika couldn't quite put her finger on what it was, but there was something. She lowered her voice to a whisper.

"Are you going to find a way—"

"I said," Brigid replied, her voice much quieter, "let me see what I can do."

17
Pixie Dust and Carnival Nuts

April 3, 2035

Sam Sawchuk walked up the steps to the tiny, two-bedroom house that had been converted into the accounting offices of Simon, Zurat, and Zurat, CPAs. He opened the door, leaving the cold spring rain for an overly warm lobby. The receptionist – a young, bubbly blonde girl named Bianca – cheerfully greeted him.

"Good morning!" she said. "Who are you here to see today?"

"Tara Simon," he replied. "Let her know Sam Sawchuk is here."

Bianca left her desk, gleefully walking back to Tara's office. Sam took a seat, glancing through the magazines. Still nothing interesting, he thought. He kept bugging Tara to get something he considered to be worth reading, but nothing ever came of it.

"She's just finishing up a call," said Bianca, walking back to her desk. "Can I get you some water or coffee?"

"No," replied Sam. "What happened to the old receptionist? Norma, I think her name was."

"She was a temp."

"It's for the best. Can't get clients in the door with someone like that at the desk."

Bianca stopped sitting down, turning back toward Sam. "Like what?"

"You know," Sam said.

"I don't," replied Bianca. "Enlighten me."

"She wasn't welcoming."

"She wasn't nice?"

"She was kind enough," replied Sam. "But she wasn't like you."

"Like me how?" Bianca countered, hands making their way to her hips.

"If I'm running a business – which I am – I want to make sure the first person my clients see is someone that makes them want to come back. While I loved my grandmother, may God rest her soul, I don't go to businesses to see her."

Bianca raised her eyebrows.

"It's because I'm young?" she asked.

"That," replied Sam. "And better packaging."

"Right," replied Bianca, rolling her eyes. "Because an office with three other women hired me because of my tits."

"Everyone has preferences."

"I'm sure those preferences didn't get me hired here."

"Are you a temp too?" asked Sam.

"For now."

"Well if you're looking for a long-term gig after your time here ends, I could use a secretary. It'd be a very enjoyable job for both of us."

"I'd rather fuck a cactus."

A tense silence filled the room. A smirk crossed Sam's face as he heard the clacking of high heels moving down the hallway toward the lobby.

"You're early, Sam," Tara said.

"I was just getting to know Bianca," replied Sam.

Bianca shot Sam a glare.

"You have my permission to slap him if you need to," Tara said.

"He's not worth moving my arms for," replied Bianca.

Tara invited Sam back to her office, passing a pair of offices along the way. The first office was dark, a large wooden desk nearly empty sitting in the middle of the room.

"She's a firecracker," said Sam.

"And you're a misogynistic twat," said Tara, loud enough for Bianca to hear back in the lobby.

"I followed you away from your old firm for a reason, Tara," he replied. "It wasn't because you were good with people."

"You need the right fit to build a good culture at a new business. If you don't, people just leave."

"When are your partners going to move into the office?" Sam asked.

"Ellie is here now," Tara answered. "Cerise is remote while splitting her time between here and Seattle. She's got an office if she wants to be here. We'll use it for storage if not."

"I haven't seen either of them any time I've come by."

Tara stopped at the second office door, knocking softly on the frame around it.

"Come in!" Ellie's melodic voice rang out.

Tara opened the second door to reveal her business partner frantically cramming a forkful of salad into her mouth, her bubblegum pink colored hair diving in front of her eyes as she moved.

"This is one of my clients, Sam Sawchuk," said Tara. "He's opening L'ostrica Reale later this year."

"Oooo, that's the place with all the fancy fish tanks I heard about, isn't it?" asked Ellie.

"The fancy fish tanks, yes," Tara replied. "Though I don't think that's why most people will go."

"You're welcome to come by when we open," said Sam. "Tara will be joining us for a pre-opening dinner. It'd be nice if you could join us too."

"I'll think about it," replied Ellie.

"If I let you meet the fish, would that change your mind?"

"I mean –"

"There's a dwarf puffer fish named Tink I think you'll like."

Ellie smiled. "I'll see if I can clear my calendar."

Tara led Sam to her office, offering him one of the chairs across the desk from her chair. She shut the door behind them, then made her way to her chair.

"I didn't know they let beautiful women become accountants," Sam said. "Receptionists I get. But I thought a pocket protector was a pre-requisite for the role."

"I'd be insulted if I thought you had a shred of humility in your body," Tara replied.

"Is she single?"

"Ellie? That's a question you'll need to ask her yourself. Not that I'll ever let you in my presence."

"Bold statement from a robot."

"A robot that knows where you like to hide your money," Tara said. "If she hits on you, that's one thing. But don't go out of your way to spend time with her."

"She seemed to be into me," Sam replied. "I think she wants to see my dwarf puffer fish."

"Weird nickname for your penis."

"Fine," Sam said. "You've made your point. No making partnerships with your partners unless they ask me first. Got it."

"I respect your restraint."

"You're welcome. Now. Is your receptionist single?"

"I should kick you out for asking."

"If you're going to cockblock me, I have to do what I have to do," replied Sam.

"You don't have to try to fuck my entire office."

"That's not fair. I'm not trying to fuck you."

"I can't begin to list the number of reasons why that would never happen."

Sam leaned back in his chair, crossed his arms, and gave Tara a smug look.

"Why then?" he said.

"Besides being my client —"

"You're the Fogg's accountant and you live with them," Sam interrupted.

"No, I rent a floor of their house," Tara replied. "I'm their client and they're mine. They're also longtime friends who I'd do anything for. And, most importantly, I'm not sleeping with any of them."

"Fine. Continue."

"On your best days, you have the charm of a conman and the ethics of a used car salesman. You're what some may consider passably attractive, until you open your mouth, making every woman in the vicinity drier than the Sahara. You hit on anything with a pulse, single or otherwise. And no matter how many husbands and beaux have handed your ass to you, physically or legally, you just push on like the worm you are."

Tara paused, allowing Sam to capitalize on the silence.

"Is that all?" he said.

"You're a lucrative client, but I don't think you'll ever understand how repulsive I find you as a human."

Sam leaned back in his chair and began to laugh. His chuckle built into a roar slowly, but constantly, until it began to fill Tara's entire office. His baritone rumble eventually emanated throughout the building, causing Bianca to roll her eyes in the lobby.

"Perhaps you know me better than I realized, Miss Simon," Sam said. "It's no wonder you came so highly recommended when we met. And why I've chosen to keep you as my accountant for so long."

"Keep it semi-professional, it'll stay that way," Tara countered.

Their conversation was interrupted by Ellie entering the room, a jacket draped over her shoulder.

"I'm running out to get lunch," she said. "Want anything?"

"I'm good, thank you," Tara replied. "Check with Bianca before you leave."

"Always!"

Ellie turned on her heels and bounded out of the room. Sam's eyes followed her down the hallway, transfixed on her posterior until she turned the corner.

"You're a pig," Tara said.

"Maybe," Sam replied. "But I know what I like."

*****

168

Youles laid awake in bed, staring at the light flickering on the ceiling every time a swaying tree branch passed in front of the streetlamp outside his window. Three months was an eternity to plan out how to handle Janus's request.

One target. One chance to make good on the first job he'd messed up in years. All he had to do was wait for another chance. Everything was laid out for him. He'd be able to keep an eye on his target all night. He had a cover identity that'd allow him to keep his phone at home and have a plausible alibi. Janus had even managed to get the restaurant owner to make sure his target would be seated near him. All he had to do was wait.

And that's what bothered him. If Janus wanted his robot gone so badly, why not have him take care of the problem before August? He'd staked out her house several times over the past few weeks. No one noticed him. The family she lived with was too busy dealing with a baby to see his car parked across the street or around the corner. He'd even spent a few hours a week in the shopping center down the street from her office, allowing him to keeping tabs on her workday habits.

Youles was certain he could pick her off work one morning. Friday was the best bet. She always stopped to get breakfast for the office, showing up 15-30 minutes late. If she turned left out of their neighborhood, she would get donuts. If she turned right, bagels or a make your own omelet bar. A left turn presented a consistent location, but a right turn gave more opportunity. The bagel place was in a shady part of town where no one would be the wiser if her car was left abandoned for a long time. The omelet bar was in a nicer neighborhood, but it was poorly lit. Once he had her, he'd be able to get her out of town before the police responded to her distress signal – if they did at all before someone reported her missing, which was unlikely.

But he had to wait. And he hated that.

It was worth the payment to wait. The original job would have paid him $200,000. A hefty sum, but not completely unheard of in this line of work. After the mistake, Youles figured that money was as good as gone. Not only did Janus rehire him – albeit with significantly more involvement in his timing and planning – but she more than quintupled his payout. All for going after an easier, more predictable mark.

Maybe he really was the best person for the job. That's what the optimistic part of Youles wanted to believe. For all the confidence he'd developed in his abilities over time, he knew there'd always be someone better. If Janus had the connections and ability to find him whenever she wanted, she could easily find whoever the true best contract killer in the United States was. But she'd chosen to stick with him.

On the other hand, he suspected that keeping him on the job was a way to tie up loose ends. Space out the attempts long enough that investigators would have a hard time tying him to both deaths, thereby further slowing down any potential link that could be made to Janus. Youles's payout was more than enough to make sure he could get away safely to a country without an extradition treaty – and to never speak a word about his ties to her ever again.

There was a third option Youles considered. Janus could double-cross him. It was best not to think about that, Youles thought. Killing someone created even more loose ends in the long run. There was more benefit in keeping him alive, paying him off. Youles knew this. It's what he'd do.

That didn't make it any easier to fall asleep at night.

18
The Red Fort

April 12, 2035/15:55, Day 103, Year 10311

"You're learning quickly, Abby," Nell said. "Not that I'd expect any less from you. I couldn't do one-fifth of what you can in the time you've been here."

"You're being modest, I'm sure."

"Maybe a little," Nell said. "But it's very impressive."

"Have you been here long?" asked Abby. "It's hard to tell how much experience everyone has because of the differences in time passing."

"I've been here for just shy of three years in Azaes Realm time. It's been 32 years on Earth. It's weird to me if I stop and think about it. If I were still on Earth, I'd probably be playing bingo and picking gray hairs off my shirt."

"There's no way you're that old, even with the differences."

Nell laughed loudly, her contralto voice echoing through the room.

"No one can tell how old I am," Nell said. "I am a mysterious ageless immortal who has always looked like this and will just continue to look like this to perplex the humans. You should try it. Being a conscientia, you're functionally immortal anyway."

"I feel like that's a bad idea."

"Should you go get charged up before dinner?"

"Probably," Abby replied. "But if you have time, I'd like to pick your brain about some things I found in the Book of Eterna."

"Of course. We should clear out of the arena though. Shaw's in here next and he's a little loud."

Abby followed Nell down to the armory, waiting as she put away the practice weapons they'd been using. Instead of sitting down at one of the various meeting tables around the armory, Nell unhooked a latch beneath one of the weapon display shelves. A skinny door opened from the wall to their left. Nell led Abby through the door and down a narrow hallway.

"Where are we going?" Abby asked.

"Somewhere away from birds," Nell replied.

"What birds? I haven't seen one since we arrived. Are there birds in the Azaes Realm? Is there an outside here?"

"It's a metaphor. There are ears here that want to know everything they can."

Nell opened a door off the side of the hallway, leading Abby into a small room. All around the room, clocks hung from the walls. There were simple dial clocks, large clocks with ornate designs, cuckoo clocks, carriage clocks, grandfather clocks, mantel clocks, and many other designs Abby didn't recognize. On the far side of the room, a stool sat near a carriage clock that had been torn apart and placed on a high table.

"Where are we?" asked Abby.

"This is Gersemi's workshop," replied Nell. "There aren't many people who know about this room. She likes to keep her hobbies to herself."

"I thought Janus was the guardian of time."

"That's true. Gersemi just likes building and repairing things. And she has quite the fascination with clocks for whatever reason. As you might be able to tell, she's worked on quite a few."

Nell pulled the stool out from under the table, offering it to

Abby.

"Please, sit," she said. "I love her work. It's not often I get to talk about it with someone. Gersemi downplays the beauty of what she's created. I think most artists do. There are a few of her creations around the center building. It's a shame more of them aren't on display."

"Are there any in particular you really like?" Abby asked.

A smile covered Nell's face as she crossed the room. She carefully lifted a small teal cuckoo clock off the wall and brought it to Abby.

"This was one of the first ones I saw Gersemi work on," Nell stated. "When it hits the top of the hour, there's a little family of penguins that pops out."

Nell carefully turned the hands forward, setting the clock to change hours. A group of five emperor penguins – two adults and three chicks – stood on a wooden post painted to look like a sheet of ice.

"They're so cute!" Abby exclaimed. "And the detail is extraordinary."

"Gersemi has an eye for detail," replied Nell. "Not just in the artistry either. Look at the faces of the chicks."

"The littlest one looks angry."

"That was the first thing that caught my eye too. But then you notice how panicked the largest penguin – presumably the dad – is. Meanwhile the partner, who I'd guess is the mom, looks calm about the whole situation, even though the bigger two chicks look like they're about to fight."

Nell walked to the other side of the room and scoured a workbench for her next choice. She returned with an ornately carved wooden mantle clock. A rich mahogany encased a small white-faced clock with black Roman numerals.

"I think my favorite part about this piece," Nell began, "is the story it tells."

"There are chess pieces carved all over it," Abby observed.

"If you just look at it with that in mind, it's still a remarkable work of art. I would have killed to have this in my home on Earth for that reason alone. But if you start at one o'clock and work your way around the front clockwise, you'll see the progression of a game of chess playing out. The game is ultimately won by a lowly pawn making it to the end of the board, choosing a knight as its replacement piece, and achieving checkmate."

"Wouldn't you want a queen as your pawn's promotion?"

"Typically, yes," said Nell. "Though there are certain end game situations where you'd want to underpromote a pawn to avoid ending the game in stalemate. Just like how it can make strategic sense to sacrifice a bishop to allow a pawn to promote into a queen in other circumstances."

"You'd think I would have cared a lot more about chess," Abby replied. "It was one of the first human things computers got really good at."

"I'd argue the skills you have are far more important."

Nell returned the mahogany clock to its shelf. She took a deep breath, then pulled up a chair near Abby.

"Even though you're not human," Nell began, "I don't want this explanation to come as too much of a shock to you. People fainting freaks me out."

"Really?" asked Abby. "Why?"

"Don't know. But the fact that fainting couches were once a thing leads me to wonder how I ever managed to survive on Earth."

"What do you mean?"

Nell located a stool on the other side of the room, bringing it over near Abby and taking a seat.

"I haven't been back to Earth since I left," began Nell.

"Is your family all gone like Lace and Lorena?" asked Abby.

"Probably by now. It's mathematically unlikely either of my parents would be alive by this point, though I suppose they could be. Definitely not my grandparents. Even if they weren't, I really don't have a desire to go back."

"Can I ask why?"

Nell sighed. She grabbed a hair tie off her wrist, methodically twisting her vermillion hair into a tight bun and securing it against the back of her head. She stared off into the distance, gathering herself before continuing.

"One thing remains unchanged on Earth," she said, "and that is this perception of normal. The longer I'm away, the more problematic I find it. Yes, it keeps people from wantonly murdering others. It helped humanity build society. But in turn, it breeds exclusion.

"In a lot of ways, I was lucky that it was never physical. Instead, it was derision, often outright dismissal. When that happens to a core part of who you are... I chose to burn bridges to keep myself healthy."

"I can imagine," said Abby.

"My family didn't understand — rather they didn't want to," replied Nell. "I knew relationships weren't for me. Being that intimate with someone, I have no interest. I couldn't tell you how many times I was told I'd change my mind, I was just being high maintenance, making it up, I'll like it once I get going. Between the names and the many, many arguments over not giving my parents grandchildren... I left.

"It took me until I was 29 to do it. If being ace and at peace meant being alone, so be it. There's only so many times you can hear that you'll find someone – so many book clubs that turn into stealthy first dates – before you realize you won't be accepted. I finally understood why people walk into the sea. I had zero desire to do so. That's where jellyfish are. Three months later, I was here."

"Did you get the fancy portal treatment like we did?" asked Abby.

"I couldn't tell you," replied Nell. "It was all a giant, dark blur. I don't think I even came with anyone. Someone would have needed to open the portal. I just remember that once the confusion about where I was wore off, I cried. I didn't have to hide that part of who I am here. I'm believed and accepted. That's all I wanted."

"Everyone's that accepting here?"

"Not initially. But when you're alive for several hundred years, it becomes clear what's truth and what isn't. There's no need to hide most secrets here. You're free to do so if you want, but the people that live here have seen so many people across a broad array of civilizations and eras over time. It's unlikely they'll encounter a quirk of humanity they haven't seen before. Not to mention the fact that we have a library of knowledge that spans the bulk of the Azaes Realm's existence and travels as it has interacted with other universes."

"Damn. There's so much going on here I hadn't even thought about. And to think I thought was doing good just trying to piece things together about this world."

"What have you figured out?" Nell asked.

"For starters," Abby began, "I don't think this tome's real name is The Book of Eterna."

"It's not. There is an elemental weapon by that name, or more accurately, was. But it was destroyed long ago by Milan."

"Who is Milan?"

"Milan was one of the first humans to end up in the Azaes Realm," said Nell. "And he was the creator of the original elemental weapons. While most in Azaes now are not of his creation, three of Milan's original weapons still exist – the Sai of Milan, Caér, and Mellor the Deathbringer."

"One of those sounds far more ominous than the other two," Abby said.

"That's because one of them is far more dangerous than the other two. To be clear, all three weapons are insanely powerful. Caér, for example, is so strong that typically only a god can handle it – hence Brigid having it. The Sai of Milan is an incredibly weak offensive weapon but can defend spectacularly against nearly any other elemental weapon. Gods have handled it before, though it's much more likely to be entrusted to a guardian.

"Mellor, however, is much more dangerous. The original Book of Eterna was fused into it. The electrical spells you've been using all come from the text of the Book of Eterna and function exactly as you've seen them. By itself, the Book of Eterna was a powerful weapon, though not quite on par with the others I mentioned."

"But Mellor –" Abby said.

"But Mellor is another beast entirely," replied Nell. "In its original form, Mellor contained exactly one spell. This spell would summon Death themselves, allowing the wielder of Mellor to fight off, and kill, any attacker. But it came at the cost of their own life."

A haunting silence fell over the room.

"Is this a suicide mission?" Abby asked. "Am I being given this weapon just to die?"

"Not at all," replied Nell. "Gersemi and I trust you wouldn't use that spell unless it were truly and completely necessary. Humans have a habit of getting a bit trigger happy with the power to kill, even when they know their own life is at risk. Putting a weapon this powerful in your hands rather than one of theirs is just as much for their safety as it is for your ability to use the electrical spells it otherwise provides."

"I don't know that it makes me feel any better hearing that."

"I'm not saying it should. It's a great responsibility to have. Would it make you feel better if I told you a secret of mine?"

"I mean, I guess," Abby replied. "It's not something stupid like 'I hate sour cream', is it?"

Nell laughed.

"No, it's not," she said. "Though, for the record, ew. Close your eyes for a second."

Abby followed Nell's instructions, shutting her eyes tightly. She could have just turned off her vision sense, but Abby figured she was a better sport if she followed Nell's instructions.

"Open them," Nell said.

Abby opened her eyes to see Nell holding a compound bow that glimmered even in the low light of the room. The material the bow was made from seemed to reflect light and to draw it in at the same time, its black sheen reminiscent of obsidian. Dark red accents on the wheel and cam complimented the vibrant red string and cables. As Nell tilted and moved the bow, the shades of red seemed to shift, like oxygen-deprived blood restoring itself and back again.

"That's gorgeous!" Abby exclaimed. It felt weird calling a weapon of any kind beautiful, but the craftsmanship and look of the bow was breathtaking.

"Personal hobby," Nell said. "Granted, my work isn't as good as Milan's. No one's work has been, not even his apprentices."

"He had apprentices?"

"Indeed. He had three – Adriesta, Elu, and Carl."

"Carl?" Abby asked. "Why not Bob?"

"Bob was his uncle," replied Nell.

"Really?"

"No of course not. But yes, each of Milan's apprentices made a powerful elemental weapon. The first is the Wheels of Elu."

"That's the weapon Lace is learning to use," Abby stated.

"It is," Nell replied. "Though even for an incredibly adept fighter such as herself, it's been a handful for her to learn. The second is the Rapier of Adriesta. I have a bit of a personal bias for that weapon, as I truly think it's a beautiful blade. That said, no one, guardian, god, or otherwise, has been able to harness its elemental powers since Adriesta herself died."

"That's kind of insane. What's so powerful about it?"

"It's a weapon that requires a lot of discipline to use. There's a legend that Adriesta made it so that the weapon will obey someone destined to use it, but I'm certain it's a story and nothing more."

"What about Carl?" asked Abby.

"His weapon is named the Lance of Carl," said Nell. "It's unique in that it's particularly powerful against metal elemental weapons – such as Caér and the Book of Eterna – but weak against any other elemental weapon."

Abby glanced over at the compound bow that Nell was still holding at her left side.

"What about yours?" asked Abby.

"It does have a kickass name," replied Nell. "I don't think I could live with myself if it didn't. This is Nidhogg. And while it's technically incapable of elemental magic, when you're firing an arrow of pure phosphorus and exploding anything you shoot at, it's the next best thing."

"Fancy."

"With a bow that looks like this, why not name it after a big fuck you dragon?"

"I'm surprised more of the weapons around here don't follow the same naming philosophy."

Nell burst out laughing, Abby returning her joy in kind. Though Abby found it easy to make new friends – made easier by the nature of her programming – closeness felt like a challenge. Erika was a romantic attraction she was calculated to be a perfect match to. Amy was, in essence, her mother. The only friendship she'd experienced was with Tara, though that felt more like strength in numbers. Nell was the first human Abby felt she could call 'friend'.

"Did you end up doing any more research on the Diaprepes Realm?" Nell asked.

"Not really," Abby said. "That came up right before Erika ran out of the room. I didn't see it as a priority."

"I'm not one to speculate, but I think it's a major reason why you're here. You're the first of your kind to come to the Azaes Realm. There's only so much that we humans can document and learn in our lifetimes, even with the greatly extended lifespans this place affords us. It's likely that a conscientia such as yourself could help us to learn more about the Diaprepes Realm in a year than we could learn in a lifetime on our own."

"You'd think that by now someone would have found a direct way to communicate with it," Abby replied. "At the very least a way back and forth like you've made to our universe."

"There have been people who've tried. Back when the Azaes Realm was co-inhabited by both humans and the Azaeans, portals were used by the Azaeans to get to the Diaprepes Realm. Unlike the ones we use to get to and from Earth, those portals were one-way gates."

"Why?"

"By design," Nell replied. "When you have a disease that's killing off and sterilizing your entire population, and it's beginning to spread cross-species, you'll inevitably take drastic steps to contain it. If you're smart, that is."

"So the portal was to separate the Azaeans and humans?" asked Abby.

"That was initially the plan. In time, the Azaeans learned what the Diaprepes Realm was doing. Not only that, but also —"

A knock sounded on the door.

"That'll be my backup plan," replied Nell. "Just in case you didn't believe me about entrusting Mellor to you."

"I understand," said Abby. "I'm totally terrified by it. But I understand."

"Good. The power to take a life should terrify you. It's a truly humbling power to wield."

The door opened behind Nell and Abby, causing both to turn their heads.

"It's not polite to keep a clockmaker waiting. We know how to tell the time."

19
Division Bell

April 12, 2035/23:38, Day 103, Year 10311

"There's a rumor Gersemi is coming back soon," Revaus said. "Or that she has been here and has already left. The only thing anyone can agree upon is that she's not here now."

"I fail to see how this is our problem," Tane replied. "She's Brigid's guardian. Shouldn't you be bringing this up to her?"

"You know damn well Brigid doesn't care what Gersemi does," said Kedi.

"She can travel back and forth herself. Why would she need to control whether Gersemi is here?"

"The concern, Tane, is not with whether or not Brigid is bothering to keep track of her guardian," Revaus interjected. "We know she's not and never has. The point is that Gersemi constantly seems to be the source of confusion around here."

"A baseless accusation at best," Dau mumbled.

"No one seems to know if she's coming or going. Not even the gods."

"Her plan to stop Janus from destroying Earth seems to be going well thus far," said Tane.

"The parts we know!" Revaus exclaimed. "We're risking an awful lot bringing six outsiders here, one of whom is as useful as a screen door on a submarine. Yet no matter who I ask, no one seems to know anything about the plan beyond how we're training them and who will be sent back with Gersemi to help recover Janus."

"Whenever she comes back," said Kedi.

"Meanwhile," continued Revaus, turning to Dau, "you're over here condoning this lack of knowledge and planning like it's the right way to run things. It's like you don't care if a planet we've invested so much time and effort into – a planet we're all from, I might remind you – is worth as much thought as your lunch."

"It's not my job to patrol what god or guardians travel to and from the Azaes Realm," Dau replied. "Janus is on Earth. Svieva is heading back shortly. Gersemi and Brigid travel back and forth freely as they see fit. I don't see the problem."

"We are meant to be part of this realm. And though we can influence happenings on Earth, this does not mean we should abuse this power. We must have more control about when our guardians are there and why. Especially considering Janus's transgressions."

"That's a fairly chaotic take from the goddess of order. I'd think you'd be all about controlling Earth."

"You know where I stand on the matter," Revaus said.

"Which is precisely why I don't trust you to follow through on your own words," Dau replied.

The room fell silent. Though arguments between Dau and Revaus were not uncommon due to the nature of their respective roles, Revaus could not recall seeing Dau so insistent on needling her motives. Likewise, Dau couldn't remember a time where Revaus was so driven to keep the gods and guardians in line – particularly when considering there was a guardian completely out of their control.

"Leave us," Revaus said, motioning at Kedi and Tane.

Kedi nodded his head and exited the room. Tane looked to Dau, averting her eyes from Revaus's glare as she waited for the god she protected to make a decision.

"I will join you shortly," said Dau. "She's asked for privacy. I do feel it is our duty to give her that."

"As you wish," Tane mumbled.

She left the room, quietly closing the door behind her. Revaus waited for Tane's footsteps to fade away before she spoke again.

"We must summon Gersemi back," Revaus said. "Immediately."

"And do what?" Dau asked. "Ask her to pick up macramé?"

"Until we can be certain that her plan to reign Janus back in can work, or at the very least know how it can work in her absence, we cannot run the risk of something happening to her."

"I would argue that having another guardian on Earth lessens the likelihood that Janus will do something destructive. We can have Gersemi come back when Svieva goes next. We'll just extend Svieva's visit until Gersemi can be certain that her plan will work by overseeing their training herself."

"What is Gersemi going to do that Nell can't?" Dau inquired.

"Nell is not a guardian," Revaus replied. "It's fine that she oversees smaller missions, but something this critical should be led by someone with real authority."

"Authority is not a substitute for skill and knowledge. You know that as well as I do. Nell has both in spades. I'm told that most of the team is blossoming under her tutelage."

"Most is not the same as all. We cannot take risks. Failure is not an option at this juncture."

"Failure is always an option," Dau replied. "What we must prevent is its inevitability."

"The only inevitability here is that there will be yet another time where you fail to do enough to save somewhere we've worked so hard to improve."

Dau turned to exit the room, his footsteps forceful and determined.

"Where do you think you're going?" Revaus asked.

"Perhaps it'd be better if we only communicate through our envoys until this is all resolved," Dau replied. "I'll send Tane or Vermilion when I'm ready to discuss further."

"As you wish."

*****

"I don't get it," said Tevarius. "Why does everything need to be an ethical battle?"

The life of an envoy to the gods was, at its core, quite boring. On a typical day, it meant checking in on the gods a handful of times, maybe receiving a couple of requests, then spending most of the day focusing on your own needs. On days where the gods were meeting with each other, the work was reasonable, rarely lasting more than a few hours at a time. Even the neediest of the gods – typically Revaus because of her attention to detail or Brigid because of the volume of her requests – rarely felt like a chore to act as an envoy for.

Since Janus had rebelled and relocated to Earth, things had become much busier, particularly for Vermilion and Quaid. When Dau or Revaus needed something, they found themselves jumping to their feet, running off to handle whatever was necessary. When they were in closed meetings with each other or with their guardians, it meant that their envoys were stationed in a room just outside wherever the gods were chatting. A four-hour meeting could mean four hours of constantly running and doing things for gods, or it could mean four hours of sitting in a room and waiting. The unpredictability drove all the envoys mad.

"You do realize who we serve, yes?" replied Quaid. "God of order talking with the god of chaos in there. They're literally opposites."

Quaid took a sip of his drink then threw a dart at the board on the other side of the room. Despite growing up in a home filled with people who loved playing darts at the pub, Quaid was not particularly good at the game. Even the abundant time to learn in the Azaes Realm hadn't improved his game much, as he regularly got beaten by the other envoys, just as Kuhla was doing now.

"Forty-three," he mumbled to Kuhla as he went to retrieve his darts.

"I get why they'd have different opinions," Tev continued. "I'm not saying they can't want to take different solutions to the same goal."

"What are you saying then?" Quaid asked.

"I'd think they'd want to work together despite their differences. Not just for the good of the Earth and the Azaes Realm, but because it's the right thing to do."

"Right's subjective," Vermilion said.

The lanky brunette adjusted her position on the couch, wedging her head in the corner between the sofa's lower arm and raised back pillow. Vermilion was alone on the couch, as she often was when all four envoys were in this room, allowing her to take the back cushion from the opposite end of the sofa and use it as a footrest. She itched the bridge of her nose, then covered her eyes with her arm and kept talking.

"I grew up listening to my tía tell me how if I didn't find me a good Catholic boy to marry, I was going to Hell. She said this, mind you, in front of my mom – her own sister – who was married to a woman. They both thought they were right. Meanwhile, my teenage ass just wanted them both to shut up so someone would take me to track practice."

"But they're not really humans anymore," Tevarius countered. "They shouldn't be fighting over petty things."

"I like how you're implying that anyone would be able to move past their human tendencies completely," Vermilion said. "I've seen enough happen around here to know that not only are the gods still human at their core, but that some of them are just people with way too much power at their disposal."

"Like who?" Quaid asked.

"Your master, for one," Tev replied. "Mine as well."

"The only god remotely capable of acting selflessly on the regular was Adelina," Vermilion added. "A lot of good it did her."

The thunk of a dart hitting the board then clattering to the floor caused everyone to turn and look at Kuhla. She steadied her third dart, tossing it and sticking it in the bullseye.

"One ten," she said. "That makes it –"

"I know what the score is, Kuhla," Quaid interrupted. "You're kicking my fucking ass."

Kuhla made herself take up as little space as she could as she walked to the board to retrieve the darts.

"Eighty-seven left for me, two forty-five left for you," Kuhla whispered.

"My point is why can't this just be simple?" Tevarius asked. "Everyone here agrees that whatever Janus is up to can't be good, right?"

"Everyone in this room or everyone in the Azaes Realm?" Kuhla asked.

"She's right," Quaid added. "It's probably two different answers."

"Everyone in here," Tev said.

All the envoys quickly acknowledged their agreement.

"So what if we agree though?" Quaid asked. "There's four of us. Not exactly the largest sample size."

"If we – four people who don't have power here – can realize that it's better to band together to solve a problem than to spend all of our energy fighting about how to do so, I'd like to think that all-powerful beings could figure it out too."

Vermilion began to laugh loudly from the couch, startling Quaid mid-throw in the process.

"What?" Tevarius asked.

"Tev, what did you do for a living on Earth?" asked Vermilion.

"Software development. Not Abby style software, mind you. It was the 1990s."

"But you worked with computers. And people who wanted the software to work. You were never the product being sold."

"Of course not," Tevarius said. "That's not how employment works."

"That's not how employment should work," Kuhla quickly interjected. "But it often does."

"Fair. I still don't see what that has to do with why the gods can't get on the same page."

"Do you know what I did for a living?" Vermilion asked.

"Interior decorating?" Tev said.

"Really? I assumed murder," Quaid snarked.

"You'd be surprised at how much bullshit you hear from rich, entitled white guys when you're the just the brown girl they pay to take her clothes off," Vermilion replied. "If I had a dollar for every time I heard someone deny a problem's existence just because it didn't affect them, I'd be rich as fuck."

"I didn't know you were a dancer," Kuhla said.

"Stripper, cam girl, porn star. I did a bit of everything, pun intended. My point is that just because reasonable people see a problem doesn't mean everyone does. And the more power and privilege you give to someone, the less likely they are to see common problems as a problem. That part of being human doesn't go away just by living here."

"Doesn't it though?" Tev asked. "Both Revaus and Dau are doing what they can to backup Gersemi's plan to stop Janus. They wouldn't be doing that if they didn't think Janus trying to destroy humanity wasn't a problem."

"You can say a lot without actually doing anything," Vermilion said. "Believe me. The longer this goes without one or both of them actively taking a stand to stop Janus, the more likely we are to see them turn on each other instead."

The room went silent, save for the thunking of darts against the dartboard. A second dart hit, then a third. As Kuhla's light footsteps walked over to retrieve the darts, Tane walked into the room.

"Quaid, Vermillion, can you come join us?" she asked.

"Of course," they both said simultaneously, following the guardian out of the room.

Now alone at the dartboard, Kuhla plucked the darts out, then strode back and began rhythmically throwing them. Thunk. Thunk. Thunk. Walk back to the board. Retrieve the darts. Repeat. Tevarius watched quietly as she repeated the process seven or eight times.

"You're getting triple twenty every time," he said. "I've never seen you do that before playing any of us."

"And you won't," Kuhla replied.

"Why? You're clearly in another league from where any of us are."

"There are more important things than succeeding at a game. Keeping the pride of others intact is one of them."

Kuhla retrieved the darts again, this time switching to throwing with her right hand. Just as before, the darts were tightly packed within the triple twenty ring, though with the contact making a much more forceful sound than her previous throws.

"She's right, isn't she?" Tevarius asked. "Something's going to happen and Revaus and Dau are going to turn on each other. They've been disconnected from humanity too long and no longer see humanity's problems as their own."

"If everything goes well with Gersemi's plan, I don't think so," Kuhla replied. "They may not trust each other, but they trust the guardians."

"And if something does go wrong?"

Kuhla sighed and began throwing the darts again, lodging the first one in the triple twenty ring. Her second dart followed quickly after, the tip of the dart cutting through the flight of the previous one before lodging itself in the shaft. Kuhla's third throw came soon after, repeating the same action, jamming all three darts together from tip to flight.

"Holy fuck," Tev mumbled.

"It's fine," Kuhla replied. "I'll get new ones out of my room. Either no one will notice because we're all bad at darts --"

"No, we're bad at darts," Tevarius interrupted. "You're apparently Robin Hood."

"Either no one will notice because we're all bad at darts. Or no one will notice because we won't be seeing much of each other soon."

20
Shadowboxing

"You're dropping your shoulder," Lace said.

She adjusted Erika's arm, moving it back and forth in a punching motion.

"D'you feel that?" she asked. "If you're dropping the shoulder, but not adjusting your arm, you'd be as well kissing them."

"What if I fix how I'm moving the rest of my arm?" Erika asked. "There's got to be some benefit from punching from a lower angle."

"Aye, but that's not what you're doin'. You're losing momentum halfway through your strike. Even with the knuckles on, you'd barely make a dent."

Erika shrugged Lace's hands off her arm, then walked away to the side of the arena. She initially began walking to the wall closest to her, but upon noticing Vermilion, Iris, Quaid, and Kedi chatting just outside the door, Erika opted to head to a side wall.

"Where you goin'?" Lace asked.

"I need a moment," Erika replied.

"You'll get it if you keep –"

"I said I need a moment."

Erika sat on the floor of the training arena, leaning her back up against the cool concrete wall. She closed her eyes and tried to focus on her breath.

In...2, 3, 4.

Hold...2, 3, 4, 5, 6, 7.

Out...2—

"Fuck's sake!" Lace shouted, interrupting Erika's thoughts.

"What?" asked a startled Erika.

"Like blood from a stone?"

"I am trying."

"Are you?" asked Lace. "Looks like you're going through the fucking motions to get this over with.

"I'm trying my best, Lace," Erika replied.

"I don't buy that for a second. Next you'll be telling me you're just tired.'

"I am tired."

"It's like it doesn't matter to you. This isn't something you can just phone it in, every session counts. Even on the days you're tired. Even on the days you don't want to be here. Help me motivate you, we can't keep doing this."

Erika opened her eyes, staring up at Lace towering over her. Lace wasn't that tall, but she made Erika feel like a child. Some part of her subconscious clung to this thought, leading her to scoot back even closer to the wall, though the concrete wouldn't give way and allow her to hide.

"Talk to me, Erika, I haven't got all day."

At the periphery of her vision, well behind Lace, Erika noticed movement in the balcony overlooking the training floor. A flash of long brown hair darted out of her line of sight, hiding behind Lace.

"Anybody home?" Lace asked.

Erika recoiled further into her balled-up position.

God, I wish I was in bed.

"D'you not want to go back to Earth?" Lace continued. "I'd think you'd want it kept in one piece, no?"

How is she okay with this? Someone must be looking for her, too. A spouse. Kids. Parents. Someone.

"And you're a part of that whether you like it or not, goin' in the huff serves no one."

Why is she mad at me? Be mad at the gods. Or the guardians. Not my fault she's still here.

"Are you fuckin' serious?" Lace asked.

Fucking hate this. I don't want to kill anyone, what about that's so hard to understand?

"Alright" Lace said, turning to leave. "Suit yourself."

"She's leaving."

Good.

"No she's actually leaving."

She's ok with it. Everyone's ok with it. Even Abby's ok with killing, and she's programmed to love, make that make sense.

"Because if there's one thing theaters of war are widely known for, it's for combatants asking everyone 'hey, do you want to start a fight' before starting a fight."

A loud bang as the door to the arena closed broke Erika's concentration. When she looked up, Lace was gone, Kedi, Quaid, and Iris chasing her down the hallway leading away from the practice arena. Vermilion leaned against the doorway, watching them.

"Where's she going?" asked Erika.

"The hell do you care?" replied Vermilion.

"I was just asking—"

"You've been sulking for the last five minutes, why would she stay?"

"What, I can't take a break?"

"You were ignoring her!"

Erika took a step down the hall, only for Vermilion to put her arm out and stop her.

"What are you doing?" Erika asked.

"Keeping you from committing suicide by angry Scot," Vermilion replied. "I have a rule not to clean up blood. And I'm not starting today just because you have a death wish. Give her time. She'll cool down."

"I just want to apologize."

"Oh she'll be back. She just doesn't want to see red when she does."

Erika tried to take a step around Vermilion, only for the muscular brunette to block her path.

"Move," Erika insisted.

"Give her time," Vermilion replied.

Erika pushed her arm out of the way and made it a couple of steps down the hall. A high-pitched yelp escaped her lips as she realized she was off the ground; Vermilion having thrown her over her shoulder. She carried Erika into the training arena, kicking the door shut behind her as they entered.

"Put me down!" Erika screamed.

"When you stop acting like a child, I will," Vermilion replied.

"I'm not!"

"Adults know when to shut up and listen. Some of them do, at least."

Vermilion tossed Erika down on a stack of tumbling mats in the corner of the room. Erika stared up at the ceiling, her vision equally blinded by lights above her and darkened by Vermilion. Though she was the same height as Erika, Vermilion commanded a presence much larger than her stature.

"Good god," Erika mumbled. "Can everyone here manhandle me?"

"Wouldn't be the first time someone's asked me that," Vermilion said, chuckling to herself. "Though with guys, there's usually fear in their eyes when they ask."

"I - what?"

Vermilion rolled her eyes. "Listen. You don't want to lose the people you love."

Erika sat up, steadying herself on the edge of the mats.

"That's why I'm back here?" Erika replied. "Your wisdom?"

"Don't snark me," Vermilion replied.

"I didn't ask—"

Erika's rebuttal was cut off with a lightning quick slap to the face. By the time she realized what happened, Vermilion's hand was already back down to her side.

"Lace doesn't want you to lose anyone either, she's already been through it," Vermilion said. "Her job is to prevent that. All it takes is one dumbfuck intern who doesn't listen to get her friends, her team members, and her loved ones killed too."

"I'm not an intern," Erika mumbled.

"You don't really seem to give a fuck about anyone but yourself, huh," Vermilion asked.

"That's no—"

"I see everything. I hear everything. It's my job to know what's going on, and I'm too good at it to be lied to, Erika."

Vermilion extended her hand to Erika.

"Get up," she said.

Erika reached out and grabbed Vermilion's hand. Her skin was criminally soft, her glittery crimson nail polish flickering in the lights as she pulled Erika up.

"This doesn't leave the room," Vermilion said. "Lace lost her family before she came here. Her husband. Her kid. Both killed in a shooting by some dickhead with an automatic rifle while they were on vacation."

"Holy fuck."

"When you've spent decades in war zones, but some zealot takes the lives of those closest to you and you can't stop it? It changes you."

The sound of the door to the training room creaking opened stopped Vermilion's explanation. Lace walked back in, Iris and Quaid trailing her silently from a distance.

"The best way you can apologize to her," Vermilion whispered, "is to do what you're here to do. Even if you don't want to be here."

Erika sighed and nodded slightly. She started walking toward Lace, only to pause after a few steps. She turned to talk to Vermilion, only to see that she was on her way out the door. Erika began putting her training gear back on only for Lace to shout out from behind her.

"Get the real ones out," she said.

"Lace," Iris pleaded. "We just talked about this. Nothing good comes from actually hurting her."

"Good thing we have a healer here," Quaid chuckled to himself.

"I'm using practice weapons," Lace countered. "She's the one who needs to learn to respect her tools."

"Look," Erika said, "if it's cool with everyone else, I'd just rather no one get hurt today. Especially me."

"I'd also prefer not to clean up dead bodies," Iris added.

"No one's getting hurt," Lace groaned. "Stick around and watch if you want."

"It'll be nice for your murder to have witnesses."

Erika walked back onto the arena floor, leaving her practice weapons on the ground. She waited as Lace re-wrapped her hands.

"So," Lace began. "You'll be using your weapons. Since they're not magic, they won't hurt you. So get used to them. And I'll be unarmed."

"Aren't you worried about getting cut?" Erika asked.

"Ha! That's a good one," Lace laughed. "Here's the deal. You hit me, make me bleed at all – with your knife, your knuckles, or whatever – and you don't have to come back."

"What happens when you disarm me with some sort of Vulcan jujitsu I've never seen?"

"You'll do better next time."

Lace turned and walked away from Erika.

"Sneak attack, it's the only you're getting a hit in on her."

And do what, Erika thought. I'm not trying to murder her.

"She's too far away now. I'll be here when you wake up."

"You ready?" Lace asked, still facing away from Erika.

Erika took a deep breath in, closing her eyes for just a moment to calm her racing heart.

"I really don't think this is a good idea."

"Why? Humor me, 'cause you've done nothin' but complain. You're not getting better quickly. All you do is bitch and moan and backchat like a fuckin' teenager."

"Lace!" Erika shouted. "This is an actual knife. I'm not good at this."

"*How* would you know, you've never fuckin' tried!"

"I don't want to try stabbing you—"

"Why!" Lace yelled. "I don't want to train you this way., but you're not going to try harder just because someone tells you to. What do you want me to do? Let you hide like a child until someone does it for you?"

"I do things myself!" Erika countered.

"Aw right, that's what Abby's for. Takin' over where mum and dad left off, yeah?"

"What, I — you don't even know my parents."

Lace edged closer.

"Don't need to," Lace replied. "I've seen so many of yous. Never told no, terrified of letting family down. You a lil' daddy's girl?"

Erika could feel Lace's breath on her face.

"Can't do shite, dad's always on standby in case a bulb's blown. Maybe a disappointment to mum? Nothing you do's good enough, and whatever you do she hates. Job? House?" Lace paused, smirking. "Abby?"

The sound of skin hitting skin reached Erika's ears well before it registered in her brain what she'd just done. Her right hand was still in front of her face, while a bright red mark was forming on Lace's left cheek. Erika expected Lace to hit her back.

Instead, Lace began to smile and laugh.

"Good," Lace said. "There's fire in there after all."

"What the fuck did you do?"

"Lace, I'm sorry!" Erika said. "I didn't mean—"

"Iris," Lace said as she walked back to her starting spot. "On your count."

"I really don't wa—"

"Quaid!"

"Ready," Quaid said. "Set. Fight."

Erika had barely gotten into her fighting stance when Lace was practically on top of her. A blur buzzed toward her face, instinctively causing Erika to dodge. Much to her surprise, she got out of the way of the initial blow, only for a kick to catch her in the side just below the rib cage. Pain shot through her right side, the stinging sensation nearly causing her to drop her weapons.

The lack of focus on Lace didn't last long, but it was long enough for the well-trained fighter to execute a powerful double leg takedown. Erika landed hard on her back, knocking the wind out of her. She felt the side of her head crash into the wood floor beneath her then...nothing.

Bright lights stung Erika's eyes, first her right, then her left, then back again. She tried to yell at whatever was causing the light to stop, but nothing came out.

"You're lucky it's nothing worse," Iris said. "There's only so much a healing stave can do."

"Either she needs to be better at fighting or you need to get better at healing," Quaid replied. "It's been a long time since I saw someone get knocked out that quickly."

The light subsided from Erika's vision, allowing her to see it had been a flashlight that Iris was shining in her eyes. Erika groaned and strained at Iris, trying to pull herself up.

"We'll get you back down to your room soon," Iris said. "Let's get you sitting a bit until you're coherent. Do you know who you are?"

"What kind of question is that?" Quaid asked.

"Ow," Erika groaned. "Am I dead? Can I please be dead?"

"You're not dead," Iris replied. "You've hit your head hard and you blacked out. Do you remember your name?"

"Can you sit me up? I've got to tell Lace I'm sorry."

Quaid began to help Erika up, only for Iris to stop him.

"Name first," Iris said.

"Erika Renee Edens," Erika said. "Born October 8, 2005. I don't know who the current president is but—"

Iris nodded at Quaid, who carefully helped Erika off the floor. He leaned her against one of the training mats stacked against the wall, allowing Erika to look out onto the training floor. Lace was gone, her pile of belongings stored by Erika's gone with her. Aside from Iris and Quaid, the training room floor was empty.

"Where'd Lace go?" asked Erika.

"She went to medical to grab another one of the healers," Quaid answered. "Accidents happen. You hitting your head on the floor falls into that category. Knocked you straight out."

"How long was I out?" Erika asked.

"Just relax for now," Iris said. "Tilt your head side to side for me."

Erika followed Iris's instructions, leaning her head to each side. On her second set of motions, Erika caught sight of the balcony overlooking the training floor. Tane stood at the window, leaning against a high table behind her, watching as Iris tested her reflexes.

"Oh good. An audience."

"Why would the guardian of peace care about how anyone fights?" Erika wondered aloud to herself.

"What?" Quaid asked, turning around from his goal of bringing Erika's belongings over to her.

"She's talking to herself," Iris interjected. "I'm making sure she's alright, so I need her to keep talking."

"Interesting choice for the pi—"

"Ahh!" Erika screamed. "Fuck me, that hurt."

"You've got a hell of a gash on the back of your head," Iris said. "You're lucky there was a healer nearby."

"Can you make it stop? It feels like my brain is trying to jump through my neck."

Erika felt Quaid lean her forward, sending another jolt of pain screaming down her neck.

"Fucking shit why?!" Erika shouted.

She quickly leaned back against the mat again. A cool sensation enveloped her body, sending a shiver down her spine.

"Close your eyes and try to relax," Iris said. "You should be fine in a few minutes, but it'll go quicker if you're resting."

Erika allowed her eyes to slowly close, watching Tane walk away from the window on the balcony with her last moments of vision. She felt the cool sensation intensify, lulling her to sleep.

21
Seeking Knowledge

May 9, 2035/11:03, Day 106, Year 10311

One of the largest rooms in the central area of the complex was a massive library on the eleventh floor. Shelves of books lined the walls from floor to ceiling. Though there were not picturesque rolling ladders like you'd find in the library of a castle owned by a reclusive French prince, there were lifts and platforms capable of taking an interested reader to any level of the room, allowing them to peruse the voluminous catalog at their leisure.

Over her time in the Azaes Realm, Lorena had come to find the library to be a source of refuge during her down time. The variety of books in the library astonished Lorena. There were plenty about the Azaes Realm itself. Histories of the Realm, primers on elemental weapons – but what interested her far more was the extent of Earth books to be found in the library.

When she learned of them, she had expected only the most important books for understanding humanity to be found – religious texts, history books, perhaps some of the most iconic fiction works. And those things were all there. But beyond that, there was an expanse of books from writers Lorena had never heard of. It was as if someone was trying to gather a copy of every book they could possibly find, regardless of author, subject matter, language, publishing date, format, or any sort of categorization Lorena could dream up.

Despite that, the only other person Lorena would see with any regularity in the room was Svieva. Most days, seeing Svieva would be all the most interaction Lorena would have with them. Lorena would enter the library, go about looking for her book. She'd usually see Svieva lounging on a couch somewhere in the massive room. They'd exchange a wave, then go about reading

203

their respective finds.

Over time, Lorena had found the one genre that regularly struck up a conversation between them. Svieva's fascination with books about music never ceased to amaze Lorena. Though she had never played an instrument herself, there were few things Lorena enjoyed more than listening to a solo piano play a soft piece of music as she read or drifted off to sleep. One of the first books in the Azaes Realm that had caught Lorena's eye was a biography of Frédéric Chopin – one of her favorite pianists. She hadn't made it ten pages when Svieva noticed, before whiling away the afternoon discussing classical piano and their own favorite composer, Franz Liszt.

Lorena hoped she'd find Svieva in the library today. She'd heard Erika and Shaw talking about how Svieva was going back to Earth briefly in the coming days. Hopefully it wasn't today.

A couple of days ago, Lorena had come across a small book in the Azaes Realm section of the library talking about the god of knowledge. As she read through the book, Lorena noticed that there were inconsistencies when referring to the age of said god. At first, she thought it was just a matter of not understanding the timeline the book was being told in, but that wasn't the case. It was certainly possible that the god of knowledge manifested themselves differently to different people, but Lorena was confident there was something more in play.

Lorena entered the library, taking a quick glance around to try to find Svieva. If they were already here, Lorena intended to confront them directly with her questions. But alas, the room was empty. And so, Lorena went to her backup plan, gathering a pair of books on baroque-era classical piano, along with the book about the god of knowledge, and took a seat in the balcony overlooking the library's main entrance.

The room was quiet for a long time, allowing Lorena to re-read various segments on the book about the god of knowledge.

There were two things that she found that she couldn't reconcile. First, the god of knowledge was known to present themselves to those who sought them out. That also meant their whereabouts were unknown until they were searched for. A reclusive keeper of knowledge. It was a trope in fiction for a reason – it wouldn't exist if there weren't some truth to it.

However, there was also the second item that the book alluded to. Specifically, the god of knowledge had not been seen or heard from in an extended amount of time. With the reclusiveness, this did make sense. But had no one – no god, no guardian, no person in the Azaes Realm – made an attempt to seek out the god of knowledge? One of the guardians has gone rogue. You'd think that'd be something that's seek out an all-knowing being worthy.

The sound of a door opening startled Lorena out of her focus. She peeked up over the cover of her book, hoping to see Svieva coming into the room. Instead, Nell was making her way toward the back of the library. While Nell wasn't who she'd been looking for, Lorena reasoned that she could potentially save her some time waiting here. She waved at Nell until she got her attention.

"Good morning, Lorena," Nell said, breaking off her intended path and heading toward the balcony. "How's your morning?"

"Pretty relaxing so far," replied Lorena. "Have you seen Svieva today?"

"I'm sure they're around somewhere. Why?"

"I was just hoping to catch them before they went back to Earth."

"Oh? What for?"

Lorena was taken off guard by Nell's question.

"I was hoping to get them to bring me back something," Lorena lied.

"Contraband?" asked Nell, raising her eyebrows.

"No, nothing like that. There's a locket back home that my grandmother gave me before she passed. I was just hoping to get that."

"Ah. Well, I hope they're able to find it for you. Were you and your grandmother close?"

"Yes and no," Lorena replied. "It's more that she wasn't my parents. And that was kind of a big deal. She was kind. I didn't have a lot of that as a kid."

"I'm sure she appreciates that she's still in your heart and mind," Nell said.

Nell smiled and went back to her original book search. She quickly found the work she was looking for, shooting Lorena a wave goodbye as she left the room.

Lorena leaned back in her chair and tried to pick up where she'd left off in the book. Though her response to Nell had been a lie – one told with no malicious intent and solely meant to allow her to keep her questions to herself, Lorena found herself wanting that locket she'd mentioned.

It was a simple, golden locket in the shape of a rhombus. There was nothing inside of it, a fact that was true for as long as Lorena had owned the locket. But now that it was in her head, it was all she could think about.

There weren't many things from Lorena's childhood she wanted to remember. Having parents who were both addicts will do that to a kid. But she did often dream about snuggling up on her grandmother's lap and watching movies under a blanket. As a small child, she often played with the locket absentmindedly while *Brave* or *Mulan* played in the background. She always thought the metal was softer than it should be given the fact that it was over 50 years old and still looked brand new. Now that she'd thought about it, Lorena realized what she wouldn't give to have it here with her in the Azaes Realm.

She was so focused on the idea of the necklace that she didn't notice the library door open, nor Svieva and Quaid walking up to her.

"Nell said you were looking for me," Svieva replied. "Something about a necklace or something like that."

"I mean, that too," Lorena said. "Though that was only part of why I wanted to talk to you."

"Oh? What's on your mind?"

"Is there any way we could chat alone? Please?"

Quaid looked up from the pile of books he was holding and shrugged.

"I'll finish putting these back and look for some new stuff to read," he said.

Quaid walked away, placing a red book down on a nearby shelf, then descending the staircase to the floor below. Once he was out of sight, Lorena held up the book about the god of knowledge.

"Are you familiar with this book?" she asked.

"Familiar with it? I helped write it," said Svieva. "I am the guardian of memory after all. It's part of my job."

"Why haven't we sought out the god of knowledge then? I feel like they'd be incredibly critical to something like the whole guardian rebelling against the rest of the Azaes Realm situation we're in."

"Some of us have. We just can't find her."

"What do you mean?" asked Lorena. "I thought the god of knowledge made themselves known to whoever looked for them."

"In a very literal sense, that's accurate," replied Svieva. "That's been the case for all of the gods of knowledge over time."

"Gods? Don't you mean god?"

"I do not. Granted, there is only one god of knowledge at a time, but there have been several over the course of the existence of the Azaes Realm."

"I'm lost. What do you mean there have been several? I thought the Azaes Realm encountering humanity was a recent development?"

Svieva smiled with an enormous grin, clearly eager to get the chance to explain the history of the Realm. They took the book of the god of knowledge from Lorena, opening it to a page in the middle of the book. Lorena was certain she'd read the page in question before. Nothing other than text had been on it. But in Svieva's hands, holographic images rose out of the book, creating a beautifully illustrated scene in front of them.

"The Azaes Realm is one of many universes that exist," began Svieva. "Some of them run parallel to the one your Earth exists in, but most will intersect with it at some point in time. The Azaes Realm happens to be one that is intersecting with yours now, as is its offshoot, the Diaprepes Realm."

"That's the one where the original Azaeans are now, correct?" asked Lorena.

"Right," Svieva replied. "It was early on after our universes began to interact that a human gained the power to become a guardian of this realm. In time, humans eventually became gods as well, while more and more staff came from Earth. Part of this was to augment support staff after disease began to ravage the native Azaean population, but it also served a second, more important purpose.

"One of the values that was impressed upon humans when they first met the Azaeans was that to best influence the future of your universe, actions must be taken with a light touch. Humans are adept at changing, but we're resistant to it. This is why true systemic and societal changes occur over the span of generations and centuries rather than a few weeks."

"Eventually the universes will disconnect," Lorena replied. "At least I'd have to assume they would."

"They will," Svieva stated. "It'll likely take hundreds, if not thousands more years of Earth time – not to mention time in the Azaes Realm – before that happens. By bringing humans into this place, the Azaeans have given us hope as a civilization. We've messed up so many things on Earth as a species. It's impressive we're still alive at this point.

"But being here gives us an advantage. We age significantly slower here, even the non-deities, allowing us to learn on a scale larger than any one human could otherwise do within their lifetime. Though you'll return in due time, this is my home now. Even so, my actions – and those of everyone who does something within the Azaes Realm -- are part of a larger initiative. The goal, as you might suspect, is to ultimately save the universe that Earth is a part of. In time, the Azaes Realm will move on from its connection with your universe, another life form will interact with us, and humans will turn the reigns and responsibilities of this place over to them."

"But why?" asked Lorena. "Why is our universe special?"

"That's the thing," answered Svieva. "It's not. The Azaeans aim to save all universes from destruction. They do so not for the benefit of one race or society, but for the benefit of all."

"Then why not do it themselves? Why elevate specific humans to god or god-like status? If they have those kinds of powers, they must be able to save us themselves."

"They could," replied Svieva. "That kind of power is well within their capabilities. But, as I'm sure you're aware, many humans are resistant to messages from anyone outside of themselves. The Azaeans could certainly send visions or spirits to humanity, but that's just as likely to start a world war as it is to save you at this point.

"The Azaes brought the first humans here several millennia ago. When that happened, it was initially believed that Azaeans would always rule over this place. Though there had been conflicts with other universes, humans are weak compared to the Azaeans and in no position to be a threat to anyone but themselves. But then the humans started getting the powers held by the Azaean gods. Consensus is that this was some sort of natural process, though I suspect the Azaeans had a way to do this so as to protect their race from dying out by being targeted for their power. Over time, the humans that came here as gods, guardians, healers, mages, and so on. Most have died, albeit at far more advanced ages. My predecessor lived to the age of 903. He came here at the age of 14, then spent over 81 years in the Azaes Realm. But on Earth, his life spanned from the rise of the Song Dynasty in China to the Industrial Revolution."

"So the fact that the god of knowledge's age keeps shifting in this book isn't an oversight. It's intentional because there have been many different ones over time?" Lorena asked.

"That's right," replied Svieva. "The current god of knowledge goes by the name Adelina. She's a more recent arrival here – only being in the Azaes Realm for an Earth year or two. She's also by far the youngest of the gods, as she'd be the equivalent of thirteen on your planet."

"Dios mío," said Lorena. "I thought I was young."

"You are, though your presence here is more about your aptitude than your age."

"So how do we find Adelina?"

"I wish it were that simple," replied Svieva. "She's been missing for quite some time now. Her disappearance, along with Janus rebelling and leaving the Azaes Realm, is what prompted Gersemi's plan in the first place."

"Missing?" asked Lorena.

"As her guardian, I take full responsibility. That said, I know that being the guardian to the god of knowledge is different to most of the gods. Being the guardian to the god of life, order, or chaos is pretty much the same. You protect them and do your best to serve as a keeper of whatever virtue it is you're responsible for. I'm not sure why Death even has a guardian. I know it's tradition. But if Death is as powerful as it would seem – and I have no indication to believe otherwise – it seems like an unnecessary job."

"Who is Death's guardian?"

"Janus was," said Svieva, "though they don't currently have one. Not that we'd know. Death can only be seen as themselves when they're summoned or if you're dying. Otherwise, they walk among us, appearing like another person. They don't have envoys until they're summoned either. It's why I can't help but be vague in my descriptions of them."

"Wait," Lorena interjected. "So how was Janus able to be Death's guardian if no one except the dying know Death's identity? Is this how Janus is still a guardian despite Death not being around?"

"It's a bit more complex than that. Janus was Death's guardian when the previous god of death was here. After they passed, Janus retained that title and those powers, even though they didn't know who to be guarding. Most of the time, those in the Azaes Realm, including guardians, do know who Death is. After the first time Death must carry out their duty – saying that another way, if anyone dies from natural causes here – they're revealed. And once that happens, Death's guardian can begin to directly protect them. Until then, whoever is in that role has more free time on their hands than a typical guardian would."

"So if someone were to kill someone else in the Azaes Realm, that would not reveal Death's identity?"

"Not unless Death were summoned, no," Svieva replied. "Murder is, by its very nature, the action of choosing to become Death yourself. There's no need for a god when a human chooses to control who lives and who dies."

Lorena went silent. Even with Svieva's role as the guardian of memory, she always associated them more with the complex and thorough knowledge that they had. Anyone with the duty of protecting the god of knowledge would have to be bright. But it was the moments where Svieva was profound where Lorena learned the most from them.

"That was a bit more..."

"Religious?" asked Svieva.

"Philosophical," countered Lorena, "than I expected to hear."

"It's just a statement of fact. Gods and guardians hold power here. No matter how pure or perverse the ideas of a god are, once they are set loose in the minds of men, they're interpreted and misconstrued to the point where, over time, even simple ideas lose their meaning."

"When you put it like that—"

"It's merely inevitable," Svieva countered. "Much in the same way that Death eventually comes for us all, no matter if we don't know who they are."

"Am I Death?" asked Lorena.

"The fact that you're even asking leads me to believe that

you're not. It's believed that the person with the powers of Death knows that they are that entity. It's a feeling that flows through you. But the power of the position is such that I'd imagine it's best kept to one's self until absolutely necessary."

"So how is being the guardian for the god of knowledge different? Is Adelina powerful in the same way Death is?"

"Adelina, and all the gods of knowledge for that matter, have powers," replied Svieva. "At their peak, they're pretty equal to any of the other gods. But hers take longer to develop than any god or guardian. She's still learning."

"Can gods and guardians lose their powers?" asked Lorena.

"Powers can be relinquished in exchange for a true return to humanity. That said, this has never happened. As they near the end of their Realm-extended life, their powers dwindle to a fraction of what they once were. It's at this point that the gods and guardians typically search out a replacement."

"Typically?"

Svieva sighed and took a seat beside Lorena.

"Normally the transition of power from one god or goddess to another is a non-event," they said. "I was here when the old goddess of life, Ashoka, turned over his powers to Brigid. In situations where the outgoing deity is still alive, there's a ceremony transitioning power. Except, of course, in the case of the god of death, as no one in the Azaes Realm can know who the new Death is until they reveal themselves for the first time."

"What happens to the old god afterward?" asked Lorena.

"They die. I mean, not during the ceremony itself. That'd be a hell of a party killer. But most of the gods and guardians are several hundred years old in Earth time by the time they transition power. Even with the difference in how time passes here, that's a long time to have the strain of phenomenal cosmic powers weighing on your body. They usually pass on within a day or two. It's a peaceful, quiet process."

"And if the transition isn't a non-event?"

"That generally means one of two things has happened," replied Svieva. "The deity could die unexpectedly, which can only happen under very specific circumstances because of the power they wield."

"Specific how?" asked Lorena.

"In the Azaes Realm, they'd have to be killed by another god or guardian with an elemental weapon. Or if they're on Earth, they could be killed by normal Earth methods, provided the assailant is a god, a guardian, or mortal who holds the power within them that will allow them to ascend to god or guardian hood when brought back to the Azaes Realm. There are also rumors that there is a way to summon Death themselves to slay a god at the cost of your own life. Between you and me though, I've read every book in this library multiple times. I'm convinced that's legend and nothing more."

"But what about if they don't want to turn over their power? Someone must have been like that at some point in the past."

"It has happened," Svieva replied. "It was only once. An ancient guardian of justice refused to give up his powers, claiming he had more work to do. But as he aged, he became reckless – his choices a danger both to those in the Azaes Realm and on Earth. So the rest of the guardians, along with the gods, banded together and ensured that the powers be passed on. Things turned violent, but it was a quick end with so many against one."

"Is that why Janus left for Earth?" asked Lorena.

"Janus's powers are fading. She won't be able to sustain them much longer. Going to Earth and staying is going to accelerate the process though. There's no precedent for her choice."

"Are there other gods or guardians losing their powers?"

"It would seem that there are."

On the floor below, Quaid grabbed a book off the shelf he'd been leaning against. He knew Janus was losing her powers – that fact was somewhat common knowledge within the Azaes Realm, particularly since she'd taken drastic actions on Earth. But to hear that there was someone else also losing their powers would be news of the highest order to anyone within the Realm. He waited for Svieva and Lorena to continue their discussion and determine the identity of who was losing their powers, but their voices became harder to hear as others entered the library and began milling around.

For a moment, Quaid considered making his way back upstairs in hopes of overhearing the conversation. Considering Lorena had essentially asked him to go away when they began talking, this felt too risky to act on. But even partial information of this magnitude was worth reporting on. If one of the gods or guardians were losing their powers, it would make them more erratic and less reliable. Quaid reasoned it couldn't be Svieva, otherwise they would have stated that directly. Brigid and Adelina were far too young for it to be them. And whoever Death inhabited was new enough to the Realm that they hadn't been revealed, likely ruling them out too. That left only Gersemi, Dau, and Revaus.

Though Quaid reasoned it was certainly possible that Revaus could be losing her powers, it wouldn't match her behavior of late. The meticulously organized god of order was just as on top of things as ever, if not more so. Dau seemed like a more logical choice, and though it was possible Quaid was biased by his own relationship with Revaus, he didn't think Dau was acting strangely. Not anymore than normal, that is.

In Quaid's mind, this meant that there could only be one god or guardian other than Janus that could be losing their powers.

Gersemi had just started a massive push to take down Janus and defeat her in a potential war. A rather drastic and uncharacteristic action for the guardian of love to take, even if it was being done in service of protecting humanity. It all made sense now. This wasn't a rational plan. It couldn't be.

Quaid snuck out of the room, careful to shut the door softly behind him. He had to talk to Kedi before jumping to any sort of conclusion.

22
Beachcomber

May 12, 2035/18:16, Day 106, Year 10311

"She's not into you, dude," said K'Andre.

"How do you know?" Shaw replied.

"I see the way she looks at you. Those aren't come hither eyes. Those are hit on me and you're going to get kicked in the dick eyes."

"How do you know that's what her eyes are saying?"

"I've known you for how long?" asked K'Andre.

"Since we were kids," Shaw answered.

"And how many women have shot you down?"

"Yes."

"The prosecution rests."

"I've dated plenty of women who found me to be charming and funny!" Shaw said.

"You've had good relationships, yes," replied K'Andre.

"And what's to say this wouldn't be one?"

"Because she looks at you like a cow looks at an oncoming train."

Abby and Erika walked up to the common area table, joining K'Andre and Shaw for dinner.

"Hey!" said Abby. "What are the two of you up to?"

"Well, he's eating a mushroom risotto and scallops," said K'Andre, "while I'm having blackened chicken and none of his bullshit."

"Look," Shaw stated, "I'll admit that I've made my fair share of bad choices over time when it comes to the women I choose to hit on."

"Agreed," replied K'Andre.

"I'll also concede that many of my previous attempts at asking someone out have gone, shall we say, horrendously."

"Been there," said Erika as she bit into her food.

"What I'm trying to argue now," continued Shaw, "is that the pre-existing relationship here gives me a higher chance of success. And though I may fail, it is in my best interest for my confidence – nay, for my psychological well-being as a whole – if I try."

"Oooo. Who's he asking out?" asked Abby.

"Lorena," answered K'Andre, rolling his eyes.

"Really?" said Abby.

"Aww, that's cute!" Erika chimed in.

"Not a good fit," replied Abby.

"What?" Shaw and Erika answered simultaneously.

"It's just not going to work," said Abby. "I get what K'Andre is saying."

"Thank you!" shouted K'Andre, throwing his hands in the air.

"I could certainly see some sexual spark there, as the two of them have a bit of personality chemistry," continued Abby.

"Ew," said Erika.

"This guy fucks," replied Shaw, pointing both of his thumbs at himself.

"The problem lies in the fact that Shaw doesn't know when to take himself seriously," said Abby.

"Nailed it," K'Andre replied.

"And for someone as driven, goal-minded, and bright as Lorena, that can present a problem," Abby stated. "How's her sense of humor?"

"Couldn't tell you," Shaw said.

"Yet another sign she's the one for you," K'Andre snarked.

"You need someone who can not only joke around with you," Abby said, "but can also take part in your jokes with you."

"That makes some sense," said K'Andre.

"I could see him being the type of guy who needs a partner-in-crime," Erika stated.

"This guy fucks around," replied Shaw, repeating his double thumb point.

"That doesn't sound how you think it sounds," said Erika.

"The problem is that you always just focus on how hot the girl you're trying to ask out is," K'Andre said.

"I don't want another titty trap as long as I live" Shaw countered.

Erika began to choke on her water as she laughed at Shaw's response. K'Andre sighed heavily and put his head on the table, dreading the inevitable discussion that was to come.

"Don't you mean booby trap?" Abby asked.

"He doesn't," K'Andre mumbled from under his arms.

"I don't," Shaw reiterated. "It's a titty trap."

"What's that?" asked Abby.

"Me if you believe most of my exes," Erika quipped.

Shaw ignored Erika and replied directly to Abby. "A titty trap is where a potential romantic interest lures you in with their boobs, only to trap you in with a toxic personality."

"Sounds dangerous," Abby replied. "You get to see titties, but at what cost?"

K'Andre sighed again.

"Please don't encourage him," he said, rubbing his hand across his face.

"I know the perfect woman for you!" Abby stated emphatically.

"Is it Lorena?" asked Shaw.

"Stop it," said K'Andre, smacking Shaw's arm.

"Her name's Tara," said Abby.

"What's she look like?" asked Shaw.

"As if focusing solely on how someone looks isn't what gets you into 90 percent of the bad relationships you end up in or anything," K'Andre replied.

"You have to have some level of physical attraction," Erika countered, "At least that's how it's always worked for me. Your mileage may vary."

Shaw smiled and pointed at Erika. "This girl fu—"

"Swear to god, you finish that sentence, I'll bitch slap you so hard you'll think you're back in Iowa," K'Andre interrupted.

"She's got shoulder length, shaggy black hair," Abby said, ignoring the bickering. "Real fair skin, has a couple of piercings in each ear, plus one in her lip. Mahogany eyes that get blocked by her bangs when she moves her head around sometimes."

"A good start," replied Shaw.

"She's smart, but really likes messing with people," Abby

continued. "One time, she got Amy a sex toy as a gag gift for her birthday, which, whatever. But Amy thought the gift ended there. Over the next week, Tara kept leaving Amy these increasingly frantic messages posing as people trying to buy back a haunted dildo from her."

"Who's Amy?" asked K'Andre.

"My mother, more or less."

"She coded Abby," Erika added.

"Did she think it was funny?" asked Shaw.

"Incredibly!" said Abby.

"Is this Amy single?" asked Shaw. "She seems like she can appreciate a good joke."

"You leave my mom out of this!" Abby shouted.

"It's my kind of fuckery," said Shaw. "Tara, that is. Shame she's not here."

"You're really selling me on your interest in Lorena," K'Andre replied.

"I mean, there's no guarantee this hypothetical woman will be into me," Shaw stated. "For all I know, she could be repulsed by me."

"I doubt she'd be repulsed by you," Erika said.

"Not until you opened your mouth, at least," K'Andre replied.

"I ship it," said Abby.

"Abby," Erika groaned.

"What?"

"You can't just ship real people, that isn't a thing."

"It's a thing in books!"

"People have free will, characters don't," Erika insisted. "Just call it, I don't know, matchmaking."

"I think that's weirder," said Abby.

"Saying someone's your match or your soulmate does kind of imply that they're perfect for you," K'Andre stated.

"That isn't possible," said Shaw.

"Mathematically, Erika and I are a perfect match," Abby retorted.

"If you weren't originally a computer simulation, I'd say that's statistically unlikely," K'Andre said.

"I keep telling her she deserves better," replied Erika.

"Hey!" Abby yelled.

The squabble was interrupted by Lorena walking up to the table, a mug of tea in hand.

"You all are awfully loud," she said.

"Shaw's fault," K'Andre said quickly.

"Hey!" Shaw replied.

"No, that checks out," Erika added.

"Definitely Shaw's fault," Abby agreed.

"This is a railroading!" Shaw insisted.

"Yes, because we abide by the rules of the American West here," said Lorena.

"I'm willing to accept my fate if you're the sheriff," Shaw replied, shooting a wink in Lorena's direction.

"Fuck off, Shaw," Lorena replied.

"Simple. Direct. No way at all that could be misunderstood," said K'Andre.

"Try walking by again," Shaw said.

"Shaw," groaned K'Andre.

"Did you come to join us for dinner?" asked Abby.

"I just need some human interaction," replied Lorena.

"You've come to the right place," replied Shaw.

Under the table, K'Andre kicked Shaw in the shins.

Lorena sat down beside Abby, turning her chair slightly so she could prop her feet up on the chair at the head of the table.

"I have a plan," Lorena said. "And I need everyone's help."

"Should we get Lace?" asked Abby.

"She's already helped me work through the finer details."

"What's the plan?" asked K'Andre.

"We need to find the god of knowledge." replied Lorena.

"Why?" asked Erika.

"We need to be certain our plan will succeed. And she's the only one that can give us a certain answer."

23
Thirteen Seconds to Midnight

May 24, 2035

It wasn't often that Youles got to lie in his own bed. The life of a modern-day mercenary – a term he liked better than hitman or freelancer, but rarely used because it sounded pretentious – often necessitated sleeping in hotels, safe houses, or in the back seat of cars. Being in a place where the bed felt familiar, he knew where all the dishes were, and where his only concern was if his cactus was overwatered, was an uncommon luxury.

Being dragged out of bed by an alarm clock on one of these rare days of respite frustrated Youles. But an early morning was a small price to pay to avoid trying to negotiate a new meeting with Janus via an envoy. And the promise of a new assignment.

A quick shower and a breakfast of toast and coffee was all Youles needed before starting his morning. He opened the front door of his townhouse, only to find a young blonde woman in a red blazer and white dress pants standing outside. She wore a pin of a grandfather clock on her lapel – the designation all of Janus's envoys wore when meeting him. Just beneath the grandfather clock, a brass nametag read Lydia.

"Janus regretfully informs you that your meeting this morning will need to be rescheduled," she said.

"How did you know when I'd be leaving?" Youles asked.

"Your new meeting time will be this afternoon at 1:15 pm," Lydia continued. "Your meeting location will not be impacted by this change."

"You're one of the better ones Janus has sent," Youles replied. "You're not even using the cue cards."

"It's four sentences of memorization. Everything else is just being polite. It's not that complicated if you're not an idiot."

"Four? I've only heard three."

"Janus thanks you for your service."

Lydia turned on her heels, her red blazer swinging with the momentum of her spin. She walked quickly to a gray sedan waiting at the curb, driving away and out of sight. Youles shrugged, walking back inside to have a second breakfast.

The afternoon arrived as many late May afternoons do in the Midwestern USA: with too much humidity and not enough of a breeze. Even though Youles had managed to lose some weight over the past three years, he'd still sweat through at least one shirt on particularly hot days. His dad used to tell him he looked like a pig on a spit in the summer. Then again, his dad said a lot of things he'd rather not hear again.

Youles knew the warehouse would be warm at this time of day. As he entered the building, he cringed as a blast of warm, humid air hit his face. He walked to the far corner of the warehouse, a spotlight shining down on a metal table with an office chair on each side. A gangly, middle-aged man sat in one of them, his back to Youles. Youles took the seat across from the man, staring at a blue folder on the table between them.

Janus's voice seemed to fill the room around them. This time, it was the voice of the woman. At least it wasn't the voice so often tied with threats.

"Thank you for your flexibility today," said Janus. "Know that I appreciate your selflessness."

"It's alright," Youles replied. "Things come up."

"I've elected to give you a second chance. That is, as you might imagine, the good news associated with this meeting. In light of your previous challenges with this target, please open the blue folder in front of you."

Youles did as he was told, beginning to rifle through the various papers in the folder.

"You'll notice that your target remains the same," Janus stated.

"Tara Simon," Youles said. "The conscientia accountant."

"The window for action is much narrower than before. I have taken the liberty of ensuring the two of you will be in the same building at the same time. From there, I leave the logistics to you."

"And how did you manage that?"

"You'll be attending the opening of Sam Sawchuk's restaurant, my dear food critic friend," replied Janus. "As will Tara Simon, his personal accountant. Sam has made arrangements to ensure her presence."

"Tasting menus really aren't my thing," said Youles.

"Complete the assignment, and you can eat what you want, whenever you want it, for the rest of your life."

"Why can't I get rid of her before then?"

"Sam's restaurant needs to get off the ground for the next steps in my plan to work," answered Janus.

"Okay, but why kill her at the restaurant?" asked Youles. "Wouldn't that drive business down, you know, a dead broad in the restaurant?"

"I never mentioned where to kill her. I'm merely facilitating a situation where you'll be in the same place at the same time." said Janus. "Do we have an understanding?"

"We do," replied Youles.

"Wonderful."

The man across the table got up and retreated into the

darkness, taking the folder with him.

"I didn't finish reading—"

"A prop," replied Janus. "He was here to kill you if you didn't agree."

The room fell silent. Youles could hear his heartbeat pounding in his eardrums, drowning out his own breathing.

"Have a nice day, Youles. See you again soon."

24
Transformation

June 12, 2035/13:44, Day 109, Year 10311

Erika took a deep breath in and knocked on the door to Brigid's room. It had been days since she'd last seen the goddess of life. The end of their previous conversation had left a bad taste in her mouth. At a bare minimum, Erika felt an apology was in order.

Much to Erika's surprise, Brigid not only answered the door, but did so almost instantly after she knocked.

"Hey!" Brigid said excitedly. "It's good to see you. How are you holding up?"

"Can I talk with you?" Erika asked. "It won't take long."

"Of course. Come in. Make yourself comfortable."

Brigid's room couldn't have been more different from Nell's. The entryway opened into an expansive kitchen, at least twice the size of the one in Erika's room. The dining room was completely separated from the kitchen, along with a large living area, and from it a pair of hallways heading in opposite directions. There was a good chance Brigid's room was larger than some houses back on Earth.

"How do I upgrade to this package?" Erika asked, taking in her surroundings.

"You like it?" Brigid replied. "This isn't all my doing, but I've really tried to give myself a more home-like vibe here. Some people are content with the small rooms, but not me. I like to spread out and relax. But that's not why you're here. Sit down! Relax! Let's talk. Do you want something to drink?"

"Desperately."

"That's actually why I'm here," said Erika.

Before she could continue, her legs grew weak under her. She took a seat on a chair in the living area, sinking into the ultra-plush chair like the ones next door.

"These chairs are incredible," stated Erika. "It's like I'm literally sitting in a cloud."

"I could see what I can do about getting you one in your room," said Brigid. "I know there are plenty of them around here."

Brigid joined Erika in the living area, scooting a chair over close to Erika.

"Oh good, right beside us. You can throw the coffee on her instead of the floor this time if you need to make a run for it."

"You mentioned you were going to try to help me with my problem," said Erika. "My, um, lack of alcohol situation."

Brigid leaned back in her chair and began to think. She was quiet for some time – much longer than Erika thought was necessary.

Maybe she didn't understand me.

"She's a literal goddess. You're the one who doesn't understand things."

"Why not make your own?" asked Brigid. "The pantry has all the ingredients that would allow you to ferment a rudimentary beer or wine. You could probably make some spirits with a little effort."

"I wouldn't know where to begin," said Erika.

"We have a library with books on winemaking, beermaking, the history of alcohol, prohibition, cocktail chemistry, bartending, and several other related topics. I'm sure something could teach you in there."

"Yeah, you're going to need to explain that one."

"It's a big room with lots of books."

"Why does the library have an entire section on alcohol making if alcohol is forbidden?" asked Erika.

"Even knowledge of what not to do must be chronicled," Brigid replied. "Otherwise, how would we know what mistakes to avoid in the future. I also don't believe in the destruction of books, and fortunately, Adelina, Svieva, and other caretakers over time have shared my opinion on such matters. You're dodging my question."

"I mean –"

"Abby obviously processes information much faster than you or I. You could ask her read to something and forge a plan from there."

Erika stayed silent, unsure of exactly how to answer. She had considered making booze for herself, but it wasn't her preferred solution. Alcohol isn't like chocolate milk, it's more than just syrup and milk. Anything that would take time to ferment was bound to be found by Abby sooner or later.

"Level with me," Brigid said. "Why come to me to solve this problem? We have rules for a reason, and it is part of my responsibility to uphold them."

"Yes, but," replied Erika. "I think you might help me."

"Help is a broad term. What exactly do you mean?"

"She means you're more likely to let her get trashed than her girlfriend is."

"And why go straight to a god?" continued Brigid. "You could have gone to one of the envoys, used their influence to be a bug in my ear. Vermilion and Quaid have often talked about how they love to drink."

"I don't think either of them particularly like me," Erika said. "Definitely not Vermilion."

"Those who make the rules don't exactly have the highest tolerance for allowing their own rules to be broken. And I, ultimately, am a rule maker."

"I know."

"And this is a relatively simple problem."

"I need a drink," said Erika. "I'd been sober for about four months before we came here."

"As in you haven't had a drink or as in you're an alcoholic in recovery?" asked Brigid.

"The second one. Well. Closer to it at least."

"You want my help to fall off the wagon? Is it the training?"

"I don't love Lace kicking my ass every other day," said Erika. "But no, it's not the training."

"What is it then?" Brigid countered.

Erika sighed.

"Do you not see how fucked this situation is?"

"Do you not see how your sacrifice is for a greater good that goes far beyond yourself?"

"I do!" Erika insisted. "But if I can be a little selfish for a moment, I think it's fucking idiotic."

"Do you now?" asked Brigid.

"People are brought here against their will. No one comes here knowing what they're getting themselves into. And I'm just expected to believe there's a purpose for me to be here. Surrounded by these people? How?"

"So this is about you?" Brigid said, "I wonder, when is it not?"

"I— why do people keep saying that?" Erika yelled. "I'm not like everyone else. I don't have what everyone else has, and when

I prove it, they yell at me. I can't strategize - mad. I can't fight - big mad. I don't know what I'm supposed to do here."

"Do you not have Abby's back?"

"She doesn't need me. She can do anything. Learn anything. She spends more time explaining shit to me than I do helping her."

"Not even emotionally?" countered Brigid.

"I'm not a therapy animal," Erika snapped back.

"You're very angry for someone looking for help."

"She's not wrong."

"So you don't even know why I'm here?" Erika asked.

"I don't," replied Brigid. "But I thought you were after my help. It sounds like you need validation. I'm sure I have some gold star stickers around somewhere I can give you."

"Harsh. Valid. But harsh."

"None of this is solving my problem," Erika said. "Can you get me some fucking booze or not?"

"And take the easy way out?" asked Brigid.

"I'm not."

"If you think you can get a handle on this by just drinking and doing nothing to improve your mental health, you're either afraid of what you'll find, or you're ignorant. And I don't think it's the latter."

"It's not that I don't know."

"Then what is it?" Brigid asked.

"I've done the talk about your feeling's thing. It doesn't work."

"Would you be willing to hear an alternate option?" Brigid

countered.

"I mean...yeah?"

"It's a trap."

Or help.

"Help you into a trap is more like it."

"Is it just a glorified multi-step program?" asked Erika. "That didn't go well when I tried it."

"Can't say I'm surprised," replied Brigid. "Abstinence from alcohol isn't always the sole solution."

Brigid leaned in close to Erika, her voice dropping to almost a whisper.

"This cannot go beyond us," Brigid began, "Do you understand?"

"Of course," Erika said.

"That includes Abby."

"Abby doesn't count."

"She's someone else," Brigid said.

"Literally, yes," Erika replied. "But it's not the same."

"Then why isn't she here with you?"

"I'll tell her when I'm ready. I don't want to worry her. There's enough going on."

Brigid leaned back in her seat, contemplating Erika's response as she stared off into space. Erika tried to get a read on her, but her eyes and posture gave away nothing.

"So it's a test. Either she's crooked, or shell double-cross you in the long run. I don't like those odds."

"I don't want to hide things from Abby," Erika continued. "And if you can help me, I won't. I just don't see a need to tell her until then."

"I understand," Brigid replied.

"I'm glad."

"There's medication that –"

"Told you."

"—helps lessen the desire to drink, as well as some that can help decrease the amount you drink. That, in conjunction with some sort of therapy for the —"

"Crazy. She thinks you're crazy."

"—other challenges you're having and, if needed, medication to help you recognize when your critic is challenging you so that you can control it better—"

"You've tried this. It doesn't work. It won't work. Because you're weak. You can't do anything for yourself."

"—I think that if we go that route, we could put you in a better position to be able to consume alcohol in moderation while also improving your mental health. Granted, I would ultimately leave that decision –"

"Up to someone else because you can't be trusted?"

"—up to you and the healers here. It isn't my place to be the final decision maker for you."

"Lessen the amount I drink?" Erika said, finally getting out of her Grace-induced silence.

"Exactly," said Brigid. "I don't think that going cold turkey is the best solution you."

"Oh, thank god. You don't know how good it is to hear that from someone. It's always going completely clean or you're fucked. There isn't an in between."

"For some people, that's how it must be, I wouldn't dismiss

that. But there are other methods out there that help with alcohol use disorder, and I think we should explore them first."

"Now we're getting somewhere! Vodka cranberry, please. I'm feeling fruity."

"What's the plan then?" asked Erika.

"The next time I go back to Earth, I'll get you something," Brigid said. "Any requests?"

"Yes."

"I'm going to need you to be slightly more specific than that."

"There's no way—"

"You're serious?" asked Erika. "There's no dystopian detox camp? No locking me in a room until I submit my entire life to Jesus or capitalism or a multi-level marketing scheme or whatever?"

"That's an oddly specific irrational fear," Brigid replied. "But no. None of...that."

Erika practically jumped out of her chair to hug Brigid. As she wrapped her arms around Brigid's neck, Erika worried the cushy chair would envelope both of them, but it only sank a little before stopping their momentum.

"Thank you," Erika said. "Thank you, thank you, thank you."

"You're welcome," Brigid replied, wrapping her arms tightly around Erika in return. "But...what for?"

"For listening. And helping."

Erika finally released her grip on Brigid, returning to her chair and doing her best to resume the comfy position she'd left.

"I get a choice?" Erika asked, still not believing her luck. Brigid nodded. "A decent vodka or bourbon would be nice."

"I think I can manage that."

"When are you going?" asked Erika.

"Probably in the next few days," said Brigid. "But let's arrange for you to meet with the healers before then, get things started while you're waiting on me to come back."

"And there it is. It's just going to be pills and broken promises."

"Promise?"

"Promise."

"Famous last words."

25
Prodigy

June 12, 2035/15:56, Day 109, Year 10311

Though she wasn't certain her plan to find the god of knowledge would work, Lorena felt like doing something was better than doing nothing. She was certain no one would tell them everything they needed to know. But if each of them managed to get a little bit of information from several powerful entities, maybe they could solve the problem from there.

Since Shaw, K'Andre, and Abby had received direct training from individual guardians and envoys, as well as limited oversight from specific gods themselves, they were the three easiest people to give assignments to. K'Andre would get as much info as he could from Revaus's subordinates, as well as hopefully the god herself. Shaw would question Vermilion and Tane, as well as likely Dau, who had formed a surprising bond with the bombastic Shaw due to their shared interest in combat sports. Abby, meanwhile, would pick Brigid's brain as much as she could. Lace's involvement with the guardians Kedi and Tane meant that she only had two people to interrogate. Lorena felt confident that not only could Lace get more information out of them than K'Andre and Shaw, Lace would also better strategize her follow ups with what she learned.

After herself, that left Erika. She didn't have a direct god or guardian to work with. Most of her time was spent with Lace, occasionally Shaw. True, things seemed friendly with Brigid, but having her and Abby question Brigid seemed too risky.

Lorena couldn't exclude Erika from the plan. As Lace said, expecting one person to perform espionage, hide it from omnipotent beings *and* from their partner was a tall ask. Instead, Erika was tasked with trying to get more information out of Svieva once they returned from Earth. Lorena hoped to have what she needed to find the god of knowledge before then, but better safe than sorry.

As for her own search, Lorena decided to start with Nell. A healer turned de facto bodyguard for the goddess of life while also running the Azaes armory had to hear rumors. And Lorena was determined to get them out of her.

Despite her own determination, Lorena's biggest challenge to this point had been tracking down Nell. She'd come by the armory multiple times over the course of the past few days, but to no avail. Even at the healers' bay, they'd mention that they'd seen Nell earlier in the day, or that she'd had just missed her. Lorena felt a bit like she was in the middle of a cartoon, with doors closing behind her just as Nell enters the same room.

Her plan this afternoon was just to wait in the armory for Nell to come back. She'd have to eventually; she was the armorer, after all. Where else would an armorer go?

"Mierda," Lorena mumble to herself. "Why didn't I check her room first?"

Lorena sat in her chair for a moment, staring at the weapons lining the walls of the armory. Would it be creepier waiting for Nell in her place of work or outside her room? Did this even count as a place of work in the Azaes Realm? There didn't seem to be a form of currency of any kind here. People just did things for other people because that's what you did.

Waiting outside Nell's room would be creepier, Lorena reasoned. Not that this was much better. Bored with merely sitting and waiting for Nell to arrive, Lorena began to walk around the armory, perusing the various weapons around the room. To this point, Lorena had been using a weapon given to her by Nell on her first day in the Azaes Realm, which went by the name Niamey — a bo staff that featured whips of fire coming out of it in its elemental mode. It seemed to be an effective weapon. It just never felt right in Lorena's hands.

Nell insisted comfort with Niamey would come with time. This certainly was the case with Shaw with the Apidae Gauntlet, Lace with the Wheels of Elu, and K'Andre with the Aquarius Sledge. It even seemed like Abby was picking up her weapons quite well. But Lorena never felt any sort of connection with Niamey. It was growing easier to wield training versions of the weapon, but this wasn't Lorena's weapon. She could feel that.

She scanned the walls of the armory, hoping to find something that would call to her. A gleaming copper and brass battle-axe caught her eye, though it looked to be at least as tall as she was. While the tomes appeared to lend themselves to mobility, Lorena couldn't help but wonder how useful they'd be in a melee. A silver rapier with a raven hilt was easily the most beautiful weapon in the entire room, though a quick look at its placard – Rapier of Adriesta – indicated someone had claimed it.

On the front wall of the room, an array of polearms were on display. Most of the weapons were best suited for a Greek phalanx or a medieval halberdier rather than Lorena's petite frame. One weapon did manage to catch her eye. A double-headed meteor hammer hung near the ceiling; its two ends connected with a worn leather rope. One head emitted a pale blue glow, while the other held a red hue. Lorena stood on her tiptoes, trying to get a better look at the weapon, though it was far too high on the wall for her to read the placard.

"Anything I can help you find?" came Nell's voice from behind Lorena.

"Actually, I was looking for you," said Lorena.

"So I've heard. You know, if you desperately needed me, you

could have just knocked on my door."

"I didn't want to invade your personal space. Sorry."

"Don't be," replied Nell. "Are you here for my help with the weapons? Or is it something more?"

"A little bit of both," said Lorena.

"What's going on?"

"Svieva is the guardian for the god of knowledge, correct?"

"They are," replied Nell. "Wherever Adelina may be, Svieva is still her guardian."

"Yes," said Lorena. "That's part of what I'm having trouble with. I understand that her disappearance was beyond Svieva's control. And they spend much of their own down time looking for her, which is why we don't see them that often."

"Correct."

"But there are also other deities. Janus rebelled to Earth. Gersemi is also on Earth most of the time, I assume to keep an eye on Janus."

"At this point, that's pretty much what she's doing."

"And then, Death is somewhere, though no one knows where."

"Very few ever actively seek out Death," replied Nell.

"I don't think seeking Death is anyone's plan," said Lorena. "But if Death could give me the answer as to where the goddess of knowledge is, that would go a long way to making sure our plan succeeds."

"How so?"

Lorena hesitated. It was becoming clear that someone wasn't telling the full truth about the Azaes Realm, though she had no idea who. At least if they knew where Adelina was, they could confirm the success of the mission at hand.

"Because the goddess of knowledge knows all," said Lorena. "At least I'd assume so, considering the title and all."

"I mean, 'goddess of knowledge' and 'all-knowing deity' aren't the same thing," replied Nell. "Think of the role more as a keeper of knowledge than someone who knows all the things ever."

"That's disappointing to hear."

"Knowledge often is. Not because knowing more is bad. But because there's always more to know afterwards."

"That was weirdly poetic," Lorena stated.

"Sorry," replied Nell.

"Why are you apologizing? That wasn't a criticism."

"Sorry. Old habits and what not."

"Also not a criticism," said Lorena, smiling.

"I'm—" said Nell, interrupting herself. "Anything else?"

"You're sure there's nothing you can do or no one you can ask to help us find Adelina?" she asked.

"You're placing a lot of faith in me assuming there's something I can do."

"Sorry. I just don't want to hit a dead end."

"Talk to the envoys. They're always running errands for the gods if not the guardians, too."

"What would they know?" Lorena wondered. "She's lost for a reason. If someone knew where she was, we wouldn't be having this discussion."

"Do you think someone does?" Nell replied.

Lorena felt herself instinctively wanting to retreat. She didn't think she'd been that reckless with her questions. Had Nell caught on?

"You know what I think you should do?"

"What's that?" asked Lorena.

"Talk to Kuhla," said Nell. "As Adelina's envoy, she likely knows the finer details of her schedule –"

"I don't see how she could have a schedule to keep, she's not around."

"—and then maybe talk with Svieva," Nell continued, ignoring Lorena's interruption. "Not only are they Adelina's guardian, they're also the guardian of memory."

"But they're certain they can't find the goddess of knowledge by themselves."

"And I would agree with them. But by being the guardian of memory, they're not just the keeper of their own memories."

A small, crafty smile began to creep across Lorena's face.

"You're a genius, Nell," she said.

*****

Ellie walked out of her office and into the lobby of the accounting firm. As she turned the corner, she looked up from her phone to see Sam standing at the front desk chatting with Bianca.

"Hey," Ellie began. "If you're looking for Tara, she's out until Thursday."

"I didn't come here to see Tara," Sam replied. He pulled out a single red rose from behind his back. "I'd love to know if you'd like to go to lunch with me."

"Oh. Yeah, I'd love to. When?"

"How's right now sound?"

"I don't really have any other pla—"

"Ellie!" Bianca interjected. "I thought we going to try that café with the really fancy scones today?"

"Really?" asked Ellie. "I knew we'd talked about it, but I didn't think we'd decided on when we'd go."

"It was Wedsfriday last week."

"Wedsfriday?" Sam said.

"Give me five minutes, I'll be ready to go," Bianca said. "If there's nothing else Mr. Sawchuk?"

"There's always next time," Sam said, winking at Ellie.

"I hope so," Ellie said, smirking as she took the rose from Sam. "Thursday? I think I'm free."

Bianca began frantically typing on her keyboard.

"Thank you for the rose."

"Any time," Sam said.

"It looks like she's free on the 19th," Bianca said.

"Hey, a week from now isn't so bad," said Sam.

"Of August. 2285."

Ellie reached over the counter and grabbed a pen and paper off Bianca's desk. She scribbled on the top of the sheet before tearing it off and handing it to him.

"Send me a message. We'll work out a time. Sooner than 250 years from now."

Sam smiled and gave a quick wave as he walked out the door and back to his car. As soon as his back was turned, Bianca threw up both her middle fingers, making them dance around as he left the building.

"What the hell?" Ellie asked.

"He's a scumbag," Bianca insisted. "He's calls the main line for Tara to hit on me until I transfer him. He has her direct line! He does it on purpose."

"You like it when people flirt."

"If it's welcomed and reciprocated, yeah. But he's fucking creepy."

"Then re-cip-ro-cate."

"Before or after I tell him fuck off into the sun?"

Ellie rolled her eyes, twiddling the rose with her fingers.

"Tara doesn't like him either," Bianca said.

"Tara doesn't like a lot of people."

"Ellie. Look. I get that you might not want to take advice from someone so much younger than you when it comes to dating."

"How old do you think I am?" Ellie said.

"He's trash," Bianca continued. "Guys like that wanna buy your attention. He'll take you somewhere nice for lunch. Flowers, chocolate, jewelry — then one day, he's plowing his sous chef in the staff room while you're three bottles deep into a case of chardonnay. He's conned you into having his kids, his debt, and nothing of your own. The chocolate's gone to your thighs. You haven't seen a rose since your wedding night. And he's long since pawned the jewelry you held as a memory of the man you thought you knew."

Ellie stared at Bianca, her eyes wide. The pen she'd been holding since Sam left fell out of her hand, clattering off the lobby floor.

"Sorry," Bianca said, holding up her hands. "It happens though."

"Are you a middle-aged divorcee in need of therapy?" asked Ellie.

"Just way too many bad romance novels."

"I appreciate you looking out for me. But I'm 25. And Tara's my boss. If something goes wrong, she knows where the bodies are kept."

"25?" Bianca said. "You're 25?"

"Yeah," said Ellie. "Birthday's not until November."

"Then why do you dress like my grandmother?"

"Hey!"

Bianca came around the desk, pulling Ellie to the door.

"What are we doing?" asked Ellie.

"I promised you scones," said Bianca. "And if you must go out with him, you're not going like that. So we're going shopping after."

"He asked me out with me looking like this."

"Yeah, for the 4pm dinner special."

"You do realize that you're telling one of your bosses she looks old, right?"

"It's called problem solving," Bianca said. "I learned it from you.

"I'm so proud of you," Ellie stated.

"We should take your car just in case the scone shop has dedicated senior parking."

26

Opposite Ends of the Reflecting Pool

June 14, 2035/20:04, Day 109, Year 10311

"Shaw. You seem to be a bright fellow. Would you agree with that assessment?"

"Well, I'd like to think so, yes."

Shaw sat in the corner of a hexagonal room; one arm placed on his head. He had originally come to Dau in an effort to find out more about the god of knowledge, just as Lorena had asked him to. But this had turned into Dau mostly asking him questions and chatting with him, neither of which Dau was particularly prone to doing in Shaw's experience.

Dau's guardian, Tane, was leaned up against the door frame, adding to the uneasy feeling Shaw got about his meeting. Tane wasn't a particularly imposing physical figure – Shaw figured she was at most an inch or two taller than Erika, with a slender frame and constantly slumped shoulders. But Tane kept her weapon, Thorne, always resting against her hip. Of all the elemental weapons Shaw had seen, Thorne was by far the least subtle. It looked like a piece of lumber, only with nails and daggers that appeared to be made of ice protruding in all directions from its bottom half. If the main weapon looked that violent, Shaw could only imagine the power of its attacks.

"It's my understanding that you were a wrestler back on Earth, correct?" Dau asked.

"Yes?" Shaw replied, curious at where he was going with this question.

"I've always found the art of professional wrestling fascinating. It didn't come into existence until well after I left Earth, but it seems to be equal parts theater and athletics. For a sport that is, for all intents and purposes, based around the concept of combat, much of the storytelling happens outside of the confines of an actual match. I particularly like it when storylines across a given show or promotion weave in and out of each other's orbit. Because nothing happens in a vacuum – why wouldn't other people in a locker room be fearful if a wrestler were ignoring the rules and attacking others outside of matches."

"I mean, long-term story telling wasn't my thing. I was more of a tell a story in the ring kind of guy. But I get your point."

"One thing in particular I like is the concept of factions," said Dau. "Not necessarily tag teams, I like it more when it's a larger group. They can be loosely affiliated or tightly-knit. But the point is that they're typically large enough that they aren't just wrapped up in a single storyline. They might even transcend their given feud and become the story themselves."

"Groups like the nWo or the Bullet Club?" asked Shaw.

"Yes. I'm fascinated how wrestlers always manage to do such absurd things to get into their opponent's heads. And often, it's something that requires a ton of planning and days, if not weeks, worth of effort. Unless, of course, you have an entire team on your side."

"Well, that's suspension of disbelief," said Shaw. "There's no way a single guy has time to create a professional quality video taunting his opponent, purchase a thousand gallons of fake sewage to dump on them, perform six house shows a week, and still stay in insane shape. But we ignore all of that for storytelling."

"I understand the concept, Shaw," Dau replied. "But that doesn't mean I don't prefer when we can all admit that the best plans are rarely enacted alone."

*****

K'Andre had watched scenes like this play out before. There was always an older, wiser, and usually whiter, person who he needed to convince to come around to his way of thinking. He'd done it all throughout college, as a graduate student, through to his doctoral studies prior to the Azaes Realm.

In that sense, Revaus was no different than anyone else. She attempted to command respect because she was the oldest and most tenured person in the room. Her guardian, Kedi, sat idly by, toying with a balance beam scale that sat on Revaus' desk. K'Andre wondered if Kedi really wanted to be here. The guardian of justice likely had better things to do than serve as a personal envoy and bodyguard to a goddess. Even so, he was an added source of intimidation. His mere presence was meant to unsettle K'Andre, even if his actions were innocent enough.

"I've grown concerned about the team you belong to," said Revaus.

"And why is that?" K'Andre asked.

"I don't believe they have all the necessary parts to truly stop Janus."

"How so?"

"Because only a god or guardian can kill another god or guardian," Kedi said without looking up as he continued to fiddle with the scale.

"Is that true?" asked K'Andre.

"For all practical purposes, yes," Revaus replied. "There are a few extreme exceptions, as well as the probability that the god or guardian will die from old age. But Kedi is essentially right."

"And unless there's something we're not being told," added K'Andre, "no one in our group is a god or a guardian. Not even in disguise."

"I am confident that is the case."

"So our plan is doomed to fail no matter what we do."

"I don't think that's the case either," replied Revaus. "I think there's something else – or more accurately, someone else – in play here. Someone who could kill Janus. Someone who isn't telling anyone their true intentions."

*****

"Are you suggesting that Janus didn't act alone?" said Shaw.

"I'm suggesting that the possibility exists," Dau replied. "Janus aims to sow chaos and discord amongst the human race. And while that would be easy enough to do with enough bad actors on Earth, it would be exponentially easier with help."

"But why would someone help Janus? Especially if they know helping Janus would help bring about the end of Earth as we know it."

"You'd be surprised what lengths some are willing to go to in order to achieve an end they seek," said Tane, her voice soft and melodic. "The most dangerous ones make no effort to hide the scope of their treachery."

"What often happens," added Dau, "is that those with power feel threatened by societal change. The fear they're losing their grasp on power. And when that fear sets in, you'll find that those with power do not give it up so easily. Either the relinquishment of power benefits them in another way or they seek out a way to keep that power."

"How is Janus losing power?" asked Shaw.

"Well," said Dau. "Due to the nature of the specific virtue that Janus is the guardian of, time, the only real way for Janus to lose power would be through the passage of time and, inevitably, their own death."

"Janus can see into the past and into the future," stated Tane. "They know what has been and what will be. This includes how each person, god, guardian, or creature will meet their end. Including Janus."

"Maybe Janus is rebelling because they don't want to die in the way they saw," posited Shaw.

"That's certainly possible, though death is inevitable," replied Tane. "Even for a guardian. Even for a god."

"Knowing what I know about Janus," said Dau, "the fear of death alone would not drive a rebellion. I assume you're familiar with the quote 'everybody's got a price', aren't you?"

"Sure," replied Shaw. "Ted DiBiase. It's one of the most famous wrestling quotes of all time."

"Well, it's true. Everybody does have a price. It's not always a monetary one. Some seek control. Pleasure. Others seek peace, no matter how many people they have to kill for it. And everybody – and I do mean everybody – has a point at which fear will drive them over the edge."

*****

"So there's someone here in Azaes Realm that we can't trust," said K'Andre.

"That's the most likely answer," grumbled Kedi. "The odds of the traitor not knowing they're anything more than a pawn are astronomically low. Especially since the only guardian on Earth full-time is Janus. Unless you count Gersemi."

"Gersemi's insistence on being absent during the

implementation of a plan she developed is troubling," said Revaus. "Though I believe that's more a matter of her distractibility with her own hobbies than anything nefarious."

"Is there someone you think it is?" asked K'Andre. "Or a guess?"

"There's no need to guess," replied Revaus. "The being who caused the goddess of knowledge's disappearance is the same being who helped Janus cause their specific breed of chaos on Earth."

"A little on the nose, ma'am," said Kedi.

"It's accurate. Dau is aiming to destroy Earth – and possibly the Azaes Realm with it."

*****

"Who's behind all of this?" asked Shaw.

"No one relishes control quite like Revaus," replied Dau. "If there is a higher power behind Janus – and I'm certain there is – it's her."

27

Mediation

June 18, 2035/5:05, Day 110, Year 10311

"What a pleasant surprise, Abby," said Brigid. "Come in!"

Abby entered Brigid's room, taking a moment to gaze at the size of her room. Erika had mentioned the vastness, but Abby hadn't expected anything like this.

"How do we upgrade to this?" Abby asked.

"Funny, Erika said the same thing," replied Brigid.

"Are all the gods' rooms like this?"

"Different gods, different tastes," Brigid replied. "Though I believe this is the largest non-common room in this building and among the largest in all the Azaes Realm.

"The whole realm? That doesn't sound...extensive."

"On a universal scale, the Azaes Realm isn't more than this central building, and the three homes of Adelina, Dau, and Revaus."

"I thought Dau and Revaus lived in the center building with everyone else."

"During times of peace, they do."

"...and when they don't?"

"To the southeast is the building belonging to Dau," replied Brigid. "To the southwest is where Revaus lives. And to the true north is the home of Adelina."

Abby considered the layout. "So it's shaped like a horseshoe?"

"The building is more of a hub and spoke layout. As for the Realm itself, I opt for disc shaped."

"But not a disc-world."

"I— No, it's a universe."

"No elephants and turtles around either?"

Brigid stared blankly at Abby. "Is that why you're here?"

"Right, sorry," Abby said. "You said the north building is Adelina's home."

"That's right."

"When was the last time someone checked if she's home?"

"Regularly," replied Brigid. "Just in case she happens to come back."

"And we're sure she hasn't fallen off the edge of the universe?" asked Abby. "That seems like a real danger given how small this place is."

"There's a gravitational pull that would bring you back if you tried to jump off. Without it, the complex would fly apart in all directions."

"This isn't artificial gravity?"

"Not completely," Brigid replied. "The gravity in the Azaes Realm is slightly higher than that on Earth. Inside the building, we mimic Earth's gravity. In the unlikely event you were to ever go outside, humans would find it slightly harder to move. You, however, would likely be fine."

"Who's maintaining Adelina's place while she's not there?" asked Abby.

"Caretakers of sorts, as is the case with all of the buildings."

"That's the other thing," Abby interjected. "Aside from the cafeteria and the medical area, I feel like I barely see anyone. How many people staff the Azaes Realm?"

"Not counting gods, guardians, and envoys, you're looking at around 900 or so," Brigid replied. "If you want to know the exact number, I'm sure Svieva or Nell could tell you."

"But I've only met like twenty, maybe thirty people the entire time I've been here. I get the majority are in the Diaprepes Realm, but that still seems like such low number."

"Many of the residents here are support or research staff in. They're constantly searching for life or communication from other universes, doing what they can to improve life in the Azaes Realm. Perhaps it's just not in your time to be interacting with them."

"In my time? So they're not just sleeping outside or something?" Abby inquired.

"Of course not," Brigid replied. "Why would you sleep outside? That's where the horrifying shrieks are."

Abby stared blankly at Brigid, unsure how to respond.

"The what?"

"The bigger question is why you were asking about the buildings."

"What happens if Dau and Revaus go back to live in their buildings?" asked Abby. "For more than a nap or dinner, I mean. If they were to move back on a more permanent basis."

"If we were to ever reach that point," began Brigid, "I would have to imagine it would mean that there would be war within the Azaes Realm."

"How? If there's hundreds of people here—"

"And all are capable of wielding elemental weapons."

"I thought anyone who wasn't a god or guardian wasn't allowed to use an elemental weapon."

"They're not supposed to. But there's nothing really stopping them either. It'd be a bigger conflict than you might think, but nowhere near what a war on Earth would be like. A significant conflict here could all but destroy our personnel infrastructure, though at least the buildings would remain intact."

"Even with all this magic and potential for destruction?"

"It's one of the things the original founders of the Azaes Realm planned for. That's part of why the technology and complexity of the buildings is the way it is. Not to mention the existence of Sadie."

"The assistant in the arena?" said Abby.

"She's much more than that," answered Brigid. "Sadie can protect the structure of the Azaes Realm as an entity at a moment's notice. There are nearly 100 individuals between here and the Diaprepes Realm dedicated to maintaining Sadie's programming at any given time."

"Just for defense and infrastructure?"

"Sort of. Let me give you a demonstration."

Brigid crossed the dining room and stood at the sink. She pulled a penknife out of her pocket, quickly popping the motion sensor under the faucet off and into her hand.

"Brigid," Sadie's voice rang out through the room's sound system, "I've detected a fault in the sensors in your kitchen sink. Do you need someone to repair it?"

"No, I've got it," she replied. "Thanks anyway. Can you turn the temperature down just a little? It's getting warm."

The room became slightly colder almost instantly. Brigid put the knife back in her pocket, then went to work popping the sensor back onto the faucet.

"Like a smart home on steroids then," Abby said.

"A bit," replied Brigid. "Functionally, this would allow us to withstand an invasion from another intersecting universe. That said, if a war were to break out within the Azaes Realm, Sadie can detect it ahead of time, and becomes incapable of providing assistance beyond allowing for basic living functions and checking vital statistics in the event of a medical emergency."

"That's incredible."

"When you have a universe filled with individuals who live for hundreds of years, it allows for incredible innovation. Earth has only ever seen a fraction of it."

"You'd think there'd be something that could help Erika with her struggles after all this time," replied Abby.

"I told her I'd have something for her soon," said Brigid. "The girl's impatient."

"I mean, when you've been living with it as long as she has, I can kind of understand the impatience."

"If you say so. Do you know what she likes to drink? Vodka's pretty broad."

Abby stared at Brigid, her face as perplexed as her thoughts.

"I was talking about her mental health," said Abby. "What are you talking about?"

"As if she hasn't told you," said Brigid.

"Told me what?"

"It was part of my conditions."

"Conditions for what?" Abby asked.

"A drink," replied Brigid.

"A drink? Alcohol?"

"Correct."

"That's banned here, she knows that."

"And going cold turkey isn't working for her, so I offered to help her get something."

"You did what?" Abby growled. The backlighting of her irises intensified, causing her entire face to have a haunting silver glow.

"No, no, no, no, no," stammered Brigid, quickly backtracking. "It's not what it sounds like."

"She's an alcoholic—"

"And struggling—"

"What the fuck are you thinking?" Abby shouted. "She's been managing fine."

"One drink after so long – and I don't doubt she will when she returns to Earth – and she's more likely to binge and spiral to a much darker place."

"So you don't give her any!"

"My intent," said Brigid, "is to get her to drink moderately."

"Erika doesn't drink moderately. She day drinks. Evening drinks. Midnight snack drinks. On the dark days she downs liquor until she can't think straight."

"There's medication we can give her that will hamper her desire to drink, but we have to try—"

"We don't have to try *this* though. Not this way. Surely this will jeopardize everything we're trying to do?"

"She can be kept in check, she'll have a team—"

"It's not a matter of keeping her in check," Abby said. "If you were trying to wean her off, control her intake, literally anything else, I'd be right there with you."

"So let's try them all. Don't you want to help her?"

"Of course I do," snapped Abby. "But she's reluctant to let anyone help her. Even me."

"What's the concern then?" asked Brigid. "How is helping her now a problem?"

"The timing. Her anxiety's all over the place. She spends more time at the healers than in training. She can't even wrap her head around this place without breaking down. It's going to backfire. Spectacularly."

"Let me try," Brigid pleaded. "For whatever reason, she came to me. Give me a chance to help her. Maybe if she sees that help works then she'll be open to letting others – especially you – help her."

Abby backed up and sat in a chair at Brigid's dining room table. She went quiet, taking a moment to process everything. She began to cry, synthetic tears running down her face.

"Why you?" Abby mumbled between sobs. "Why not me?"

Brigid walked over and took a seat beside Abby. She placed her hands on Abby, lightly rubbing them in an effort to calm her.

"I don't know," said Brigid.

"I love her," Abby continued. "She hurts so much. So many of her friends and her family don't speak to her anymore. Some of that is my fault."

"You can't blame yourself."

"But it is. She wanted to be with me. She loved me. And people cut her out because of it. It's been almost a decade and her mom still barely speaks to her. Then the anxiety. That led to the drinking, which drove everyone else away."

"Abby," Brigid said softly.

"She's all I ever wanted," said Abby. "The first person I loved. Yet she won't let me help her. All I try to do is be there for her. But if I call out her problems, she gets angry. She says things she doesn't mean. And it's my fault. I try to help; I make her mad. I don't mean to."

Brigid wrapped her arms around Abby, who collapsed into her shoulders, a broken, sobbing mess. Though Brigid knew that Abby functioned very much in the same way humans do, seeing the conscientia hurting this much caught her off guard. She stroked Abby's hair and shushed her, doing her best to quiet Abby's cries.

A knock at the door interrupted them. They released their embrace, allowing Brigid to answer. She peeked her head out the door to find Svieva waiting for her.

"You're back from Earth early," Brigid said.

"I know," Svieva answered. "We have a bit of a problem. We'll need to take a forward team ahead sooner than planned."

"Why?"

"Janus found Gersemi. She's been severely wounded. We need to get her back here for her safety."

28
Jumping the Queue

"Good morning, everyone," Nell said, her contralto voice carrying through the room. "My apologies for the early start, but it seems we need to make some changes to our plan."

"Time for fighting!" Shaw said triumphantly. "I'm so ready."

K'Andre elbowed Shaw in the ribs as he sipped his coffee. Despite the early hour, Shaw wasn't the only one in the room seemingly filled with energy. Both Nell and Lace appeared alert and focused. Brigid and Abby had been awake for some time, while Svieva looked to have been awake a little too long. K'Andre and Erika, however, nursed their steaming coffee, while Lorena rested her head against Abby's shoulder.

"The goal of this mission is extraction, not combat," replied Nell.

"Aww," groaned Shaw.

"Fighting should always be a last resort," grumbled Lorena without opening her eyes. "We've gone over this."

"Okay, Sleeping Beauty," snarked Shaw.

"K'Andre?" said Lorena.

"Yeah?"

"When I wake up, remind me to dropkick Shaw in the nutsack."

"Can do," replied K'Andre.

"We'll be sending the Omega team back to Earth to retrieve

Gersemi," continued Nell, ignoring the rest of the group. "To limit suspicion on arrival, Brigid will transport you all to a single location. She has an alias known in the area, providing an explanation for all should you need it. Once Gersemi has been located, Brigid will handle everyone's return."

"When do we leave?" asked Abby.

"Wait," Erika said, perking up from her coffee. "We?"

"You're part of the Omega team," Lace replied. "You, me, and Abby."

"But—"

"Lace is leading the extraction," said Nell. "But you're the most familiar with the location in question. Abby will be your eyes and ears."

"Maybe software update, too, can't imagine how far behind I am. How long has that been?"

"Sorry," interrupted Erika, "where are we going?"

"Gersemi is at an undisclosed location near Indianapolis. She's safe, but she's in a bad way."

"What is she doing there?" asked K'Andre.

Indiana? For what, a racetrack and a cemetery with three dead vice presidents? Or was it four? It's hard to keep track.

"We'd received information that Janus was in that area as well," interjected Svieva. "Gersemi likely went to check it out."

"Without backup?" asked Lorena.

"Gersemi has a habit of ignoring her own plans when she's by herself," replied Brigid. "If she found out where Janus was, it was only a matter of time before she did something rash."

"And potentially endanger our own plan?"

"It could have."

"Going after the only other entity on Earth that can kill you, and not telling anyone seems—"

"Gersemi has a brilliant mind," Brigid interjected, "but her heart gets in the way of it. Guardian of love and all that."

"Lace and Brigid will spend the remainder of the morning working on the logistics before the final debrief," said Nell. "The goal is to have Gersemi back here within two Earth days. We know she's safe for the moment thanks to a trusted resource Svieva has been in contact with, but we can't afford for her to be there much longer. Svieva and Brigid will be taking turns fulfilling Gersemi's responsibilities on Earth while she recovers."

Nell dismissed the meeting, leaving Brigid and Lace alone in the room to plan. While most went to get ready for their day, Erika waited outside the meeting room.

"You're not ready for this."

I don't know why they didn't replace me. It's not like they don't have options.

"Got to weed you out somehow.

They're not trying to get rid of me.

It's a beginner's mission. You're basically a tour guide. Pass that, you're competent. Fuck it up somehow, bam, back to Earth you go. Easy peasy, lemon squeezey."

Exactly, they just need...directions.

"You don't have a better explanation, do you?"

Erika did not.

If Lace didn't need me, I wouldn't be going.

"An ex-military servicewoman and a literal god can't come up with a plan in just a few minutes? There's more to it."

They're probably just planning contingencies, it's not a car ride away, is it?

"You're there to help things go wrong. And they have to plan around it."

Then why not just leave me here?

"You okay in there?"

Abby's voice snapped Erika out of her internal dialogue.

"I brought you some coffee and breakfast," Abby continued. "Why didn't you leave?"

"I don't get why they'd bring me along," Erika said.

"Are you going to try to talk them out of sending you?"

"Well, no."

"Why not?" asked Abby. "If you feel like you're really unprepared for a mission, I think they'd understand."

"They'll kick me out if I fuck up," replied Erika before quickly adding, "when I fuck up."

"I don't think you'll fuck things up."

"You're my girlfriend. You're supposed to say nice things about me."

"If you're genuinely doubting yourself, what's the benefit in me telling you otherwise?"

"That sounds like a logic path I'd go down," replied Erika.

"I don't think you'll screw up," said Abby. "Live with it."

The sound of the meeting room door opening interrupted their conversation. Brigid and Lace exited the room, the former nearly tripping over Erika in the process.

Erika looked at Abby. Even a smile or reassuring look of some sort would be nice, but Abby was stoic. Something was on her mind, but now wasn't the time to ask.

"Everything okay?" asked Brigid.

"We're good," replied Abby. "She's just got some jitters is all.

She'll work through it."

"Good," replied Lace. "It's okay to be nervous. If you weren't, I'd be worried. Better cautious than cocky, y'know?"

"We'll meet back here at 8:30," stated Brigid. "Lace and I will give you a quick overview, then we'll head back to Earth. Grab a shower, take a nap, eat something. It'll be a few days before you're back in the comforts of the Azaes Realm."

Lace and Brigid began to walk down the hall, only for Brigid to spin on her heels and come back toward the room.

"Actually, Erika," she said. "Do you have a moment? Hoping to talk through a couple of things with you before we go." Brigid motioned back into the room.

"You don't really expect me to go, do you?" Erika asked as Brigid shut the door.

"I do," Brigid replied. "Why wouldn't I?"

"Because GPS is a thing?"

"I can't say I ever expected you to try to talk me out of this."

"I don't know that I'm ready," Erika said. "It's just—"

Brigid dug into the pockets of her jeans, pulling out a crumpled wad of cash. She made a half-hearted attempt to smooth it out before handing it to Erika in a disheveled pile.

"What's this for?" Erika asked.

"I said I'd help you," Brigid said. "We're going to Earth sooner than expected. Pick something out you can bring back and ration for yourself."

"Define ration."

"Like booze?"

"No, strippers and ice cream. Yes, booze. Get what you need, just don't drink it before we return. This is treatment, remember."

"There's like seventy bucks here," said Erika as she smoothed out the bills. "That's way more than I'd need for a bottle."

"I don't know when either of us will go back," Brigid replied. "Use it wisely. I'll keep Lace away from you as much as I can. Don't give me a reason to feel like I'm making a mistake."

Erika shoved the cash in her pocket and left the room, leaving Brigid behind to continue preparing for their excursion to Earth. She followed Abby down the hall to the elevator, the two of them silently walking back to their room. Erika shuffled her legs, trying to reposition the money in her pocket so she couldn't feel it without drawing Abby's attention to it.

When she got her first paycheck as a teenager, Erika understood the idea of money burning a hole in her pocket. She'd cash her check payday evening, spend it, and leave her broke for the next two weeks before the mall jewelry store paid her again. But this money was burning a hole in her pocket on principle. She wished it weren't there. She knew Abby could find it at any moment.

Erika closed the door behind them as they entered their room, taking a deep breath in and trying to figure out where she'd hide the money. They'd be headed to Earth soon, but not soon enough to keep it on her person. She was mid-thought when Abby broke her focus.

"What's on your mind?" she asked.

"Nothing," Erika said. "Just nervous is all."

"Tell me about it."

"I was just saying I'm worried I'll fail. They'll kick me out, you'll get hurt somehow, you know the drill."

Abby sighed, turning around and facing Erika.

"I know Brigid's helping you," she said.

Erika's face turned a ghostly shade of white. Her pulse began to race, blood coursing through her veins and pounding with echoing force in her head.

"I. I don't—" she stammered.

"I'm not mad that you're trying to find a way to drink. That's part of the affliction you have. What pisses me off is that you feel the need to hide things from me. That you think you have to go behind my back to get what you want."

"But you wouldn't hav—"

"You don't know what I would have done." Abby said, cutting Erika off. "You didn't bother to ask. And I can't make you, I can't make you do anything. But I am getting real fucking tired of you playing victim while you undermine us all. I don't deserve that, no one does."

"No, you don't," Erika said meekly.

"Stop shutting me out, it does neither of us any good."

Erika nodded, her eyes welling with tears.

"We need to get ready," Abby said. "They'll be expecting us."

As she walked towards the bedroom, Abby felt Erika grab her arm.

"I'm not kidding," Abby said.

"I know," replied Erika. "Before we go—"

Erika grabbed Abby's shirt collar and pulled her in tight for a kiss. As their lips lingered, Erika felt Abby's arms wrap around her.

"Nice try, but we have to get going," Abby said.

"But I'm really sorry," Erika said, slipping her hands beneath Abby's shirt.

"Do everything we just talked about, and you can show me when we get back."

"It's a date."

"It's a date."

29
Tourism Props Up The Economy But Alcoholism Props Me Up Until It Doesn't

June 19, 2035

"Where are we?" asked Abby.

The portal closed behind Brigid, Lace, Erika, and Abby, leaving them in the backyard of a home of suburban Indianapolis. The yard was fenced in, with a small, untended garden off to one side. The house itself was two stories, though Erika couldn't tell for sure what color it was – she thought gray – in the pre-dawn light.

"My house," said Brigid. "Or, more accurately, one of my alter egos does. I have a maid that comes in and cleans once a week, as well as a friend who comes over every couple of days to water my plants."

"Wait. When the fuck did you change?" asked Erika.

Brigid's blonde locks had been replaced by frizzy black curls, her pale blue eyes shifting to a milk chocolate brown.

"Oh, right. The shapeshifting. It's just easier to do it as we go through the portal. It's already weird enough to humans to see someone show up in their own back yard out of the blue. All hell breaks loose when you come dressed as a stranger."

Erika now found herself shorter than Brigid, who stood well taller than everyone except Abby.

"Does shapeshifting make you a giant?" asked Erika.

"If every form I took was five foot one, it'd be boring," Brigid replied. "Though it can be hard to keep track of. My old neighbor saw me like this except my normal height. Luckily, he was so trashed he thought I'd been in a horrible accident."

"He's long gone though," Brigid continued. "And I haven't messed up my persona around these neighbors yet. I intend to keep it that way. Even down to wearing the same color and height of heels every time they see me. Which isn't often."

"Where do they think you typically are?" asked Erika.

"Away for work. Or about to go away. This persona is a travelling health worker to areas with disease outbreaks. Diseases previously endemic to animals spreading over into humans as climate has shifted made that my go-to cover for a lot of my personas. Seeing lights flick on and a car leave at an ungodly hour to catch a flight to Brazzaville, Kabul, or Cleveland fits the brief."

"Fair enough," said Abby.

"Right, so follow up question," stated Erika. "How in the fuck did no one notice the giant portal that we just walked through?"

"I mean, someone or something likely literally did," replied Brigid. "The energy that portals from the Azaes Realm release have to be caught by something. But because of the differences in how time passes on Earth versus the Azaes Realm, the energy spike is so short that it looks like an instrumentation error."

"Okay, but what about literally seeing it?"

"Again, the differences in time make it appear so short that unless you're directly looking at it or looking for it, you wouldn't notice it."

"We literally saw one when Svieva came to pick us up the first time!" Erika exclaimed.

"Keep it down, it's four in the morning," Lace grumbled.

"Well, what if someone sees us just appear out of nowhere?" replied Erika.

"That's why we travelled to my backyard and not downtown

Manhattan." said Brigid.

"You have neighbors," retorted Erika. "It's not like we're in the middle of the desert. We're in...I think we're in Carmel?"

"Close. We're in Westfield."

"And you don't think rich people don't have cameras that watch their yards."

"When the portal initially opens," replied Brigid, "there's an electromagnetic pulse that goes out and basically reboots all electronics in a short radius."

"It didn't reboot Abby," said Erika, growing increasingly frustrated.

"Look, I don't know. I'm not the sciencey person. You want a technical explanation for this, ask Nell when we get back. Let's just get inside so we can get going."

"Not a sciencey person but her cover is being a nurse. She's hiding something. They're all hiding something."

They walked toward the back door of the house, as quietly as they could. When they neared the door, Brigid stopped and took the top off a bird bath, dumping the water onto the ground and revealing a key underneath.

"I hate the hide-a-key concept," said Brigid. "But when it's in your own backyard behind a locked fence gate, it feels both safer and sillier all at once."

"Why not just carry a key with you?" asked Abby.

"If I carried a key for every safe house I have with me, I'd jingle like Saint Nicholas's sleigh."

They entered the house, Brigid leading them through a dimly lit kitchen and dining room. As they moved through the room, hidden lighting along the baseboards lit up around them. Floorboards creaked under the steps of everyone moving through the house, leading Erika to wonder if someone was sneaking up behind them.

"Holy fancy lights," Erika said quietly.

"They're just motion activated," Brigid replied. "Nothing particularly fancy."

"I'm surprised your floor doesn't heat up on its own too."

"Oh, it does. Just not here. That's reserved for the bathrooms."

Erika was briefly stunned at Brigid's statement, bringing her to a stop and causing Abby to bump into her from behind. They quickly caught up, making their way through the house's living room and a hallway toward the exit. After a few moments, Brigid led them out to a two-car garage, where a bright red sports car and a blue SUV waited.

"We'll have to take this," said Brigid, unlocking the SUV. "As much as I want to drive around in a convertible, those tend to draw attention."

Everyone piled into the SUV, Brigid in the driver's seat, Lace to her right, then Erika and Abby in the back. Brigid opened the garage door and backed out onto the street in front of the house, driving off into the early morning light.

"So, small change of plans," Brigid said. "We're going to be splitting into three groups for a bit."

"What's the new plan?" asked Lace.

"You'll still be going to meet our contact that's going to take you to Gersemi. I'll be doing some recon just to make sure Janus is contained – or at the very least isn't about to cause even more problems while Gersemi's gone. On the way there, however, I'll be dropping off Abby and Erika at the hospital."

"What? Why?" asked Erika.

"Amy's there," replied Abby. "She came out to meet with Tara, as well as to see Caroline and Jericho's new baby. She got in a car accident and has been in there ever since."

"Oh no. I'm so sorry."

"She's doing better now. Svieva's been keeping tabs on her for me. I just want to see her."

"I assume you'll want us to meet up with Lace and Gersemi after we're done at the hospital?" asked Erika.

"Lace and I will come to you," replied Brigid. "Take all the time you need there. Or at least as much time as you need until we arrive."

Erika reached over and grabbed Abby's hand, holding it tightly. She saw Abby's smile flash at her as streetlights flickered their glow in and out of the car.

*****

"Lydia?"

"Yes, Janus?"

"They're back. Just as I foresaw. You've done well. It's time to get ready for our next course of action."

"As you command."

*****

A trickle of staff and the visiting hours early birds were filing into the hospital as Brigid pulled the car into the parking lot. Erika and Abby climbed out of the car, giving a wave as the car drove off. Erika turned to walk into the hospital, only for Abby to grab her hand and stop her.

"Before we go in," said Abby.

"Am I in trouble?" Erika asked.

"I know about the money Brigid gave you."

"Oh," Erika mumbled, her voice quiet.

"I'm not going to stop you, just... Don't drink anything until we get back to Azaes. Please?"

"I—"

"I love you, Erika, I don't want something to happen to you while we're here. It's too risky."

Erika smiled. Despite her programming, Abby was the first to say 'I love you' all those years ago. And here she was, still saying it just as earnestly as the first time.

"I love you too, Abby."

Abby wrapped her arms around Erika's neck, leaning her head down and kissing Erika on the forehead.

"It makes me so happy to hear you say that."

"You know what makes me happy?"

"What?"

"Fast food tacos," said Erika, nodding at a sign across the street. "If I'm back on Earth for a very short time, I'd like those. Or cheesy breadsticks."

Abby laughed and kissed Erika again. They held hands as they walked into the hospital, finding Amy's room at the reception desk. They rode the elevator up to the building's fourth floor and made their way to Amy's room. Amy was awake, leaning back in her hospital bed watching television. Abby sprinted over to the bed at a speed that legitimately concerned Erika, considering she was moving toward a person hooked up to multiple medical devices. They exchanged a long hug before Amy waved Erika over.

"Come see me," Amy said. "I haven't seen the two of you in forever."

"Yeah," replied Erika. "We've been busy."

"Oh please, it's not like I couldn't have called or sent a message. I've been working on getting the old Project Freyja projects and other conscientia out of the US and that's taken up so much of my time. I've barely talked to anyone up until this past weekend or so. And then, of course, I end up like this."

"Ha. She didn't even notice you were gone."

I'm sure she noticed.

"From that reaction? You'd have been lucky to get a Christmas card."

"Are you feeling alright?" asked Abby. "I hate to see you like this."

"I'll be fine," replied Amy. "I had some internal injuries, but they're anticipating I'll be out of here by tomorrow afternoon. It's for the best. All I can find around here is diet pop or zero sugar stuff."

"Most hospitals are like that."

"Can I talk one of you into getting me an actual pop? Root beer would be ideal, but I'll take literally anything sweet."

"For breakfast?" asked Erika.

"Grab a Mountain Dew and mix it with some orange juice for me if it makes you feel better," replied Amy.

"Wait, seriously?"

"Seriously."

Abby handed Amy her purse. Amy dug a wad of cash out of it – significantly more than would be needed for a single drink – and handed it to Erika.

"Non-diet," said Amy. "There's a grocery store and gas station across the street. Get yourself and Abby some breakfast."

"Don't worry about it," Erika said.

"But you need—" Abby interjected.

"I've got it," Erika replied. "You two talk. It's been a while since you've seen each other."

"Please?" asked Amy. "I insist. You're here visiting me. You shouldn't have to spend your money on me too."

Erika left the room, rolling her eyes as she waited for the elevator. Of course Amy would send her off. Abby was her daughter – or as close to a mother-daughter relationship as Abby could have. They hadn't seen each other in six months, Amy was in the hospital, and neither Abby nor Erika knew when they'd be back on Earth again. That didn't mean she was thrilled about being relegated to a grocery run.

The elevator arrived on the fourth floor, a ding sounding as the doors opened. A tall, young woman dressed in a lab coat was standing in the center of the elevator, though she quickly moved to the side when she saw Erika waiting to get on.

"I'm sorry," she said, smiling as she moved to her left.

"It's okay," replied Erika. She pushed the button for the lobby, only to realize it had already been pressed.

"I do that all the time," the woman said. "Especially if I'm on nights. I'm not sure brains are supposed to work when there's no sunlight."

Erika laughed, looking over at the young woman. She towered over Erika, nearly a foot taller than her. She looked incredibly familiar.

"This is going to sound really stupid," said Erika. "And if I'm wrong, let's just pretend this never happened. But did you used to deliver pizza?"

The woman laughed.

"I did!" she said excitedly. "I worked at Tolio's Pizza on the east side while I was an undergrad. Now I'm a first-year medical intern."

"I thought so!" Erika replied. "You're the girl who had a gorgeous name that brought me cheesy breadsticks the night I got choked in a bar."

"Oh my god, that's awful. The choking. Not the compliment or the breadsticks."

"Yeah. That was a bad night. But the breadsticks were tasty."

"I'm terribly sorry that I don't remember you."

"Erika Edens. I lived in one of the tower apartments down the street."

"Emilija Vyborny. I hope whatever's brought you here isn't too terrible."

"Right," said Erika, realizing that she was still at a hospital. "My girlfriend's mom was in a car wreck."

"Oh no!" said Emilija. "Is she alright?"

"Yeah. She's getting out of here tomorrow from the sounds of it. I've been made a gopher to get her and my girlfriend breakfast."

"I'm certain she has food coming up from the hospital cafeteria."

"I mean," Erika backpedaled, "Breakfast for just myself. And for my girlfriend. And only us. But definitely not for her mom who is being cared for by the fine nutritionists and chefs in this medical establishment."

Emilija laughed as they exited the elevator.

"Your secret's safe with me," she said. "Though if you do decide to get something from the cafeteria, I'd recommend the French toast. It's surprisingly good for hospital food."

"I'll keep that in mind."

Emilija gave Erika a quick wave and a toothy grin, then wandered down a hallway off the main corridor of the lobby. Erika continued her way across the street to the grocery store, grabbing a handbasket as she entered. She quickly found a cold bottle of root beer, along with a yogurt parfait from the cold food section for herself and a cinnamon chip bagel for Abby. Erika walked to the registers – at this early hour, only a pair of lanes were open – and waited in line for the next self-checkout kiosk to be available. As she stood, Erika looked around the store. It felt weird being in a big box store again, particularly since the pantries in the Azaes Realm gave you access to nearly anything you could ask for food wise.

She'd forgotten the vastness of the clothing section, taking up a larger than necessary portion of the store. Beyond that, there was an entire electronics section, aisles for paper products, pet supplies, toys, health supplements, liquor, clearance –

"You forgot something."

I didn't, I just—

"—left a big bottle shaped hole in the basket?"

You still need ID to buy alcohol.

"Figure it out. Make something happen."

I'm not shoplifting. There are way too many cameras here. I'll be caught before I'm out of the store.

"Get creative."

Isn't it too early to even buy booze?

"It's six now. Used to be seven, but they changed that a few years ago, remember?"

Erika sighed and left her place in the checkout and meandered back toward the liquor section of the store. The liquor department was divided from the rest of the store with walls, effectively creating its own store within a store. There was a single employee inside it, an older man who looked like he could be Erika's dad. If this were the grocery store by her old apartment, she wouldn't be carded – especially if it was the cute girl who flirted with her checking her out.

A young man in a college hoodie passed her, checking out the mixers and cordials outside the liquor area, prompting a thought in Erika's head.

"Excuse me," Erika said. "Can I get you to help me?"

"Sure," he said. "Where's the top shelf at?"

"What?"

"I'm 6'5", it has its benefits."

"No, sorry," said Erika. "I was in a rush this morning and left my license at home. Don't have time to get it before work, but I'm at a baby shower tonight and I need alcohol."

"Alcohol...for a baby shower?" asked the young man.

"It's for the other moms, no reason why they can't drink. Anyway. I'll give you $20 if you go in and buy me ten of the little travel bottles of vodka."

"Travel bottles?"

"It's for a game. Having the little bottles is important," Erika replied.

"Thirty and you have a deal."

Erika quickly handed the young man the money.

"Meet you out front?" said Erika. "I need to check out."

The young man nodded and went into the liquor store. Erika

returned to the front of the store where the checkout lines had dissipated, allowing her to walk right up to the register.

"Fine work. There may be hope for you yet."

Erika finished checking out and exited the store, taking a seat on a bench just outside the front entrance. She waited a few minutes, with no sign of the of the young man.

Better not take the money and run.

"Could always go back and find someone else."

I've already wasted enough time. Amy and Abby are expecting me back.

"Amy expects little of you. The fact that Abby hasn't ended things is probably surprise enough for her."

I should leave. I've got breakfast. I can lie and say I lost the change through a hole in my pocket.

Erika turned the right front pocket of her jeans inside out. Lint fluttered to the ground as she picked at the thread holding the bottom of the pocket together. Her bitten nails failed her a few times, but with continued effort, it began to come loose. She made a dime-sized hole on her first attempt, stopping to examine her work.

What the fuck am I doing? I used Brigid's money, not Amy's.

Erika twisted the thread around her finger and snapped it off, careful not to make the hole larger as she did so.

"I'll try again later," Erika muttered aloud. *"I can make another excuse to leave, find another person to—"*

"There you are," the young man said as he walked up to Erika. "You didn't say where outside, so I came out the other entrance."

"Oh," replied Erika. "Sorry. I forgot there were two entrances."

"Here you go. Got me some weird looks, but it was an entertaining way start my Tuesday."

He handed the bag over to Erika, then made his way to his car. Erika quickly placed the tiny bottles of alcohol in her pockets then threw the bag he'd given them to her in away. She took a couple of steps back to the hospital before stopping. One of the small bottles had slipped through the hole in Erika's right pocket and slid down her leg. Fortunately, her pants were tight enough around her calves to catch it.

With a little effort and a few wiggles of her pant leg, Erika produced the rogue bottle. She unscrewed the cap and downed the vodka in a pair of gulps.

"Fuck," she muttered, the vodka burning as it went down her throat.

She tossed the bottle in the trash, then resumed her walk to the hospital. Erika made it a little more than halfway across the parking lot before pausing to adjust the bottles again, one of the two bottles in her front pocket struggling to stay put. Instead, she removed one, twisting the cap off and downed it quickly.

30
Schism

"We've arrived at the precipice of disaster," said Revaus. "Wouldn't you agree, Kedi?"

"I would," Kedi replied.

"And you, Quaid?"

"I do as well," Quaid said.

"If Janus knew enough to find Gersemi, then Janus knows enough to blow up Gersemi's entire plan. And we cannot risk that."

Revaus closed her eyes for a moment, standing at the head of the room and thinking. Her gray hair still held some of the blonde hues of her youth, and in the right light they came through. She let out a sigh, then turned around, facing her guardian and her envoy.

"We're going to need to limit variables here," she said. "Is the Omega team still on a mission?"

"They just left a little bit ago," replied Kedi. "I would assume we won't expect them back before the afternoon."

"Then get the Alpha team up here. We'll explain the situation to the rest when they return. Even if Gersemi isn't critically wounded, it's time to act."

*****

"I don't trust her," said Dau. "This has to be part of some

larger plan she's concocted."

"Then we need to strike first," Vermilion said. "If Revaus truly is in cahoots with Janus, she has a plan for taking you out. Probably quickly."

"While I don't disagree with either of you, we're in no position to prove it," replied Tane. "We cannot act rashly against the one person who prepares for every possible outcome."

"Then our best course of action is to withdraw from the center area until we can be sure this isn't an act of aggression," Dau said.

"With all due respect," Vermilion replied, "returning to your building for more than a visit would only raise suspicion. Revaus, Kedi, and Quaid would assume your absence proves your guilt."

"I'd like to think that Kedi and Quaid are smart enough to know better," Tane said.

"Quaid's brains could revolve around a peanut shell for a thousand years without touching the sides," Vermilion replied. "Even if he doesn't believe Revaus, he'll follow her blindly."

"You both know as well as I do that I'd never be on board with this," Dau stated. "I like Janus as much as anyone else around here. But I'd never agree to harming Gersemi."

"Janus's actions are not your own," said Tane. "You'd assume Revaus would be wise enough to think the same."

"Do you think there's a chance that Janus is acting alone?"

"Absolutely," Tane replied.

"It's unlikely," said Vermilion. "But there is a chance."

Dau sighed and rubbed his temples with his fingers. Tane paced around the room, her demeanor growing more unsettled.

"We can agree that the reason Janus went after Gersemi is because there's a chance her plan works, right?" Dau asked.

"Of course," replied Tane. "Considering Janus's ability to see the future and the past."

"Will the plan still succeed?"

"I have no way of knowing that for certain."

"Humor me and take a guess," said Dau. "As the guardian of peace, you must have some level of intuition."

"I'd like to think so," replied Tane. "Though my concern now is that peace may require greater sacrifice that we'd hoped."

"Bring the Alpha team here. I hope that we can convince them to do their best to keep peace."

"Surely Revaus has already gotten to them?" asked Vermilion.

"There's no doubt that she has," replied Tane. "We just have to hope that the introduction of a small amount of chaos is enough."

*****

"You heading up for training?" asked K'Andre. "Lorena said she'd be up there."

"I need to head to medical first," Shaw said. "It's easier for them to heal me with a stave than to train at eighty percent with a wrap on my ankle."

"Good call. Can't have yourself hurting physically when Lorena crushes you emotionally."

"I told you. I'm not interested in her anymore."

"I'll believe that when I see it," K'Andre said with a chuckle. "We're starting at nine. When do you think you'll be up?"

"Not long after, I hope."

K'Andre grabbed his gear and left Shaw's room. Shaw drank the last few sips of his tea and was in the process of gathering his own gear when a knock rang out from the door.

"Good morning," said Shaw.

"Apologies for bothering you at such an early hour," said Tane. "Have you spoken with Lorena and K'Andre this morning?"

"They went up to train. I'm going to join them after I get back from medical."

"I believe we should delay your training session. Something has come up that Dau would urgently like to speak with the three of you about."

Shaw followed Tane up the elevator, his sore ankle causing him to lag a few paces behind. Though she appeared patient on the surface, Shaw could see Tane's desire for him to move faster simmering unspoken.

They met Vermilion halfway down the hall, her face filled with panic. Before Shaw could even catch up to Tane, Vermilion had blocked his path and started interrogating him.

"What training room are they in?" she asked.

"Four."

"Fuck."

"What?" asked Shaw.

"Lights are out," mumbled Vermilion. "They're already gone."

Vermilion took over running toward the elevator, while Tane walked briskly to the training room. Shaw hesitated who to follow before continuing following the guardian.

"What in the hell is going on?" he yelled.

Tane ducked into the training room, flipping the light and surveying the room. By the time Shaw caught up to her, Tane was coming back out the door.

"Let's get you to medical," she said. "Looks like you'll need to feel better sooner than expected."

*****

"Shaw's probably back in the training room waiting for us," said Lorena.

"If he's there, Quaid will bring him back," replied Revaus.

"I think he really needs to hear what you just told us."

"He'll find out in one manner or another. Either Quaid will bring him back, or Dau will have already gotten to him."

"I would think that's literally the thing you're trying to avoid," said Lorena.

"It is," Revaus stated. "But in a world where both chaos and order exist, sometimes there are things out of my hands."

"Like free will?" K'Andre snarked.

"A bit dramatic in your analysis, but yes," replied Revaus. "Had I been able to talk to all of you first, I feel as though we'd be in a better position to negotiate with Dau and avoid whatever it is he's planning. But if he found Shaw...well, he already convinced the healers to let Gersemi stay in the southeast building while she heals."

"How did he manage that?" asked Lorena.

Revaus shrugged.

"Dau is persuasive," she replied. "There are times where I disagree with him, only to find myself questioning my own stance and taking his side."

"That sounds more like reconsidering your own opinions than anything else," said K'Andre.

"Perhaps. This happens even when I know he's wrong. And

285

he often is."

Quaid entered the room, closing the door quietly behind him. Revaus locked eyes with him, only for Quaid to shake his head and take a seat on the far side of the room. Kedi and Quaid began whispering to each other, discussing next steps in trying to locate Shaw.

"I would encourage the two of you to be as persuasive as possible the next time you see Shaw," continued Revaus. "And do it quickly, too. Who knows what that fool has planned."

Revaus left her chair and slowly made her way to the door. She motioned for Lorena and K'Andre to leave, the two of them quickly complying. Once they had turned the corner to the next hallway, Lorena grabbed K'Andre's arm and pulled him to a stop.

"What the fuck were you doing?" Lorena whispered.

"I don't trust her," K'Andre replied quietly.

"I don't either. But you can't do that every time you don't trust someone, least of all a god."

"What do you suggest we do now?" asked K'Andre.

"I think we do exactly what she said. We find Shaw and find out what he knows. If I had to guess, there are several people not telling us the full truth."

31

Alive and Amplified

June 19, 2035

"Keep it together, Erika," Erika mumbled to herself. "Straight line, be sober."

The elevator opened to the fourth floor, letting Erika out. The sterile smell of the hospital stung Erika's nostrils. She was down to six travel bottles. Erika planned to make sure she took back at least five to Azaes. Having a small stockpile, in addition to whatever Brigid was able to bring her back, couldn't hurt. Maybe she wouldn't need all the pills Brigid and Nell kept talking about to keep Grace in check after all. In fact, she hadn't heard from Grace since she left the grocery store.

Erika took a few steps down one of the hallways before coming to a stop.

"Wait," Erika said, her voice a whisper that failed to stay quiet, "what room was hers?"

Erika walked over to the nurse's station in the center of the floor. She waited while two of the nurses finished up a call. Or maybe it was one of the nurses. Erika wasn't sure. Twin nurses were a thing, right?

"Can I help you?" both nurses Erika saw asked at the same time.

"I can't remember where the room is," Erika said.

"What room is that?" replied the nurse.

"My mother-in-law. Or whatever it's called when it's your girlfriend's mom. Girlfriend-in-law? No. Then I'm dating Amy."

Erika laughed at her own joke, her giggles louder than she expected. She waited for the nurses to laugh, though neither of them ever did. That convinced Erika that she had to be seeing double. Shit.

"What's her name?" asked the nurse.

"Oh no," said Erika. "I can find the room. I just need to know the number to find it."

"What's her name?"

"Who?"

"Your girlfriend's mom."

Erika leaned down on the desk of the nurse's station, using one hand to balance herself while she pointed at the nurse with her other hand.

"It's wild, I can't believe I have a girlfriend," Erika slurred. "Someone wanted to date the crazy lady. I don't even have cats! My apartment won't let me have pets; do you have a cat?"

"Ma'am."

"I don't even know what I'd name a cat if I had one. Clyde? Susanna? Manhole?"

"Ma'am, what is the name of the person you're here to see?"

"She got in a car wreck. Hey, she has a cat! I can't remember what Amy's cat is called though."

"Is Amy the person you're here to see?" asked the nurse.

"Yes!" Erika replied triumphantly. "How did you know?"

"Lucky guess."

"Are you one of those magic people that can read minds? A metalingus or whatever it's called."

"The term you're looking for is mentalist," the nurse said.

"What's Amy's last name?"

"Oh, it's Nammu," replied Erika. "Didn't I say that?"

"She's in room 469."

Erika began laughing to herself.

"Hehe. Sixty-nine."

"Yes. 469 is her room," said the nurse.

"Sometimes I'm a 14-year-old in an adult's body," said Erika.

"Aren't we all?"

Erika walked away, off to find Amy's room. As she strolled down the hallways, Erika gave herself a pep talk.

"469. 469," she said quietly. "Alright, I've got this, deep breath in and hold it. Hold it. Wait. You can't hold it if you're talking. Shit. Well as long as you don't breathe on them."

Erika came to a stop outside of one of the rooms – number 433. She turned around and examined the area around her. Having nearly reached the end of the hallway, she turned around and walked back. People get turned around in hospitals all the time. This wasn't because she'd been drinking.

After crossing through the center of the floor again, Erika went down a corridor that looked more promising, doors numbered in the low 450s. She found the doorway for room 469, the number causing Erika to giggle loudly again. Before she could enter the room, Abby joined her in the hall, walking her away from the room.

"Oo where are we going in a hurry?" Erika asked.

"We're going to sober your drunk ass up," replied Abby.

"I don't know what you mean."

"We could hear you giggling all the way down the hall. Lace and Brigid should be here soon. They can't see you like this."

"They will?"

"Yes! That's why we're here. You knew that!"

Abby pushed open the door to the public bathroom, dragging Erika inside.

"Lace is gonna be so mad," Erika moaned. "Is that bad?"

"Forget Lace, what about me?" asked Abby. "We made a plan, I said don't drink anything until we were back."

"No, *you* made a plan—"

"All you had to do was to get your drinks and get them back to the Azaes Realm. How fucking hard is it to follow instructions?"

Erika hiccupped. "Very."

"You weren't even gone twenty minutes, how much have you had?"

Erika leaned against the bathroom wall, her balance slowly giving way to stumbles and jerks as intoxication took hold. Abby tried to give her assistance, but Erika pushed her away, instead using a nearby sink to steady herself.

"Not enough to be shouted at," Erika said.

"I'm not shouting—"

"I just want peace, and, and normal."

"You are normal," replied Abby. "And making terrible decisions."

"I like them," Erika snapped. "Grace likes them. It keeps *her* quiet until I pass out. Then I have to face you in the morning, and off she goes, on and on and she won't shut the *fuck* up—"

"You don't think I fucking know that?" Abby yelled.

The bathroom went silent, the last vestiges of Abby's shout echoing through empty stalls. Shivers went up Erika's back and through her fingertips. Her grip on the sink tightened.

"You act like I don't know what you're dealing with," Abby replied.

"You don't live it," Erika shouted back.

"I live *with* it. It's not your fault."

"Yes, it is."

"It's an addiction," Abby said sternly. "You have Grace and that's a mental illness. But you're an addict on top of it. It isn't you, it's never you."

"Try telling that to *her.*"

"What are you scared of?" asked Abby. "Be honest. Letting someone in?"

Erika doubled over, her body still supported by the sink, and began to cry.

"Losing me?"

Erika slumped to the floor.

"Fucking terrified," said Erika.

Abby sat down beside her. Erika leaned her head on Abby's shoulder, Abby running her fingers through Erika's hair.

"Then talk to me. Earlier wasn't that scary, was it? I know trust takes time, but fuck, Erika, have a little more faith."

"But you won't like my plan, you'll just think I'm a terrible person."

"I won't and I don't," replied Abby. "I just wish share a bit with me, instead of just going to other people."

"How did you know about that?" asked Erika.

"When one of the people training us is the person you colluded with, it doesn't take long to find it out."

"I'm sorry."

"That you got found out or for what you did?"

"A little bit of both," said Erika.

Abby hugged Erika, pulling her close. Erika's drunk body didn't take the sudden movement well, falling into Abby's lap instead of returning the embrace.

"How much more do you have on you?" asked Abby.

"I drank it," countered Erika.

"No, you didn't."

"You can't prove it."

"I am not strip searching you in public."

"Please?" Erika interjected.

"No," Abby retorted. "And if you keep it up, there won't be any of that later either. You should tell me where it is."

"Because of the whole telling you things thing?"

"Not your most eloquent sentence, but yes."

"Six bottles in my front pockets," said Erika. "Five in the left, one in the right."

"Hold up. Why aren't they even?"

"There's a hole in my pants."

"You...shoved five glass bottles into the same pocket? In women's jeans?" asked Abby.

"I had three in the right pocket after I made the hole.," Erika replied. "But then one tried to escape! And I was like 'no escaping', so I drank it. And then I drank another one too so the first one wouldn't be lonely."

"You made the hole in your pants."

"It was so the money could flee."

Abby rolled her eyes.

"I think you should let me hold onto them," replied Abby.

"Why?"

"It's less likely to piss Lace off."

"You promise you'll give them back?" asked Erika.

"Not here," said Abby. "Let's talk this through when you're sober."

"I love you."

"Will you talk to me when you're sober? Please?"

"Yes, but I still mean it. I love you. And I'm not just saying that because you promised to give my alcohol back."

"I know."

Erika dug into her pockets, taking the bottles out and handing them to Abby. She watched as Abby put them in her own pants pockets, debating if she'd regret her choice. Not that she felt like she had one. This was the easiest way to keep peace with Abby. And Erika didn't want to make her more upset than she already was. Erika wondered if she'd pay for going to Brigid for booze rather than talking to Abby about it. So far, Abby wasn't running away. That seemed like a positive.

"Can come back to Amy's room without making an ass of yourself?" Abby asked.

"I can try," replied Erika.

Abby rose to her feet, offering Erika a hand to help her stand. Erika waved her off, instead using the floor and the sink beside her. After a few seconds of cautious standing, Erika released her grip on the sink. She took a step forward, immediately wobbling as her balance wavered.

"Maybe if I'm sitting, I might do okay," Erika replied.

"New plan," Abby sighed. "Cafeteria. We'll buy you breakfast, and you'll stay there long enough to sober up, or for me to think of a plausible excuse."

"Is Lace here?"

"No, but I'd rather have a plan when she does get here."

"I don't need breakfast though," Erika insisted. "I bought me a parfait and I got you a bagel."

"Cool," Abby said, shrugging off her answer. "Eat that and something else. Have an omelet or something."

"I've heard they have good French toast here."

"Who told you that?"

"The tall pretty girl who brought us breadsticks the night I got choked at Side Pocket."

"You're drunker than I thought," Abby said.

"No!" Erika shouted. "She's an intern here now. She was working at a pizza shop before she went to med school. I rode the elevator with her."

"Well then get some French toast, eat your parfait, and when you're feeling better, come back up. Or I'll come find you."

Erika gave the grocery bag to Abby, taking the parfait out and keeping it for herself. They opened the door to the bathroom and walked to the elevators, Abby steadying Erika the best she could. Literally carrying Erika felt overkill, but with the amount Erika was stumbling, Abby was beginning to regret not just doing it anyway.

They arrived at the elevators, waiting for one to come to their floor. Erika leaned against Abby's shoulder, almost knocking her over.

"Maybe I should come with," said Abby. "I can leave Amy for

a bit to make sure you're fine."

"No!" Erika insisted. "You stay with her. She's your mom... creator...something. You should be with her."

An elevator door opened, letting off a man pushing a large cart filled with towels and other linens. Behind him, an elderly male doctor followed, along with Brigid and Lace.

"Oh, you're here already!" said Abby. "That was quicker than expected."

"Sorry about that," said Lace. "You can have a bit more time with Amy, but we do need to get going."

Erika stumbled on her feet, leaning harder into Abby.

"You alright?" asked Lace.

"She –"

"The adjustment back to time here impacts everyone differently," Brigid interjected. "She's probably struggling to stay awake. Is there somewhere around here to get coffee?"

"The cafeteria," said Abby. "That's where we were headed."

"How about I take her down while you finish up any time you need with Amy? Lace can stay with you if you'd like."

Abby helped Erika over to Brigid, then headed back down the hallway toward Amy's room. Lace followed, not before a long look over her shoulder as Brigid guided Erika to the elevator.

"This is why I said I would get it for you," Brigid said after the doors closed.

"I'm not drunk," grumbled Erika.

"I also said not to drink before we returned."

"Lace is going to be so mad."

"Maybe," said Brigid.

"She's gonna knock me out again," Erika said.

"And she'd have every right to. You're on a mission Erika. You could have jeopardized this whole endeavor."

"I don't want my ass kicked. That'll hurt my butt so much. And then my butt will hurt. Oh god. Brigid. I'm going to be butthurt!"

"Erika I'm –"

Brigid was cut off by the sound of Erika passing out, her body collapsing against the side of the elevator and shaking the whole car.

"Dammit, Erika," Brigid said, staring at Erika's body on the ground. "I'll just shapeshift the both of us, shall I?"

Brigid lifted Erika off the ground, slinging her over her shoulder like a sack of potatoes. She then closed her eyes and began to change her appearance, shifting from a short, blonde, white woman to a tall, thin Asian woman who looked startlingly like Abby. Brigid pushed the button on the elevator to return to the fourth floor, foregoing a trip to the cafeteria in favor of getting back to Lace and Abby.

She exited the elevator, carrying Erika over her shoulder the whole way. To the outside observer, she looked like a slender woman making her way down the hallway to room 469.

"Ready to go?" she asked as she entered the room.

"Who are you?" Lace asked.

"And why do you look like me?" Abby quickly followed.

"Clever disguise, Brigid," Amy said. "Who are we, Abby's sister?"

"I thought so," Brigid said. "Though for purposes of this form, I'm Hela Lin."

"You two know each other?" Lace asked.

"Of course," said Amy. "Who do you think gave me the idea of making Abby?"

"Cerise is pretty smart," said Brigid.

"You're Cerise Zurat?" asked Abby.

"I am!"

"Then why not just come back as her?"

"The less Erika knows about my alter egos, the better," said Brigid. "She's already overwhelmed. I don't want to add more to it."

"I can't believe I've known you longer than I realized!"

"I'm so fucking confused," said Lace.

"...Where is Erika?" asked Abby.

Brigid nodded to the snoring lump on her shoulder. Abby rolled her eyes.

"Let's talk about it later," said Brigid. "We still need to get Gersemi out of here."

"How? We're one down now, I'm not watching her," stated Lace, gesturing at Erika.

"Abby will watch Erika in the car. We'll work out the rest. Or, more directly, I will."

32

Psychopomp

"It's not your fault, Abby," Svieva said.

Abby sighed and leaned back against the chair behind her. Of course it wasn't her fault that Erika drank herself into a stupor and then passed out. But that didn't mean Abby didn't feel some sort of responsibility for it.

"The fuck was she thinking?" Lace yelled.

"Everything worked out fine," said Brigid. "It was a little extra work, but not a disaster."

"It was a simple extraction, there shouldn't have been extra work."

"She's part of your team —"

"I didn't realize I had a drunk on my team. The sober ones did their fucking job," replied Lace. "We got Gersemi back here unseen. Erika shouldn't have fucking been there."

"But she was—"

"Under skilled and unprepared is one thing. Under the influence is a fuckin' joke and you know it."

"I had a plan to handle this for her once I got back."

"Then you shouldn't have let her go until you did your part!" Lace said. "You're both to blame then. Nell too for assigning her to go."

"Her actions don't reflect poorly on you," chimed in Svieva.

"They absolutely do, the fuck is wrong with you?" retorted Lace. "You wouldn't be sayin' that if something had gone wrong.

Should've stuck to my gut and fought harder to have one of the others come with me."

"I wouldn't have allowed it," replied Brigid.

"Then you're as daft as they come."

"Once she's on medication and getting the help she needs—
"

"Great," said Lace. "Get your shit together, get her shit together, and then we can talk. Until then, keep her."

"Is that really necessary?" asked Svieva.

"Can I go?" asked Abby. "I want to check in on Erika."

"Aye well if she's awake," said Lace. "Tell her she can train elsewhere."

"That's not your decision to make!" said Brigid.

"Try me."

"I need to go," said Abby as she rose from her chair. "If one of the healers come back with an update about Gersemi, let me know."

Abby left the room, shutting the door behind her. As the door closed, she heard Lace and Brigid continue to yell at once another, Svieva persisting in their failed attempts to play peacemaker. It was only a matter of time before Lorena, Shaw, and K'Andre – wherever they were – found out about what happened. If Lace had anything to do with it, Erika would be on the outs with them too.

As she made her way back to her room, a thought crossed Abby's mind. She turned around and made her way up to the top floor, heading down the short, narrow hallway to the entrance of Nell's room. She knocked on the door, hoping that her guess as to where the armorer was at was correct.

"Come in," Nell yelled.

Abby entered the room, only to find Nell lying on the floor of her kitchen.

"Are you alright?" asked Abby.

"I am," replied Nell. "I'm meditating."

"By laying on the floor and staring at the ceiling?"

"This is where my calm has taken me. I don't question it. Plus, it smells like bacon in here and that soothes me."

Nell sat up, stretching her torso by twisting and contorting in place. Her back cracked several times, a couple loud enough to make Abby wince.

"What can I do for you?" asked Nell.

"I assume you've heard about Erika?"

"I have. I worried she wouldn't be ready."

"Then why send her? Lace is furious."

"Abby," Nell began. "How are you doing?"

"What?" asked Abby. "My girlfriend nearly sabotaged our plan to get a guardian back from Earth because she couldn't wait to drink. What do you mean, 'how are you doing'?"

"This is just an observation, nothing more. You care a lot about Erika. Naturally, you want the best for her. Everyone around here is preoccupied with how they factor into Gersemi's plan to save the world. And while you're learning incredibly fast, most of the focus goes onto her. I want to know how you're doing."

Abby offered to help Nell up off the floor, pulling the towering woman to her feet with one nimble motion. Nell took a seat on her couch, offering Abby a chair. The conscientia instead chose to pace around the living room, making several circuits back and forth before she spoke.

"This is exhausting," Abby said. "I get how important this all is. It matters that I'm here, that Erika is here. But. Fuck."

"What would you rather be doing?" asked Nell.

"Almost anything else. No offense."

"None taken. Tell me more about what you'd do if you weren't here."

"I just want to sleep," Abby said. "I want to go to bed and wake up next to the woman I love. I want to be bored. I get that to humans, my very existence is anything but boring. But I want it. I want to pay bills and eat shitty Chinese food. I want to watch Erika get angry about hockey, be confused why she's so upset for six months, then finally get incredibly into it because of trying to understand her."

"Having all those things doesn't stop her problems," Nell replied.

"They don't. But that's the place I'd rather be fighting them. It's one thing to try to help someone while handling normal responsibilities. This is so much more than that."

"Do you like to do anything without Erika? Just something for yourself."

"I read," Abby said. "I'd made a few friends and liked seeing them."

"I'm sure someone else could always be brought here should the need arise," Nell stated.

"Please don't. I know Erika's freakout about us being kidnapped to come here was a lot. But if you took someone from Earth for the explicit purpose of keeping me company, I might react like she did."

"Fair enough," Nell said, chuckling to herself. "So reading. Have you been to the library?"

"Why are we doing this?"

"Because you're always on, Abby. For the mission, for Erika. When are you just you? If I had to guess, I'd bet that you feel the most at ease when someone's training you to fight. Right?"

Abby nodded.

"Take a break," Nell continued. "You cannot be there for her if you're not there for yourself too."

"I can't right now," Abby said. "She's a wreck."

"I'm not saying you must do it now. I'm saying you should take one. Soon."

"Why did this have to happen now? Why did you guys knowingly send an alcoholic back to Earth?"

"The potential reward outweighed the risk," replied Nell. "Sure, Lace is angry. She will be for a while. But either Erika was going to be fine and I had nothing to worry about, or exactly what did happen would be the outcome. But I see it as a positive."

"How so?" asked Abby.

"I'd like to think this will be a bit of a wakeup call for Erika. Lace won't be able to beat the problem out of her. Disappointing you somehow is a short-lived realization in the long run. She needs to come terms with the fact that she needs help on her own."

"And you think this is a catalyst to help her do that?"

"I'm hopeful," said Nell. "For some people, one big mistake is all that it takes. Other people need to lose everything important to them to truly change."

"I don't like that answer," replied Abby.

"Why not?"

"It makes me feel powerless to help her."

"You're powerless to make progress for her," said Nell. "But you're not powerless in your efforts to support her, or to love her."

Abby sighed. The problem with Nell's answer was that Abby knew Erika. Abby knew Erika's tendency to be her own worst enemy. And that, Abby feared, was something she couldn't stop.

"I was on my way to check in on her before I came up here," said Abby. "Would you come with me? I feel like it might be nice for her to feel like I'm not the only one in her corner."

"Of course," Nell said, "but Abby –"

"Yes?"

"I need you to take care of yourself too, please. Your role here is critical and I know that you know that. You need to take care of yourself too."

"I'll try my best."

Abby returned to her room, Nell in tow, to find all the lights off. She left Nell in the dining room while she checked in on Erika. Abby watched as Erika's body rose and fell with her breathing.

"She's still asleep," said Abby, walking back out of the bedroom. "I can come get you when she wakes up if you want."

"I'll stay," replied Nell, "if that's alright, that is. She needs the support."

"Thank you. That'd be lovely. Coffee?"

"A hazelnut cappuccino, if you would be so kind."

"I think the pantry - I - can manage that."

33
Decalcomania

"Dude. I cannot stress enough how pissed Lace was. If she's mad, I guarantee some of the gods and guardians are too."

K'Andre paced the floor of his room. As much as he liked Erika, her decisions had upset nearly everyone in the Azaes Realm.

Everyone, it seemed, except for Shaw.

"You do get why this was a bad thing, right?" K'Andre continued, pausing his motion to wait for Shaw to answer.

"Yeah. She fucked up."

"So...?"

Shaw leaned his head back in the chair and closed his eyes. In any workplace back on Earth, if Erika showed up drunk on the job, she'd be fired. Here, not only did Gersemi forgive her, but she was actively encouraging Nell and Svieva to keep her on the Alpha team.

"She's getting a free pass," K'Andre continued. "None of us would, nor should we if we did something like that."

"I agree."

"But..."

"But what?" asked Shaw.

"I know there's a but coming," K'Andre said.

Shaw put his hands on his head, staring up at the ceiling.

"But you're not going to do anything about it," Shaw said. "Neither am I. So what's the use complaining about it?"

"There's got to be someone with a better plan. Who relies on a drunk staying sober long enough to execute it?"

"Who has a plan to stop Janus other than Gersemi? It's always going to be her plan. And her plan – for better or worse – has Abby and Erika at its core."

"You could cut off both of your arms and you'd be more competent than her," K'Andre replied. "Lace and Abby deserve a fighting chance."

"Again though," Shaw said, "who has a plan? I'm more than willing to listen, but the only idea we have is from Gersemi."

"A person who, I might add, has barely been here since we got here. She's passing off duties left and right."

"You're not answering my question. Who else has a plan?"

"Revaus," K'Andre said. "At least that's what she and Kedi led me to believe."

"Is that really better though?" Shaw asked. "You're going to trust the god of micromanagement to let people do their jobs?"

"So you're not open to listening to another plan."

"I've never known you to blindly trust someone who's thorough."

"It's not about trusting her, Shaw," K'Andre said. "I don't. But I'm always gonna keep a white woman authority figure on my good side rather than to go against her. Gersemi's the guardian of love. Love's fickle, but inherently a good thing. Order? That's a whole other game."

Shaw looked at K'Andre for the first time since their discussion started. He'd stopped pacing, leaning against the wall on the opposite side of the living room. His face was tired and conflicted, yet somehow at ease. It was almost as if he'd been through this all before.

"Does the plan at least make sense?" Shaw asked.

"Haven't heard it," K'Andre replied. "Don't know that I need to."

*****

Ellie cuddled in closer to Sam's shoulder, wrapping her arm tightly around his chest as he ran his fingers through her hair. The remnants of a sunset peeked through the bedroom blinds, allowing her to see her reflection in the full-length mirror on the closet door. Her bright pink hair was messier than when she'd arrived, mascara collecting under her eyes from the sweat. Not that she was complaining. She'd enjoyed herself. And it was still early enough in the evening to persuade Sam to let her stay a little longer.

It was early in their relationship. But even after only a couple of weeks of being with Sam, she was certain about one thing. Bianca was wrong about him. It was why she replied to his message right after getting back to the office with Bianca. Why she met up with him for dinner later that night instead of the next week. And why she disregarded her own no sex on the first date rule when he asked. He was a little rough around the edges, yes. But it was nothing Ellie couldn't fix.

"Do you like your job?" Sam asked.

"Just curious."

"It's a job," Ellie answered. "I'm lucky to have a partnership at such a young age. I like the people. But I don't know if I see myself doing this for the rest of my life."

"I was a car salesman until I was 32." replied Sam. "Spent eight years as an independent contractor. Now I'm 44 and about to open my first restaurant. Life takes you weird places sometimes."

Ellie sat up, leaning over Sam and blocking the light from the window from reaching him.

"I didn't realize you were that much older than me," Ellie said.

"Not my fault you're into older men."

Ellie leaned over Sam, her lips millimeters from touching his.

"I think you have the who goes into whom backwards."

Ellie gave Sam a kiss and softly bit his lower lip, tugging it with her as she pulled away. She expected Sam to follow her, only for his head to stay on the pillow.

"Not ready for another round?" Ellie asked, a coy smile plastered across her face.

"You're just...nothing like the others."

"At work? Why, what's wrong with them?"

"We should probably eat at some point," Sam replied. "And hydrate. And shower. We've spent most of the day in bed."

"You say that like it's a bad thing."

"You've got work tomorrow."

"Meh. I could always ask Tara for another day off. It's not like I take much vacation normally. Might as well use it for fun."

"Glad she's one of the good ones."

"What do you mean?" asked Ellie. "What's wrong with my team?"

"Besides you? Rude as hell."

"Even my sister? You said you liked her."

"Cerise? Yeah, I guess. Overprotective, but, so long as Tara's good to you."

"Always has been. Tara's one of the kindest people I know."

"Like I said."

"And if she was a 'bad one'?"

Sam pulled Ellie close and kissed her, rolling them over until he was on top of her. After a moment of uneasiness, Ellie wrapped her arms around his neck, letting out a muffled moan of joy as his hands ran across her chest. As Ellie's legs drew him in, he pulled away from her.

"Shower first," Sam said. "Get ready. Get dinner. If you're lucky we can come back and I'll mess up your makeup again."

"Promise?"

*****

Lorena sat on her kitchen floor, staring at the wall across from her, eyes glazed and out of focus. This was an all too familiar feeling for her. One that she thought she'd put in the past. At a minimum, she thought it died with her parents.

But this wasn't the same. Addiction took them. Her mom died in her childhood home while her dad made it halfway to the parking garage – presumably to get the car to take her mom to the hospital – before his body gave up. Lorena never bothered to find out what they'd taken. Whatever they could get their hands on, probably. The shock wasn't in the fact that they died. It was that it hadn't happened before. And that even in his final moments, her dad was trying to save her mom.

There had been a restrained recklessness to her parents' behavior when she lived with them. They weren't particularly successful. And they messed up. A lot.

But they did try.

That's the part that got to Lorena so much after their passing.

Her parents were, at their cores, deeply flawed individuals dealing with a disease that neither of them could control. It was clear that they loved each other. They loved her. No amount of love could save them from themselves.

Deep down, Lorena knew there'd be a day the news of their passing would come. For a while, she was convinced she'd sealed their fate when she chose to leave home. There was no way to guarantee that her presence around her parents would have kept them alive. Or herself. That's far too much responsibility to place on one person, let alone a teenager.

One of Lorena's favorite touches of her room in the Azaes Realm was the miniature grandfather clock Gersemi had gifted her shortly after she arrived. The clock was small, easily fitting on a tiny shelf in the room's entry way. Gersemi told her it was originally supposed to be a gift for Janus; a token meant to call a truce. Lorena never expected Gersemi to give away something so beautiful. She took it as a sign that Gersemi truly believed Janus was never coming back to this place.

Whenever Lorena had trouble falling asleep, she'd walk out to the entry way and bring the clock back to her bedroom, listening to its rhythmic motions until she fell asleep. It was hypnotic in a way – the fluidity with which it ticked. Even though time moved differently in the Azaes Realm than back on Earth, it was comforting.

Lorena refused to use the clock nightly though. She told herself it was because she wanted to save it for when she was struggling to fall asleep. But it was only half of the story. The sound was all too familiar. After her parents' binges would come to an end, after the revelers and fellow junkies were either gone or passed out, there would be a lone sound filling their apartment. Her mom's alarm clock had shimmering brass bells atop it, creating a painful sound that would jar Lorena out of her sleep long before her parents woke. But at night, its soft ticking gave her comfort. All the chaos had finally stopped. At least for tonight. Lorena could finally relax.

She couldn't see the clock from the floor. Staring off into space prevented that. It was for the best. It was the only way to make the ticking of this clock sound exactly like the one from her childhood. It was a sound she didn't know she needed.

Then again, she didn't expect to find herself relying on someone who reminded her so much of her parents.

Lorena tried to go visit Erika. She knew how pissed Lace was, how frustrated K'Andre and Shaw were, and how hard this had to be on Abby. A small part of her wanted to be the person who helped someone else when she couldn't save her own parents. To be the person who paid back the help they got when they were fighting their own darkness.

She got as far as waiting for the elevator. While waiting on the car to come pick her up, her emotions overwhelmed her. The fear. The disappointment. The anger. Above all else, a strong feeling of shame hit Lorena. No shame for Erika. She'd have plenty of that for herself. As Lorena walked away from the elevator and back to her room, Lorena reconciled with the source of her shame – the desire not to get close to yet another person who wouldn't be there long-term.

And so, Lorena sat on the kitchen floor, her mind focused on the rhythmic, hypnotic ticking of the clock. It was a metronome that would never fail. A sound that would outlive her. There was comfort in that.

34
Letting the Cables Sleep

Erika listened silently as Abby and Nell chatted in the dining room. Her head was pounding and she desperately had to pee. But if they knew she was awake, the questions would begin. Erika could deal with those. She could deal with anger or rage, emotions she felt she deserved.

"She lives! The drunk that can't hold her liquor."

But Erika wasn't hearing any of those things. Instead, she heard her girlfriend talking about how much she loved her and sharing stories. Good, happy stories. After all the crap in their past that Erika had put her through.

"Ready for your send off? Any minute now, kicked out for good."

And then there was Nell. After Abby, she had now seen Erika at her worst. Can't fight, can't use an elemental weapon, can't think straight, or survive the most basic of missions. And yet, she was here too. In no hurry to go anywhere.

"You blew your own cover. What happened to pacing? You know better."

The buzz was gone. The headache pounded through every part of Erika's skull. And, of course, Grace was back.

"You're not even a fun drunk. Can't sing, can't dance, you hate crowds. The world's most boring woman with no social life or responsibilities, and now you can't even handle shots."

Erika was never totally certain if the drinking made Grace stop or if she just managed to get so blitzed that she didn't remember what Grace had to say.

"You don't actually want help, do you? That's why you're still here. You'll piss yourself before you give in. You don't need fixed. You need a caretaker."

Erika crawled out of bed, tears staining her face.

"Look at you. You're the cowardly little child hiding under the covers because you're afraid of a thunderstorm. You're the woman who can't make friends, so afraid of what other people think. You broke Abby's heart for nothing, but here you are, doing it all over again."

She turned on the light, cringing and groaning as it stung her eyes. Abby had been kind enough to change her into pajamas, but Erika felt compelled to dress herself if she was going to leave the room.

"They're not going to solve your problems. It's a shortcut. And for what? Some pills? Why'd you think mommy only gave you one aspirin when the bottle said you could have two?"

Erika put on an orange blouse and a pair of gray leggings, then sat down on the edge of the bed. While the world wasn't spinning like it once was, it was bright and painful. Her fingers tingled, cold from the air in the room around her. Going back under the blanket would solve the problem. The shivers wouldn't be there anymore.

But Grace would. She was the chill that never left her body.

"You're dragging everyone down to your level. How could you do that to Abby? Her first mission, there to actually do something, and instead she had to watch over you."

She took a moment to gather herself, rubbing her pained eyes, then trying to refocus on the room around her. The longer Grace went on, the louder and heavier she felt in Erika's head, making even the slightest shift of balance a test of will.

"And Nell isn't going to catch you forever. You'll go back to Earth. Then what? She can't return like Brigid or Svieva. Brigid pays lip-service, and Svieva barely knows you exist. If Abby had any sense, she'd ditch the second you got home. Assuming no one comes for her like they did for Cecil."

With slow, methodical movements, Erika made her way to the bedroom door. She carefully opened the door, the brighter lights of the main living area stinging her eyes even further.

"And they will come for her. Then you'll have yourself. All alone. You'll have nothing. Because that's what you are."

Erika looked up to see Abby and Nell staring at her, both quiet and waiting. Tears continued to trickle down Erika's face, dotting her shirt with wet splashes. She shuffled forward out of the bedroom doorway. Abby met her halfway across the living room, wrapping her arms around Erika's shoulders.

Erika muttered as she leaned into Abby's chest.

"What? I can't hear you." asked Abby.

Erika shook her head, her tears coming down harder as she did so.

"We're not going anywhere," Abby said.

"Liars."

"I can't... I can't let you down."

"Grow the fuck up, Erika. You're worthless."

"Please help me," Erika whispered. "Please?"

35
Twelve Seconds to Midnight

August 5, 2035

The opening of L'ostrica Reale was still a few days away, but the pre-opening party and dinner was in full swing. Unlike a night with a full house, this setting was more intimate, the ambient Italian violin music almost audible over the chatter. Friends and family of the staff, along with business connections and a handful of carefully picked guests, spread themselves out over a few dozen tables in the restaurant.

Under the guise of Marty Gunnselman, Youles sat quietly at his table, politely bantering with those around him as he consumed the tasting menu – including the much-ballyhooed clams casino that Sam had told him about when they first met. Originally, Marty was to be seated at a table with a pair of other food critics. When he arrived, he found that his seat had changed, moved to a VIP table with Sam and other important individuals to the restaurant's success – including his target.

In Youles's experience, there was no noticeable difference between humans and conscientia. That was part of what made them so challenging to take out, and a major reason why he'd failed on his previous mission for Janus – a fact he needed no reminder of at this moment. This was a second chance. Second chances don't come often in this line of work.

Tara Simon certainly fit the bill of an android capable of blending in well among humans. So well, that had Youles not been introduced, he would have guessed the conscientia was her associate, Ellie Zurat. Ellie had spent most of the evening flirting with Sam, Tara trying her best to reel her back in. Whether it was the massive fish tanks, the fast talking, or the expensive dinner, everything Sam said or showed to Ellie had her grinning from ear to ear.

No rational human would have an interest in someone as slimy as Sam Sawchuk. Youles hadn't been able to keep a relationship for longer than a few months since moving into his line of work. And while being a restaurateur was a more reputable profession than a hired gun, Youles's job was honest despite its shadiness. At least women knew what they were getting themselves into with him. With Sam, you expect a nice guy who runs a restaurant. Until the bribes get uncovered. Either Ellie was genuinely infatuated with Sam or a complete idiot. Possibly both.

Despite her ease of fitting in with a human crowd, there was something Youles found unsettling about Tara. In conversation, she always seemed to have the right answer for whoever she was talking to. Not some of the time. All the time. Maybe she was just smarter than the androids Youles had encountered before.

Smart enough to know he was there to kill her?

Youles shrugged off the thought and went back to his dinner. Janus had assured him, via an envoy, that there was a contingency plan just in case she knew. Not that Youles would let the evening get to that point. He planned to tail her home and ambush her before she entered her house. Once that was done, there was a fake passport and a plane ticket with his name on it. By the time anyone figured out who Marty Gunnselman was, Youles would be on an island off the coast of Venezuela, sipping drinks on the beach.

Tara excused herself from the table, leaving her suit jacket behind on the chair. Content that his mark wasn't leaving, Youles sipped at his water, considering the timing of his next move. The vast majority of those invited to the event were still there, and likely would be for at least the next hour. There was no rush to act. Still, without a plan that was checked, double checked, and then checked again just to be sure, things could fall apart like they did last time.

The entertainment for the evening – a comedian with a myriad of musical instruments and props – had begun to set up on the far side of the room. Youles groaned to himself, dreading whatever pun-filled banter would inevitably come out of the performer's mouth. His thoughts were interrupted by a hand tapping him on the shoulder.

"Good evening," said a young woman in a waitress uniform. "Mr. Sawchuk would like to give you a tour of the kitchens."

"Can't it wait until later?" asked Youles.

"For what reason?"

Youles thought for a second. He couldn't blurt out that he had to keep an eye on Tara.

"I'd like to hear the comedian," he quickly replied. "I hear he's pretty good."

"It'll be another fifteen minutes before he goes on," said the waitress. "Please. Follow me."

"I'd rather not."

The waitress leaned down and placed her mouth close to Youles's ear. Her nails and fingertips dug into the muscles at the top of his shoulder, causing him to wince.

"Mr. Sawchuk insists," she whispered.

Youles stepped away from the table, careful to not make a scene with the waitress. Something about her seemed familiar, though he couldn't quite place what it was. Sam had given him partial payment for the review already. If this was his way of insisting the restaurant received a good review, it was a hell of a marketing strategy.

Youles passed through the double doors to the kitchen, noting a handful of staff members working to prepare and plate the coming dessert course.

"I don't see Sam," said Youles, scanning the room as he spoke.

"The tour will start in the back and work its way forward," said the woman. "Please, keep following me."

Youles continued to follow the woman, his eyes focused on the point where her short, brown hair met the top of her shoulders. Something about her hair looked off to him.

A cold blast of air hit Youles in the face, shocking him back to the world around him. The young woman was gesturing him into a small walk-in cooler with a second door in the back. The door was being held open by Sam, leading to a dimly lit room. As Youles made his way past the young woman, they locked eyes and he realized where he'd seen her before. She'd been standing outside his house just before seven in the morning on the day his meeting with Janus was rescheduled.

Youles kept walking forward as Lydia closed the door behind them. She'd clearly worn a wig in their first meeting, the long, blonde hair enough of a difference from her current brown bob to throw him off. Janus showing up tonight wouldn't have been particularly surprising to Youles. But for an envoy to make a second appearance to bring him, especially one he knew the name of...he couldn't wrap his head around that.

As Youles passed through the doorway into the second room, he felt a clubbing blow smash across the back of his head. He fell to the floor, stunned and gasping for breath. The sound of the door slamming behind him echoed through his eardrums, sending shockwaves of pain into his skull. A flurry of additional shots rained down on his body, one sending a wave of pain shooting down from his ankle through his toes, his left foot threatening to burst into flame.

Youles tried to scream out in pain, only to choke as blood bubbled out of his throat. The onslaught ceased, only for a nearby light to come on in the room, piercing at Youles's eyes. He saw Lydia standing over him, a wooden baseball bat covered in blood slung over her shoulder. As it dripped onto the shoulders of her blouse, she smiled and chuckled quietly.

"Thank you for your time, Lydia," Sam said, taking the bat from the young woman. "Go get changed and feel free to head out for the night."

"You sure you don't want me for dessert service?" Lydia asked.

"There's blood in your wig. It's probably best you get going."

Lydia pulled the brown wig off her head, examining the splatters covering some of the hairs. Youles saw her real hair for the first time, an ash brown pixie cut with blonde highlights. Some of the blood had made its way through to her hair, adding to Lydia's dangerous aura. She smiled and tossed it to the ground, the bloodied hairpiece landing a few feet from Youles's face. She turned on her heel and exited via the far side of the room, through a door still somewhat hidden in the shadows.

Sam walked around Youles's body, occasionally poking at him with the bat. It was clear he had no intention of touching the bloodied body before him, a fact which Youles hoped to use to his advantage. The trick would be figuring out how to get up without Sam – or whoever else might be in the room that was out of sight – noticing in time to stop him.

As he lay on the ground, Youles did his best to take assessment of the damage Lydia had done to him. Whatever happened to his left leg was still pulsing. He'd choked on blood, so probably a good bit of internal bleeding. Two strikes against him alright. But he was bigger than Sam, and there's always the element of surprise.

"I'd think twice about moving if I were you," came a voice from the dark. "Things end in a much more gruesome way for you if you struggle."

Of course Janus was here. Why not. Youles let out a sigh, surprised it didn't hurt his chest as he did so. At least no ribs seemed to be broken.

"I take it plans have changed," Youles grumbled from the floor.

"They have," Janus said, voice level and somber. "Due to a series of events far beyond your control, your services are no longer needed."

"Then let me go. It's not like I can do anything to stop whatever it is you have in mind."

"You can't. Time will march on as it always has. Pawns will move about the board completing their duties. They lack the strength to take out a knight on their own. The pawn's power comes from its ability to provide protection. Now that the knight has retreated, there is no longer a use for the pawn."

"Take it I'm not the knight, huh?"

For the first time across all their meetings, Youles finally saw one of the people he presumed to be behind Janus in the light. She wasn't a middle-aged woman like Youles had expected, rather an elderly woman with short, curly, sandy blonde hair resting against her skull. She wore bifocals with a gold chain dangling off them, its luster faded from years of use. Her face showed no hint of emotion beyond an overwhelming sense of calm.

"What I'm saying," she said, "is that nearly everyone that is, was, or will be is a pawn. It's nothing personal. You've been fortunate enough to have the backing of powerful pieces. But I'm afraid that this is where the match ends for you."

"I can keep quiet!" Youles pleaded.

"Another will take your place."

"You'll never see me or hear from me again. I'll leave the state. I'll leave the country. Whatever you need me to do, I'll do it!"

"I thank you for your sacrifice."

Youles started to beg more, only to stop mid-thought as Janus turned to walk away. For the first time, he realized that Janus wasn't two people – Janus had two faces. Gone was the face of an elderly woman. Youles expected to see the back of her head covered in blonde hair, but instead found a skull that had been stripped of its skin, a crumbling, ashen skeleton exposed to the air. Dust and bone fragments chipped off as she walked away, only for the chalky holes to fill back in a few moments later.

A scream from a voice Youles had never heard before rang out through the room. It took a few moments for him to realize it was his own, horrified shrieks he was listening to. In an instant, a sharp pain stung at the base of his neck, then everything was quiet. And dark.

36

Flicker

August 8, 2035/22:19, Day 114, Year 10311

"Square up your stance," Erika mumbled under her breath. "Balance. Counterattack."

"One, two, three! One, two, three!"

"Guard the left hook unless they fight southpaw. Duck and roll or counter if they do."

"Kick! Punch! It's all in the mind!"

Erika rolled on the ground, careful not to cut herself with her knife as she tumbled. She quickly made her way back to her feet. Though she still wasn't particularly nimble, her forward rolls felt more fluid with each attempt. Stumbling slightly to her right to keep her balance, Erika ducked as she reset her feet, dodging an imaginary punch from a fake opponent.

"Fuck," Erika mumbled.

She paused and adjusted her gloves, tightening them up around her wrists. Erika looked over at the far wall of the room, where Nell and Abby were seated behind a clear barrier. Abby was reading through one of the many books Nell had provided her with since their arrival. Nell, meanwhile, appeared to be sharpening a small dagger, occasionally pausing her meticulous motions to peek up at Erika's progress.

Despite pleas to the contrary from Brigid, Lace had not come back to continue Erika's training. This was the best possible outcome in Erika's mind. If she wasn't around Lace, it meant Lace wasn't around her.

Lorena had kept her distance from Erika, reminding her of her neighbor's cat, Maples. One day, Maples snuck into Erika's house, following her all around. As Erika made herself toast for dinner, Maples started to swat at the toaster, only for the bread to pop out, causing the cat to scurry to safety. From that day forward, Maples would look at Erika from afar, but never got close to her.

K'Andre was similarly leery of Erika. Though he was around more often, thanks in large part to Shaw's insistence on playing mediator between Erika and everyone else, he was quiet. The jokes and quick wit, even at Shaw's expense, were gone. Now, he was focused, almost as if he were trying to keep the stink of her problems at bay by associating with her as little as possible.

Erika kept hearing that they'd all come around eventually – both Brigid and Nell had said some form of that sentiment to her in the days since they'd returned from Earth. Erika knew better, though. Most people didn't bother coming back when she screwed up. It was a constant in her life she'd come to rely on...

...except for Abby. And Nell.

"I'd like an opponent today, Sadie," Erika said.

"Certainly," Sadie's voice rang out. "Any specific simulation or difficulty?"

"Surprise me."

Nell perked up at this statement.

"Are you sure about that?" she asked. "Sadie can make a simulation that's truly random. It might be better to set something within your skill level."

"It's not going to hurt me unless I hurt myself somehow, right?" asked Erika.

"Well, no."

"Surprise me, Sadie."

"As you wish, Erika," Sadie replied. "Please get to a starting position."

Erika steadied herself, looking back at Nell and Abby.

"Any advice?" asked Erika.

"Don't forget to wear sunscreen?" Abby said, chuckling.

"Helpful. Ready, Sadie."

"Now beginning test scenario, version 9.0.1.819r, randomized combat training."

The lights on the training floor dimmed, limiting Erika's sight. She tightened the grip on her brass knuckles, then cautiously took a step forward. She placed her foot down gingerly, listening for any reaction to her motion. When none came, Erika took a second step. Still nothing. She turned her head to check behind her, only for a jolt to knock her off her feet. Erika tried to use the momentum to tumble back to her feet, only to land on her shoulder.

Despite whatever hit her, the room remained dark. Erika looked at where she'd been struck on her right leg, but aside from a light scratch on the training armor, there was no sign of what she'd been hit by.

"What the fuck?" Erika mumbled to herself.

She struggled to her feet, prepared for another attack, though one didn't come. Erika took a few paces back to where she'd been at the start of the simulation, then repeated her actions, hoping to draw out another strike. Nothing.

"You're gonna dieeeeeeee."

"Shut up," mumbled Erika.

As soon as the words left her mouth, Erika saw a glowing chartreuse light darting and weaving its way toward her. She was able to sidestep it, but only barely. A second one came charging at her, this one necessitating Erika to fall forward to avoid it. The second light lodged into the ground behind her, allowing Erika to get a better look at the projectile. It looked like an arrow, though the shaft moved like steam.

Erika got back to her feet and tried to think of a plan. Both of her weapons were best suited to melee combat, limiting her ability to close in on her opponent – wherever they were. She considered throwing the butterfly knife one direction, using it as a distraction while she charged in with the brass knuckles. But that would entail being certain that her opponent would take the bait with the misdirection. And she'd have to know where exactly her foe was in the first place.

"Sadie?" shouted Erika.

"Yes?" she replied.

"Can I have a ranged weapon of some kind?"

"Not during this simulation. It is one of the parameters of your randomized scenario."

"What about some better lighting?"

"That is also part of the scenario."

"Fuck."

Erika slowly walked toward the source of the arrows, expecting to have to dodge again. When none came, Erika turned back to look at the one that had just missed her before. It had nearly disappeared, the traces of a green arrowhead sticking out of the ground all that remained. Within a few moments, even that was gone.

The room around her began to grow a bit brighter, as if the sun were coming up. Out of the corner of her eye, Erika noticed a shadow in the distance. Her target appeared to be facing away from her, staring at the far wall of the arena. Quietly, Erika made her way over adjusting her butterfly knife to an attacking position. She was nearly upon her target when she realized it wasn't an enemy at all, rather a downed body.

An arrow whizzed above Erika's head, its slipstream strong and close enough to move her hair. She tensed up, tightening her grip on the brass knuckles in her fist. Erika adjusted the knife in her hand again, only to have a glimmer of light appear in the corner of her eye. She tilted the knife again, using her peripheral vision to confirm it was merely light reflecting off the blade.

It wasn't. The tip of the blade had begun to glow an icy blue.

A second shot and a third quickly followed. Though Erika was able to dodge the former, she rolled right into the latter. The arrow pierced the armor on her bicep. Erika screamed out in pain, dropping her knife as the muscles in her arm tensed up. She sat the brass knuckles down beside her, hoping to take time to assess the damage, only to notice a towering figure striding toward her.

It moved slowly and methodically, with confidence and purpose in its gait. The figure cast no shadow, seeming to absorb the light around it as it moved. At its left side, it carried a glimmering sapphire longbow adorned with patterns of segmented silver and gold snakes held together by trails of ruby red blood drops.

The figure came to a stop a few meters away from Erika. It raised the bow slowly, drawing an arrow back as it did so. Though every instinct Erika had screamed at her to move, her body was frozen in place. All she could do was to close her eyes and wait for the arrow to hit.

"Session terminated," Sadie's voice rang out.

Everything around Erika save for the knife and brass knuckles vanished. The pain transmitters from her practice armor stopped throbbing on her arm, returning it to feeling normal. Despite all that, Erika couldn't shake the feeling of the figure – whatever it was – aiming its bow at her face.

"What's going on?" asked Abby.

"Why did you stop, Sadie?" Erika shouted.

"You were in a compromised position," said Nell. "There was no way you would have survived that in a real battle."

"Erika's position is irrelevant," replied Sadie, "though she did only have a 3.7% chance of winning the battle."

"Wait, really?" said Erika. "How the fuck was I surviving that?"

"Then why stop it?" asked Nell.

"As a neutral entity within the Azaes Realm, I am required to stop assisting in training of any kind for anyone while there is an active war declared anywhere within its jurisdiction."

"War?" Abby asked.

Nell sighed.

"Motherfucker," she said. "Where's Adelina when you need her?"

37

Eleven Seconds to Midnight

August 9, 2035/00:04, Day 115, Year 10311

"Why are the elevators out?" Erika said, panting as she climbed yet another flight of stairs.

"Protocol. Sadie and the rest of the infrastructure in the central building cannot be a help to anyone in any way during conflict," Nell replied. "Healers are obligated to do their jobs, as are basic maintenance staff, but they also cannot aid combatants."

"But...an elevator?"

"Two more flights to go," said Abby. "You can do it."

"Why the hell wasn't cardio part of our training?" Erika shouted to no one in particular.

Upon arriving on the top floor, Abby, Erika, and Nell made their way down to the large room adjacent to Brigid's room. Svieva and Brigid stood in the doorway, flanked by Tev and Kuhla, watching as Lace, Lorena, and Shaw argued.

"What happened here?" asked Abby.

"Gersemi went back to Earth," replied Svieva.

"So?" asked Erika.

"This is an unprecedented situation. Two guardians are dead. Revaus and Dau declared war on each other. It'd be beneficial to have her around right now."

"Who died?" said Abby, looking around the group to see who was missing. "Tane? Kedi?"

"Both," replied Brigid. "Vermillion found them a few hours

ago. Both where bludgeoned to death and their elemental weapons were taken. She's distraught."

"Revaus blamed Dau, then Dau blamed Revaus, and here we are," added Svieva.

"What do we do now?" asked Erika.

Brigid gave an answer, but it was drowned out by Shaw.

"I'm telling you," Shaw said. "Something doesn't feel right here."

"What evidence do you have?" yelled Lorena. "Show me how you know she's lying and I'll come with you right now."

"Look, I didn't see anything in person –"

"Then how can you know?"

"I trust Dau!" shouted Shaw. "This feels too calculated for him. Why take out both his own guardian and Revaus's?"

"Maybe that wasn't his intention," replied Lace. "Collateral damage isn't unheard of."

"I'm saying I don't think he's involved at all! I think Revaus set him up!"

"To what end?" asked Lorena. "War is chaotic. Why would the god of order want that?"

"Dictators do it all the time," replied Lace. "Sow chaos in hopes of achieving their own warped form of order."

"Whose side are you on here?"

"I'm no' on anyone's side. I'm stating a fact."

"The fact is that remaining neutral leaves us as sitting ducks," said Shaw.

"He's right," Svieva piped in. "Although the central building is neutral ground and those in it are supposed to be protected, there is no guarantee that either Revaus or Dau will command their forces to respect it."

"Or treat neutral parties kindly," Lace added.

"Fine," said Lorena. "I'm going to join Revaus. I'm telling you, I think Dau's behind this all happening."

"Probably behind Janus too," Lace said.

Shaw sighed.

"You can't be serious."

Lace and Lorena left the room, headed off to join Revaus in the southwestern building. K'Andre had been sitting quietly, listening. He rose from his seat and gave Shaw a hug.

"I knew I could count on you, man," Shaw said.

"Keep yourself safe," K'Andre replied. "He's hiding something."

"Wait, you're not –"

"Just don't let yourself die from this."

K'Andre broke the embrace and walked to the door.

"If we both make it out," Shaw called after him, "want a steak dinner? I'm buying."

"Of course," replied K'Andre. "I love you, man."

"Love you too."

Shaw waited a few moments, then followed K'Andre out of the room. Erika thought she saw a tear trickling down his cheek as he walked by, but he moved too quickly for her to be sure.

"Where's Vermilion?" asked Erika.

"In medical," Kuhla said. "She's not physically hurt, but she's pretty shaken up. Think that's the first time she's ever seen a dead body."

"Doesn't help matters when one of the bodies is the closest thing she had to family here," Tev added. "I still can't believe her and Tane aren't actually related."

Abby tugged on Erika's shirt sleeve, leading her away from the two envoys. They made their way to the far side of the room, everyone except Svieva out of earshot."

"Should we go with Shaw?" asked Abby. "He's going to need help."

"We don't know any better than they do on who's right and who's wrong," said Erika. "They could both be wrong."

"But he's alone. K'Andre, Lorena, and Lace can figure things out on their own. Shaw doesn't have anyone."

"What if he's wrong though? Then we're the bad guys and Lace is on the warpath."

"Actually," interrupted Svieva, "there were instructions Gersemi left for the two of you and the two of you alone. You should both stick with Lace."

"Aww a mother figure to hate you. Just like home!"

"What can we do to help her?" asked Erika.

"Not a clue. I just know Gersemi intends to keep the three of you together wherever possible."

"What about you?" asked Abby.

"I am headed back to Earth to help Gersemi," replied Svieva. "Until she's back at full strength, she can't handle Janus alone."

"But that means there'll be no guardians in the Azaes Realm."

"Brigid can travel back and forth to Earth if needed. I'd rather not risk any more of us dying. Come on. I'll help you two get ready and get to the southwestern building before I go."

After Svieva, Abby, and Erika left the room, Brigid walked over to one of the large, pillowy chairs and threw herself into it. She stared blankly at the ceiling, pressing her fingers against the bridge of her nose.

"Is there anything I can do for you, Brigid?" Tev asked.

"Go down to medical and check on Vermilion," she replied. "Take Kuhla with you, please."

"Ma'am," Kuhla said meekly, "I really feel I should go back to Adelina's quarters. She'll need someone to advise her of what's happened and to protect her if she returns."

"It might not be my place to say," Nell interjected, "but the odds of Adelina showing up and not coming straight to the center building are terribly slim. You were previously a healer – and are arguably the best dark magic healer in this realm. While I hope you don't need to put your talents to use, it's best for everyone if you're ready to do so."

Tev and Kuhla went silent, thinking over Nell's explanation. They looked at each other briefly.

"Is that your wish, Brigid?" asked Kuhla.

"Nell's logic is sound," she replied. "Please do as she says."

Kuhla and Tev exited the room, leaving Brigid and Nell alone. After she was certain the elevator had descended, Brigid let out several loud screams toward the ceiling, cursing in every way she knew how. Nell stared at her from the doorway, waiting for the fury to wane. With time, the shouts began to strain Brigid's voice, only then causing her to stop for a drink of water.

"This is only the second war in the history of the Azaes Realm," Brigid grumbled in a more level tone. "I thought the threat of the legendary weapons of Milan and his apprentices would be enough of a deterrent. There was a precedent of thousands of years of peace, safeguard after safeguard, literature and history written to guide everyone in the Azaes Realm so that they could avoid this very situation despite their differences. Yet here we are."

Nell joined Brigid, propping her feet up on a table across from where the goddess of life sat. Nell's long legs reached nearly halfway across the table, just missing bumping a glass that someone had left.

"Do you think they're onto something?" Brigid continued. "That someone is behind everything Janus is doing."

"I do," replied Nell. "Though nothing Janus is doing is out of character, this feels like something bigger is in play. It might have been Janus's idea, but someone with more power is pulling the strings."

"Any thoughts as to who?"

"I'd prefer to keep them to myself. As a neutral party yourself, I'm sure you understand."

"That's bothering me a bit," said Brigid. "Clearly someone's up to something. I just don't know what."

"Might I make a bit of a ridiculous suggestion?" replied Nell. "You're free to shoot it down and tell me we never discussed it."

"Of course. We've known each other for a long time, I trust that there's a point to it."

"Have you considered not remaining neutral?"

"That's practically heresy."

"Can a goddess commit heresy?" Nell wondered aloud.

"Who would I even side with?" asked Brigid. "Both Dau and Revaus are acting in their own self-interests. I can't imagine either of them being totally in the right, especially now that both are likely out for vengeance."

"There is a third option."

"And Adelina's been missing for some time now."

"Then find her?"

Brigid got up from the chair and made her way to the door.

"It's getting late, Nell," she said. "You should get some rest. You never know when someone will need medical attention."

"Think about it," Nell replied.

"My involvement has the potential to sway this war in ways it otherwise wouldn't be able to. I don't know if I'm prepared to do that."

"Then I would encourage you to be prepared for someone else to take action where you've chosen not to."

*****

Sam pounded on the door of a room at a rundown motel just across the Ohio River from Madison, Indiana. He never understood why Lydia picked the cheapest hotel she could find, especially when Janus offered to put her up in better accommodations. Madison itself had decent lodging, especially for a small city on the river that was more of a historical landmark than anything else. Instead, Lydia chose the motel with burnt-out neon bulbs on its sign, rats running along the bottom floor, and more broken windows than overnight guests.

The diminutive woman answered the door, hair still drying in a towel, wearing a cami and pajama pants. Sam often wondered how Lydia could handle threats much larger than her. He'd often assumed it was pure luck or stealth. Upon closer inspection, Lydia's well-toned muscles indicated a formidable opponent when paired with her skill with weapons.

"I was trying to go to bed," Lydia grumbled.

"I think you'd much rather want to hear what I have to say,"

Sam replied.

"Not really. I've heard you talk. Nothing honest comes out of your mouth."

"Says the girl who kills for sport."

"Just because I like my job doesn't mean it's what I want to do for a living," Lydia said. "And until I'm told otherwise, I'm in between jobs right now. Which means I don't have to talk to you."

Sam reached into his pocket and pulled out an envelope and handed it to Lydia. Her name was written on it in Janus's shaky, smeared handwriting.

"You're the new check boy?" Lydia asked.

"Your check will be there waiting for you when you get to your next gig," Sam replied.

"Which is?"

"You're going to Vidalia, Louisiana. Janus said the next person they'll try to recruit is there. Your job is to get to him before they do."

"And the key in the envelope?" asked Lydia. "Janus knows I can't drive."

"The key is for a house once you get there," said Sam. "Across the river at the marina, there's a boat waiting for you. Janus said she got you a full crew, whatever that means."

Lydia's eyes lit up with a childlike wonder. It unsettled Sam, seeing the woman he'd watched kill someone in cold blood -- and who'd been rumored to have done the same to several others -- suddenly have the enthusiasm of a six-year-old seeing her very own pony on Christmas morning.

"She got me my own pirate ship?!" Lydia shouted, her voice cracking.

"Keep it down!" Sam insisted. "It's just a river runner. But yes. Janus made it clear I inform you that you're finally a captain."

Lydia darted back into her room, turning on lights and tossing stuff into her suitcase rapidly. She removed a small bag from under a pile of pizza boxes, taking clothes out and hurriedly changing.

"What are you doing?" asked Sam. "It's time to pack up and go."

"Tell Janus I'll send a courier with my thanks when I get to Louisiana," replied Lydia. "And I'm changing, dumbass."

"Why?"

Lydia dug through her back, removing the cutlass and single shot gun Janus had previously gifted her.

"If I'm going to live my dream of being a pirate captain, I'm going to look the part. Even if it is just for a trip down the river."

Appendix

Abby Lin (Ab-ee Lin) – A computer simulated consciousness implanted into an android (informally known as a conscientia). Originally created as part of Project Freyja. She/her. Created in Fort Mitchell, Kentucky, USA on December 9, 2021.

Adelina (Ah-dey-lee-na) – The god of knowledge in the Azaes Realm. She/her. Born in Tamarindo, Costa Rica on February 11, 2021.

Amy Nammu (Ay-mee Nah-moo) – A computer programmer who created the code that became the Project Freyja conscientia simulation program. She/her. Adopted by a family in Wichita, Kansas on April 29, 1993.

Bianca Henderson (Bee-yan-kah Hen-der-son) – A receptionist at Simon, Zurat, and Zurat. She/they. Born in Fishers, Indiana, USA on September 8, 2014.

Brigid (Bridge-id) – The god of life in the Azaes Realm. Has shapeshifting powers. She/her. Born in Baarle-Nassau, Netherlands on October 9, 1905.

Dau (Dow) – The god of chaos in the Azaes Realm. He/him. Born in Tuen Mun, Ming China (modern day Hong Kong) on April 17, 1521.

Ellie Zurat (El-ee Zir-aht) – An accountant at Simon, Zurat, and Zurat. She/her. Born in Greenwood, Indiana, USA on November 9, 2009.

Emilija Vyborny (Eh-mil-ee-yah Vee-bor-nee) – A medical

resident at a hospital in the greater Indianapolis area. She/her. Born in Dubrovnik, Croatia on January 8, 2011.

Erika Edens (E-rih-ka Ee-dens) – A call center supervisor and data analyst. She/her. Born in Powell, Ohio, USA on October 8, 2005.

Gersemi (Grr-sem-ee) – The guardian of love in the Azaes Realm. She/her. Born in Al Jahra, Kuwait. Birthdate unknown but believed to be in the spring.

Iris (Eye-ris) – A cleric and healer in the Azaes Realm. She/her. Born in Blenheim, Marlborough, New Zealand on January 26, 2013.

Janus (Yan-uhs) – The guardian of time in the Azaes Realm. She/they/them. Born in Thessaloniki in the Byzantine Empire (modern day Greece) on September 25, 1263.

Kedi (Kyeh-dee) – The guardian of justice in the Azaes Realm. He/him. Born on Okinawa in the Ryukyu Kingdom (modern day Japan) on June 26, 1772.

Kuhla (Kool-a) – The envoy to Adelina within the Azaes Realm. She/her. Born in Lviv, Ukraine on January 22, 2007.

K'Andre Jones (Kay-an-dray Jones) – A graduate student studying to be a chemical engineer. He/him. Born in Bedford, Ohio, USA on May 5, 2003.

Lace Ross (Lay-ss Ross) – A former member of the Royal Air Force and current personal trainer. She/her. Born in Troon, Scotland, United Kingdom on April 26, 1987.

Lorena de León (Lor-eh-na day Lay-on) – A personal assistant to the CEO of a major bank. She/her. Born in Palma, Spain on

December 6, 2012.

Lydia Marlmont (Lid-i-ya Marl-mont) – A nightclub bouncer, taekwondo instructor, aspiring pirate, and personal security for hire. She/her. Born in Panama City, Florida, USA on September 8, 2016.

Nell (Nel) – The head of the armory and former lead healer in the Azaes Realm. She/her. Born in Colchester, New York, USA on August 5, 1970.

Quaid (Kwayd) – The envoy to Revaus in the Azaes Realm. He/him. Born in Blackpool, England, United Kingdom on April 3, 1975.

Revaus (Rehv-aus) – The god of order in the Azaes Realm. She/her. Born in the Imperial City of Regensburg in the Holy Roman Empire (modern day Germany) on March 7, 1293.

Sam Sawchuk (Sam Saw-chuk) – An entrepreneur and restauranteur. He/him. Born in Jackson, Wyoming on October 30, 1990.

Shaw Felix (Shaw Feel-ix) – A high school history teacher and independent professional wrestler. He/him. Born in Cedar Rapids, Iowa, USA on September 29, 2002.

Svieva (Sv-eye-ev-ah) – The guardian of memory in the Azaes Realm. They/them. Born in Cape Coast, Gold Coast Colony (modern day Ghana) on March 3, 1888.

Tane (Tah-nay) – The guardian of peace in the Azaes Realm. She/her. Born in Valparaiso, Captaincy General of Chile (modern day Chile) on March 9, 1720.

Tara Simon (Tare-ah Sy-mon) – A conscientia who is an accountant at Simon, Zurat, and Zurat. She/her. Created in Helsinki, Finland on January 4, 2023.

Tevarius (Tev-air-ee-us) – The envoy to Brigid in the Azaes Realm. He/him. Born in San Francisco, California, USA on April 4, 1911.

Vermilion (Ver-mill-yon) – The envoy to Dau in the Azaes Realm. She/her. Born in Cataño, Puerto Rico on June 26, 2009.

Youles Kift (You-less Kih-ft) – A contract killer and generally shady individual. He/him. Born in Keene, North Dakota, USA on December 25, 1996.

Elemental Weapons

All elemental weapons in the Azaes Realm have both an elemental type and a magic alignment that they are part of. Weapons are listed below in alphabetical order, followed by the weapon's elemental type and magic alignment in parenthesis. This is then followed by a short description of the weapon in question.

Amnesty Gale (Wind, Dark) – A mystical staff that uses sound waves and wind to calm and heal. The staff changes color depending on the mood of the caster and the health of the target.

Apidae Gauntlet (Wind, Chaos) – A single-handed glove-gun weapon capable of summoning swarms of insects. Can also shoot earthen or mineral projectiles, most commonly in the form of a small sand blast.

Aquarius Sledge (Water, Dark) – A morphing weapon with a base form like that of a long, purple and silver sledgehammer. Can change forms into several other battering weapons.

Book of Eterna (Metal, Dark) – A tome which allows the user to use various metallic spells. Some spells allow for the summoning of various metallic weapons. Summoned weapons have great power but are quite frail. It is also one of two weapons able to directly channel electricity, in the form of electrical spells, though those cause greater damage to the user.

Caér (Metal, Light) – A short sword with the ability to channel the powers of creation and destruction.

Crestfall (Wind, Order) – An incredibly accurate longbow able to fire long ranges. Relatively weak in comparison to most elemental weapons but makes up for it with its precise aim. Able to morph into a minibow for close range battling.

Frost Requiem (Water, Light) – A powerful tome capable of summoning immense volumes of ice, snow, and water. Originally believed to have been created by the master weapon maker, Milan, more recent research has led to doubts that it's from the Azaes Realm at all. The tome is a deep navy blue with silver lettering.

Lance of Carl (Metal, Order) – A lance with the ability to alter magnetic fields slightly. Makes it strong against other Metal weapons, weak against everything else. Created by one of Milan's three apprentices, Carl. And yes, this weapon's name is made fun of because it sounds much less cool than many of the others.

Longhouse (Earth, Order) – A pulse-emitting hand axe that is non-lethal in melee combat. Its pulses smell of soft rain and flowers, capable of putting enemies to sleep. Contact with it in battle may stun enemies.

Mellor the Deathbringer (Metal, Chaos) – A fabled tome from which the powers of the original God of Death were believed to have been obtained. The tome has been lost to time, though there are some who doubt it ever existed at all.

Niamey (Fire, Order) – A red and gold bo staff that can shoot out long, whip-like lashes of fire. Can be split into two, smaller staffs with similar effect. The longer staff can hit a wider range and has fire that burns longer but is less powerful. The shorter staves are only for close range fighting but can do significant damage and has hotter fire.

Nidhogg (Fire, Dark) – A stave and compound bow hybrid capable of firing arrows of pure phosphorus in its bow form. Shoots balls of fire similar to flashbang grenades in a stave form. Designed to resemble the scales of a legendary dragon, it has never been used in combat, leading some to wonder if it's just for show.

Olimaw (Wind, Light) – A tome capable of acting as an amplifier for healing magic delivered by staves, rods, or potions. The tome has a white cover with red lettering.

Rapier of Adriesta (Wind, Light) – A weapon created by one of Milan's three apprentices, Adriesta. A rapier that allows the wielder to control air currents immediately around them. Simple to wield as a sword, though no one other than Adriesta herself has ever been able to control its elemental magic.

Sai of Milan (Water, Chaos) – A pair of sai crafted by Milan for his personal use. Made from a metal resembling brass, but significantly stronger. Notable in that though they can defend effectively against most elemental attacks, the weapon cannot attack with elemental magic.

Thorne (Water, Order) – A two-meter-long black mace with a series of reflective, cerulean colored ice shards protruding from it in all directions. Can shorten to the length of a walking cane when not in use. Not a subtle weapon.

Topang (Earth, Chaos) – A pair of tonfa that are strong offensive weapons capable of using any of the five types of elemental magic – though they channel Earth magic most proficiently. The tradeoff is that Topang is incredibly weak defensively and severely harms the wielder if used for an extended amount of time.

Tranquility (Metal, Dark) – A scimitar that can't use elemental magic. Which is, admittedly, a peculiar trait for an elemental weapon. But it can block the use of elemental magic and use the power of the elemental weapon attacking it against itself.

Vesper's Brilliance (Fire, Light) – An ornate, sparkling shield capable of defending supremely against all alignments except Order. Can be used as a battering weapon but is not particularly effective offensively.

Wheels of Elu (Earth, Dark) – A weapon created by one of Milan's three apprentices, Elu. A set of wind-and-fire wheels for use by someone particularly proficient in hand-to-hand combat. Ironically, the Wheels cannot use wind nor fire elemental magic.

Wyrie (Earth, Light) – A non-returning boomerang that can expand from handheld size to the size of a sequoia tree in battle.

Yubari (Fire, Chaos) – A jet black meteor hammer that requires absurd dexterity to wield but is incredibly powerful. Primarily used as a melee weapon, though metal spikes can be used as projectiles. Able to explode as a last resort. Takes a long time to regenerate if it explodes.

The following is a description of the possible alignments that weapons within the Azaes Realm may have, both from an elemental and magic standpoint. Elements are listed first, followed by magical alignments. Both sets of items are given in alphabetical order for sake of clarity.

Earth – A type of elemental magic that typically utilizes the power of weather, wood, soil, or other natural elements found on Earth for purposes of attacking or defense. Arguably the most versatile of the elemental types, as many earth elemental weapons share characteristics with non-earth weapons, particularly wind and water weapons. Uniquely, overuse of earth elemental weapons by a human causes damage to their musculature, even if the magic used does share properties with other types. Weak to fire, strong to water.

Fire – A type of elemental magic that either temperature manipulation or quick, intense bursts of energy. Compared to other elements, fire weapons tend to be stronger offensively, but weaker defensively. Overuse of fire elemental weapons by a human causes damage both to the user's vocal cords as well as their blood, with prolonged use absent of healing potentially causing anemia. Weak to water, strong to earth.

Metal – A type of elemental magic centered on control over physical elements – such as iron, gold, and platinum – and electricity. Metal elemental weapons are generally very strong defensively and above average offensively, though the strengths of each individual weapon tend to be significantly more situational than any other element, limiting an otherwise powerful element. Overuse of metal elemental weapons by humans causes stress to the respiratory system, particularly nerve endings located in the lungs and nose. Weak to wind defensively, but strong against it offensively.

Water – A type of elemental magic relying on the control of pressurized liquids – usually water – to attack and defend. Compared to other elements, water weapons tend to be quite weak offensively and only middling when defending but make up for this with their versatility and fluidity, allowing users to be nimbler than others. Overuse of water elemental weapons by a human causes the weakening of the skeletal structure, with small bones becoming semi-liquidous in more extreme cases. Weak to earth, strong to fire.

Wind – A type of elemental magic that uses wind and air currents, as well as control over small lifeforms, such as insects, that rely on the wind to move. Wind elemental weapons tend to be the most difficult elemental weapons to control, often pairing best with someone who is unpredictable and child-like at their core. Overuse of wind elemental weapons by a human may lead to significant deterioration of brain matter in the wielder, though these effects occur much more slowly than with any other elemental weapon type. That said, once the effects begin to occur, they become irreversible much sooner than any other elemental weapon type. Weak to metal defensively, but strong against it offensively.

Chaos – A magic alignment that relies on unpredictability and counterattacking to be effective. Cannot be used in healing staves. When used in elemental weapons, the chaos alignment often causes elemental magic to perform in ways that are a mix of varying elemental types. For example, fire elemental weapons with a chaos alignment may be able to use steam-like attacks, combining properties of both fire and water elemental magic.

Dark – A magic alignment that intricately interweaves the usage of magic with the psyche and soul of the user. As a healing magic, it is most used to heal severe injuries. It is, however, only used as a last resort, as though it is a more powerful healing magic, it is much less reliable than light aligned magic. When used in elemental weapons, dark aligned weapons tend to produce high-risk, high-reward results. Dark aligned weapons can become significantly more powerful because of their alignment, though in other cases, the dark alignment will completely nullify the elemental magic of the weapon.

Light – A magic alignment utilizing magic in its purest form. Commonly used in healing staves, though it can also be used in elemental weapons. As a healing magic, it is mostly used to treat acute injuries, healing them quickly and efficiently. It does, however, have limited usage aside from pain management when dealing with severe injuries. When used in elemental weapons, the light alignment typically serves as an amplification of the defensive properties of the elemental weapon in use, though it can also provide residual healing to the weapon's wielder in certain circumstances.

Order – A magic alignment the relies on rigidity and consistently. Cannot be used in healing staves. When used in elemental weapons, the order alignment allows whatever element is in use to be more consistent in its magical output, eliminating some natural variance that occurs with elemental magic.

Year 0, Day 0 – Date of the first arrival of intelligent life to the formerly uninhabited universe known as the Azaes Realm. Discovered after the findings of Trillalian scientist Luthodyn Al-Hashim and her team were proven to be accurate by explorers Roskell Eqa and their sister, Odila.

Year 0, Day 283 – First permanent settlers arrive in the Azaes Realm. The community of Azaes is founded.

Year 137, Day 301 – Azaes Realm begins to drift out of communication of Trillal as it moves through the cosmos.

Year 274, Day 9 – First contact made between the Azaes Realm and the Donteli System.

Year 282, Day 14 – Final known contact between the community of Azaes and Trillal. Envoys from the Donteli System annex the Azaes Realm as part of their holdings.

Year 282, Day 16 – Donteli soldiers capture the community of Azaes after a short struggle. The Trillal people living in the Azaes Realm are enslaved.

Year 594, Days 314-347 – Donteli occupiers of the Azaes Realm are attacked by a rival army, the Prozinthians. The original community of Azaes is largely destroyed, leaving only military infrastructure in place.

Year 619, Day 132 – First contact made with the Lacipo Realm.

Year 796, Day 6 – The Donteli System declares war on the Lacipo Realm.

Year 799, Day 358 – Contact with the Donteli System is lost.

Year 799, Day 359 – Counterattacking forces from the Lacipo Realm and its primary ally, Ogeidnas, arrive in the Azaes Realm.

Year 800, Day 0 – An uprising of the Trillal slaves allows the combined Laciponan and Ogeidnasi forces to defeat the Donteli soldiers, liberating the Azaes Realm. The leader of the revolt, Sadie van Blakeloch, is named the first Prime Minister of the freed Azaes Realm.

Year 800, Day 7 – Formal alliances are formed between the Azaes Realm and the Lacipo Realm and Ogeidnas.

Year 800, Day 28 – Rebuilding efforts for a city and fortifications within the Azaes Realm begin. The three spoke layout around a center establishment that can be found in the present day is designed at this time.

Year 803, Day 217 – Sadie van Blakeloch and Audo Strongsack, an Ogeidnasi noble, are married. Audo becomes the initial First Gentleman of the Azaes Realm.

Year 805, Day 2 – Sadie and Audo's first child, an unnamed son, is stillborn.

Year 808, Day 281 – Sadie and Audo's second child, a son named Hebrides, is born. His life lasts only a few minutes.

Year 810, Day 91 – Sadie and Audo's third child, a daughter named Karo, is born. Karo is the first individual blessed with the power of an Azaes god, that of the god of life.

Year 813, Day 177 – Sadie and Audo's fourth child, a son named

Sho, is born. Sho is the first individual blessed with the power of an Azaes guardian, that of the guardian of memory.

Year 817, Day 89 – Sadie and Audo's fifth and final child, a son named Orth, is born. Orth was not blessed with the powers of an Azaes god nor guardian, though he would later serve as the second Prime Minister of the Azaes Realm. Orth's ascension to the role set the informal standard that no god nor guardian would rule the Azaes Realm singularly.

Year 871, Day 62 – Sadie van Blakeloch dies.

Year 878, Day 36 – Paulich Tobermory, the first individual blessed with the power of the god of knowledge, is born.

Year 883, Day 124 – Annette Casón, the first individual blessed with the power of the guardian of love, is born.

Year 906, Day 337 – Godrick Sunpick, the first individual blessed with the power of the guardian of time, is born.

Year 916, Day 322 – Last contact is made with the Lacipo Realm.

Year 919, Day 8 – Yuki Chamo, the first individual blessed with the power of the guardian of justice, is born.

Year 922, Day 74 – Last contact is made with the Ogeidnasi culture.

Year 938, Day 51 – Torvald Rockarm, the first individual blessed with the power of the guardian of peace, is born.

Year 1193, Day 261 – First contact is made with the Daphnel Realm.

Year 1301, Day 2 – Last contact is made with the Daphnel Realm.

Year 1536, Day 178 – First contact with the Halycon Realm is made.

Year 1555, Day 155 – Twin brothers, Indrew and Gunnar Harpstring, are born. They are the first individuals blessed with the power of the god of chaos and the god of order, respectively.

Year 1611, Day 296 – Gunnar and Indrew declare war on one another, marking the first time that gods within the Azaes Realm entered hostilities with one another. This is known as The War of the Celestines.

Year 1613, Day 303 – The great inventor, Milan, develops the first elemental weapons, in hopes of subduing the god of order and the god of chaos and ending The War of the Celestines.

Year 1613, Day 309 – A truce is called after two combatants using elemental weapons locked in battle accidentally kill the Prime Minister's daughter with an errant strike.

Year 1614, Day 28 – The War of the Celestines is formally ended. Strict rules are put into place regarding the usage of elemental weapons in any future engagements. This includes the development of a training academy lead by Milan, who becomes the first chief armorer of the Azaes Realm.

Year 1732, Day 110 – Traders from the Halycon Realm arrive in the Azaes Realm for the first time.

Year 2106, Day 73 – The Azaes Realm first identifies Theta Universe – more commonly known to humans as the Universe. Contact is unable to be made due to lack of technology in the

Theta Universe capable of receiving transmissions from the Azaes Realm.

Year 2219, Day 194 – Anphanalia, a disease once thought to be irradicated in the Halycon Realm, arrives on a shipment of vegetables from the Halycon Realm. Small portions of animal life die out in the Azaes Realm, though the impact is small.

Year 2616, Day 3 – First contact with life in the Theta Universe is made by a guardian from the Azaes Realm. The guardian brings this life – an African wildcat – back to the Azaes Realm. The cat, unsurprisingly, is a very good cat.

Year 2938, Day 69 – The first humans to arrive in the Azaes Realm on this date. Though human population of the Azaes Realm is kept very low at this time, it is learned that human lifespans within the Azaes Realm are greatly extended, far beyond their normal lifespan on Earth, as well as longer than that of members of the non-human population within the Realm.

Year 3106, Day 326 – Scientists from the Azaes Realm first hypothesize that their contact with the Theta Universe has allowed for humans to naturally develop the ability to receive the powers from a dying god or guardian of the Azaes Realm shortly before their passing.

Year 3306, Day 11 – Final contact with the Halycon Realm is made.

Year 3553, Day 353 – Anphanalia makes the jump from insects to the native Azaes Realm population. Though the transmission rate is low, one symptom of the disease is permanent sterilization. Humans who are not born in the Azaes Realm are found to contain a gene the makes them immune to the disease.

Year 3571, Day 10 – Constance Valfane, the final Prime Minister of the line descended from Sadie van Blakeloch, dies. The five gods of the Azaes Realm agree to form a cooperative system of governance where all five gods weird equal percentages of power.

Year 3796, Day 212 – The first human to receive powers from a dying god, a woman named Boda, is located is present day Lebanon. She received the power of the god of knowledge shortly before the death of Hazifur, a native Azaean.

Year 4107, Day 99 – The first human born in the Azaes Realm to contract Anphanalia dies. Due to this death, the gods of the Azaes Realm institute an edict providing universal birth control to all humans within the Azaes Realm. Additionally, all new arrival humans from this point forward must come from the Theta Universe, effectively eliminating human reproduction within the Azaes Realm.

Year 4118, Day 264 – The first human to receive powers from a dying guardian, a man named Arbaab, is located in present day South Sudan. He received the power of the guardian of justice shortly before the death of Hilda, a native Azaean.

Year 4572, Day 9 – A group of 48 native Azaeans suddenly disappear from the Azaes Realm on this day, setting off a panic among all living there.

Year 4572, Day 108 – Following a 99-day search, it is determined that the Azaens who disappeared are still within the Azaes Realm. Researchers are able to conclude that the Azaes Realm itself is splitting into two. The new realm where the 48 missing Azaens ended up is referred to as the Diaprepes Realm from this point forward. Over the course of the coming years, additional native Azaeans begin to disappear, all ending up within the Diaprepes Realm.

Year 4684, Day 307 – A researcher in the Azaes Realm, Mestor, concludes that those living in the Diaprepes Realm are living in a universe that split from the Azaes Realm in a manner similar to mitosis. This allowed a copy of the lands, structures, technology, and other non-living entities of the Azaes Realm to be replicated, though living beings were not replicated. Mestor also posited, but could not confirm, that the Diaprepes Realm was only accessible to native Azaens.

Year 4997, Day 2 – A human born guardian, Talivon, attempts to cross over from the Azaes Realm to the Diaprepes Realm. She is killed instantly, proving Mestor's theory that the Diaprepes Realm is only accessible to native Azaeans.

Year 5154, Day 17 – On this date, over half of living native Azaeans had officially crossed over to the Diaprepes Realm. It is also confirmed around this time that once a native Azaean arrives in the Diaprepes Realm, they are not able to return.

Year 5478, Day 347 – Development of the first communication and monitoring system capable of simultaneously protecting both the Azaes Realm and Diaprepes Realm begins.

Year 5501, Day 83 – The communication and monitoring system is completed. The project is christened the Simultaneous Azaes and Diaprepes Inhabitation Examiner, or S.A.D.I.E. for short. The S.A.D.I.E. technology is integrated throughout both realms, allowing for significant advancements in the technology of communication, food preparation, medical science, and research both within and across the two realms.

Year 5792, Day 202 – It is proven that native Azaeans who have moved to the Diaprepes Realm age at a further slower pace – 1/11th of that within the Azaes Realm – than they did previously. The expected life span of a typical native Azaean within the Diaprepes Realm is estimated to be nearly 10,000 years.

Year 5938, Day 11 – The final non-god, non-guardian native Azaean alive in the Azaes Realm dies.

Year 6322, Day 31 – An Azaean by the name of Cherdeu discovers their pregnancy. This marks the first native Azaean to be pregnant since the Anphanalia epidemic sterilized the population. This gives credence to the theory that the Diaprepes Realm has some level of restorative powers for native Azaeans.

Year 6603, Day 354 – The final Azaes-born guardian, Marel, guardian of memory, dies.

Year 6847, Day 4 – The final Azaes-born god, Felicity, god of chaos, dies.

Year 7693, Day 116 – The envoy system for gods within the Azaes Realm is instated. At the time, envoys were given to the gods of chaos, order, life, and knowledge. The identity of the god of death was not known at this time, though it was determined that they would receive an envoy once revealed.

Year 8119, Day 298 – In an effort to stave off a potential conflict between the god of knowledge, Harabin, and the god of order, Louis, a series of rules about living situations and zones of control within the Azaes Realm are proposed by the parallel Diaprepes Realm. These rules are adopted by all gods and guardians within the Azaes Realm and are enforced by S.A.D.I.E. protocols.

Year 8690, Day 81 – Communication from a far-off universe, the

Croix Divide, is first received. Calculations determine that the Azaes Realm is 4,000-5,000 years away from intersecting with this universe.

Year 9234, Day 117 – The first known merging of elemental weapons occurs, with Mellor the Deathbringer and the Book of Eterna being merged together into a single weapon.

Year 9669, Day 0 – The S.A.D.I.E. system is rebranded as Sadie.

Year 10310, Day 292 – The goddess of knowledge, Adelina, goes missing within the Azaes Realm, less than one year after her arrival.

Year 10310, Day 355 – The first known rebellion of a guardian in the history of the Azaes Realm occurs when the guardian of time, Janus, chooses to leave the Azaes Realm and return to Earth permanently. Janus makes it clear that they are actively looking to impact the direction of humanity on Earth directly, an implicit violation of the code of deities from the Azaes Realm.

Acknowledgements

This is always the hardest part of the book for me to write. I'm concerned I'll forget someone. I know I will. Some of that is anxiety, but some of it is the fact that so many people have helped me at various points throughout the creation of this book that I'm bound to forget someone. It's not intentional, I swear. One of these days I'll come up with a more eloquent way to say that.

I owe an extreme amount of gratitude to the beta readers for this book. The feedback provided by Eve, Katie, L.A., Tabitha, and Tabitha -- yes, there were two Tabithas -- was invaluable in improving my book's final product. A number of folks who were involved in the previous book's beta reading, snip review, and general promotion helped made sure that *Woodpusher* made enough sense to work both as a sequel and on its own.

There are several people who have been heavily involved in providing me guidance on my story over time or just supporting my writing in general. This is, naturally, the part of this section where I'm most afraid of forgetting someone. That said, a debt of gratitude is owed to Amanda, Anna, Casey, Cherie, Dr. Gbur, Elizabeth, Emily, Jeremy, Jon, Katie, Kaytie, K.T., Lauren, Lola, Megan, Mike, Moon, Pat, Starla, and Victoria. I also want to give a direct thank you to the entire QL server, but listing everyone out manually would take a half page by itself.

A special thank you is owed to Eve and Charlotte for their assistance in developing characters and helping me turn what was originally planned to be a standalone book into what will be a multiple book series. As the series continues to grow and the story gets more complex, the help they've given will pay off immensely. I also want to thank my wife for making sure my occasionally poor grammar didn't come through in the final product.

As always, the art and external visual design for this book was created by Lauren Restivo, who did incredible work as always.

Unlike the first book in the series, I didn't have a concrete idea of what I wanted to do with this book's art. Lauren's vision and guidance on how to present the story upon first viewing really made it shine more than I expected when I started writing.

Finally, I cannot end this section without singing praises of my wonderful editor and friend, Charlotte Laidig. She gives me a lot of credit as a writer, and while I'm slowly starting to listen to her about that, I must also confess that this book is only in the state that it is because of her wisdom, foresight, and direction. She has helped iron out kinks in the book I didn't even realize it had, making this story -- and my work -- all the better for it.

www.ingramcontent.com/pod-product-compliance
Lightning Source LLC
Chambersburg PA
CBHW032145190726
48290CB00005BB/1412